They all had something to hide—the society belles, the carriage-trade surgeon, the suave Foreign Minister, the General . . .

Each socialite knew more than the next on the point of Lord Gospell's grisly end. Now Inspector Alleyn must hit on the method of murder—before the killer could strike again . . .

"Well up to Miss Marsh's previous high standard."—LONDON TIMES

Ngaio Marsh's mysteries are
"a joy absolute!"—THE NEW YORK TIMES

"Clever and pointed."—THE NEW YORKER

Also by Ngaio Marsh from Jove

DEATH IN A WHITE TIE

NGAIO MARSH

A JOVE BOOK

Five previous printings
First Jove edition published September 1977

New Jove edition published July 1980

10 9 8 7 6 5

Printed in the United States of America

Jove books are published by Jove Publications, Inc.,
200 Madison Avenue, New York, NY 10016

**For
NELLY
To whom this book
owes its existence**

Contents

CONTENTS

DEATH
IN A
WHITE TIE

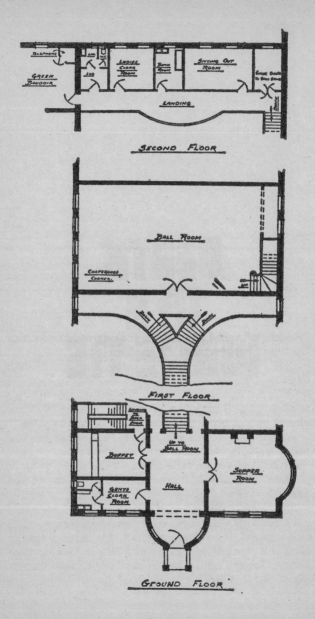

SECOND FLOOR

FIRST FLOOR

GROUND FLOOR

1

The Protagonists

"Roderick," said Lady Alleyn, looking at her son over the top of her spectacles, "I am coming out."

"Out?" repeated Chief Detective-Inspector Alleyn vaguely. "Out where, mama? Out of what?"

"Out into the world. Out of retirement. Out into the season. Out. Dear me," she added confusedly, "how absurd a word becomes if one says it repeatedly. Out."

Alleyn laid an official-looking document on the breakfast-table and stared at his mother.

"What can you be talking about?" he said.

"Don't be stupid, darling. I am going to do the London season."

"Have you taken leave of your senses?"

"I think perhaps I have. I have told George and Grace that I will bring Sarah out this coming season. Here is a letter from George and here is another from Grace. Government House, Suva. They think it charming of me to offer."

"Good Lord, mama," said Alleyn, "you must be demented. Do you know what this means?"

"I believe I do. It means that I must take a flat in London. It means that I must look up all sorts of people who will turn out to be dead or divorced or remarried. It means that I must give little luncheon-parties and cocktail-parties and exchange cutlets with hard-working mothers. It means that I must sit in ballrooms praising other women's granddaughters and securing young men for my own. I shall be up until four o'clock five nights out of seven and I'm afraid, darling, that my black lace and my silver charmeuse will not be quite equal to the strain. So that in addition to buying clothes for Sarah I shall have to buy some for myself. And I should like to know what you think about that, Roderick."

"I think it is all utterly preposterous. Why the devil can't George and Grace bring Sarah out themselves?"

"Because they are in Fiji, darling."

"Well, why can't she stay in until they return?"

"George's appointment is for four years. In four years your niece will be twenty-two. An elderly sort of débutante."

"*Why* has Sarah got to come out? Why can't she simply emerge?"

"That I cannot tell you, but George and Grace certainly could. I rather see it, I must say, Roderick. A girl has such fun doing her first season. There is nothing like it, ever again. And now we have gone back to chaperones and all the rest of it, it really does seem to have some of the old glamour."

"You mean débutantes have gone back to being treated like hothouse flowers for three months and taking their chance as hardy perennials for the rest of their lives."

"If you choose to put it like that. The system is not without merit, my dear."

"It may be quite admirable, but isn't it going to be a bit too exhausting for you? Where is Sarah, by the way?"

"She is always rather late for breakfast. How wonderfully these children sleep, don't they? But we were talking about the season, weren't we? I think I shall enjoy it, Rory. And really and truly it won't be such hard work. I've heard this morning from Evelyn Carrados. She was Evelyn O'Brien, you know. Evelyn Curtis, of course, in the *first* instance, but that's so long ago nobody bothers about it. Not that she's as old as all that, poor girl. She can't be forty yet. Quite a chicken, in fact. Her mother was my greatest friend. We did the season together when we came out. And now here's Evelyn bringing her own girl out and offering to help with Sarah. Could anything be more fortunate?"

"Nothing," responded Alleyn dryly. "I remember Evelyn O'Brien."

"I should hope you do. I did my best to persuade you to fall in love with her."

"Did I fall in love with her?"

"No. I could never imagine why, as she was quite lovely and very charming. Now I come to think of it, you hadn't much chance as she herself fell madly in love with Paddy O'Brien who returned suddenly from Australia."

"I remember. A romantic sort of bloke, wasn't he?"

"Yes. They were married after a short engagement. Five months later he was killed in a motor accident. Wasn't it awful?"

"Awful."

"And then in six months or so along came this girl, Bridget. Evelyn called her Bridget because Paddy was Irish. And then, poor Evelyn, she married Herbert Carrados. Nobody ever knew why."

"I'm not surprised. He's a frightful bore. He must be a great deal older than Evelyn."

"A thousand years and so pompous you can't believe he's true. You know him evidently."

"Vaguely. He's something pretty grand in the City."

Alleyn lit his mother's cigarette and his own. He

walked over to the french window and looked across the lawn.

"Your garden is getting ready to come out, too," he said. "I wish I hadn't got to go back to the Yard."

"Now, darling? This minute?"

"Afraid so. It's this case." He waved the papers in his hand. "Fox rang up late last night. Something's cropped up."

"What sort of case is it?"

"Blackmail, but you're not allowed to ask questions."

"Rory, how exciting. Who's being blackmailed? Somebody frightfully important, I hope?"

"Do you remember Lord Robert Gospell?"

"*Bunchy* Gospell, do you mean? Surely he's not being blackmailed. A more innocent creature——"

"No, mama, he isn't. Nor is he a blackmailer."

"He's a dear little man," said Lady Alleyn emphatically. "The nicest possible little man."

"Not so little nowadays. He's very plump and wears a cloak and a sombrero like G.K.C."

"Really?"

"You must have seen photographs of him in your horrible illustrated papers. They catch him when they can. 'Lord Robert ("Bunchy") Gospell tells one of his famous stories.' That sort of thing."

"Yes, but what's he got to do with blackmail?"

"Nothing. He is, as you say, an extremely nice little man."

"Roderick, don't be infuriating. Has Bunchy Gospell got anything to do with Scotland Yard?"

Alleyn was staring out into the garden.

"You might say," he said at last, "that we have a very great respect for him at the Yard. Not only is he charming—he is also, in his own way, a rather remarkable personage."

Lady Alleyn looked at her son meditatively for some seconds.

"Are you meeting him to-day?" she asked.

"I think so."

"Why?"

"Why, darling, to listen to one of his famous stories, I suppose."

It was Miss Harris's first day in her new job. She was secretary to Lady Carrados and had been engaged for the London season. Miss Harris knew quite well what this meant. It was not, in a secretarial sense, by any means her first season. She was a competent young woman, almost frighteningly unimaginative, with a brain that was divided into neat pigeon-holes, and a mind that might be said to label all questions "answered" or "unanswered." If a speculative or unconventional idea came Miss Harris's way, it was promptly dealt with or promptly shut up in a dark pigeon-hole and never taken out again. If Miss Harris had not been able to answer it immediately, it was unanswerable and therefore of no importance. Owing perhaps to her intensive training as a member of the large family of a Buckinghamshire clergyman she never for a moment asked herself why she should go through life organising fun for other people and having comparatively little herself. That would have seemed to Miss Harris an irrelevant and rather stupid speculation. One's job was a collection of neatly filed duties, suitable to one's station in life, and therefore respectable. It had no wider ethical interest of any sort at all. This is not to say Miss Harris was insensitive. On the contrary, she was rather touchy on all sorts of points of etiquette relating to her position in the houses in which she was employed. Where she had her lunch, with whom she had it, and who served it, were matters of great importance to her and she was painfully aware of the subtlest nuances in her employers' attitude towards herself. About her new job she was neatly optimistic. Lady Carrados had impressed her favourably, had treated her, in her own phrase, like a perfect lady. Miss Harris walked briskly along an upstairs passage and tapped twice, not too loud and not too timidly, on a white door.

"Come in," cried a far-away voice.

Miss Harris obeyed and found herself in a large white bedroom. The carpet, the walls and the chairs were all white. A cedar-wood fire crackled beneath the white Adams mantelpiece, a white bearskin rug nearly tripped Miss Harris up as she crossed the floor to the large white bed where her employer sat propped up with pillows. The bed was strewn about with sheets of notepaper.

"Oh, good morning, Miss Harris," said Lady Carrados. "You can't think how glad I am to see you. *Do* you mind waiting a moment while I finish this note? Please sit down."

Miss Harris sat discreetly on a small chair. Lady Carrados gave her a vague, brilliant smile, and turned again to her writing. Miss Harris with a single inoffensive glance had taken in every detail of her employer's appearance.

Evelyn Carrados was thirty-seven years old, and on her good days looked rather less. She was a dark, tall woman with little colour but a beautiful pallor. Paddy O'Brien had once shown her a copy of the Madonna di San Sisto and had told her that she was looking at herself. This was not quite true. Her face was longer and had more edge and character than Raphael's complacent virgin, but the large dark eyes were like those in the painting and the sleek hair parted down the centre. Paddy had taken to calling her "Donna" after that and she still had his letters beginning: "Darling Donna." Oddly enough Bridget, his daughter, who had never seen him, called her mother "Donna" too. She had come into the room on the day Miss Harris was interviewed and had sat on the arm of her mother's chair. A still girl with a lovely voice. Miss Harris looking straight in front of her remembered this interview now while she waited. "*He* hasn't appeared yet," thought Miss Harris, meaning Sir Herbert Carrados whose photograph faced her in a silver frame on his wife's dressing-table.

Lady Carrados signed her name and hunted about the

counterpane for blotting-paper. Miss Harris instantly placed her own pad on the bed.

"Oh," said her employer with an air of pleased astonishment, "you've got some! Thank you so much. There, that's settled *her*, hasn't it?"

Miss Harris smiled brightly. Lady Carrados licked the flap of an envelope and stared at her secretary over the top.

"I see you've brought up my mail," she said.

"Yes, Lady Carrados. I did not know if you would prefer me to open all——"

"No, no. No, please not."

Miss Harris did not visibly bridle, she was much too competent to do anything of the sort, but she was at once hurt in her feelings. A miserable, a hateful, little needle of mortification jabbed her thin skin. She had overstepped her mark.

"Very well, Lady Carrados," said Miss Harris politely.

Lady Carrados bent forward.

"I know I'm all wrong," she said quickly. "I know I'm not behaving a bit as one should when one is lucky enough to have a secretary but, you see, I'm not used to such luxuries, and I still like to pretend I'm doing everything myself. So I shall have all the fun of opening my letters and all the joy of handing them over to you. Which is very unfair, but you'll have to put up with it, poor Miss Harris."

She watched her secretary smile and replied with a charming look of understanding.

"And now," she said, "we may as well get it done, mayn't we?"

Miss Harris laid the letters in three neat heaps on the writing-pad and soon began to make shorthand notes of the answers she was to write for her employer. Lady Carrados kept up a sort of running commentary.

"Lucy Lorrimer. Who is Lucy Lorrimer, Miss Harris? I know she's that old Lady Lorrimer who talks as if everybody was dead. What does she want? 'Hear you

are bringing out your girl and would be so glad——'
Well, we'll have to see about that, won't we? If it's a free
afternoon we'd be delighted. There you are. Now, this
one. Oh, *yes*, Miss Harris, now this is most important.
It's from Lady Alleyn who is a *great* friend of mine. Do
you know who I mean? One of her sons is a deadly
baronet and the other is a detective. Do you know?"

"Is it Chief Inspector Alleyn, Lady Carrados? The
famous one?"

"That's it. Terribly good-looking and remote. He was
in the Foreign Office when the war broke out and then
after the war he suddenly became a detective. I can't
tell you why. Not that it matters," continued Lady
Carrados, glancing at the attentive face of her secretary,
"because this letter has nothing to do with him. It's
about his brother George's girl whom his mother is
bringing out and I said I'd help. So you must remember,
Miss Harris, that Sarah Alleyn is to be asked to
everything. And Lady Alleyn to the mothers' lunches
and all those games. Have you got that? There's her
address. And remind me to write personally. Now away
we go again and——"

She stopped so suddenly that Miss Harris glanced up
in surprise. Lady Carrados was staring at a letter which
she held in her long white fingers. The fingers trembled
slightly. Miss Harris with a sort of fascination looked at
them and at the square envelope. There was a silence in
the white room—a silence broken only by the hurried
inconsequent ticking of a little china clock on the
mantelpiece. With a sharp click the envelope fell on the
heap of letters.

"Excuse me, Lady Carrados," said Miss Harris, "but
are you feeling unwell?"

"What? No. No, thank you."

She put the letter aside and picked up another. Soon
Miss Harris's pen was travelling busily over her pad.
She made notes for the acceptance, refusal, and issuing
of invitations. She made lists of names with notes

beside them and she entered into a long discussion about Lady Carrados's ball.

"I'm getting Dimitri—the Shepherd Market caterer, you know—to do the whole thing," explained Lady Carrados. "It seems to be the—" she paused oddly—"the safest way."

"Well, he *is* the best," agreed Miss Harris. "You were speaking of expense, Lady Carrados. Dimitri works out at about twenty-five shillings a head. But that's *everything*. You do know where you are and he is good."

"Twenty-five? Four hundred, there'll be, I think. How much is that?"

"Five hundred pounds," said Miss Harris calmly.

"Oh dear, it is a lot, isn't it? And then there's the band. I do think we must have champagne at the buffet. It saves that endless procession to the supper-room which I always think is such a bore."

"Champagne at the buffet," said Miss Harris crisply. "That will mean thirty shillings a head, I'm afraid."

"*Oh,* how awful!"

"That makes Dimitri's bill six hundred. But, of course, as I say, Lady Carrados, that will be every penny you pay."

Lady Carrados stared at her secretary without replying. For some reason Miss Harris felt as if she had made another *faux pas*. There was, she thought, such a very singular expression in her employer's eyes.

"I should think a thousand pounds would cover the whole of the expenses, band and everything," she added hurriedly.

"Yes, I see," said Lady Carrados. "A thousand."

There was a tap at the door and a voice called: "Donna!"

"Come in, darling!"

A tall, dark girl carrying a pile of letters came into the room. Bridget was very like her mother but nobody would have thought of comparing her to the Sistine Madonna. She had inherited too much of Paddy

O'Brien's brilliance for that. There was a fine-drawn look about her mouth. Her eyes, set wide apart, were deep under strongly marked brows. She had the quality of repose but when she smiled all the corners of her face tipped up and then she looked more like her father than her mother. "Sensitive," thought Miss Harris, with a mild flash of illumination. "I hope she stands up to it all right. Nuisance when they get nerves." She returned Bridget's punctilious "Good morning" and watched her kiss her mother.

"Darling Donna," said Bridget, "you are so sweet."

"Hullo, my darling," said Lady Carrados, "here we are plotting away for all we're worth. Miss Harris and I have decided on the eighth for your dance. Uncle Arthur writes that we may have his house on that date. That's General Marsdon, Miss Harris. I explained, didn't I, that he is lending us Marsdon House in Belgrave Square? Or did I?"

"Yes, thank you, Lady Carrados. I've got all that."

"Of course you have."

"It's a mausoleum," said Bridget, "but it'll do. I've got a letter from Sarah Alleyn, Donna. Her grandmother, your Lady Alleyn, you know, is taking a flat for the season. Donna, please, I want Sarah asked for *everything*. Does Miss Harris know?"

"Yes, thank you, Miss Carrados. I beg pardon," said Miss Harris in some confusion, "I should have said, Miss O'Brien, shouldn't I?"

"Help, yes! Don't fall into that trap whatever you do," cried Bridget. "Sorry, Donna darling, but really!"

"Ssh!" said Lady Carrados mildly. "Are those your letters?"

"Yes. All the invitations. I've put a black mark against the ones I really do jib at and all the rest will just have to be sorted out. Oh, and I've put a big Y on the ones I want specially not to miss. And——"

The door opened again and the photograph on the dressing-table limped into the room.

Sir Herbert Carrados was just a little too good to be

true. He was tall and soldierly and good-looking. He had thin sandy hair, a large guardsman's moustache, heavy eyebrows and rather foolish light eyes. You did not notice they were foolish because his eyebrows gave them a spurious fierceness. He was not, however, a stupid man but only a rather vain and pompous one. It was his pride that he looked like a soldier and not like a successful financier. During the Great War he had held down a staff appointment of bewildering unimportance which had kept him in Tunbridge Wells for the duration and which had not hampered his sound and at times brilliant activities in the City. He limped a little and used a stick. Most people took it as a matter of course that he had been wounded in the leg and so he had—by a careless gamekeeper. He attended military reunions with the greatest assiduity and was about to stand for Parliament.

Bridget called him Bart, which he rather liked, but he occasionally surprised a look of irony in her eyes and that he did not at all enjoy.

This morning he had *The Times* under his arm and an expression of forbearance on his face. He kissed his wife, greeted Miss Harris with precisely the correct shade of cordiality, and raised his eyebrows at his stepdaughter.

"Good morning, Bridget. I thought you were still in bed."

"Good morning, Bart," said Bridget. "Why?"

"You were not at breakfast. Don't you think perhaps it would be more considerate to the servants if you breakfasted before you started making plans?"

"I expect it would," agreed Bridget and went as far as the door.

"What are your plans for to-day, darling?" continued Sir Herbert, smiling at his wife.

"Oh—everything. Bridget's dance. Miss Harris and I are—are going into expense, Herbert."

"Ah, yes?" murmured Sir Herbert. "I'm sure Miss

Harris is a perfect dragon with figures. What's the total, Miss Harris?"

"For the ball, Sir Herbert?" Miss Harris glanced at Lady Carrados who nodded a little nervously. "It's about a thousand pounds."

"Good God!" exclaimed Sir Herbert and let his eyeglass fall.

"You see, darling," began his wife in a hurry, "it just *won't* come down to less. Even with Arthur's house. And if we have champagne at the buffet——"

"I cannot see the smallest necessity for champagne at the buffet, Evelyn. If these young cubs can't get enough to drink in the supper-room all I can say is, they drink a great deal too much. I must say," continued Sir Herbert with an air of discovery, "that I do not understand the mentality of modern youths. Gambling too much, drinking too much, no object in life—look at that young Potter."

"If you mean Donald Potter," said Bridget dangerously, "I must——"

"Bridgie!" said her mother.

"You're wandering from the point, Bridget," said her stepfather.

"Me!"

"My point is," said Sir Herbert with a martyred glance at his wife, "that the young people expect a great deal too much nowadays. Champagne at every table——"

"It's not that——" began Bridget from the door.

"It's only that it saves——" interrupted her mother.

"However," continued Sir Herbert with an air of patient courtesy, "if you feel that you can afford to spend a thousand pounds of an evening, my dear——"

"But it isn't all Donna's money," objected Bridget. "It's half mine. Daddy left——"

"Bridget, darling," said Lady Carrados, "breakfast."

"Sorry, Donna," said Bridget. "All right." She went out.

Miss Harris wondered if she too had better go, but

nobody seemed to remember she was in the room and she did not quite like to remind them of her presence by making a move. Lady Carrados with an odd mixture of nervousness and determination was talking rapidly.

"I know Paddy would have meant some of Bridgie's money to be used for her coming out, Herbert. It isn't as if——"

"My dear," said Sir Herbert with an ineffable air of tactful reproach, and a glance at Miss Harris. "Of course. It's entirely for you and Bridget to decide. Naturally. I wouldn't dream of interfering. I'm just rather an old fool and like to give any help I can. Don't pay any attention."

Lady Carrados was saved the necessity of making any reply to this embarrassing speech by the entrance of the maid.

"Lord Robert Gospell has called, m'lady, and wonders if——"

" 'Morning, Evelyn," said an extraordinarily high-pitched voice outside the door. "I've come up. Do let me in."

"Bunchy!" cried Lady Carrados in delight. "How lovely! Come in!"

And Lord Robert Gospell, panting a little under the burden of an enormous bunch of daffodils, toddled into the room.

On the same day that Lord Robert Gospell called on Lady Carrados, Lady Carrados herself called on Sir Daniel Davidson in his consulting-rooms in Harley Street. She talked to him for a long time and at the end of half an hour sat staring rather desperately across the desk into his large black eyes.

"I'm frightfully anxious, naturally, that Bridgie shouldn't get the idea that there's anything the matter with me," she said.

"There is nothing *specifically* wrong with you," said Davidson, spreading out his long hands. "Nothing, I mean, in the sense of your heart being overworked or

your lungs at all unsound or any nonsense of that sort. I
don't think you are anaemic. The blood test will clear all
that up. But"—and he leant forward and pointed a
finger at her—"*but* you are very tired. You're altogether
too tired. If I was an honest physician I'd tell you to go
into a nursing-home and lead the life of a placid cow for
three weeks."

"I can't do that."

"Can't your daughter come out next year? What
about the little season?"

"Oh, no, it's impossible. Really. My uncle has lent us
his house for the dance. She's planned everything. It
would be almost as much trouble to put things off as it is
to go on with them. I'll be all right, only I do rather feel
as if I've got a jellyfish instead of a brain. A wobbly
jellyfish. I get these curious giddy attacks. And I simply
can't stop bothering about things."

"I know. What about this ball? I suppose you're hard
at it over that?"

"I'm handing it over to my secretary and Dimitri. I
hope you're coming. You'll get a card."

"I shall be delighted, but I wish you'd give it up."

"Truly I can't."

"Have you got any particular worry?"

There was a long pause.

"Yes," said Evelyn Carrados, "but I can't tell you
about that."

"Ah, well," said Sir Daniel, shrugging up his
shoulders. "*Les maladies suspendent nos vertus et nos
vices.*"

She rose and he at once leapt to his feet as if she was
royalty.

"You will get that prescription made up at once," he
said, glaring down at her. "And, if you please, I should
like to see you again. I suppose I had better not call?"

"No, please. I'll come here."

"*C'est entendu.*"

Lady Carrados left him, wishing vaguely that he was
a little less florid and longing devoutly for her bed.

Agatha Troy hunched up her shoulders, pulled her smart new cap over one eye and walked into her one-man show at the Wiltshire Galleries in Bond Street. It always embarrassed her intensely to put in these duty appearances at her own exhibitions. People felt they had to say something to her about her pictures and they never knew what to say and she never knew how to reply. She became gruff with shyness and her incoherence was mistaken for intellectual snobbishness. Like most painters she was singularly inarticulate on the subject of her work. The careful phrases of literary appreciation showered upon her by highbrow critics threw Troy into an agony of embarrassment. She minded less the bland commonplaces of the philistines though for these also she had great difficulty in finding suitable replies.

She slipped in at the door, winked at the young man who sat at the reception desk and shied away as a large American woman bore down upon him with a white-gloved finger firmly planted on a price in her catalogue.

Troy hurriedly looked away and in a corner of the crowded room, sitting on a chair that was not big enough for him, she saw a smallish round gentleman whose head was aslant, his eyes closed, and his mouth peacefully open. Troy made for him.

"Bunchy!" she said.

Lord Robert Gospell opened his eyes very wide and moved his lips like a rabbit.

"Hullo!" he said. "What a scrimmage, ain't it? Pretty good."

"You were asleep."

"May have been having a nap."

"That's a pretty compliment," said Troy without rancour.

"I had a good prowl first. Just thought I'd pop in," explained Lord Robert. "Enjoyed myself." He balanced his glasses across his nose, flung his head back and with an air of placid approval contemplated a large landscape. Without any of her usual embarrassment Troy looked with him.

"Pretty good," repeated Bunchy. "Ain't it?"

He had an odd trick of using Victorian colloquialisms; legacies, he would explain, from his distinguished father. " 'Lor'!" was his favourite ejaculation. He kept up little Victorian politenesses, always leaving cards after a ball and often sending flowers to the hostesses who dined him. His clothes were famous—a rather high, close-buttoned jacket and narrowish trousers by day, a soft wide hat and a cloak in the evening. Troy turned from her picture to her companion. He twinkled through his glasses and pointed a fat finger at the landscape.

"Nice and clean," he said. "I like 'em clean. Come and have tea."

"I've only just arrived," said Troy, "but I'd love to."

"I've got the Potters," said Bunchy. "My sister and her boy. Wait a bit. I'll fetch 'em."

"Mildred and Donald?" asked Troy.

"Mildred and Donald. They live with me, you know, since poor Potter died. Donald's just been sent down for some gambling scrape or other. Nice young scamp. No harm in him. Only don't mention Oxford."

"I'll remember."

"He'll probably save you the trouble by talking about it himself. I like having young people about. Gay. Keep one up to scratch. Can you see 'em anywhere? Mildred's wearing a puce toque."

"Not a *toque,* Bunchy," said Troy. "There she is. It's a very smart purple beret. She's seen us. She's coming."

Lord Robert's widowed sister came billowing through the crowd followed by her extremely good-looking son. She greeted Troy breathlessly but affectionately. Donald bowed, grinned and said: "Oh, I say, I say! The distinguished artist in person. We *have* been enjoying ourselves. Frightfully good!"

"Fat lot you know about it," said Troy good-humouredly. "Mildred, Bunchy suggests tea."

"I must say I should be glad of it," said Lady Mildred Potter. "Looking at pictures is the most exhausting pastime, even when they are your pictures, dear."

"There's a restaurant down below," squeaked Lord Robert. "Follow me."

They worked their way through the crowd and downstairs. Donald, who was separated from them by several strangers, shouted: "I say, Troy, did you hear I was sent down?" This had the effect of drawing everyone's attention first to himself and then to Troy.

"Yes, I did," said Troy severely.

"Wasn't it awful?" continued Donald, coming alongside and speaking more quietly. "Uncle Bunch is *furious* and says I'm no longer The Heir. It's not true, of course. He's leaving me a princely fortune, aren't you, Uncle Bunch, my dear?"

"Here we are," said Lord Robert thankfully as they reached the door of the restaurant. "Will you all sit down. I'm afraid I must be rather quick." He pulled out his watch and blinked at it. "I've an appointment in twenty minutes."

"Where?" said Troy. "I'll drive you."

"Matter of fact," said Lord Robert, "it's at Scotland Yard. Meeting an old friend of mine called Alleyn."

2

Bunchy

"Lord Robert Gospell to see you, Mr. Alleyn," said a voice in Alleyn's desk telephone.

"Bring him up, please," said Alleyn.

He pulled a file out of the top drawer and laid it open before him. Then he rang through to his particular Assistant Commissioner.

"Lord Robert has just arrived, sir. You asked me to let you know."

"All right, Rory, I'll leave him to you, on second thoughts. Fox is here with the report on the Temple case and it's urgent. Make my apologies. Say I'll call on him any time that suits him if he thinks it would be any good. You know him, don't you? Personally, I mean?"

"Yes. He's asked for me."

"That's all right, then. Bring him along here if it's advisable, of course, but I'm snowed under."

"Very good, sir," said Alleyn.

A police sergeant tapped, and opened the door.

"Lord Robert Gospell, sir."

Lord Robert entered twinkling and a little breathless. "Hullo, Roderick. How-de-do," he said.

"Hullo, Bunchy. This is extraordinarily good of you."

"Not a bit. Like to keep in touch. Enjoy having a finger in the pie, you know. Always did." He sat down and clasped his little hands over his stomach. "How's your mother?" he asked.

"She's very well. She knows we are meeting to-day and sent you her love."

"Thank yer. Delightful woman, your mother. Afraid I'm a bit late. Took tea with another delightful woman."

"Did you indeed?"

"Yes. Agatha Troy. Know her?"

There was a short silence.

"Yes," said Alleyn.

"Lor', yes. Of course you do. Didn't you look after that case where her model was knifed?"

"Yes, I did."

"Charming," said Lord Robert. "Ain't she?"

"Yes," said Alleyn, "she is."

"I like her awfully. M'sister Mildred and her boy Donald and I had been to Troy's show. You know m'sister Mildred, don't you?"

"Yes," said Alleyn, smiling.

"Yes. No end of a donkey in many ways but a good woman. The boy's a young dog."

"Bunchy," said Alleyn, "you're better than Victorian, you're Regency."

"Think so? Tell me what, Roderick, I've got to come out of my shell and do the season a bit."

"You always do the season, don't you?"

"I get about a bit. Enjoy myself. Young Donald's paying his addresses to a gel called Bridget O'Brien. Know her?"

"That's funny," said Alleyn. "My mama is bringing out brother George's girl and it appears she's the bosom friend of Bridget O'Brien. She's Evelyn and Paddy O'Brien's daughter, you know."

"I know. Called on Evelyn this morning. She married that ass Carrados. Pompous. Clever in the City, I'm told. I had a look at the gel. Nice gel, but there's something wrong somewhere in that family. Carrados, I suppose. D'you like the gel?"

"I don't know her. My niece Sarah likes her."

"Look here," said Lord Robert spreading out his hands and staring at them in mild surprise. "Look here. Dine with us for Lady C.'s dance. Will you? Do."

"My dear Bunchy, I'm not asked."

"Isn't your niece goin'?"

"Yes, I expect she is."

"Get you a card. Easy as winking. Do come. Troy's dining, too. Donald and I persuaded her."

"Troy," said Alleyn. "Troy."

Lord Robert looked sharply at him for about two seconds.

"Never mind if you'd rather not," he said.

"I can't tell you how much I should like to come," said Alleyn slowly, "but you see I'm afraid I might remind Miss Troy of—of that very unpleasant case."

"Oh. 'M. Well, leave it open. Think it over. You're sure to get a card. Now—what about business?"

He made a funny eager grimace, pursed his lips, and with a deft movement of his hand slung his glasses over his nose. "What's up?" he asked.

"We rather think blackmail," said Alleyn.

"Lor'," said Lord Robert. "Where?"

"Here, there and everywhere in high society."

"How d'yer know?"

"Well." Alleyn laid a thin hand on the file. "This is rather more than usually confidential, Bunchy."

"Yes, yes, yes. All right. I'll be as silent," said Lord Robert, "as the grave. Mum's the word. Let's have the names and all the rest of it. None of your Mr. and Mrs. Xes."

"All right. You know Mrs. Halcut-Hackett? Old General Halcut-Hackett's wife?"

"Yes. American actress. Twenty years younger than H.-H. Gorgeous creature."

"That's the one. She came to us last week with a story of blackmail. Here it is in this file. I'll tell you briefly what she said, but I'm afraid you'll have to put up with one Madame X."

"Phoo!" said Lord Robert.

"She told us that a very great woman-friend of hers had confided in her that she was being blackmailed. Mrs. H.-H. wouldn't give this lady's name so there's your Mrs. X."

"Um," said Lord Robert doubtfully. "Otherwise Mrs. 'Arris?"

"Possibly," said Alleyn, "but that's the story and I give it to you as Mrs. H.-H. gave it to me. Mrs. X, who has an important and imperious husband, received a blackmailing letter on the first of this month. It was written on Woolworth paper. The writer said he or she had possession of an extremely compromising letter written to Mrs. X by a man-friend. The writer was willing to sell it for £500. Mrs. X's account is gone into very thoroughly every month by her husband and she was afraid to stump up. In her distress (so the story went) she flew to Mrs. Halcut-Hackett who couldn't provide £500 but persuaded Mrs. X to let her come to us with the whole affair. She gave us the letter. Here it is."

Alleyn laid the file on Lord Robert's plump little knees. Lord Robert touched his glasses and stared for quite thirty seconds at the first page in the file. He opened his mouth, shut it again, darted a glance at Alleyn, touched his glasses again and finally read under his breath:

" 'If you would care to buy a letter dated April 20th, written from the Bucks Club addressed to Darling Dodo and signed M., you may do so by leaving £ 500 in notes of small denomination in your purse behind the picture of the Dutch funeral above the fireplace in the ballroom of Comstock House on the evening of next Monday fortnight.' "

Lord Robert looked up.

"That was the night the Comstocks ran their charity bridge-party," he said. "Big show. Thirty tables. Let's see, it was last Monday."

"It was. On the strength of this letter we saw the Comstocks, told them a fairy-story and asked them to let us send in a man dressed as a waiter. We asked Mrs. H.-H. to get her distressed friend to put the purse full of notes which we dusted with the usual powder behind the Dutch funeral. Mrs. H.-H. said she would save her friend much agony and humiliation by doing this office for her." Alleyn raised one eyebrow and bestowed a very slow wink upon Lord Robert.

"Poor thing," said Lord Robert. "Did she suppose she'd taken you in?"

"I don't know. I kept up a polite pretence. Our man, who I may say is a good man, attended the party, saw Mrs. H.-H. tuck away the bag, and waited to see what would happen."

"What did happen?"

"Nothing. Our man was there all night and saw a maid discover the bag next morning, put it unopened on the mantelpiece and call Mrs. Comstock's attention to it. Mrs. Comstock, in the presence of our man and the maid, opened it, saw the paper, was surprised, could find nothing to indicate the owner and told the maid to put it aside in case it was asked for."

"And what," asked Lord Robert, suddenly hugging himself with his short arms, "what do you deduce from that, my dear Roderick?"

"They rumbled our man."

"Is it one of the Comstocks' servants?"

"The whole show was done by Dimitri, the Shepherd Market caterer. You know who I mean, of course. He does most of the big parties nowadays. Supplies service, food, and everything."

"One of Dimitri's men?"

"We've made extremely careful enquiries. They've all got splendid references. I've actually spoken to Dimitri himself. I told him that there had been one or two thefts lately at large functions and we were bound to make enquiries. He got in no end of a tig, of course, and showed me a mass of references for all his people. We followed them up. They're genuine enough. He employs the best that can be found in the world. There's a strict rule that all objects left lying about at these shows should be brought at once to him. He then, himself, looks to see if he can find the owner and in the case of a lost purse or bag returns it in person or else, having seen the contents, sends it by one of his men. He explained that he did this to protect both his men and himself. He always asks the owner to examine a bag the moment it is handed to her."

"Still——"

"I know it's by no means watertight but we've taken a lot of trouble over the Dimitri staff and in my opinion there's not a likely man among 'em."

"Dimitri himself?"

Alleyn grimaced.

"Wonders will never cease, my dear Bunchy, but ——"

"Yes, yes, of course, I quite see. He's a bit too dem' grand for those capers, you'd imagine. Anything else?"

"We've been troubled by rumours of blackmail from other sources. You can see the file if you like. Briefly they all point to someone who works in the way suggested by Mrs. Halcut-Hackett alias Mrs. X. There's one anonymous letter sent to the Yard, presumably by a victim. It simply says that a blackmailer is at work among society people. Nothing more. We haven't been able to trace it. Then young Kremorn shot himself the other day and we found out that he had been drawing very large sums in bank-notes for no known reason. His

servant said he'd suspected blackmail for some time."
Alleyn rubbed his nose. "It's the devil. And of all the
filthy crimes this to my mind is the filthiest. I don't mind
telling you we're in a great tig over it."

"Bad!" said Lord Robert, opening his eyes very wide.
"Disgusting! Where do I come in?"

"Everywhere, if you will. You've helped us before
and we'll be damn' glad if you help us again. You go
everywhere, Bunchy," said Alleyn with a smile at his
little friend. "You toddle in and out of all the smart
houses. Lovely ladies confide in you. Heavy colonels
weep on your bosom. See what you can see."

"Can't break confidences, you know, can I? Sup-
posing I get 'em."

"Of course you can't, but you can do a little quiet
investigation on your own account and tell us as much
as——" Alleyn paused and added quickly: "As much as
a man of integrity may. Will you?"

"Love to!" said Lord Robert with a great deal of
energy. "Matter of fact, but it'd be a rum go if it
was—coincidence."

"What?"

"Well. Well, see here, Roderick, this is between
ourselves. Thing is, as I told you, I called on Evelyn
Carrados this morning. Passing that way and saw a
feller selling daffodils so thought I'd take her some.
Damn' pretty woman, Evelyn, but——" He screwed up
his face. "Saddish. Never got over Paddy's death, if you
ask me. Devoted to the gel and the gel to her, but if you
ask me Carrados comes the high horse a bit. Great
pompous exacting touchy sort of feller, ain't he? Evelyn
was in bed. Snowed under with letters. Secretary.
Carrados on the hearth-rug looking injured. Bridget
came in later on. Well now. Carrados said he'd be off to
the City. Came over to the bed and gave her the sort of a
kiss a woman doesn't thank you for. Hand each side of
her. Right hand under the pillow."

Lord Robert's voice suddenly skipped an octave and
became high-pitched. He leant forward with his hands

on his knees, looking very earnestly at Alleyn. He moved his lips rather in the manner of a rabbit and then said explosively:

"It was singular. It was demmed odd. He must have touched a letter under her pillow because when he straightened up it was in his right hand—a common-looking envelope addressed in a sort of script—letters like they print 'em, only done by hand."

Alleyn glanced quickly at the file but said nothing.

"Carrados said: 'Oh, one of your letters, m'dear,' squinting at it through his glass and then putting it down on the counterpane. 'Beg pardon,' or something. Thing is, she turned as white as the sheet. I promise you as white as anything, on my honour. And she said: 'It's from one of my lame ducks. I must deal with it,' and slid it under the others. Off he went, and that was that. I talked about their ball and so on and paid my respects and pretended I'd noticed nothing, of course, and, in short, I came away."

Still Alleyn did not speak. Suddenly Lord Robert jabbed at the letter in the file with his fat finger.

"Thing is," he said most emphatically. "Same sort of script."

"Exactly the same? I mean, would you swear to the same writer?"

"No, no! 'Course not. Only got a glimpse of the other, but I rather fancy myself on handwriting, you know."

"We rather fancy you, too."

"It was very similar," said Lord Robert. "It was exceedingly similar. On my honour."

"Good Lord," said Alleyn mildly. "That's what the Americans call a break. Coincidence stretches out a long arm. So does the law. 'Shake,' says Coincidence. Not such a very long arm, after all, if this pretty fellow is working among one class only and it looks as if he is." He shoved a box of cigarettes in Lord Robert's direction. "We had an expert at that letter—the Mrs. H.-H. one you've got there. Woolworth paper. She didn't show us the envelope, of course. Woolworth ink and the sort of nib they use for script writing. It's square with a feeder. You notice the letters are all neatly fitted between the ruled lines. That and the script nib and the fact that the letters are careful copies of ordinary print completely knocks out any sort of individuality. There were no finger-prints and Mrs. Halcut-Hackett hadn't noticed the postmark. Come in!"

A police constable marched in with a packet of letters, laid them on the desk and marched out again.

"Half a moment while I have a look at my mail, Bunchy; there may just be—yes, by gum, there is!"

He opened an envelope, glanced at a short note, unfolded an enclosure, raised his eyebrows and handed it to Lord Robert.

"Wheeoo!" whistled Lord Robert.

It was a sheet of common ruled paper. Three or four rows of script were fitted neatly between the lines. Lord Robert read aloud:

> " 'Unforeseen circumstances prevented collection on Monday night. Please leave bag with same sum down between seat and left-hand arm of blue sofa in concert-room, 57, Constance Street, next Thursday afternoon.' "

"Mrs. Halcut-Hackett," said Alleyn, holding out the note, "explains that her unfortunate friend received this letter by yesterday evening's post. What's happening on Thursday at 57, Constance Street? Do you know?"

"Those new concert-rooms. Very smart. It's another charity show. Tickets on sale everywhere. Three guineas each. Chamber music. Bach. Sirmione Quartette. I'm going."

"Bunchy," said Alleyn, "let nothing wean you from the blue sofa. Talk to Mrs. Halcut-Hackett. Share the blue sofa with her and when the austere delights of Bach knock at your heart pay no attention but with the very comment of your soul——"

"Yes, yes, yes. Don't quote now, Roderick, or somebody may think you're a detective."

"Blast you!" said Alleyn.

Lord Robert gave a little crowing laugh and rose from his chair.

"I'm off," he said. Alleyn walked with him into the corridor. They shook hands. Alleyn stood looking after him as he walked away with small steps, a quaint out-of-date figure, black against a window at the end of the long passage. The figure grew smaller and smaller, paused for a second at the end of the passage, turned the corner and was gone.

3

Sequence to a Cocktail-Party

A few days after his visit to the yard, Lord Robert
Gospell attended a cocktail-party given by Mrs. Halcut-
Hackett for her plain protégée. Who this plain protégée
was, nobody seemed to know, but it was generally
supposed that Mrs. Halcut-Hackett's object in bringing her out was not entirely philanthropic. At the
moment nobody even remembered the girl's name but
merely recognised her as a kind of coda to Mrs.
Halcut-Hackett's social activities.

This was one of the first large cocktail-parties of the
season and there were as many as two hundred and fifty
guests there. Lord Robert adored parties of all kinds
and was, as Alleyn had pointed out, asked everywhere.
He knew intimately that section of people to whom the
London season is a sort of colossal hurdle to be taken in
an exhilarating leap or floundered over as well as may

be. He was in tremendous demand as a chaperone's partner, could be depended on to help with those unfortunate children of seventeen who, in spite of all the efforts of finishing schools, dressmakers, hairdressers, face-specialists and their unflagging mothers, were apt to be seen standing alone nervously smiling on the outskirts of groups. With these unhappy débutantes Lord Robert took infinite trouble. He would tell them harmless little stories and when they laughed would respond as if they themselves had said something amusing. His sharp little eyes would search about for younger men than himself and he would draw them into a group round himself and the girl. Because of his reputation as a gentle wit, the wariest and most conceited young men were always glad to be seen talking to Lord Robert, and soon the débutante would find herself the only girl in a group of men who seemed to be enjoying themselves. Her nervous smile would vanish and a delicious feeling of confidence would inspire her. And when Lord Robert saw her eyes grow bright and her hands relax, he would slip away and join the cluster of chaperones where he told stories a little less harmless and equally diverting.

But in the plain protégée of General and Mrs. Halcut-Hackett he met his Waterloo. She was not so very plain but only rather disastrously uneventful. Every inch of this unhappy child had been prepared for the cocktail-party with passionate care and at great expense by her chaperone—one of those important American women with lovely faces and cast-iron figures. Lord Robert was greeted by Mrs. Halcut-Hackett, who looked a little older than usual, and by her husband the General, a notable fire-eater who bawled "What!" two or three times and burst into loud surprising laughter which was his method of circulating massed gaiety. Lord Robert twinkled at him and passed on into the thick of the party. A servant whom he recognised as the Halcut-Hackett's butler gave him a drink. "Then they're not having Dimitri or anybody like that," thought Lord

Robert. He looked about him. On the right-hand side of the enormous room were collected the débutantes, and the young men who, in the last analysis, could make the antics of the best dance-bands in London, all the efforts of all the Dimitris, Miss Harrises, and Mrs. Halcut-Hacketts to the tune of a thousand pounds, look like a single impotent gesture. Among them were the young men who were spoken of, in varying degrees of irony, as "The Debs' Delight." Lord Robert half suspected his nephew Donald of being a Debs' Delight. There he was in the middle of it all with Bridget O'Brien, making himself agreeable. Very popular, evidently. "He'll have to settle down," thought Lord Robert. "He's altogether too irresponsible and he's beginning to look dissipated. Don't like it."

Then he saw the plain protégée of Mrs. Halcut-Hackett. She had just met a trio of incoming débutantes and had taken them to their right side of the room. He saw how they all spoke politely and pleasantly to her but without any air of intimacy. He saw her linger a moment while they were drawn into the whirlpool of high-pitched conversation. Then she turned away and stood looking towards the door where her chaperone dealt faithfully with the arrivals. She seemed utterly lost. Lord Robert crossed the room and greeted her with his old-fashioned bow.

"How-de-do. This *is* a good party," he said, with a beaming smile.

"Oh! Oh—I'm so glad."

"I'm an old hand, y'know," continued Lord Robert, "and I always judge a cocktail-party by the time that elapses between one's paying one's respects and getting a drink. Now this evening I was given this excellent drink within two minutes of shaking hands with the General. Being a thirsty, greedy old customer, I said to myself: 'Good party.' "

"I'm so glad," repeated the child.

She was staring, he noticed, at her chaperone, and he saw that Mrs. Halcut-Hackett was talking to a tall smooth man with a heavy face, lack-lustre eyes and a proprietary manner. Lord Robert looked fixedly at this individual.

"Do tell me," he said, "who is that man with our hostess?"

The girl started violently and without taking her gaze off Mrs. Halcut-Hackett, said woodenly: "It's Captain Withers."

"Ah," thought Lord Robert, "I fancied it was." Aloud he said: "Withers? Then it's not the same feller. I rather thought I knew him."

"Oh," said the protégée. She had turned her head slightly and he saw that she now looked at the General. "Like a frightened rabbit," thought Lord Robert. "For all the world like a frightened rabbit." The General had borne down upon his wife and Captain Withers. Lord Robert now witnessed a curious little scene. General Halcut-Hackett glared for three seconds at Captain Withers who smiled, bowed, and moved away. The General then spoke to his wife and immediately, for a fraction of a second, the terror—Lord Robert decided that terror was not too strong a word—that shone in the protégée's eyes was reflected in the chaperone's. Only for a second, and then with her husband she turned to greet a new arrival who Lord Robert saw with pleasure was Lady Alleyn. She was followed by a thin girl with copper-coloured hair and slanting eyebrows that at once reminded him of his friend Roderick. "Must be the niece," he decided. The girl at his side suddenly murmured an excuse and hurried away to greet Sarah Alleyn. Lord Robert finished his drink and was given another. In a few minutes he was surrounded by acquaintances and was embarked upon one of his new stories. He made his point very neatly, drifted away on the wave of laughter that greeted it, and found Lady Alleyn.

"My dear Bunchy," she said, "you are the very person I hoped to see. Come and gossip with me. I feel like a phoenix."

"You look like a princess," he said. "Why do we meet so seldom? Where shall we go?"

"If there is a corner reserved for grandmothers I ought to be in it. Good heavens, how everybody screams. How old are you, Bunchy?"

"Fifty-five, m'dear."

"I'm sixty-five. Do you find people very noisy nowadays or are you still too much of a chicken?"

"I enjoy parties, awfully, but I agree that there ain't much repose in modern intercourse."

"That's it," said Lady Alleyn, settling herself in a chair. "No repose. All the same I like the moderns, especially the fledgelings. As Roderick says, they finish their thoughts. *We* only did that in the privacy of our bedrooms and very often asked forgiveness of our Creator for doing it. What do you think of Sarah?"

"She looks a darling," said Lord Robert emphatically.

"She's a pleasant creature. Amazingly casual but she's got character and, I think, looks," said her grandmother. "Who are those young things she's talking to?"

"Bridget O'Brien and my young scapegrace of a nephew."

"So that's Evelyn Carrados's girl. She's like Paddy, isn't she?"

"She's very like both of 'em. Have you seen Evelyn lately?"

"We dined there last night for the play. What's the matter with Evelyn?"

"Eh?" exclaimed Lord Robert. "You've spotted it, have you? You're a wise woman, m'dear."

"She's all over the place. Does Carrados bully her?"

"Bully ain't quite the word. He's devilish grand and patient, though. But——"

"But there's something more. What was the reason for your meeting with Roderick the other day?"

"Hi!" expostulated Lord Robert in a hurry. "What are you up to?"

"I shouldn't let you tell me if you tried. I trust," said Lady Alleyn untruthfully but with great dignity, "that I am not a curious woman."

"That's pretty rich."

"I don't know what you mean," said Lady Alleyn grandly. "But I tell you what, Bunchy. I've got neurotic women on the brain. Nervous women. Women that are on their guard. It's a most extraordinary thing," she continued, rubbing her nose with a gesture that reminded Lord Robert of her son, "but there's precisely the same look in our hostess's mascaraed eyes as Evelyn Carrados had in her naturally beautiful ones. Or has this extraordinary drink gone to my head?"

"The drink," said Lord Robert firmly, "has gone to your head."

"Dear Bunchy," murmured Lady Alleyn. Their eyes met and they exchanged smiles. The cocktail-party surged politely about them. The noise, the smoke, the festive smell of flowers and alcohol, seemed to increase every moment. Wandering parents eddied round Lady Alleyn's chair. Lord Robert remained beside her listening with pleasure to her cool light voice and looking out of the corner of his eye at Mrs. Halcut-Hackett. Apparently all the guests had arrived. She was moving into the room. This was his chance. He turned round and suddenly found himself face to face with Captain Withers. For a moment they stood and looked at each other. Withers was a tall man and Lord Robert was obliged to tilt his head back a little. Withers was a fine arrogant figure, Lord Robert a plump and comical one. But oddly enough it was Lord Robert who seemed the more dominant and more dignified of these two men and before his mild glare the other suddenly looked furtive. His coarse, handsome face became quite white. Some seconds elapsed before he spoke.

"Oh—ah—how do you do?" said Captain Withers very heartily.

"Good evening," said Lord Robert and turned back to Lady Alleyn. Captain Withers walked quickly away.

"Why, Bunchy," said Lady Alleyn softly, "I've never seen you snub anybody before."

"D'you know who that was?"

"No."

"Feller called Maurice Withers. He's a throw-back to my Foreign Office days."

"He's frightened of you."

"I hope so," said Lord Robert. "I'll trot along and pay my respects to my hostess. It's been charming seeing you. Will you dine one evening? Bring Roderick. Can you give me an evening? Now?"

"I'm so busy with Sarah. May we ring you up? If it can be managed——"

"It must be, *Au 'voir,* m'dear."

"Good-bye, Bunchy."

He made his little bow and picked his way through the crowd to Mrs. Halcut-Hackett.

"I'm on my way out," he said, "but I hoped to get a word with you. Perfectly splendid party."

She turned all the headlights of her social manner full on him. It was, he decided compassionately, a bogus manner. An imitation, but what a good imitation. She called him "dear Lord Robert" like a grande dame in a slightly dated comedy. Her American voice, which he remembered thinking charming in her theatrical days, was now much disciplined and none the better for it. She asked him if he was doing the season very thoroughly and he replied with his usual twinkle that he got about a bit.

"Are you going to the show at the Constance Street Rooms on Thursday afternoon?" he asked. "I'm looking forward to that awfully."

Her eyes went blank but she scarcely paused before answering yes, she believed she was.

"It's the Sirmione Quartette," said Lord Robert. "Awfully good, ain't they? Real top-notchers."

Mrs. Halcut-Hackett said she adored music, especially classical music.

"Well," said Lord Robert, "I'll give myself the

pleasure of looking out for you there if it wouldn't bore you. Not so many people nowadays enjoy Bach."

Mrs. Halcut-Hackett said she thought Bach was marvellous.

"Do tell me," said Lord Robert with his engaging air of enjoying a gossip. "I've just run into a feller whose face looked as familiar as anything, but I can't place him. Feller over there talking to the girl in red."

He saw the patches of rouge on her cheeks suddenly start up in hard isolation and he thought: "That's shaken her, poor thing."

She said: "Do you mean Captain Maurice Withers?"

"May be. The name don't strike a chord, though. I've got a shocking memory. Better be getting along. May I look out for you on Thursday? Thank you so much. Good-bye."

"Good-bye, dear Lord Robert," said Mrs. Halcut-Hackett.

He edged his way out and was waiting patiently for his hat and umbrella when someone at his elbow said:

"Hullo, Uncle Bunch, are you going home?"

Lord Robert turned slowly and saw his nephew.

"What? Oh, it's you, Donald! Yes, I am! Taking a cab. Want a lift?"

"Yes, please," said Donald.

Lord Robert looked over his glasses at his nephew and remarked that he seemed rather agitated. He thought: "What the deuce is the matter with everybody?" but he only said: "Come along, then," and together they went out into the street. Lord Robert held up his umbrella and a taxi drew in to the kerb.

" 'Evening, m'lord," said the driver.

"Oh, it's you, is it?" said Lord Robert. " 'Evening. We're going home."

"Two hundred, Cheyne Walk. Very good, m'lord," wheezed the driver. He was a goggle-eyed, grey-haired, mottle-faced taximan with an air of good-humoured truculence about him. He slammed the door on them, jerked down the lever of his meter, and started up his engine.

"Everybody knows you, Uncle Bunch," said Donald in a voice that was not quite natural. "Even the casual taxi-driver."

"This feller cruises about in our part of the world," said Lord Robert. He twisted himself round in his seat and again looked at his nephew over the top of his glasses. "What's up?" he asked.

"I—well—nothing. I mean, why do you think anything's up?"

"Now then," said Lord Robert. "No jiggery-pokery. What's up?"

"Well, as a matter of fact," answered Donald, kicking the turned-up seat in front of him, "I did rather want a word with you. I—I'm in a bit of a tight corner, Uncle Bunch."

"Money?" asked his uncle.

"How did you guess?"

"Don't be an ass, my boy. What is it?"

"I—well, I was wondering if you would mind—I mean, I know I've been a bit extravagant. I'm damn' sorry it's happened. I suppose I've been a fool but I'm simply draped in sackcloth and steeped in ashes. Never again!"

"Come, come, come," said Lord Robert crisply. "What is it? Gambling?"

"Well—yes. With a slight hint of riotous living. Gambling mostly."

"Racing? Cards?"

"A bit, but actually I dropped the worst packet at roulette."

"Good Gad!" exclaimed Lord Robert with surprising violence. "Where the devil do you play roulette?"

"Well, actually it was at a house out at Leatherhead. It belongs to a man who was at that party. Some people I know took me there. It turned out to be a rather enterprising sort of gamble with a roulette-table and six fellows doing croupier. All in order, you know. I mean it's not run for anything but fun naturally, and Captain Withers simply takes on the bank——"

"*Who?*"

"The person's name is Withers."

"When was this party?"

"Oh, a week or so ago. They have them fairly regularly. I paid all right, but—but it just about cleaned me up. I had the most amazing bad luck, actually. Would you believe it there was a run of seventeen against me on the even chances? Bad. Very bad," said Donald with an unconvincing return to his lighter manner. "Disastrous, in fact."

"You're shying about," said Lord Robert. "What's the real trouble?"

"One of my cheques has been returned R.D. I'm bust."

"I paid your Oxford debts and started you off with five hundred as a yearly allowance. Are you telling me you've gone through five hundred since you came down?"

"I'm sorry," said Donald. "Yes."

"Your mother gives you four pounds a week, don't she?"

"Yes."

Lord Robert suddenly whisked out a notebook.

"How much was this returned cheque?"

"Fifty quid. Awful, isn't it?" He glanced at his uncle's profile and saw his lips were pursed in a soundless whistle. Donald decided that it was not as bad as he had feared and said more hopefully: "Isn't it a bore?"

Lord Robert, his pencil poised, said: "Who was it made out to?"

"To Wits—Withers—everyone calls him Wits. You see, I had a side bet with him."

Lord Robert wrote, turned, and looked over his spectacles at his nephew.

"I'll send Withers a cheque to-night," he said.

"Thank you so much, Uncle Bunch."

"What's the address?"

"Shackleton House, Leatherhead. He's got a flat in town but the Leatherhead address is all right."

"Any other debts?"

"One or two shops. They seem to be getting rather testy about it. And a restaurant or two."

"Here we are," said Lord Robert abruptly.

The taxi drew up outside the house he shared with his sister. They got out. Lord Robert paid and tipped the driver.

"How's the lumbago?" he asked.

"Not too bad, m'lord, thank you, m'lord."

"Good. 'Evening to you."

"Good evening, m'lord."

They entered the house in silence. Lord Robert said over his shoulder: "Come to my room."

He led the way, a small, comic, but somehow a rather resolute figure. Donald followed him into an old-fashioned study. Lord Robert sat at his desk and wrote a cheque with finicky movements of his fat hands. He blotted it meticulously, and swung round in his chair to face his nephew.

"You still of the same mind about this doctoring?" he asked.

"Well, that's the big idea," said Donald.

"Passed some examination for it, didn't you?"

"Medical prelim," said Donald easily. "Yes, I've got that."

"Before you were sent down for losing your mother's money. And mine."

Donald was silent.

"I'll get you out of this mess on one condition. I don't know the way you set about working for a medical degree. Our family's been in the diplomatic for a good many generations. High time we did something else, I dare say. You'll start work at Edinburgh as soon as they'll have you. If that's not at once I'll get a coach and you'll go to Archery and work there. I'll allow you as much as the usual medical student gets and I'll advise your mother to give you no more. That's all."

"Edinburgh! Archery!" Donald's voice was shrill with dismay. "But I don't want to go to Edinburgh for my training. I want to go to Thomas's."

"You're better away from London. There's one other thing I must absolutely insist upon, Donald. You are to drop this feller Withers."

"Why should I?"

"Because the feller's a bad 'un. I know something about him. I have never interfered in the matter of your friendships before, but I'd be neglectin' my duty like anything if I didn't step in here."

"I won't give up a friend simply because you choose to say he's no good."

"I give you my word of honour this man's a rotter—a criminal rotter. I was amazed when I recognised Withers this afternoon. My information dates from my Foreign Office days. It's unimpeachable. Very bad record. Come now, be sensible. Make a clean break and forget all about him. Archery's a nice old house. Your mother can use it as a *pied-à-terre* and see you sometimes. It's only ten miles out of Edinburgh."

"But——"

"Afraid it's definite."

"But—I don't want to leave London. I don't want to muck about with a lot of earnest Scots from God knows where. I mean the sort of people who go there are just simply The End!"

"Why?" asked Lord Robert.

"Well, because I mean, you know what I mean. They'll be the most unspeakable curiosities. No doubt perfectly splendid but——"

"But not in the same class with young men who contract debts of honour which they cannot meet and do the London season on their mother's money?"

"That's not fair," cried Donald hotly.

"Why?" repeated Lord Robert.

"I'll bet you got into the same sort of jams when you were my age."

"You're wrong," said Lord Robert mildly. "I did as

many silly things as most young men of my day. But I did not contract debts that I was unable to settle. It seemed to me that sort of thing amounted to theft. I didn't steal clothes from my tailor, drink from my hotel, or money from my friends."

"But I knew it would be all right in the end."

"You mean, you knew I'd pay?"

"I'm not ungrateful," said Donald angrily.

"My dear fellow, I don't want you to be grateful."

"But I won't go and stay in a deserted mausoleum of a Scotch house in the middle of the season. There's—there's Bridget."

"Lady Carrados's gel? Is she fond of you?"

"Yes."

"She seems a nice creature. You're fortunate. Not one of these screeching rattles. She'll wait for you."

"I won't go."

"M'dear boy, I'm sorry, but you've no alternative."

Donald's face was white but two scarlet patches burned on his cheek-bones. His lips trembled. Suddenly he burst out violently.

"You can keep your filthy money," he shouted. "By God, I'll look after myself. I'll borrow from someone who's not a bloody complacent Edwardian relic and I'll get a job and pay them back as I can."

"Jobs aren't to be had for the asking. Come now——"

"Oh, shut up!" bawled Donald and flung out of the room.

Lord Robert stared at the door which his nephew had not neglected to slam. The room was very quiet. The fire settled down with a small whisper of ashes and Lord Robert's clock ticked on the mantelpiece. It ticked very loudly. The plump figure, only half-lit by the lamp on the desk, was quite still, the head resting on the hand. Lord Robert sighed, a slight mournful sound. At last he pulled an envelope towards him and in his finicky writing addressed it to Captain Withers, Shackleton House, Leatherhead. Then he wrote a short note, folded

a cheque into it and put them both in the envelope. He
rang for his butler.

"Has Mr. Donald gone out?"

"Yes, m'lord. He said he would not be returning."

"I see," said Lord Robert. "Thank you. Will you see
that this letter is posted immediately?"

4

Blackmail to Music

Lord Robert had sat on the blue sofa since two o'clock but he was not tired of it. He enjoyed watching the patrons of music arriving and he amused himself with idle speculations on the subject of intellectual snobbishness. He also explored the blue sofa, sliding his hands cautiously over the surface of the seat and down between the seat and the arms. He had taken the precaution of leaving his gloves on a chair on the left of the sofa and a little behind it. A number of people came and spoke to him, among them Lady Carrados who was looking tired.

"You're overdoing it, Evelyn," he told her. "You look charming—that's a delightful gown, ain't it?—but you're too fragile, m'dear."

"I'm all right, Bunchy," she said. "You've got a nice way of telling a woman she's getting older."

"No, I say! It wasn't that. Matter of fact it rather suits you bein' so fine-drawn, but you are too thin, you know. Where's Bridgie?"

"At a matinée."

"Evelyn, do you know if she sees anything of my nephew?"

"Donald Potter? Yes. We've heard all about it, Bunchy."

"He's written to his mother who no doubt is giving him money. I suppose you know he's sharing rooms with some other feller?"

"Yes. Bridgie sees him."

"Does Bridgie know where he is?"

"I think so. She hasn't told me."

"Is she fond of the boy, Evelyn?"

"Yes."

"What do you think of him?"

"I don't know. He's got a lot of charm, but I wish he'd settle down."

"Is it botherin' you much?"

"That?" She caught her breath. "A little, naturally. Oh, *there's* Lady Alleyn! We're supposed to be together."

"Delightful woman, ain't she? I'm waiting for Mrs. Halcut-Hackett."

"I shouldn't have thought her quite your cup of tea," said Lady Carrados vaguely.

Lord Robert made his rabbit-face and winked.

"We go into mutual raptures over Bach," he said.

"I must join Lady Alleyn. Good-bye, Bunchy."

"Good-bye, Evelyn. Don't worry too much—over anything."

She gave him a startled look and went away. Lord Robert sat down again. The room was nearly full and in ten minutes the Sirmione Quartette would appear on the modern dais.

"Is she waiting for the lights to go down?" wondered Lord Robert. He saw Agatha Troy come in, tried to catch her eye, and failed. People were beginning to settle down in the rows of gilt chairs and in the odd armchairs and sofas round the walls. Lord Robert looked restlessly towards the door and saw Sir Daniel Davidson. Davidson made straight for him. Sir Daniel had once cured Lord Robert's sister of indigestion and Mildred, who was an emotional woman, had asked him to dinner. Lord Robert had been amused and interested by Davidson. His technique as a fashionable doctor was superb. "If Disraeli had taken to medicine instead of primroses," Lord Robert had said, "he would have been just such another." And he had encouraged Davidson to launch out on his favourite subject, The Arts, with rather emphatic capitals. He had capped Davidson's Latin tags, quoted Congreve against him, and listened with amusement to a preposterous parallel drawn between Rubens and Dürer. "The extrovert and the introvert of Art," Davidson had cried, waving his beautiful hands, and Lord Robert had twinkled and said: "You are talking above my head." "I'm talking nonsense," Davidson had replied abruptly, "and you know it." But in a minute or two he had been off again as flamboyantly as ever and had left at one o'clock in the morning, very pleased with himself and overflowing with phrases.

"Ah!" he said now as he shook hands. "I might have guessed I should find you here. Doing the fashionable thing for the unfashionable reason. Music! My God!"

"What's wrong?" asked Lord Robert.

"My dear Lord Robert, how many of these people will know what they are listening to, or even listen? Not one in fifty."

"Oh, come now!"

"Not one in fifty! There goes that fellow Withers whose aesthetic appreciation is less than that of a monkey on a barrel-organ. What's he here for? I repeat, not one in fifty of these humbugs knows what he's listening to. And how many of the forty-nine have the courage to confess themselves honest philistines?"

"Quite a number, I should have thought," said Lord Robert cheerfully. "Myself for one. I'm inclined to go to sleep."

"Now, why say that? You know perfectly well——What's the matter?"

"Sorry. I was looking at Evelyn Carrados. She looks

damn' seedy," said Lord Robert. Davidson followed his glance to where Lady Carrados sat beside Lady Alleyn. Davidson watched her for a moment and then said quietly:

"Yes. She's overdoing it. I shall have to scold her. My seat is somewhere over there, I believe." He made an impatient gesture. "They all overdo it, these mothers, and the girls overdo it, and the husbands get rattled and the young men neglect their work and then there are half a dozen smart weddings, as many nervous breakdowns and there's your London season."

"Lor'!" said Lord Robert mildly.

"It's the truth. In my job one sees it over and over again. Yes, yes, yes, I know! I am a smart West End doctor and I encourage all these women to fancy themselves ill. That's what you may very well think, but I assure you, my dear Lord Robert, that one sees cases of nervous exhaustion that are enough to make a cynic of the youngest ingenue. And they are so charming, these mamas. I mean really charming. Women like Lady Carrados. They help each other so much. It is not all a cutlet for cutlet. But"—he spread out his hands—"what is it for? What is it all about? The same people meeting each other over and over again at great expense to the accompaniment of loud negroid noises on jazz bands. For what?"

"Damned if I know," said Lord Robert cheerfully. "Who's that feller who came in behind Withers? Tall, dark feller with the extraordinary hands. I seem to know him."

"Where? Ah, I see." Davidson picked up his glasses which he wore on a wide black ribbon. "Who is it, now! I'll tell you who it is. It's the catering fellow, Dimitri. He's having his three guineas' worth of Bach with the *haute monde* and, by God, I'll wager you anything you like that he's got more appreciation in his extraordinary little finger—you are very observant, it *is* an odd hand—than most of them have in the whole of their pampered carcasses. How do you do, Mrs. Halcut-Hackett?"

She had come up so quietly that Lord Robert had actually missed her. She looked magnificent. Davidson, to Lord Robert's amusement, kissed her hand.

"Have you come to worship?" he asked.

"Why, certainly," she said and turned to Lord Robert. "I see you have not forgotten."

"How could I?"

"Now isn't that nice?" asked Mrs. Halcut-Hackett, looking slantways at the blue sofa. Lord Robert moved aside and she at once sat down, spreading her furs.

"I must find my seat," said Davidson. "They are going to begin."

He went to a chair beside Lady Carrados on the far side of the room. Mrs. Halcut-Hackett asked Lord Robert if he did not think Sir Daniel a delightful personality. He noticed that her American accent was not quite so strictly repressed as usual and that her hands moved restlessly. She motioned him to sit on her right.

"If you don't mind," he said, "I'll stick to my chair. I like straight backs."

He saw her glance nervously at his chair which was a little behind the left arm of the sofa. Her bag was on her lap. It was a large bag and looked well filled. She settled her furs again so that they fell across it. Lord Robert perched on his hideously uncomfortable chair. He noticed that Dimitri had sat down at the end of a row of seats close by. He found himself idly watching Dimitri. "Wonder what he thinks of us. Always arranging food for our parties and he could buy most of us up and not notice it, I shouldn't mind betting. They *are* rum hands and no mistake. The little finger's the same length as the third."

A flutter of polite clapping broke out and the Sirmione String Quartette walked on to the dais. The concealed lights of the concert chamber were dimmed into darkness, leaving the performers brilliantly lit. Lord Robert experienced thaf familiar thrill that follows the glorious scrape of tuning strings. But he told himself he had not come to listen to music and he was careful not to look towards the dais lest his eyes should be blinded by the light. Instead he looked towards the left-hand arm of the blue sofa. The darkness gradually thinned and presently he could make out the dim sheen of brocade and the thick depth of blackness that was Mrs. Halcut-Hackett's furs. The shape of this blackness shifted. Something glinted. He bent forward. Closer than the exquisite pattern of the music he caught the sound made by one fabric rubbed against another, a sliding rustle. The outline of the mass that was Mrs. Halcut-Hackett went tense and then relaxed. "She's stowed it away," thought Lord Robert.

Nobody came near them until the lights went up for the interval and then Lord Robert realised how very well the blackmailer had chosen when he hit upon the blue sofa as a postbox, for the side door beyond it was thrown open during the interval and instead of going out into the lounge by the main entrance many people passed behind the blue sofa and out by this side door. And as the interval drew to a close people came in and stood behind the sofa gossiping. Lord Robert felt sure that his man had gone into the lounge. He would wait until the lights were lowered and come in with the rest of the stragglers, pass behind the sofa and slip his hand over the arm. Most of the men and many of the women had gone out to smoke, but Lord Robert remained uncomfortably wedded to his chair. He knew very well that Mrs. Halcut-Hackett writhed under the pressure of conflicting desires. She wished to be alone when the bag was taken and she dearly loved a title. She was to have the title. Suddenly she murmured something about powdering her nose. She got up and left by the side door.

Lord Robert rested his head on his hand and devoted the last few minutes of the interval to a neat imitation of an elderly gentleman dropping off to sleep. The lights were lowered again. The stragglers, with mumbled apologies, came back. There was a little group of people still standing in the darkness behind the sofa. The performers returned to the dais.

Someone had advanced from behind Lord Robert and stood beside the sofa.

Lord Robert felt his heart jump. He had placed his chair carefully, leaving a space between himself and the left-hand arm of the sofa. Into this space the shadowy figure now moved. It was a man. He stood with his back to the lighted dais and he seemed to lean forward a little as though he searched the darkness for something. Lord Robert also leant forward. He emitted the most delicate hint of a snore. His right hand propped his head. Through the cracks of his fat fingers he watched the left arm of the sofa. Into this small realm of twilight came the shape of a hand. It was a curiously thin hand and he could see quite clearly that the little finger was as long as the third.

Lord Robert snored.

The hand slid over into the darkness and when it came back it held Mrs. Halcut-Hackett's bag.

As if in ironic appreciation the music on the dais swept up a sharp crescendo into a triumphant blare. Mrs. Halcut-Hackett returned from powdering her nose.

5

Unqualified Success

The ball given by Lady Carrados for her daughter
Bridget O'Brien was an unqualified success. That is
to say that from half-past ten when Sir Herbert
and Lady Carrados took up their stand at the
head of the double staircase and shook hands with the
first guests until half-past three the next morning when
the band, white about the gills and faintly glistening,
played the National Anthem, there was not a moment
when it was not difficult for a young man to find the
débutantes with whom he wished to dance and easy for
him to avoid those by whom he was not attracted. There
was no ominous aftermath when the guests began to
slide away to other parties, to slip through the doors
with the uncontrollable heartlessness of the unamused.
The elaborate structure, built to pattern by Lady
Carrados, Miss Harris and Dimitri, did not slide away
like a sand-castle before a wave of unpopularity, but
held up bravely till the end. It was, therefore, an
unqualified success.

In the matter of champagne Lady Carrados and Miss Harris had triumphed. It flowed not only in the supper-room but also at the buffet. In spite of the undoubted fact that débutantes do not drink, Dimitri's men opened two hundred bottles of Heidsieck '28 that night and Sir Herbert afterwards took a sort of well-bred pride in the rows of empty bottles he happened to see in a glimpse behind the scenes.

Outside the house it was unseasonably chilly. The mist made by the breathing of the watchers mingled with drifts of light fog. As the guests walked up the strip of red carpet from their cars to the great door they passed between two wavering masses of dim faces. And while the warmth and festive smell of flowers and expensive scents reached the noses of the watchers, through the great doors was driven the smell of mist so that the footmen in the hall told each other from time to time that for June it was an uncommonly thickish night outside.

By midnight everybody knew the ball was a success and was able when an opportunity presented itself to say so to Lady Carrados. Leaving her post at the stair-head she came into the ballroom looking very beautiful and made her way towards the far end where most of the chaperones were assembled. On her way she passed her daughter dancing with Donald Potter. Bridget smiled brilliantly at her mother, and raised her left hand in gay salute. Her right hand was crushed against Donald's chest and round the misty white nonsense of her dress was his black arm and his hard masculine hand was pressed against her ribs. "She's in love with him," thought Lady Carrados. And up through the maze of troubled thoughts that kept her company came the remembrance of her conversation with Donald's uncle. She wondered suddenly if women ever fainted from worry alone and as she smiled and bowed her way along the ballroom she saw herself suddenly crumpling down among the dancers. She would lie there while the band played on and presently she would open her eyes and see people's legs and then some one would help her to her feet and she would beg them to get her away quickly before anything was noticed. Her fingers tightened on her bag. Five hundred pounds! She had told the man at the bank that she wanted to pay some of the expenses of the ball in cash. That had been a mistake. She should have sent Miss Harris with the cheque and made no explanation to anybody. It was twelve o'clock. The letter had said she was to leave her bag on the little Sheraton writing-table in the green room before one o'clock. She would do it on her way to supper. There was that plain Halcut-Hackett protégée without a partner again. Lady Carrados looked round desperately and to her relief saw her husband making his way towards the girl. She felt a sudden wave of affection for her husband. Should she go to him to-night and tell him everything? And just sit back and take the blow? She must be very ill indeed to dream of such a thing. Here she was in the chaperones' corner and there, thank God, was Lady Alleyn with an empty chair beside her.

"Evelyn!" cried Lady Alleyn. "Come and sit down, my dear, in all your triumph. My granddaughter has just told me this is the very pinnacle of all balls. Everybody is saying so."

"I'm so thankful. It's such a toss-up nowadays. One never knows."

"Of course one doesn't. Last Tuesday at the Gainscotts' by one o'clock there were only the three Gainscott girls, a few desperate couples who hadn't the heart to escape, and my Sarah and her partner whom I had kept there by sheer terrorism. Of course, they didn't have Dimitri, and I must say I think he *is* a perfect magician. Dear me," said Lady Alleyn, "I *am* enjoying myself."

"I'm so glad."

"I hope you are enjoying yourself, too, Evelyn. They say the secret of being a good hostess is to enjoy yourself at your own parties. I have never believed it. Mine were always a nightmare to me and I refuse to admit they were failures. But they are so exhausting. I suppose you wouldn't come down to Danes Court with me and turn yourself into an amiable cow for the week-end?"

"Oh," said Lady Carrados, "I wish I could."

"Do."

"That's what Sir Daniel Davidson said I should do—lead the life of a placid cow for a bit."

"It's settled, then."

"But——"

"Nonsense. There is Davidson, isn't it? That dark flamboyant-looking man talking to Lucy Lorrimer. On my left."

"Yes."

"Is he clever? Everyone seems to go to him. I might show him my leg one of these days. If you don't promise to come, Evelyn, I shall call him over here and make a scene. Here comes Bunchy Gospell," continued Lady Alleyn with a quick glance at her hostess's trembling fingers, "and I feel sure he's going to ask you to sup with him. Why, if that isn't Agatha Troy with him!"

"The painter?" said Lady Carrados faintly. "Yes. Bridgie knows her. She's going to paint Bridgie."

"She did a sketch portrait of my son Roderick. It's amazingly good."

Lord Robert, looking, with so large an expanse of white under his chin, rather like Mr. Pickwick, came beaming towards them with Troy at his side. Lady Alleyn held out her hand and drew Troy down to a stool beside her. She looked at the short dark hair, the long neck and the spare grace that was Troy's and wished, not for the first time, that it was her daughter-in-law that sat at her feet. Troy was the very wife she would have chosen for her son, and, so she believed, the wife that he would have chosen for himself. She rubbed her nose vexedly. "If it hadn't been for that wretched case!" she thought. And she said:

"I'm so pleased to see you, my dear. I hear the exhibition is the greatest success."

Troy gave her a sideways smile.

"I wonder," continued Lady Alleyn, "which of us is

the most surprised at seeing the other. I have bounced out of retirement to launch my granddaughter."

"I was brought by Bunchy Gospell," said Troy. "I'm so seldom smart and gay that I'm rather enjoying it."

"Roderick had actually consented to come but he's got a tricky case on his hands and has to go away again to-morrow at the crack of dawn."

"Oh," said Troy.

Lord Robert began to talk excitedly to Lady Carrados.

"Gorgeous!" he cried, pitching his voice very high in order to top the band which had suddenly begun to make a terrific din. "Gorgeous, Evelyn! Haven't enjoyed anything—ages—superb!" He bent his knees and placed his face rather close to Lady Carrados's. "Supper!" he squeaked. "Do say you will! In half an hour or so. Will you?"

She smiled and nodded. He sat down between Lady Carrados and Lady Alleyn and gave them each a little pat. His hand alighted on Lady Carrados's bag. She moved it quickly. He was beaming out into the ballroom and seemed lost in a mild ecstasy.

"Champagne!" he said. "Can't beat it! I'm not inebriated, my dears, but I am, I proudly confess, a little exalted. What I believe is nowadays called nicely thank you. How-de-do? Gorgeous, ain't it?"

General and Mrs. Halcut-Hackett bowed. Their smiling lips moved in a soundless assent. They sat down between Lady Alleyn and Sir Daniel Davidson and his partner, Lady Lorrimer.

Lucy, Dowager Marchioness of Lorrimer, was a woman of eighty. She dressed almost entirely in veils and untidy jewellery. She was enormously rich and not a little eccentric. Sir Daniel attended to her lumbago. She was now talking to him earnestly and confusedly and he listened with an air of enraptured attention. Lord Robert turned with a small bounce and made two bobs in their direction.

"There's Davidson," he said delightedly, "and Lucy Lorrimer. How are you, Lucy?"

"What?" shouted Lucy Lorrimer.

"How are yer?"

"Busy. I thought you were in Australia."

"Why?"

"What?"

"Why?"

"Don't interrupt," shouted Lucy Lorrimer. "I'm talking."

"Never been there," said Lord Robert; "the woman's mad." The Halcut-Hacketts smiled uncomfortably. Lucy Lorrimer leant across Davidson and bawled: "Don't forget to-morrow night!"

"Who? Me?" asked Lord Robert. "Of course not."

"Eight-thirty sharp."

"I know. Though how you could think I was in Australia——"

"I didn't see it was you," screamed Lucy Lorrimer. "Don't forget now." The band stopped as abruptly as it had begun and her voice rang out piercingly. "It wouldn't be the first night you had disapponted me."

She leant back chuckling and fanning herself. Lord Robert took the rest of the party in with a comical glance.

"Honestly, Lucy!" said Lady Alleyn.

"He's the most absent-minded creature in the world," added Lucy Lorrimer.

"Now to that," said Lord Robert, "I do take exception. I am above all things a creature of habit, upon my honour. I could tell you, if it wasn't a very boring sort of story, exactly to the minute what I shall do with myself to-morrow evening and how I shall ensure my punctual arrival at Lucy Lorrimer's party."

"Suddenly remember it at a quarter to nine and take a cab," said Lucy Lorrimer.

"Not a bit of it."

Mrs. Halcut-Hackett suddenly joined in the conversation.

"I can vouch for Lord Robert's punctuality," she said loudly. "He always keeps his appointments." She laughed a little too shrilly and for some unaccountable reason created an uncomfortable atmosphere. Lady Alleyn glanced sharply at her. Lucy Lorrimer stopped short in the middle of a hopelessly involved sentence; Davidson put up his glass and stared. General Halcut-Hackett said "What!" loudly and uneasily. Lord Robert examined hs fat little hands with an air of complacent astonishment. The inexplicable tension was relieved by the arrival of Sir Herbert Carrados with the plain protégée of the Halcut-Hacketts. She held her long chiffon handkerchief to her face and she looked a little desperately at her chaperone. Carrados who had her by the elbow was the very picture of British chivalry.

"A casualty!" he said archly. "Mrs. Halcut-Hackett, I'm afraid you are going to be very angry with me!"

"Why, Sir Herbert!" said Mrs. Halcut-Hackett; "that's surely an impossibility."

The General said "What!"

"This young lady," continued Carrados, squeezing her elbow, "no sooner began to dance with me than she developed toothache. Frightfully bad luck—for both of us."

Mrs. Halcut-Hackett eyed her charge with something very like angry despair.

"What's the matter," she said, "darling?"

"I'm afraid I'd better go home."

Lady Carrados took her hand.

"That *is* bad luck," she said. "Shall we see if we can find something to——"

"No, no, please," said the child. "I think really, I'd better go home. I—I'm sure I'd better. Really."

The General suddenly became human. He stood up, took the girl by the shoulders, and addressed Lady Carrados.

"Better at home," he said. "What? Brandy and oil of cloves. Damn' bad show. Will you excuse us?" He addressed his wife. "I'll take her home. You stay on. Come back for you." He addressed his charge: "Come on, child. Get your wrap."

"You need not come back for me, dear," said Mrs. Halcut-Hackett. "I shall be quite all right. Stay with Rose."

"If I may," squeaked Lord Robert, "I'll give myself the pleasure of driving your wife home, Halcut-Hackett."

"No, no," began Mrs. Halcut-Hackett, "I— please——"

"Well," said the General. "Suit splendidly. What? Say good night. What?" They bowed and shook hands. Sir Herbert walked away with both of them. Mrs. Halcut-Hackett embarked on a long polite explanation and apology to Lady Carrados.

"Poor child!" whispered Lady Alleyn.

"Poor child, indeed," murmured Troy.

Mrs. Halcut-Hackett had made no further reply to Lord Robert's offer. Now, as he turned to her, she hurriedly addressed herself to Davidson.

"I must take the poor lamb to a dentist," she said. "Too awful if her face should swell half-way through the season. Her mother is my dearest friend but she'd never forgive me. A major tragedy."

"Quite," said Sir Daniel rather dryly.

"Well," said Lucy Lorrimer beginning to collect her scarves, "I shall expect you at eight twenty-seven. It's only me and my brother, you know. The one that got into difficulties. I want some supper. Where is Mrs. Halcut-Hackett? I suppose I must congratulate her on her ball, though I must say I always think it's the greatest mistake——"

Sir Daniel Davidson hurriedly shouted her down.

"Let me take you down and give you some supper," he suggested loudly with an agonised glance at Mrs. Halcut-Hackett and Lady Carrados. He carried Lucy Lorrimer away.

"Poor Lucy!" said Lady Alleyn. "She never has the remotest idea where she is. I wish, Evelyn, that he hadn't stopped her. What fault do you suppose she was about to find in your hospitality?"

"Let's follow them, Evelyn," said Lord Robert, "and

no doubt we shall find out. Troy m'dear, there's a young man making for you. May we dance again?"

"Yes, of course, Bunchy dear," said Troy, and went off with her partner.

Lady Carrados said she would meet Lord Robert in the supper-room in ten minutes. She left them, threading her way down the ballroom, her fingers clutching her bag. At the far end she overtook Sir Daniel and Lucy Lorrimer.

Lady Alleyn, looking anxiously after her, saw her sway a little. Davidson stepped up to her quickly and took her arm, steadying her. Lady Alleyn saw him speak to her with a quick look of concern. She saw Evelyn Carrados shake her head, smiling at him. He spoke again with emphasis and then Lucy Lorrimer shouted at him and he shrugged his shoulders and moved away. After a moment Lady Carrados, too, left the ballroom.

Lord Robert asked Mrs. Halcut-Hackett if she would "take a turn" with him once round the room. She excused herself, making rather an awkward business of it:

"I fancy I said that I would keep this one for—I'm so sorry——Oh, yes—here he comes right now."

Captain Withers had come from the farther side of the ballroom. Mrs. Halcut-Hackett hurriedly got up and went to meet him. Without a word he placed his arm round her and they moved off together, Withers looking straight in front of him.

"Where's Rory?" Lord Robert asked Lady Alleyn. "I expected to find him here to-night. He refused to dine with us."

"Working at the Yard. He's going north early to-morrow. Bunchy, that was your Captain Withers, wasn't it? The man we saw at the Halcut-Hackett's cocktail-party?"

"Yes."

"Is she having an affair with him, do you suppose? They've got that sort of look."

Lord Robert pursed his lips and contemplated his hands.

"It's *not* malicious curiosity," said Lady Alleyn. "I'm worried about those women. Especially Evelyn."

"You don't suggest Evelyn——?"

"Of course not. But they've both got the same haunted look. And if I'm not mistaken Evelyn nearly fainted just then. Your friend Davidson noticed it and I think he gave her the scolding she needs. She's at the end of her tether, Bunchy."

"I'll get hold of her and take her into the supper-room."

"Do. Go after her now, like a dear man. There comes my Sarah."

Lord Robert hurried away. It took him some time to get round the ballroom and as he edged past dancing couples and over the feet of sitting chaperones he suddenly felt as if an intruder had thrust open all the windows of this neat little world and let in a flood of uncompromising light. In this cruel light he saw the people he liked best and they were changed and belittled. He saw his nephew Donald, who had turned aside when they met in the hall, as a spoilt, selfish boy with no honesty or ambition. He saw Evelyn Carrados as a woman haunted by some memory that was discreditable, and rag-ridden by a blackmailer. His imagination leapt into extravagance, and in many of the men he fancied he saw something of the unscrupulousness of Withers, the pomposity of Carrados, and the stupidity of old General Halcut-Hackett. He was plunged into a violent depression that had a sort of nightmare-ish quality. How many of these women were what he still thought of as "virtuous?" And the débutantes? They had gone back to chaperones and were guided and guarded by women, many of whose own private lives would look ugly in this flood of hard light that had been let in on Lord Robert's world. The girls were sheltered by a convention for three months but at the same time they heard all sorts of things that would have horrified and bewildered his sister Mildred at their age. And he wondered if the Victorian and

Edwardian eras had been no more than freakish incidents in the history of society and if their proprieties
had been as artificial as the paint on a modern woman's
lips. This idea seemed abominable to Lord Robert and
he felt old and lonely for the first time in his life. "It's
the business with Donald and this blackmailing game,"
he thought as he twisted aside to avoid a couple who
were dancing the rumba. He had reached the door. He
went into the lounge which opened off the ballroom, saw
that Evelyn Carrados was not there, and made for the
staircase. The stairs were covered with couples sitting
out. He picked his way down and passed his nephew
Donald who looked at him as if they were strangers.

"No good trying to break that down," thought Lord
Robert. "Not here. He'd only cut me and someone
would notice." He felt wretchedly depressed and tired,
and was filled with a premonition of disaster that quite
astonished himself. "Good God," he thought suddenly,
"I must be going to be ill." And oddly enough this
comforted him a little. In the lower hall he found
Bridget O'Brien with a neat, competent-looking young
woman whose face he dimly remembered.

"Now, Miss Harris," Bridgie was saying, "are you
sure you're getting on all right? Have you had supper?"

"Well, thank you so much Miss O'Brien, but really it
doesn't matter——"

Of course, it was Evelyn's secretary. Nice of Evelyn to
ask her. Nice of Bridgie to take trouble. He said:

"Hullo, m'dear. What a grand ball. Has your mother
come this way?"

"She's in the supper-room," said Bridget without
looking at him and he realised that of course she had
heard Donald's side of their quarrel. He said:

"Thank you, Bridgie, I'll find her." He saw Miss
Harris was looking a little like a lost child so he said:
"Wonder if you'd be very nice and give me a dance later
on? Would you?"

Miss Harris turned scarlet and said she would be very
pleased thank you, Lord—Lord Gospell.

"Got it wrong," thought Lord Robert. "Poor things, they don't get much fun. Wonder what *they* think of it all. Not much, you may depend upon it."

He found Lady Carrados in the supper-room. He took her to a corner table, made her drink champagne and tried to persuade her to eat.

"I know what you're all like," he told her. "Nothing all day in your tummies and then get through the night on your nerves. I remember mama used to have the vapours whenever she gave a big party. She always came round in time to receive the guests."

He chattered away, eating a good deal himself and getting over his own unaccountable fit of depression in his effort to help Lady Carrados. He looked round and saw that the supper-room was inhabited by only a few chaperones and their partners. Poor Davidson was still in Lucy Lorrimer's toils. Withers and Mrs. Halcut-Hackett were tucked away in a corner. She was talking to him earnestly and apparently with great emphasis. He glowered at the table and laughed unpleasantly.

"Lor!" thought Lord Robert, "she's giving him his marching order. Now why's that? Afraid of the General or of—what? Of the blackmailer? I wonder if Withers is the subject of those letters. I wonder if Dimitri has seen her with him some time. I'll swear it was Dimitri's hand. But what does he know about Evelyn? The least likely woman in the world to have a guilty secret. And, damme, there is the fellow as large as you please, running the whole show."

Dimitri had come into the supper-room. He gave a professional look around, spoke to one of his waiters, came across to Lady Carrados and bowed tentatively and then went out again.

"Dimitri is a great blessing to all of us," said Lady Carrados. She said it so simply that he knew at once that if Dimitri was blackmailing her she had no idea of it. He was hunting in his mind for something to reply when Bridget came into the supper-room.

She was carrying her mother's bag.

Everything seemed to happen at the same moment. Bridget calling gaily: "Really, Donna darling, you're *hopeless*. There was your bag, simply preggy with banknotes, lying on the writing-table in the green boudoir. And I *bet* you didn't know where you'd left it." Then Bridget seeing her mother's face and crying out: "Darling, what's the matter?" Lord Robert himself getting up and interposing his bulk between Lady Carrados and the other tables. Lady Carrados half laughing, half crying and reaching out frantically for the bag. Himself saying: "Run away, Bridget, I'll look after your mother." And Lady Carrados, in a whisper: "I'm all right. Run upstairs, darling, and get my smelling-salts."

Somehow they persuaded Bridget to go. The next thing that happened was Sir Daniel Davidson who stood over Evelyn Carrados like an elegant dragon.

"You're all right," he said. "Lord Robert, see if you can open that window."

Lord Robert succeeded in opening the window. A damp hand seemed to be laid on his face. He caught sight of street lamps blurred by impalpable mist.

Davidson held Lady Carrado's wrist in his long fingers and looked at her with a sort of compassionate exasperation.

"You women," he said. "You impossible women."

"I'm all right. I simply felt giddy."

"You ought to lie down. You'll faint and make an exhibition of yourself."

"No I won't. Has anybody——?"

"Nobody's noticed anything. Will you go up to your room for half an hour?"

"I haven't got a room. It's not my house."

"Of course it's not. The cloakroom, then."

"I—yes. Yes, I'll do that."

"Sir Daniel!" shouted Lucy Lorrimer in the corner.

"For Heaven's sake go back to her," implored Lady Carrados, "or she'll be here."

"Sir Daniel!"

"Damn!" whispered Davidson. "Very well, I'll go back to her. I expect your maid's here, isn't she? Good. Lord Robert, will you take Lady Carrados?"

"I'd rather go alone. Please!"

"Obstinate woman. Promise you'll send your maid if you want me."

"Very well. But *please go.*"

He made a grimace and returned to Lucy Lorrimer.

Lady Carrados stood up, holding her bag.

"Come on," said Lord Robert. "Nobody's paying any attention."

He took her elbow and they went out into the hall. It was deserted. Two men stood just in the entrance to the cloakroom. They were Captain Withers and Donald Potter. Donald glanced round, saw his uncle, and at once began to move upstairs. Withers followed him. Dimitri came out of the buffet and also went upstairs. The hall was filled with the sound of the band and with the thick confusion of voices and sliding feet.

"Bunchy," whispered Lady Carrados. "You must do as I ask you. Leave me for three minutes. I——"

"I know what's up, m'dear. Don't do it. Don't leave your bag. Face it and let him go to the devil."

She pressed her hand against her mouth and looked wildly at him.

"You *know?*"

"Yes, and I'll help. I know who it is. You don't, do you? See here—there's a man at the Yard—whatever it is——"

A look of something like relief came into her eyes.

"But you don't know what it's about. Let me go. I've *got* to do it. Just this once more."

She pulled her arm away and he watched her cross the hall and slowly climb the stairs.

After a moment's hesitation he followed her.

6

Bunchy Goes Back to the Yard

Alleyn closed his file and looked at his watch. Two
minutes to one. Time for him to pack up and go home.
He yawned, stretched his cramped fingers, walked
over to the window and pulled aside the blind. The row
of lamps hung like a necklace of misty globes along the
margin of the Embankment.

"Fog in June," muttered Alleyn. "This England!"

Out there in the cold Big Ben tolled one. At that
moment, three miles away at Lady Carrados's ball, Lord
Robert Gospell was slowly climbing the stairs to the top
landing and the little drawing-room.

Alleyn filled his pipe slowly and lit it. An early start
to-morrow, a long journey, and a piece of dull routine at
the end of it. He held his fingers to the heater and fell
into a long meditation. Sarah had told him Troy was
going to the ball. She was there now, no doubt.

"Oh, well!" he thought and turned off his heater.

The desk telephone rang. He answered it.

"Hullo?"

"Mr. Alleyn? I thought you were still there, sir. Lord Robert Gospell."

"Right."

A pause and then a squeaky voice.

"Rory?"

"Bunchy?"

"You said you'd be at it till late. I'm in a room by myself at the Carrados's show. Thing is, I think I've got him. Are you working for much longer?"

"I can."

"May I come round to the Yard?"

"Do!"

"I'll go home first, get out of this boiled shirt and pick up my notes."

"Right. I'll wait."

"It's the cakes-and-ale feller."

"Good Lord! No names, Bunchy."

" 'Course not. I'll come round to the Yard. Upon my soul it's worse than murder. Might as well mix his damn' brews with poison. And he's working with—Hullo! Didn't hear you come in."

"Is someone there?" asked Alleyn sharply.

"Yes."

"Good-bye," said Alleyn, "I'll wait for you."

"Thank you so much," squeaked the voice. "Much obliged. Wouldn't have lost it for anything. Very smart work, officer. See you get the reward."

Alleyn smiled and hung up his receiver.

Up in the ballroom Hughie Bronx's Band packed up. Their faces were the colour of raw cod and shone with a fishy glitter, but the hair on their heads remained as smooth as patent leather. The four experts who only ten minutes ago had jigged together with linked arms in a hot rhythm argued wearily about the way to go home. Hughie Bronx himself wiped his celebrated face with a beautiful handkerchief and lit a cigarette.

"O.K., boys," he sighed. "Eight-thirty to-morrow and

if any——calls for 'My Girl's Cutie' more than six times running we'll quit and learn anthems."

Dimitri crossed the ballroom.

"Her ladyship particularly asked me to tell you," he said, "that there is something for you gentlemen at the buffet."

"Thanks a lot, Dim," said Mr. Bronx. "We'll be there."

Dimitri glanced round the ballroom, walked out, and descended the stairs.

Down in the entrance hall the last of the guests were collected. They looked wan and a little raffish but they shouted cheerfully, telling each other what a good party it had been. Among them, blinking sleepily through his glasses, was Lord Robert. His celebrated cape hung from his shoulders and in his hands he clasped his broad-brimmed black hat. Through the open doors came wreaths of mist. The sound of people coughing as they went into the raw air was mingled with the noise of taxi engines in low gear and the voices of the departing guests.

Lord Robert was among the last to go.

He asked several people, rather plaintively, if they had seen Mrs. Halcut-Hackett. "I'm supposed to be taking her home."

Dimitri came up to him.

"Excuse me, my lord, I think Mrs. Halcut-Hackett has just left. She asked me if I had seen you, my lord."

Lord Robert blinked up at him. For a moment their eyes met.

"Oh. Thank you," said Lord Robert. "I'll see if I can find her."

Dimitri bowed.

Lord Robert walked out into the mist.

His figure, looking a little like a plump antic from one of Verlaine's poems, moved down the broad steps. He passed a crowd of stragglers who were entering their taxis. He peered at them, watched them go off, and looked up and down the street. Lord Robert walked slowly down the street, seemed to turn into an insubstantial wraith, was hidden for a moment by a drift of mist, reappeared much farther away, walking steadily into nothingness, and was gone.

In his room at the Yard Alleyn woke with a start, rushing up on a wave of clamour from the darkness of profound sleep. The desk telephone was pealing. He reached out for it, caught sight of his watch and exclaimed aloud. Four o'clock! He spoke into the receiver.

"Hullo?"

"Mr. Alleyn?"

"Yes."

He thought: "It's Bunchy. What the devil——!"

But the voice in the receiver said:

"There's a case come in, sir. I thought I'd better report to you at once. Taxi with a fare. Says the fare's been murdered and has driven straight here with the body."

"I'll come down," said Alleyn.

He went down thinking with dismay that another case would be most unwelcome and hoping that it would be handed on to someone else. His mind was full of the blackmail business. Bunchy Gospell wouldn't have said he'd found his man unless he was damn' certain of him. The cakes-and-ale fellow. Dimitri. Well, he'd have opportunities, but what sort of evidence had Bunchy got? And where the devil was Bunchy? A uniformed sergeant waited for Alleyn in the entrance hall.

"Funny sort of business, Mr. Alleyn. The gentleman's dead all right. Looks to me as if he'd had a heart attack or some thing, but the cabby insists it was murder and won't say a word till he sees you. Didn't want me to open the door. I did, though, just to make sure. Held my watch-glass to the mouth and listened for the heart. Nothing! The old cabby didn't half go off pop. He's a character."

"Where's the taxi?"

"In the yard, sir. I told him to drive through."

They went out to the yard.

"Dampish," said the sergeant and coughed.

It was very misty down there near the river. Wreaths of mist that were almost rain drifted round them and changed on their faces into cold spangles of moisture. A corpse-like pallor had crept into the darkness and the vague shapes of roofs and chimneys waited for the dawn. Far down the river a steamer hooted. The air smelt dank and unwholesome.

A vague huge melancholy possessed Alleyn. He felt at once nerveless and over-sensitised. His spirit seemed to rise thinly and separate itself from his body. He saw himself as a stranger. It was a familar experience and he had grown to regard it as a precursor of evil. "I must get back," cried his mind and with the thought the return was accomplished. He was in the yard. The stones rang under his feet. A taxi loomed up vaguely with the overcoated figure of its driver standing motionless by the door as if on guard.

"Cold," said the sergeant.

"It's the dead hour of the night," said Alleyn.

The taxi-driver did not move until they came right up to him.

"Hullo," said Alleyn, "what's it all about?"

" 'Morning, governor." It was the traditional hoarse voice. He sounded like a cabby in a play. "Are you one of the inspectors?"

"I am."

"I won't make no report to any copper. I got to look after meself, see? What's more, the little gent was a friend of mine, see?"

"This is Chief Inspector-Detective Alleyn, daddy," said the sergeant.

"All right. That's the stuff. I got to protect meself, ain't I? Wiv a blinking stiff for a fare."

He suddenly reached out a gloved hand and with a quick turn flung open the door.

"I ain't disturbed 'im," he said. "Will you switch on the glim?"

Alleyn's hand reached out into the darkness of the cab. He smelt leather, cigars, and petrol. His fingers touched a button and a dim light came to life in the roof of the taxi.

He was motionless and silent for so long that at last the sergeant said loudly:

"Mr. Alleyn?"

But Alleyn did not answer. He was alone with his friend. The small fat hands were limp. The feet were turned in pathetically, like the feet of a child. The head leant sideways, languidly, as a sick child will lean its head. He could see the bare patch on the crown and the thin ruffled hair.

"If you look froo the other winder," said the driver, "you'll see 'is face. 'E's dead all right. Murdered!"

Alleyn said: "I can see his face."

He had leant forward and for a minute or two he was busy. Then he drew back. He stretched out his hand as if to close the lids over the congested eyes. His fingers trembled.

He said: "I mustn't touch him any more." He drew his hand away and backed out of the taxi. The sergeant was staring in astonishment at his face.

"Dead," said the taxi-driver. "Ain't he?"

"——you!" said Alleyn with a violent oath. "Can't I see he's dead without——"

He broke off and took three or four uncertain steps away from them. He passed his hand over his face and then stared at his fingers with an air of bewilderment.

"Wait a moment, will you?" he said.

The other two waited uncomfortably.

"I'm sorry," said Alleyn at last. "Give me a moment."

"Shall I get someone else, sir?" asked the sergeant. "It's a friend of yours, isn't it?"

"Yes," said Alleyn. "It's a friend of mine."

He turned on the taxi-driver and took him fiercely by the arm.

"Come here," he said and marched him to the front of the car.

"Switch on the headlights," he said.

The sergeant reached inside the taxi and in a moment the driver stood blinking in a white flood of light.

"Now," said Alleyn. "Why are you so certain it was murder?"

"Gorblimy, governor," said the driver, "ain't I seen wiv me own eyes 'ow the uvver bloke gets in wiv 'im, and ain't I seen wiv me own eyes 'ow the uvver bloke gets out at 'is lordship's 'ouse dressed up in 'is lordship's cloak and 'at and squeaks at me in a rum little voice same as 'is lordship: 'Sixty-three Jobbers Row, Queens Gate'? Ain't I driven 'is corpse all the way there, not knowing? 'Ere! You say 'is lordship was a friend of yours. So 'e was o' mine. This is bloody murder, this is, and I want to see this Mr. Clever, what's diddled me and done in as nice a little gent as ever I see, swing for it. That's me."

"I see," said Alleyn. "All right. I'll get a statement from you. We must get to work. Call up the usual lot. Get them all here. Get Dr. Curtis. Photograph the body from every angle. Note the position of the head. Look for signs of violence. Routine. Case of homicide. Take the name, will you? Lord Robert Gospell, two hundred, Cheyne Walk——"

7

Stop Press News

LORD ROBERT GOSPELL DIES IN TAXI
Society Shocked   Foul Play Suspected
Full story of Ball on Page 5

Evelyn Carrados let the paper fall on the counterpane
and stared at her husband.

"The papers are full of it," she said woodenly.

"Good God, my dear Evelyn, of course they are! And
this is only the ten o'clock racing edition brought in by a
damn' pup of a footman with my breakfast. Wait till we
see the evening papers! Isn't it enough, my God, that I
should be rung up by some jack-in-office from Scotland
Yard at five o'clock in the morning and cross-examined
about my own guests without having the whole thing
thrust under my nose in some insulting bloody
broadsheet."

He limped angrily about the room.

"It's perfectly obvious that the man has been
murdered. Do you realise that at any moment we'll have

some damned fellow from Scotland Yard cross-questioning us and that all the scavengers in Fleet Street will be hanging about our doors for days together? Do you realise——"

"I think he was perhaps my greatest friend," said Evelyn Carrados.

"If you look at their damned impertinent drivel on page five you will see the friendship well advertised. My God, it's intolerable. Do you realise that the police rang up Marsdon House at half-past four—five minutes after we'd gone, thank God!—and asked when Robert Gospell left? Some fellow of Dimitri's answered them and now a blasted snivelling journalist has got hold of it. Do you realise——"

"I only realise," said Evelyn Carrados, "that Bunchy Gospell is dead."

Bridget burst into the room, a paper in her hands.

"Donna! Oh, Donna—it's our funny little Bunchy. Our funny little Bunchy's dead! Donna!"

"Darling—I know."

"But, Donna—*Bunchy!*"

"Bridget," said her stepfather, "please don't be hysterical. The point we have to consider is——"

Bridget's arm went round her mother's shoulders.

"But we *mind,*" she said. "Can't you see—Donna minds *awfully.*"

Her mother said: "Of course we mind, darling, but Bart's thinking about something else. You see, Bart thinks there will be dreadful trouble——"

"About what?"

Bridget's eyes blazed in her white face as she turned on Carrados.

"Do you mean Donald? *Do you?* Do you dare to suggest that Donald would—would——"

"Bridgie!" cried her mother, "what are you saying!"

"Wait a miment, Evelyn," said Carrados. "What is all this about young Potter?"

Bridget pressed the back of her hand against her mouth, looked distractedly from her mother to her stepfather, burst into tears and ran out of the room.

*   *   *   *   *

"BUNCHY" GOSPELL DEAD
Mysterious death in Taxi
Sequel to the Carrados Ball

Mrs. Halcut-Hackett's beautifully manicured hands closed like claws on the newspaper. Her lips were stretched in a smile that emphasised the carefully suppressed lines from her nostrils to the corners of her mouth. She stared at nothing.

General Halcut-Hackett's dressing-room door was flung open and the General, wearing a dressing-gown, but few teeth, marched into the room. He carried a copy of a ten o'clock sporting edition.

"What!" he shouted indistinctly. "See here! By God!"

"I know," said Mrs. Halcut-Hackett. "Sad, isn't it?"

"Sad! Bloody outrage! What!"

"Shocking," said Mrs. Halcut-Hackett.

"Shocking!" echoed the General, "preposterous!" and the explosive consonants pronounced through the gap in his teeth blew his moustache out like a banner. His bloodshot eyes goggled at his wife. He pointed a stubby forefinger at her.

"He said he'd bring you home," he spluttered.

"He didn't do so."

"When did you come home?"

"I didn't notice. Late."

"Alone?"

Her face was white but she looked steadily at him.

"Yes," she said. "Don't be a fool."

*   *   *   *   *

STRANGE FATALITY
Lord Robert Gospell dies
after Ball
Full Story.

Donald Potter read the four headlines over and over again. From the centre of the page his uncle's face twinkled at him. Donald's cigarette-butt burnt his lips. He spat it into his empty cup, and lit another. He was shivering as if he had a rigor. He read the four lines again. In the next room somebody yawned horribly.

Donald's head jerked back.

"Wits!" he said. "Wits! Come here!"

"What's wrong?"

"Come here!"

Captain Withers clad in an orange silk dressing-gown appeared in the doorway.

"What the hell's the matter with you?" he enquired.

"Look here."

Captain Withers, whistling between his teeth, strolled up and looked over Donald's shoulder. His whistling stopped. He reached out his hand, took the newspaper, and began to read. Donald watched him.

"Dead!" said Donald. "Uncle Bunch! Dead!"

Withers glanced at him and returned to the paper. Presently he began again to whistle through his teeth.

*   *   *   *   *

DEATH OF LORD ROBERT GOSPELL
Tragic end to a distinguished career
Suspicious Circumstances

Lady Mildred Potter beat her plump hands on the proofs of the *Evening Chronicle* obituary notice and turned upon Alleyn a face streaming with tears.

"But who could have *wanted* to hurt Bunchy, Roderick? Everyone adored him. He hadn't an enemy in the world. Look what the *Chronicle* says—and I must say I think it charming of them to let me see the things they propose to say about him—but look what it says: 'Beloved by all his friends!' And so he was. So he was. By all his friends."

"He must have had one enemy, Mildred," said Alleyn.

"I can't believe it. I'll never believe it. It must be an escaped lunatic." She pressed her handkerchief to her eyes and sobbed violently. "I shall never be able to face all this dreadful publicity. The police! I don't mean you, Roderick, naturally. But everything—the papers, everyone poking and prying. Bunchy would have detested it. I can't face it, I can't."

"Where's Donald?"

"He rang up. He's coming."

"From where?"

"From this friend's flat, wherever it is."

"He's away from home?"

"Didn't Bunchy tell you? Ever since that awful afternoon when he was so cross with Donald. Bunchy didn't understand."

"Why was Bunchy cross with him?"

"He had run into debt rather. And now, poor boy, he is no doubt feeling too dreadfully remorseful."

Alleyn did not answer immediately. He walked over to the window and looked out.

"It will be easier for you," he said at last, "when Donald gets here. I suppose the rest of the family will come too?"

"Yes. All our old cousins and aunts. They have already rung up—Broomfield—Bunchy's eldest nephew, you know—I mean my eldest brother's son is away on the Continent. He's the head of the family, of course. I suppose I shall have to make all the arrangements and—and I'm so dreadfully shaken."

"I'll do as much as I can. There are some things that I must do. I'm afraid, Mildred, I shall have to ask you to let me look at Bunchy's things. His papers and so on."

"I'm sure," said Lady Mildred, "he would have preferred you to anyone else, Roderick."

"You make it very easy for me. Shall I get it done now?"

Lady Mildred looked helplessly about her.

"Yes. Yes, please. You'll want his keys, won't you?"

"I've got the keys, Mildred," said Alleyn gently.

"But—where——?" She gave a little cry. "Oh, poor

darling. He always took them with him everywhere."
She broke down completely. Alleyn waited for a
moment and then he said:

"I shan't attempt the impertinence of condoling
phrases. There is small comfort in scavenging in this
mess for crumbs of consolation. But I tell you this,
Mildred, if it takes me the rest of my life, and if it costs
me my job, by God! if I have to do the killing myself, I'll
get this murderer and see him suffer for it." He paused
and made a grimace. "Good Lord, what a speech!
Bunchy *would* have laughed at it. It's a curious thing
that when one speaks from the heart it is invariably in
the worst of taste."

He looked at her grey hair arranged neatly and
unfashionably and enclosed in a net. She peered at him
over the top of her drenched handkerchief and he saw
that she had not listened to him.

"I'll get on with it," said Alleyn, and made his way
alone to Lord Robert's study.

*   *   *   *   *

LORD ROBERT GOSPELL
DIES IN TAXI
Last night's shocking Fatality
Who was the Second Passenger?

Sir Daniel Davidson arrived at his consulting-rooms
at half-past ten. At his front door he caught sight of the
news placard and, for the first time in his life, bought a
sporting edition. He now folded the paper carefully and
laid it on top of his desk. He lit a cigarette, and glanced
at his servant.

"I shan't see any patients," he said. "If anybody rings
up—I'm out. Thank you."

"Thank you, sir," said the servant and removed
himself.

Sir Daniel sat thinking. He had trained himself to
think methodically and he hated slipshod ideas as much

as he despised a vague diagnosis. He was, he liked to tell his friends, above all things a creature of method and routine. He prided himself upon his memory. His memory was busy now with events only five hours old. He closed his eyes and saw himself in the entrance hall of Marsdon House at four o'clock that morning. The last guests, wrapped in coats and furs, shouted cheerfully to each other and passed through the great doors in groups of twos and threes. Dimitri stood at the foot of the stairs. He himself was near the entrance to the men's cloakroom. He was bent on avoiding Lucy Lorrimer who had stayed to the bitter end and would offer to drive him home if she saw him. There she was, just going through the double door. He hung back. Drifts of fog were blown in from the street. He remembered that he had wrapped his scarf over his mouth when he noticed the fog. It was at that precise moment he had seen Mrs. Halcut-Hackett, embedded in furs, slip through the entrance alone. He had thought there was something a little odd about this. The collar of her fur wrap turned up, no doubt against the fog, and the manner in which she slipped, if so majestic a woman could be said to slip, round the outside of the group! There was something furtive about it. And then he himself had been jostled by that fellow Withers, coming out of the cloakroom. Withers had scarcely apologised but had looked quickly round the melting group in the hall and up the stairs.

It was at that moment that Lord Robert Gospell had come downstairs. Sir Daniel twisted the heavy signet ring on his little finger and still with closed eyes he peered back into his memory. Withers had seen Lord Robert. There was no doubt of that. Sir Daniel heard again that swift intake of breath and noticed the quick glance before the fellow unceremoniously shoved his way through the crowd and disappeared into the fog. Then Lord Robert's nephew, young Donald Potter, came out of the buffet near the stairs. Bridget O'Brien was with him. They almost ran into Lord Robert, but when Donald saw his uncle he sheered off, said something to Bridget, and then went out by the front entrance. One more picture remained.

Bunchy Gospell speaking to Dimitri at the foot of the stairs. This was the last thing Sir Daniel saw before he too went out into the fog.

He supposed that those moments in the hall would be regarded by the police as highly significant. The papers said that the police wished to establish the identity of the second fare. Naturally, since he was obviously the murderer! The taxi-driver had described him as a well-dressed gentleman who, with Lord Robert, had entered the cab about two hundred yards up the street from Marsdon House. "Was it one of the guests?" asked the paper. That meant the police would get statements from everyone who left the house about the same time as Lord Robert. The last thing in the world that Sir Daniel wanted was to appear as a principal witness at the inquest. That sort of publicity did a fashionable physician no good. His name in block capitals, as likely as not, across the front sheets of the penny press and before you knew where you were some fool would say: "Davidson? Wasn't he mixed up in that murder case?" He might even have to say he saw the Halcut-Hackett woman go out, with Withers in hot pursuit. Mrs. Halcut-Hackett was one of his most lucrative patients. On the other hand, he would look extremely undignified if they found out that he was one of the last to leave and had not come forward to say so. It might even look suspicious. Sir Daniel swore picturesquely in French, reached for his telephone and dialled WHI1212.

*　　*　　*　　*　　*

MYSTERY IN MAYFAIR
Lord Robert Gospell suffocated in Taxi
Who was the second fare?

Colombo Dimitri in his smart flat in the Cromwell Road drew the attention of his confidential servant to the headlines.

"What a tragedy," he said. "It may be bad for us at the beginning of the season. Nobody feels very gay after a murder. He was so popular, too. It is most unfortunate."

"Yes, monsieur," said the confidential servant.

"I must have been almost the last person to speak with him," continued Dimitri, "unless, of course, this dastardly assassin addressed him. Lord Robert came to me in the hall and asked me if I had seen Mrs. Halcut-Hackett. I told him I had just seen her go away. He thanked me and left. I, of course, remained in the hall. Several of the guests spoke to me after that, I recollect. And then, an hour later, when I had left, but my men were still busy, the police rang up. Then they rang me up. It is all extremely sad. He was a charming personality. I am very, very sorry."

"Yes, monsieur."

"It would be a pleasant gesture for us to send flowers. Remind me of it. In the meantime, if you please, no gossip. I must instruct the staff on this point. I absolutely insist upon it. The affair must not be discussed."

"C'est entendu, monsieur."

"In respect of malicious tittle-tattle," said Dimitri virtuously, "our firm is in the well-known position of Caesar's wife." He glanced at his servant's face. It wore a puzzled expression. "She did not appear in gossip columns," explained Dimitri.

* * * * *

MYSTERY OF THE UNKNOWN FARE
"Bunchy" Gospell dead
Who was the Man in Dress Clothes?

Miss Harris finished her cup of tea but her bread and butter remained untasted on her plate. She told herself she did not fancy it. Miss Harris was gravely upset. She had encountered a question to which she did not know the answer and she found herself unable to stuff it away in one of her pigeon-holes. The truth was Miss Harris's heart was touched. She had seen Lord Robert several times in Lady Carrados's house and last night Lord Robert had danced with her. When Lady Carrados asked Miss Harris if she would like to come to the ball she had never for a moment expected to dance at it. She had expected to spend a gratifying but exceedingly lonely night watching the fruits of her own labours. Her expectations had been realised until the moment when Lord Robert asked her to dance and from then onwards Miss Harris had known a sort of respectable rapture. He had found her on the upper landing where she was sitting by herself outside the little green boudoir. She had just come out of the "Ladies" and had had an embarrassing experience practically in the doorway. So she had sat on a chair on the landing to recover her poise and because there did not seem to be anywhere else much to go. Then she had pulled herself together and gone down to the ballroom. She was trying to look happy and not lost when Lord Robert came up and remembered his request that they should dance. And dance they did, round and round in the fast Viennese waltz, and Lord Robert had said he hadn't enjoyed himself so much for ages. They had joined a group of dizzily "right" people and one of them, Miss Agatha Troy the famous painter it was, had talked to her as if they had been introduced. And then, when the band played another fast Viennese Waltz because they were fashionable, Miss Harris and Lord Robert had danced again and had afterwards taken champagne at the buffet. That had been quite late—not long before the ball ended. How charming he had been, making her laugh a great deal and feel like a human young woman of thirty and not a dependent young lady of no age at all.

And now, here he was, murdered.

Miss Harris was so upset that she could not eat her breakfast. She glanced automatically at her watch. Twelve o'clock. She was to be at Lady Carrados's house by two in case she was needed. If she was quick she would have time to write an exciting letter home to the

Buckinghamshire vicarage. The girlfriend with whom she shared the flatlette was still asleep. She was a night operator in a telephone exchange. But Miss Harris's bosom could contain this dreadful news no longer. She rose, opened the bedroom door and said:

"Smithy!"

"Uh!"

"Smithy, something awful has happened. Listen!"

"Uh?"

"The girl has just brought in a paper. It's about Lord Gospell. I mean Lord Robert Gospell. You know. I told you about him last night——"

"For God's sake!" said Miss Smith. "Did you have to wake me up again to hear all about your social successes?"

"No, but Smithy, *listen!* It's simply frightful! He's murdered."

Miss Smith sat up in bed looking like a sort of fabulous goddess in her mass of tin curling-pins.

"My dear, he isn't," said Miss Smith.

"My dear, he is!" said Miss Harris.

8

Troy and Alleyn

When Alleyn had finished his examination of the study he sat at Lord Robert's desk and telephoned to Mardson House. He was answered by one of his own men.

"Is Mr. Fox there, Bailey?"

"Yes, sir. He's upstairs. I'll just tell him."

Alleyn waited. Before him on the desk was a small, fat notebook and upon the opened page he read again in Lord Robert's finicky writing the notes he had made on his case:

"*Saturday, May 8th.* Cocktail-party at Mrs. H.-H.'s house in Halkin Street. Arrived 6.15. Mrs. H.-H. *distraite.* Arranged to meet her June 3rd, Constance Street Hall. Saw Maurice Withers, ref. drug affair 1924. Bad lot. Seems thick with Mrs. H.-H. Shied off me. *Mem.* Tell Alleyn about W.'s gambling hell at L.

"Thursday, June 3rd. Constance Street Hall. Recital by Sirmione Quartette. Arrived 2.15. Met Mrs. H.-H. 2.30 Mrs. H.-H. sat on left-hand end of blue sofa (occupant's left). Sofa about 7 feet inside main entrance and 8 feet to right as you enter. Sofa placed at right angles to right-hand corner of room. Side entrance on right-hand wall about ten feet behind sofa. My position in chair behind left arm of sofa. At 3.35 immediately after interval observed Mrs. H.-H.'s bag taken from left end of sofa where previously I watched her place it. She had left the room during interval and returned after bag had gone. Will swear that hand taking the bag was that of Dimitri of Shepherd Market Catering Company. Saw him there. Seat nearby. Little finger same length as next and markedly crooked. Withers was there. *N.B.* Think Mrs. H.-H. suspects me of blackmail. R.G."

Fox's voice came through the receiver.

"Hullo, sir?"

"Hullo, Fox. Have you seen the room where he telephoned to me?"

"Yes. It's a room on the top landing. One of Dimitri's waiters saw him go in and the man on the house switchboard remembers that he got the Yard number about that time. The room hasn't been touched."

"Right. Anything else?"

"Nothing much. The house is pretty well as it was when the guests left. You saw to that, sir."

"Is Dimitri there?"

"No."

"Get him, Fox. I'll see him at the Yard at twelve o'clock. That'll do him for the moment. Tell Bailey to go all over the telephone-room for prints. We've got to find out who interrupted that call to the Yard. And, Fox——"

"Sir?"

"Can you come round here? I'd like a word with you."

"I'll be there."

"Thank you," said Alleyn and hung up the receiver.

He looked again at the document he had found in the central drawer of Lord Robert's desk. It was his will. A very simple little will. After one or two legacies he left all his possessions and the life interest on £40,000 to his sister, Lady Mildred Potter, to revert to her son on her death, and the remainder of his estate, £20,000, to that same son, his nephew Donald Potter. The will was dated January 1st of that year.

"His good deed for the New Year," thought Alleyn.

He looked at the two photographs in leather frames that stood on Lord Robert's desk. One was of the Lady Mildred Potter in the presentation dress of her girlhood. Mildred had been rather pretty in those days. The other was of a young man of about twenty. Alleyn noted the short Gospell nose and wide-set eyes. The mouth was pleasant and weak, the chin one of those jutting affairs that look determined and are too often merely obstinate. It was rather an attractive face. Donald had written his name across the corner with the date, January Ist.

"I hope to God," thought Alleyn, "that he can give a good account of himself."

"Good morning," said a voice from the doorway.

He swung round in his chair and saw Agatha Troy. She was dressed in green and had a little velvet cap on her dark head and green gloves on her hands.

"Troy!"

"I came in to see if there was anything I could do for Mildred."

"You didn't know I was here?"

"Not till she told me. She asked me to see if you had everything you wanted."

"Everything I wanted," repeated Alleyn.

"If you have," said Troy, "that's all right. I won't interrupt."

"Please," said Alleyn, "could you *not* go just for a second?"

"What is it?"

"Nothing. I mean, I've no excuse for asking you to

stay, unless, if you will forgive me, the excuse of wanting to look at you and listen for a moment to your
voice." He held up his hand. "No more than that. You
liked Bunchy and so did I. He talked about you the last
time I saw him."

"A few hours ago," said Troy, "I was dancing with
him."

Alleyn moved to the tall windows. . . . They looked
out over the charming little garden to the Chelsea
reaches of the Thames.

"A few hours ago"—he repeated her words
slowly—"the river was breathing mist. The air was
threaded with mist and as cold as the grave. That was
before dawn broke. It was beginning to get light when I
saw him. And look at it now. Not a cloud. The damned
river's positively sparkling in the sunlight. Come here,
Troy."

She stood beside him.

"Look down there into the street. Through the side
window. At half-past three this morning the river mist
lay like a pall along Cheyne Walk. If anybody was
awake at that mongrel hour or abroad in the deserted
streets they would have heard a taxi come along Cheyne
Walk and stop outside this gate. If anybody in this house
had had the curiosity to look out of one of the top
windows they would have seen the door of the taxi open
and a quaint figure in a cloak and wide-brimmed hat get
out."

"What do you mean? *He got out?*"

"The watcher would have seen this figure wave a
gloved hand and heard him call to the driver in a shrill
voice: 'Sixty-three, Jobbers Row, Queens Gate.' He
would have seen the taxi drive away into the mist—and
then—what? What did the figure do? Did it run like a
grotesque with flapping cloak towards the river to be
swallowed up in vapour? Or did it walk off sedately into
Chelsea? Did it wait for a moment, staring after the
taxi? Did Bunchy's murderer pull off his cloak, fold it
and walk away with it over his arm? Did he hide his own

tall hat under the cloak before he got out of the taxi, and afterwards change back into it? And where are Bunchy's cloak and hat, Troy? Where are they?"

"What did the taxi driver say?" asked Troy. "There's nothing coherent in the papers. I don't understand."

"I'll tell you. Fox will be here soon. Before he comes I can allow myself a few minutes to unload my mind, if you'll let me. I've done that before—once—haven't I?"

"Yes," murmured Troy. "Once."

"There is nobody in the world who can listen as you can. I wish I had something better to tell you. Well, here it is. The taxi-driver brought Bunchy to the Yard at four o'clock this morning, saying he was murdered. This was his story. He picked Bunchy up at three-thirty some two hundred yards from the doors of Marsdon House. There was a shortage of taxis and we suppose Bunchy had walked so far, hoping to pick one up in a side street, when this fellow came along. The unnatural mist that hung over London last night was thick in Belgrave Square. As the taximan drove towards Bunchy he saw another figure in an overcoat and top-hat loom through the mist and stand beside him. They appeared to speak together. Bunchy held up his stick. The cabby knew him by sight and addressed him:

" " 'Morning, m'lord. Two hundred, Cheyne Walk?'

" 'Please,' said Bunchy.

"The two men got into the taxi. The cabby never had a clear view of the second man. He had his back turned as the taxi approached and when it stopped he stood towards the rear in shadow. Before the door was slammed the cabby heard Bunchy say: 'You can take him on.' The cabby drove to Cheyne Walk by way of Chesham Place, Cliveden Place, Lower Sloane Street and Chelsea Hospital and across Tite Street. He says it took about twelve minutes. He stopped here at Bunchy's gate and in a few moments Lord Robert, as he supposed him to be, got out and slammed the door. A voice squeaked through a muffler: 'Sixty-three, Jobbers Row, Queens Gate,' and the cabby drove away. He arrived at

Jobbers Row ten minutes later, waited for his fare to get out and at last got out himself and opened the door. He found Bunchy."

Alleyn waited for a moment, looking gravely at Troy's white face. She said:

"There was no doubt——"

"None. The cabby is an obstinate, opinionated, cantankerous old oddity, but he's no fool. He satisfied himself. He explained that he once drove an ambulance and knew certain things. He headed as fast as he could for the Yard. A sergeant saw him; saw everything; made sure it was—what it was, and got me. I made sure, too."

"What had been done to Bunchy?"

"You want to know? Yes, of course you do. You're too intelligent to nurse your sensibilities."

"Mildred will ask me about it. What had happened?"

"We think he was struck on the temple, stunned and then suffocated," said Alleyn, without emphasis. "We shall know more when the doctors have finished."

"Struck?"

"Yes. With something that had a pretty sharp edge. About as sharp as the back of a thick knife-blade."

"Did he suffer?"

"Not very much. Hardly at all. He wouldn't know what happened."

"His heart was weak," said Troy suddenly.

"His heart? Are you sure of that?"

"Mildred told me the other day. She tried to persuade him to see a specialist."

"I wonder," said Alleyn, "if that made it easier—for both of them."

Troy said:

"I haven't seen you look like that before."

"What do you mean, Troy?"

He turned to her a face so suddenly translated into gentleness that she could not answer him.

"I—it's gone now."

"When I look at you I suppose all other expression is lost in an effect of general besottedness."

"How can I answer that?" said Troy.

"Don't. I'm sorry. What *did* you mean?"

"You looked savage."

"I feel it when I think of Bunchy."

"I can understand that."

"The hunt is up," said Alleyn. "Have you ever read in the crime books about the relentless detective who swears he'll get his man if it takes him the rest of his life? That's me, Troy, and I always thought it rather a bogus idea. It is bogus in a way, too. The real heroes of criminal investigation are Detective-Constables X, Y and Z—the men in the ranks who follow up all the dreary threads of routine without any personal feeling or interest, who swear no full round oaths, but who, nevertheless, *do* get their men in the end; with a bit of luck and the infinite capacity for taking pains. Detective-Constables X, Y and Z are going to be kept damned busy until this gentleman is laid by the heels. I can promise them that."

"I don't feel like that," said Troy. "I mean, I don't feel anything in particular about this murderer except that I think he must be mad. I know he should be found but I can't feel savage about him. It's simply Bunchy who did no harm in this world; no harm at all, lying dead and lonely. I must go now, and see what I can do for Mildred. Has Donald come in?"

"Not yet. Do you know where he is staying?"

"He wouldn't tell Mildred because he thought she would tell Bunchy, and he wanted to be independent. She's got the telephone number. I've seen it written on the memorandum in her room. I suppose you heard about the difference?"

"Yes, from Mildred. It was his debts, wasn't it?"

"Yes. Mildred has always spoilt Donald. He's not a bad child, really. He will be terribly upset."

Alleyn looked at the photograph.

"Did you see him at the dance?"

"Yes. He danced a lot with Bridgie O'Brien."

"Did he stay until the end, do you know?"

"I didn't stay till the end myself. Mildred and I left at half-past one. She dropped me at my club. Bunchy—Bunchy—was seeing us home, but he came and asked us if we'd mind going without him. He said he was feeling gay."

"Did you see much of him, please?"

"I danced three times with him. He *was* very gay."

"Troy, did you notice anything? Anything at all?"

"What sort of things?"

"Did there seem to be any hint of something behind his gaiety? As if, do you know, he was thinking in the back of his head?"

Troy sat on the edge of the desk and pulled off her cap. The morning sun came through the window and dappled her short dark hair with blue lights. It caught the fine angle of her jaw and her cheek-bone. It shone into her eyes, making her screw them up as she did when she painted. She drew off her green gloves and Alleyn watched her thin intelligent hands slide out of their sheaths and lie delicately in the fur of her green jacket. He wondered if he would ever recover from the love of her.

He said: "Tell me everything that happened last night while you were with Bunchy. Look back into your memory before it loses its edge and see if there is anything there that seemed a little out of the ordinary. Anything, no matter how insignificant."

"I'll try," said Troy. "There was nothing when we danced except—yes. We collided once with another couple. It was a Mrs. Halcut-Hackett. Do you know her?"

"Yes. Well?"

"It's a tiny thing but you say that doesn't matter. She was dancing with a tall coarse-looking man. Bunchy apologised before he saw who they were. He danced very bouncily, you know, and always apologised when there were collisions. Then we swung round and he saw them. I felt his hand tighten suddenly and I looked over his shoulder at them. The man's red face had gone quite pale and Mrs. Halcut-Hackett looked very odd. Frightened. I asked Bunchy who the man was and he said: 'Feller called Withers,' in a queer frozen little voice. I said: 'Don't you like him?' and he said: 'Not much, m'dear,' and then began to talk about something else."

"Yes," said Alleyn. "That's interesting. Anything more?"

"Later on, Bunchy and I went to chaperones' corner. You know, the end of the ballroom where they all sit. Your mother was there. Mrs. Halcut-Hackett came up with her husband and then the girl she's bringing out arrived with that old ass Carrados. The girl had toothache, she said, but I'm afraid the wretched child was really not having a great success. There's something so blasted cruel and barbaric about this season game," said Troy vigorously.

"I know."

"Your mother noticed it. We said something to each other. Well, General Halcut-Hackett said he'd take the girl home and Bunchy offered to take Mrs. Halcut-Hackett home later on. The General thanked him but *she* looked extraordinarily put out and seemed to me to avoid answering. I got the impression that she hated the idea. There was one other thing just about then. Wait a second! Bunchy started a conversation about punctuality with old Lucy Lorrimer. You know?"

"Lord, yes. She's a friend of my mama's."

"That's her. She twitted Bunchy about being late or something and Mrs. Halcut-Hackett suddenly said in a loud, high voice that she knew all about Bunchy's punctual habits and could vouch for them. It sounds nothing, but for some extraordinary reason it made everybody feel uncomfortable."

"Can you remember exactly what she said?"

Troy ran her fingers through her hair and scowled thoughtfully.

"No, not exactly. It was just that she knew he always kept appointments. Your mother might remember. I went away to dance soon after that. Evelyn Carrados was there but———"

"But what?"

"You'll think I'm inventing vague mysteries but I thought she seemed very upset, too. Nothing to do with Bunchy. She looked ill. I heard someone say afterwards that she nearly fainted in the supper-room. She looked rather as if she might when I saw her. I noticed her hands were tense. I've often thought I'd like to paint Evelyn's hands. They're beautiful. I watched them last night. She kept clutching a great fat bag in her lap. Bunchy sat between her and your mother and he gave each of them a little pat—you know Bunchy's way. His hand touched Evelyn's bag and she started as if he'd hurt her and her fingers tightened. I can see them now, white, with highlights on the knuckles, dug into the gold stuff of the bag. I thought again I'd like to paint them and call the thing: 'Hands of a frightened woman.' And then later on—but look here," said Troy, "I'm simply maundering."

"God bless your good painter's eyes, you're not. Go on."

"Well, some time after supper when I'd danced again with Bunchy, I sat out with him in the ballroom. We were talking away and he was telling me one of his little stories, a ridiculous one about Lucy Lorrimer sending a wreath to a wedding and a toasting-fork to a funeral, when he suddenly stopped dead and stared over my shoulder. I turned and saw he was looking at Evelyn Carrados. There was nothing much to stare at. She still looked shaken, but that was all. Dimitri, the catering man you know, was giving her back that bag. I suppose she'd left it somewhere. What's the matter?"

Alleyn had made a little exclamation.

He said: "That great fat bag you had noticed earlier in the evening?"

"Yes. But it wasn't so fat this time," said Troy quickly. "Now I think of it, it was quite limp and flat. You see, I was looking at her hands again. I remember thinking subconsciously that it seemed such a large bag for a ball-dress. Mildred came up and we left soon after that. I'm afraid that's all."

"Afraid? Troy, you don't know what an important person you are."

"Don't I?"

She looked at him with an air of bewildered friendliness and at once his whole face was lit by his fierce awareness of her. Troy's eyes suddenly filled with tears. She reached out her hand and touched him.

"I'll go," she said. "I'm so sorry."

Alleyn drew back. He struck one hand against the palm of the other and said violently:

"For God's sake, don't be kind! What is this intolerable love that forces me to do the very things I wish with all my soul to avoid? Yes, Troy, please go now."

Troy went without another word.

9

Report from Mr. Fox

Alleyn walked about the room swearing under his breath. He was found at this employment by Detective-Inspector Fox who arrived looking solid and respectable.

"Good morning, sir," said Fox.

"Hullo, Fox. Sit down. I've found the will. Everything goes to his sister and her son. The boy's in debt and has quarrelled with his uncle. He's living away from home but will be in any moment. I've found Lord Robert's notes on the blackmail case. He told me when he rang up at one o'clock this morning that he'd call here first to get out of his boiled shirt and collect the notes. There they are. Look at 'em."

Fox put on his spectacles and took the little notebook

in his enormous fist. He read solemnly with his head thrown back a little and his eyebrows raised.

"Yes," he said when he had finished. "Well now, Mr. Alleyn, that's quite an interesting little bit of evidence, isn't it? It puts this Mr. Dimitri in what you might call a very unfavourable light. We can get him for blackmail on this information if the lady doesn't let us down. This Mrs. Halcut-Hackett, I mean."

"You notice Lord Robert thought she suspected him himself of taking the bag at the concert."

"Yes. That's awkward. You might say it gives her a motive for the murder."

"If you can conceive of Mrs. Halcut-Hackett, who is what the drapers call a queenly woman, dressing up as a man during the ball, accosting Lord Robert in the street, getting him to give her a lift, knocking him out, smothering him, and striding home in the light of dawn in somebody's trousers."

"That's right," said Fox. "I can't. She might have an accomplice."

"So she might."

"Still, I must say Dimitri looks likelier," Fox plodded on thoughtfully. "If he found out Lord Robert had a line on him. But how would he find out?"

"See here," said Alleyn. "I want you to listen while I go over that telephone call. I was working late at the Yard on the Temple case. I would have gone north today, as you know, if this hadn't happened. At one o'clock Lord Robert rang me up from a room at Marsdon House. He told me he had proof positive that Dimitri was our man. Then he said he'd come round to the Yard. And then——" Alleyn shut his eyes and screwed his face sideways. "I want to get his exact words," he said. "I'm my own witness here. Wait, now, wait. Yes. He said: 'I'll come round to the Yard. Upon my soul it's worse than murder. Might as well mix his damn' brews with poison,' and then, Fox, he added this phrase: 'And he's working with——' He never finished it. He broke off and said: 'Hallo, I didn't hear you come in.' I asked if anyone was there and he said yes and pretended he'd rung up about lost property. He must have done that because he realised this new arrival had overheard him mention the Yard. See here, Fox, we've got to get the man or woman who overheard that call."

"If it was Dimitri," began Fox.

"Yes, I know. If it was Dimitri! And yet, somehow, he sounded as if he was speaking to a friend. 'Hallo, I didn't hear you come in.' Might have been. But we've got to get at it, Fox."

" 'And he's working with——' " quoted Fox. "What do you reckon he was going to say? Name an accomplice?"

"No. He was too old a hand to use names on the telephone. It might have been 'with somebody else,' or it might have been 'with devilish ingenuity.' I wish to God we knew. And now what have you done?"

Fox unhooked his glasses.

"Following your instructions," he said, "I went to Marsdon House. I got there at eight o'clock. I found two of our chaps in charge, and got a report from them. They arrived there at four-twenty, a quarter of an hour after the taxi got to the Yard and five minutes after you rang up. Dimitri had left the house, but our chaps, having the office from you, sir, telephoned him at his flat to make sure he was there and sent a plain-clothes man round to watch it. He's being relieved at ten o'clock by that new chap, Carewe. I thought he might take it on. He's a bit too fanciful for my liking. Well, to go back to Marsdon House. They took statements from the men Dimitri had left to clear up the house, sent them away, and remained in charge until I got there at eight. We've located the room where Lord Robert rang you up. The telephone was left switched through there for the whole evening. We've sealed it up. I've got a guest list. Bit of luck, that. We found it in the buffet. Names and addresses all typed out, very methodical. It's a carbon copy. I suppose Lady Carrados's secretary must have done it. I found out from Dimitri's men some of the people who had left early. The men's cloakroom attendant was still there and could remember about twenty of them. He managed to recollect most of the men who were the last to go. I started off on them. Rang them up and asked if they noticed Lord Robert Gospell. Several of them remembered him standing in the hall at the very end. Most of the people left in parties and we were able to check up on these at once. We found that Dimitri was in the hall at this time. I called in at his flat just now before I came here. You'll notice he's a witness of some importance as well as, on the strength of what you've told me, a prime suspect. I've got a list, very likely incomplete, of the guests who left alone about the same time as Lord Robert. Here it is. A bit rough. I've put it together from notes on my way here."

Fox took out a fat notebook, opened it and handed it to Alleyn who read:

"Mrs. Halcut-Hackett. Seen leaving alone by footman at door, Dimitri, and linkman who offered to call a taxi for her. She refused and walked away. Lord Robert had not left. Dimitri says he thinks Lord Robert came downstairs about this time.

"Captain Maurice Withers. Seen leaving alone by Dimitri, footman and by several members of a party whom he passed on the steps outside the house. Refused a lift. Footman thinks Capt. W. left after Mrs. H.-H. Impression confirmed by Dimitri. Lord Robert at foot of stairs.

"Mr. Donald Potter. Seen saying good-bye to Miss O'Brien by Dimitri and by two servants near door into buffet at foot of stairs. Dimitri noticed him meet Lord Robert, appear to avoid him, and go away hurriedly.

"Sir Daniel Davidson. Seen leaving alone immediately after this by Dimitri and two of the servants.

"Mr. Percy Percival. Young gentleman suspected of having taken too much. Tripped in doorway and offered

to embrace footman who remembers him. Heard calling for taxi outside.

"*Miss Violet Harris.* Secretary to Lady Carrados, seen leaving alone by cloakroom attendant standing at door, to whom she said good night. Unnoticed by anyone else.

"*Mr. Trelawny-Caper.* Young gentleman who had lost Mr. Percy Percival. Asked repeatedly for him. Handed a ten-shilling note to footman who remembers him. Described by footman as being 'nicely decorated but not drunk.'

"*Lord Robert Gospell.* Both footmen and a linkman saw him go. One footman places his departure immediately after Sir Daniel Davidson's. The other says it was some minutes later. The cloakroom attendant says it was about two minutes after Miss Harris and five after Sir D.D."

Alleyn looked up.

"Where was Dimitri, then?" he asked. "He seems to have faded out."

"I asked him," said Fox. "He said he went into the buffet about the time Sir Daniel left and was kept there for some time. The buffet's at the foot of the stairs."

"Any confirmation of that?"

"One of his men remembers him there but can't say exactly when or for how long. He was talking to Sir Herbert Carrados."

"To Carrados? I see. How did Dimitri shape when you saw him?"

"Well," said Fox slowly, "he's a pretty cool customer, isn't he? Foreign, half Italian, half Greek, but that's hardly noticeable in his speech. He answered everything very smooth and kept saying it was all very regrettable."

"I trust he'll find it even more so," said Alleyn and returned to the notebook.

"The rest," said Fox, "left after Lord Robert and as far as we can make out, some time after. There are only three names and I don't fancy they'll amount to much but I thought we'd better have them."

"When did the Carrados party go? Last of all, of course?"

"Yes. Sir Herbert and Lady Carrados were at the head of the stairs on the ballroom landing saying good-bye most of this time, but Sir Herbert must have come down to the buffet if it's right that Dimitri talked to him there. I've left Sir Herbert to you, Mr. Alleyn. From what I hear of him he'll need handling."

"Extraordinarily kind of you," said Alleyn grimly. "Is there any exit from the buffet other than the one into the hall?"

"Yes, there is. A door that gives on to the back stairs down to the basement."

"So it's conceivable that Dimitri might have gone out into the street that way?"

"Yes," agreed Fox. "It's possible all right. And come back."

"He would have been away at least forty minutes," said Alleyn, "if he's our man. If, if, if! Would he be able to get hold of a topper? The murderer wore one. What would he say to Bunchy to persuade him to give him a lift? 'I want to talk to you about blackmail?' Well—that might work."

"For all we know," said Fox, "it may not have been any of the guests or Dimitri."

"True enough. For all we know. All the same, Fox, it looks as if it was. It's not easy to fit an outsider into what facts we've got. Try. An unknown in full evening dress wearing an overcoat and a top-hat stands outside Marsdon House waiting for Lord Robert to come out and on the off-chance of getting a lift. He doesn't know when Lord Robert will leave so he has to hang about for three hours. He doesn't know if he'll get a chance to speak to Lord Robert, whether Lord Robert will leave in a party or alone, in a private car or a taxi. He doesn't know a heavy mist is going to crawl over London at one o'clock."

"He might have just happened to come up," said Fox and added immediately: "All right, all right, sir. I won't press it. We've got plenty to go on from inside and it's a bit far-fetched, I will allow."

"The whole thing's too damn' far-fetched, in my opinion, said Alleyn. "We're up against a murder that was very nearly unpremeditated."

"How do you make that out?"

"Why, Fox, for the reasons we've just ticked off. Lord Robert's movements could not be anticipated. I have just learned that he had intended to leave much earlier with his sister, Lady Mildred Potter, and Miss Troy."

"Miss Agatha Troy!"

"Yes, Fox." Alleyn turned aside and looked out of the window. "She's a friend of the family. I've spoken to her. She's here."

"Fancy that, now," said Fox comfortably.

"I think," continued Alleyn after a pause, "that when the murderer went out from the lighted house into that unwholesome air he perhaps knew that Bunchy—Lord Robert—was returning alone. He may have seen him alone in the hall. That's why your little list is important. If the man was Dimitri he went out with the deliberate intention of accomplishing his crime. If it was one of the guests he may have made up his mind only when he caught a glimpse of Bunchy standing alone in the mist, waiting for a taxi. He may have meant to threaten, or reason, or plead. He may have found Bunchy obdurate and on an impulse, killed him."

"How do you reckon he brought it off?" With what?"

"Back to the jurists' maxim," said Alleyn with a slight smile: *"Quis, quid, ubi, quibus auxiliis, cur, quamodo, quando?"*

"I never can remember it that way," said Fox, "knowing no Latin. But I've got old Gross's rhyme all right:

"What was the crime, who did it, when was it done, and where?

How done, and with what motive, who in the deed did share?"

"Yes," said Alleyn. "We've got *quid, quamodo and ubi,* but we're not so sure of *quibus auxiliis.* Dr. Curtis says the abrasion on the temple is two and a half inches long and one-twelfth of an inch across. The blow, he thinks, was not necessarily very heavy, but sharp and extremely accurate. What sort of implement does that suggest to you, Fox?"

"I've been thinking that——"

The desk telephone rang. Alleyn answered it.

"Hullo?"

"Mr. Alleyn? The Yard here. Sir Daniel Davidson has rung up and says he may have something to tell you. He'll be in all day."

"Where is he?"

"In his rooms, number fifty, St. Luke's Chambers, Harley Street."

"Say I'll call at two o'clock. Thank him." Alleyn put the receiver down.

"Davidson," he said, "thinks he may have something to relate. I bet he had a heart-to-heart talk with himself before he decided to ring up."

"Why?" asked Fox. "Do you mean he feels shaky?"

"I mean he's a fashionable doctor and they don't care for the kind of publicity you get from criminal investigation. If he's a clever fellow, and I imagine he must be to have got where he is, he's realised he was one of the last people to see Lord Robert. He's decided to come to us before we go to him. According to your notes, Fox, Sir Daniel was the first of the last three people to leave before Lord Robert. The other two were a tight young gentleman and a female secretary. Sir Daniel would have seen Lord Robert was alone and about to leave. He could have waited outside in the mist and asked for a lift in the taxi as easily as anybody. I wonder if he realises that."

"No motive," said Fox.

"None, I should imagine. I mustn't gat fantastic, must I? Damn young Potter, why doesn't he come?"

"Have you finished here, sir?"

"Yes. I got here at five o'clock this morning, broke the news to Lady Mildred, and settled down to Lord Robert's dressing-room, bedroom and this study. There's nothing at all to be found except his notes and the will. From seven until ten I looked in their garden, the neighbouring gardens, and up and down the Embankment for a cloak and a soft hat. With no success. I've got a squad of men at it now."

"He may not have got rid of them."

"No. He may have been afraid of leaving some trace of himself. If that's the case he'll want to destroy or lose them. It was low tide at three o'clock this morning. To drop them in the river he'd have to get to a bridge. What sort of house is Dimitri's?"

"It's a small two-roomed flat in the Cromwell Road. He keeps a servant. French, I should say."

"We'll go round there at noon when he's due at the Yard, and see if we can find anything. You've seen the flat. Where's his telephone?"

"On the landing."

"Right. You'd better ring from the nearest call-box as soon as I've gone in. Keep the servant on the telephone as long as possible. You can put a string of questions about the time Dimitri got in, ask for the names of some of the men, anything. I'll have a quick look round for a possible spot to hide a largish parcel. We must get the dust-bins watched though he's not likely to risk that. Blast this nephew. Fox, go and do your stuff with the maids. Don't disturb Lady Mildred but ask for Mr. Donald's telephone number. It's written on a memorandum in her room but they may have it, too."

Fox went out and returned in a few minutes.

"Sloane 8405."

Alleyn reached for the telephone and dialled a number.

"Chief Detective-Inspector Alleyn, Scotland Yard. I want you to trace Sloane 8405 at once, please. I'll hang on."

He waited, staring absently at Fox who was reading his own notes with an air of complacent detachment.

"What?" said Alleyn suddenly. "Yes. Will you repeat that? Thank you very much. Good-bye."

He put back the receiver.

"Mr. Donald Potter's telephone number," he said, "is that of Captain Maurice Withers, one hundred and ten, Grandison Mansions, Sling Street, Chelsea. Captain Maurice Withers, as you will have noticed, appears in Lord Robert's notes. He was at the cocktail-party at Mrs. Halcut-Hackett's and 'seemed thick with her.' He was at the concert when Dimitri took her bag. Now look at this——"

Alleyn took a cheque-book from a drawer in the desk and handed it to Fox.

"Look at the heel of the book. Turn up June 8th, last Saturday."

Fox thumbed over the leaves of the heel until he found it.

"Fifty pounds. M. Withers. (D) Shackleton House, Leatherhead."

"That's the day of the cocktail-party at Mrs. Halcut-Hackett's. This case is beginning to make a pattern."

Fox, who had returned to Lord Robert's notes, asked:

"What's this he says about Captain Withers being mixed up in a drug affair in 1924?"

"It was rather in my salad days at the Yard, Fox, but I remember and so will you. The Bouchier-Watson lot. They had their headquarters at Marseilles and Port Said, but they operated all over the shop. Heroin mostly. The F.O. took a hand. Bunchy was there in those days and helped us enormously. Captain Withers was undoubtedly up to his nasty neck in it but we never quite got enough to pull him in. A very dubious person. And young Donald's flown to him for sanctuary. Besotted young ninny! Oh, blast! Fox, blast!"

"Do you know the young gentleman, sir?"

"What? Yes. Oh, yes, I know him vaguely. What's going to come of this? I'll have to probe. A filthy crime dentist! And quite possibly I'll haul up young Potter wriggling like a nerve on the end of a wire. These people are supposed to be my friends! Fun, isn't it? All right, Fox, don't looked perturbed. But if Donald Potter doesn't show up here before——"

The door was suddenly flung open and Donald walked into the room.

He took half a dozen steps, pulled up short, and glared at Alleyn and Fox. He looked awful. His eyes were blood-shot and his face pallid.

He said: "Where's my mother?"

Alleyn said: "Agatha Troy's looking after her. I want to speak to you."

"I want to see my mother."

"You'll have to wait," said Alleyn.

10

Donald

Donald Potter sat on a chair facing the window. Alleyn
was at Lord Robert's desk. Fox sat in the window, his
notebook on his knees, his pencil in his hand. Donald
lit one cigarette from the butt of another. His fingers
shook.

"Before we begin," said Alleyn, "I should like to
make one point quite clear to you. Your uncle has been
murdered. The circumstances under which he was
murdered oblige us to go most thoroughly into the
movements of every person who was near to him within
an hour of his death. We shall also find it necessary to
make exhaustive enquiries into his private affairs, his
relationship with members of his own family, and his
movements, conversation, and interests during the last
weeks or perhaps months of his life. Nothing will be
sacred. You, of course, are most anxious that his
murderer should be arrested?"

Alleyn paused. Donald wetted his lips and said:

"Naturally."

"Naturally. You will therefore give us all the help you can at no matter what cost to yourself?"

"Of course."

"You will understand, I am sure, that everything the police do is done with one purpose only. If some of our enquiries seem impertinent or irrelevant that cannot be helped. We must do our job."

"Need we go into all this?" said Donald.

"I hope it has been quite unnecessary. When did you last speak to your uncle?"

"About ten days ago."

"When did you leave this house?"

"On the same day," said Donald breathlessly.

"You left as the result of a misunderstanding with your uncle?"

"Yes."

"I'm afraid I shall have to ask you to tell me about it."

"I—it's got nothing to do with this—this awful business. It's not too pleasant to remember. I'd rather not——"

"You see," said Alleyn, "there was some point in my solemn opening speech." He got up and reached out a long hand, and touched Donald's shoulder. "Come," he said. "I know it's not easy."

"It wasn't that I didn't like him."

"I can't believe anyone could dislike him. What was the trouble? Your debts?"

"Yes."

"Did he pay them?"

"Yes."

"Then why did you quarrel?"

"He wanted me to go to Edinburgh to take my medical."

"And you didn't want to go?"

"No."

"Why?"

"I thought it would be so damned dull. I wanted to go to Thomas's. He had agreed to that."

Alleyn returned to his seat at the desk. "What made him change his mind?" he asked.

"This business about my debts."

"Nothing else?"

Donald ground out his cigarette with a trembling hand and shook his head.

"Did he object to any of your friends, for instance?" Alleyn asked.

"I—well he may have thought—I mean, it wasn't that."

"Did he know you were acquainted with Captain Maurice Withers?"

Donald darted a glance of profound astonishment at Alleyn, opened his mouth, shut it again, and finally said:

"I think so."

"Aren't you certain?"

"He knew I was friendly with Withers. Yes."

"Did he object to this friendship?"

"He did say something, now I come to think about it."

"It didn't leave any particular impression on you?"

"Oh, no," said Donald.

Alleyn brought his hand down sharply on Lord Robert's cheque-book.

"Then, I take it," he said, "you have forgotten a certain cheque for fifty pounds?"

Donald stared at the long thin hand lying across the blue cover. A dull flush mounted to the roots of his hair.

"No," he said, "I remember."

"Did he pay this amount to Withers on your behalf?"

"Yes."

"And yet it left no particular impression on you?"

"There were," said Donald, "so many debts."

"Your uncle knew you were friendly with this man. He had certain information about him. I know that. I ask you, whether, in fact, he did not object most strongly to your connection with Withers?"

"If you like to put it that way."

"For God's sake," said Alleyn, "don't hedge with me. I want to give you every chance."

"You—don't—think—I——"

"You're his heir. You quarrelled with him. You've been in debt. You are sharing rooms with a man against whom he warned you. You're in no position to try and save your face over smaller matters. You want to spare your mother as much as possible, don't you? Of course you do, and so do I. I ask you most earnestly as a friend, which I should not do, to tell me the whole truth."

"Very well," said Donald.

"You're living in the same flat as Captain Withers. What have you been doing there?"

"I—we—I was waiting to see if I couldn't perhaps go to Thomas's, after all."

"How could you afford to do that?"

"My mother would have helped. I've got my Prelim, and I thought if I read a bit and tried to earn a bit, later on I could start."

"How did you propose to earn a bit?"

"Wits was helping me—Captain Withers, I mean. He's been perfectly splendid. I don't care what anybody says about him, he's not a crook."

"What suggestions did he make?"

Donald fidgeted.

"Oh, nothing definite. We were going to talk it over."

"I see. Is Captain Withers doing a job of work himself?"

"Well, not exactly. He's got a pretty decent income, but he's thinking of doing something one of these days. He hates being idle, really."

"Will you tell me, please, why you were in debt to him for fifty pounds?"

"I—I simply owed it to him."

"Evidently. For what? Was it a bet?"

"Yes. Well, one or two side bets, actually."

"On what—horses?"

"Yes," said Donald quickly.

"Anything else?"

Silence.

"Anything else?"

"No. I mean . . . I can't remember exactly."

"You must remember. Was it at poker? Cards of any sort?"

"Yes, poker."

"There's something else," said Alleyn. "Donald, I can't exaggerate the harm you may do if you insist on hedging with us. Don't you see that with every fresh evasion you put your friend in an even more dubious light than the one in which he already appears? For God's sake, think of your uncle's death and your mother's sensibilities and your own foolish skin. How else did you lose money to Captain Withers?"

Alleyn watched Donald raise his head, knit his brows, and put his fingers to his lips. His eyes were blank but they were fixed on Alleyn's and presently an expression of doubtful astonishment crept into them.

"I don't know what to do," he said naïvely.

"You mean you owe something to Withers. You have made some promise, I suppose. Is that it?"

"Yes."

"To me the young men of your generation are rather bewildering. You seem to be a great deal more knowing than we were and yet I swear I would never have been taken in by a flashy gentleman with persuasive manners and no occupation, unless running an illicit hole-and-corner casino may be called an occupation."

"I never mentioned roulette," said Donald in a hurry.

"It is indeed a shame to take your money," rejoined Alleyn.

Fox gave a curious little cough and turned a page of his notebook.

Alleyn said: "Has Captain Withers, by any chance, suggested that you should earn an honest penny by assisting him?"

"I can't answer any more questions about him," said Donald in a high voice. He looked as if he would either fly into a violent rage or burst into tears.

"Very well," said Alleyn. "When did you hear of this tragedy?"

"This morning when the sporting edition came in."

"About an hour and a half ago?"

"Yes."

"How long does it take to get here from Captain Withers's flat? It's in Sling Street, Chelsea, isn't it? About five minutes' walk. Why were you so long coming here?"

"I wasn't dressed and though you may not believe it, I got a shock when I heard of my uncle's death."

"No doubt. So did your mother. I wonder she didn't ring you up."

"The telephone's disconnected," said Donald.

"Indeed? Why is that?"

"I forgot to pay the bloody bill. Wits left it to me. I rang her from a call-box."

"I see. Fox, one of our men is out there. Ask him to go to one hundred and ten Grandison Mansions, Sling Street, and tell Captain Withers I shall call on him in a few minutes and will be obliged if he remains indoors."

"Very good, Mr. Alleyn," said Fox, and went out.

"Now then," Alleyn continued. "I understand you were among the last to leave Marsdon House this morning. Correct?"

"Yes."

"I want you to tell me exactly what happened just before you left. Come now, will you try and give me a clear account?"

Donald looked slightly more at his ease. Fox came back and resumed his seat.

"I'll try, certainly," said Donald. "Where do you want me to begin?"

"From the moment when you came into the hall to go out."

"I was with Bridget O'Brien. I had the last dance with her and then we went into the buffet downstairs for soup."

"Anybody else there?"

"Her stepfather. I said good-night to him and then Bridgie and I went into the hall."

"Who was in the hall?"

"I don't remember except——"

"Yes?"

"Uncle Bunch was there."

"Did you speak to him?"

"No. I wish to God I had."

"What was he doing?"

"He had his cloak on. You know that extraordinary garment he wears? I think I heard him asking people if they'd seen Mrs. Halcut-Hackett."

"Had you seen her?"

"Not for some time, I think."

"So you remember nobody in the hall except your uncle and Miss O'Brien?"

"That's right. I said good-night to Bridgie and went away."

"Alone?"

"Yes."

"Captain Withers was not at the ball?"

"Yes, but he'd gone."

"Why did you not go away together?"

"Wits was going on somewhere. He had a date."

"Do you know where he went and with whom?"

"No."

"When you left Marsdon House what did you do?"

"Some people waiting outside for a taxi asked me to go on with them to the Sauce Boat, but I didn't want to. To get rid of them I walked to the corner to look for a taxi."

"Which corner?"

"First on the left as you come out of Marsdon House. Belgrave Road, I think it is."

"Anyone see you?"

"I don't know. Shouldn't think so. There was a damned heavy mist lying like a blanket over everything."

"We'll have to find your taxi."

"But I didn't get a taxi."

"What!"

Donald began to speak rapidly, his words tumbling over each other, as though he had suddenly opened all the doors of his thoughts.

"There wasn't a taxi at the corner, so I walked. I walked on and on through Eaton Square. It was late—after three o'clock. Lots of taxis passed me, of course, but they were all engaged. I was thinking about things. About Bridget. I meant to keep her out of this but I suppose you'll hear everything now. Everything will be dragged out and—and made to look awful. Bridgie, and—and Uncle Bunch—and taking my medical—and everything. I hardly noticed where I was going. It's queer walking through mist. Your footsteps sound odd. Everything seemed thin and simple. I can't describe it. I went on and on and presently there weren't any more taxis and I was in the Kings Road so I just walked home. Past the Chelsea Palace and then off to the right into Sling Street. That's all."

"Did you meet anyone?"

"I suppose I must have met a few people. I didn't notice."

"What time did you get home?"

"I didn't notice."

Alleyn looked gravely at him.

"I want you, please, to try very hard to remember if you met anybody on that walk, particularly in the early stages, just after you left Marsdon House. I see no reason why I should not point out the importance of this. As far as we can make out your uncle left the house a few minutes after you did. He, too, walked a short way round the square. He hailed a taxi and was joined at the last minute by a man in evening dress who got into the taxi with him. It is the identity of this man that we are anxious to establish."

"You can't think I would do it!" Donald said. "You can't! You've been our friend. You can't treat me like this, as though I was just anybody under suspicion. You *know* us! Surely to God——!"

Alleyn's voice cut coldly across his protestations.

"I am an investigating officer employed by the police. I must behave as if I had no friends while I am working on this case. If you think for a little you will see that this must be so. At the risk of sounding pompous I must go a bit further and tell you that if I found my friendship with your uncle, your mother, or yourself, was in any way influencing my conduct of this case I should be obliged to give up. Ask to be relieved of the job. Already I have spoken to you as a friend—I should not have done this. If you are innocent you are in no danger unless you prevaricate or shift ground, particularly in matters relating to your acquaintance with Captain Withers."

"You can't suspect Withers! Why should he want to kill Uncle Bunch? It's got nothing to do with him."

"In that case he has nothing to fear."

"On that account, of course, he hasn't. I mean—oh, hell!"

"Where were you when you lost this money to him?"

"In a private house."

"Where was it?"

"Somewhere near Leatherhead. Shackleton House, I think it's called."

"Was it his house?"

"Ask him. *Ask him.* Why do you badger me with all this! My God, isn't it enough that I should be faced with the other business! I can't stand any more of it. Let me out of this."

"You may go, certainly. There will be a statement for you to sign later on."

Donald got up and walked to the door. He turned and faced Alleyn.

"I'm as anxious as you," he said, "that the man should be caught. Naturally, I'm as anxious as anybody."

"Good," said Alleyn.

Donald's face was puckered into the sort of grimace a small boy makes when he is trying not to cry. For some reason this gave him a strong resemblance to his uncle. Alleyn felt his heart turn over. He got up, crossed the room in six long strides, and took Donald roughly by the arm.

"There!" he said, "if you're innocent you're safe. As for this other mess you've got yourself into, stick to the truth and we'll do what we can for you. Tell your mama the house is rid of us for the time being. Now, march!"

He turned Donald round, shoved him through the door, and slammed it behind him.

"Come on, Fox," he said. "Pack up those things—the will and the notes. Ring up the Yard and see if the post-mortem report is through, tell them to look Withers up in the record, and if one of my men is free, send him straight off to Shackleton House, Leatherhead. He'd better take a search-warrant, but he's not to use it without ringing me up first. If the place is locked up he's to stay there and report to me by telephone. Tell him we want evidence of a gambling hell. Fix that while I see the men outside, and then we'll be off."

"To see Withers?"

"Yes. To see Captain Maurice Withers who, unless I'm much mistaken, has added a gambling hell to his list of iniquitous sources of livelihood. My God, Fox, as someone was out for blood, why the hell couldn't they widen their field to include Captain Maurice Withers? Come on."

11

Captain Withers at Home

The report on the post-mortem was ready. Fox took it down over the telephone and he and Alleyn discussed it on their way to Sling Street.

"Dr. Curtis," said Fox, "says there's no doubt that he was suffocated. They've found"—and here Fox consulted his book—"Tardieu's ecchymosis on the congested lungs and on the heart. There were signs of fatty degeneration in the heart. The blood was dark-coloured and very liquid——"

"All right," said Alleyn violently. "Never mind that. Sorry, Fox. On you go."

"Well, sir, they seem to think that the condition of the heart would make everything much more rapid. That's what you might call a merciful thing, isn't it?"

"Yes."

"Yes. Barring the scar on the temple, Dr. Curtis says there are no marks on the face. The mucous membrane in the forepart of the palate is slightly congested. Posteriorly it is rather bleached. But there are no marks of violence."

"I noticed that. There was no struggle. He was unconscious after the blow on the temple," said Alleyn.

"That's what Dr. Curtis thinks."

"This murderer knew what he was about," said Alleyn. "Usually your asphyxiating homicide merchant goes in for a lot of unnecessary violence. You get marks round the mouth. Has Curtis any idea what was used?"

"He says possibly a plug of soft material introduced into the mouth and held over the nostrils."

"Yes. Not Bunchy's handkerchief. That was uncreased."

"Perhaps his own handkerchief."

"I don't think so, Fox. I found a trace of fine black woollen fluff in the mouth."

"The cloak?"

"Looks like it. It might be. One of the reasons why the cloak was got out of the way. By the way, Fox, did you get a report from that P.C. in Belgrave Square last night?"

"Yes. Nothing suspicious."

They plodded on, working out lines to take in the endless interviews. They correlated, sorted, and discussed each fragment of information. "Finding the pattern of the case," Alleyn called it. A five minutes' walk brought them to Sling Street and to a large block of rather pretentious service flats. They took the lift up to 110 and rang the bell.

"I'm going to take some risks here," said Alleyn.

The door was opened by Captain Withers himself.

He said. "Good morning. Want to see me?"

"Good morning, sir," said Alleyn. "Yes. You had our message just now, I hope. May we come in?"

"Certainly," said Withers and walked away from the door with his hands in his pockets.

Alleyn and Fox went in. They found themselves in a mass-production furnished sitting-room with a divan bed against one wall, three uniform armchairs, a desk, a table, and built-in cupboards. It had started off by being an almost exact replica of all the other "bachelor flats" in Grandison Mansions but since it is impossible to live in any place without leaving some print of yourself upon it, this room bore the impress of Captain Maurice Withers. It smelt of hairwash, cigars and whiskey. On one wall hung a framed photograph of the sort advertised in magazines as "artistic studio studies from the nude." On the bookshelves guides to the Turf stood between shabby copies of novels Captain Withers had bought on the Riviera and, for some reason, troubled to smuggle into England. On a table by the divan bed were three or four medical text-books: "Donald Potter's," thought Alleyn. Through a half-open door Alleyn caught a glimpse of a small bedroom and a second masterpiece that may have been a studio study but appeared to be an exercise in pornographic photography.

Captain Withers caught Fox's bland gaze directed at this picture and shut the bedroom door.

"Have a drink?" he said.

"No, thank you," said Alleyn.

"Well, sit down then."

Alleyn and Fox sat down, Fox with extreme propriety, Alleyn with an air of leisurely fastidiousness. He crossed one long leg over the other, hung his hat on his knee, pulled off his gloves, and contemplated Captain Withers. They made a curious contrast. Withers was the sort of man who breathes vulgarity into good clothes. His neck was too thick, his fingers too flat and pale and his hair shone too much; his eyes were baggy and his eyelashes were white. Yet in spite of these defects he was a powerful dominant animal with a certain coarse arrogance that was effective. Alleyn, by contrast, looked fine drawn, a cross between a monk and a grandee. The planes of Alleyn's face and head were emphatically defined, the boney structure showed clearly. There was a certain austerity in the chilly blue of his eyes and in the sharp blackness of his hair. Albrecht Dürer would have made a magnificent drawing of him, and Agatha Troy's sketch portrait of Alleyn is one of the best things she has ever done.

Withers lit a cigarette, blew the smoke down his nose and said:

"What's it all about?"

Fox produced his official notebook. Captain Withers eyed the letters M.P. on the cover and then looked at the carpet.

"First, if I may," said Alleyn, "I should like your full name and address."

"Maurice Withers and this address."

"May we have the address of your Leatherhead house as well, please?"

"What the hell d'you mean?" asked Withers quite pleasantly. He looked quickly at the table by the divan and then full in Alleyn's face.

"My information," lied Alleyn, "does not come from the source you suppose, Captain Withers. The address, please."

"If you mean Shackleton House, it is not mine. It was lent to me."

"By whom?"

"For personal reasons, I'm afraid I can't tell you that."

"I see. Do you use it much?"

"Borrow it for week-ends sometimes."

"Thank you," said Alleyn. "Now, if you please, I want to ask you one or two questions about this morning. The early hours of this morning."

"Oh, yes," said Withers, "I suppose you're thinking of the murder."

"Whose murder?"

"Why, Bunchy Gospell's."

"Was Lord Robert Gospell a personal friend of yours, Captain Withers?"

"I didn't know him."

"I see. Why do you think he was murdered?"

"Well, wasn't it?"

"I think so. Evidently you think so. Why?"

"Judging from the papers it looks like it."

"Yes, doesn't it?" said Alleyn. "Won't you sit down, Captain Withers?"

"No, thanks. What about this morning?"

"When did you leave Marsdon House?"

"After the ball was over."

"Did you leave alone?"

Withers threw his cigarette with great accuracy into a tin waste-paper bin.

"Yes," he said.

"Can you remember who was in the hall when you went away?"

"What? I don't know that I can. Oh, yes. I bumped into Dan Davidson. You know. The fashionable quack."

"Is Sir Daniel Davidson a friend of yours?"

"Not really. I just know him."

"Did you notice Lord Robert in the hall as you left?"

"Can't say I did."

"You went out alone. Did you take a taxi?"

"No. I had my own car. It was parked in Belgrave Road."

"So you turned to the left when you went away from Marsdon House. That," said Alleyn, "is what the murderer, if there is, as you say, a murderer, must have done."

"Better choose your words a bit more carefully, hadn't you?" enquired Captain Withers.

"I don't think so. As far as I can see my remark was well within the rules. Did you see any solitary man in evening dress as you walked from Marsdon House to Belgrave Road? Did you overtake or pass any such person?"

Withers sat on the edge of the table and swung his foot. The fat on his thighs bulged through his plaid trouser leg.

"I might have. I don't remember. It was misty."

"Where did you go in your car?"

"To the Matador."

"The night club in Sampler Street?"

"That's right."

"Did you meet anybody there?"

"About a hundred and fifty people."

"I mean," said Alleyn with perfect courtesy, "did you meet a partner there by arrangement?"

"Yes."

"May I have her name?"

"No."

"I shall have to find out by the usual routine," murmured Alleyn. "Make a note of it, will you, Fox?"

"Very good, Mr. Alleyn," said Fox.

"You can produce no witness to support your statement that you drove to the Matador from Marsdon House?"

The swinging foot was suddenly motionless. Withers waited a moment and then said: "No."

"Perhaps your partner was waiting in your car, Captain Withers. Are you sure you did not drive her there? Remember there is a commissionaire at the Matador?"

"Is there?"

"Well?"

"All right," said Withers. "I did drive my partner to the Matador but I shan't give you her name."

"Why not?"

"You seem to be a gentleman. One of the new breed at the Yard, aren't you? I should have thought you'd have understood."

"You are very good," said Alleyn, "but I am afraid you are mistaken. We shall have to use other methods, but we shall find out the name of your partner. Have you ever studied wrestling, Captain Withers?"

"What? What the hell has that got to do with it?"

"I should be obliged if you would answer."

"I've never taken it up. Seen a bit out East."

"Ju-jitsu?"

"Yes."

"Do they ever use the side of the hand to knock a man out? On one of the vulnerable points or whatever you call them? Such as the temple?"

"I've no idea."

"Have you any medical knowledge?"

"No."

"I see some text-books over there by the bed."

"They don't belong to me."

"To Mr. Donald Potter?"

"That's right."

"He is living here?"

"You've been talking to him, haven't you? You must be a bloody bad detective if you haven't nosed that out."

"Do you consider that you have a strong influence over Mr. Potter?"

"I'm not a bear leader!"

"You prefer fleecing lambs, perhaps?"

"Is that where we laugh?" asked Withers.

"Only, I am afraid, on the wrong side of our faces. Captain Withers, do you recollect the Bouchier-Watson drug-running affair of 1924?"

"No."

"You are fortunate. We have longer memories at the Yard. I am reminded of it this morning by certain notes left in his private papers by Lord Robert Gospell. He mentions the case in connection with recent information he gleaned about an illicit gambling club at Leatherhead."

The coarse white hands made a convulsive movement which was immediately checked. Alleyn rose to his feet.

"There is only one other point," he said. "I believe your telephone is disconnected. Inspector Fox will fix that. Fox, will you go out to the post office at the corner. Wait a second."

Alleyn took out his notebook, scribbled: "Get Thompson to tail W. at once," and showed it to Fox. "Give that message, will you, and see that Captain Withers's telephone is re-connected immediately. As soon as it's through, ring me here. What's the number?"

"Sloane 8405," said Withers.

"Right. I'll join you, Fox."

"Very good sir," said Fox. "Good morning, sir."

Withers did not answer. Fox departed.

"When your telephone is working again," Alleyn said, "I would be glad if you'd ring up Mr. Donald Potter to suggest that as his mother is in great distress, you think it would be well if he stayed with her for the time being. You will send his property to Cheyne Walk in a taxi."

"Are you threatening me?"

"No. I am warning you. You are in rather uncertain country at the moment, you know."

Alleyn walked over to the divan bed and looked at the books.

"Taylor's *Medical Jurisprudence*," he murmured. "Is Mr. Potter thinking of becoming a medical jurist?"

"I haven't the slightest idea."

Alleyn ruffled the pages of a large blue volume.

"Here we have the fullest information on asphyxia. Very interesting. May I borrow this book? I'll return it to Mr. Potter."

"I've no objection. Nothing to do with me."

"Splendid. Have you any objection to my looking at your dress clothes?"

"None," said Withers.

"Thank you so much. If you wouldn't mind showing them to me."

Withers walked into the bedroom and Alleyn followed him. While Withers opened his wardrobe and pulled open drawers Alleyn had a quick look round the room. Apart from the photograph, which was frankly infamous, the only item of interest was a row of paper-bound banned novels of peculiar indecency and no literary merit whatsoever.

Withers threw a tail coat, a white waistcoat and a pair of trousers on the bed. Alleyn examined them with great care, smelt the coat and turned out the pockets which were empty.

"Had you a cigarette-case?" he asked.

"Yes."

"May I see it?"

"It's in the next room."

Withers went into the sitting-room. Alleyn, with a catlike swiftness, looked under the bed and in at a cupboard door.

Withers produced a small, flat silver case.

"Is this the only case you possess?"

"It is."

Alleyn opened it. The inside lid was inscribed: "Maurice from Estelle." He returned it and took another from his pocket.

"Will you look at this case carefully, please, and tell me if you have seen it before?"

Withers took it. It was a thin, smooth, gold case, uninscribed, but with a small crest in one corner.

"Open it, will you, please?"

Withers opened it.

"Do you know it?"

"No."

"You don't by any chance recognise the crest?"

"No."

"It is not Mr. Donald Potter's crest, for instance?"

Withers made a quick movement, opened his mouth, shut it again and said:

"It isn't his. I've seen his. It's on his links. They're here somewhere."

"May I see them?" asked Alleyn, taking the case.

Withers crossed to the dressing-table. Alleyn rapidly wrapped his silk handkerchief round the case and put it in his pocket.

"Here they are," said Withers.

Alleyn solemnly inspected Donald's links and returned them.

The telephone rang in the next room.

"Will you answer it, please?" said Alleyn.

Withers went into the sitting-room. Alleyn whipped off the dust jacket from one of the banned novels and coolly slipped it in his overcoat pocket. He then followed Withers.

"It's for you," Withers said, "if you're Alleyn."

"Thank you."

It was Fox; to say in an extremely low voice that Thompson was well on his way.

"Splendid," said Alleyn. "Captain Withers wanted to use it at once."

He hung up the receiver and turned to Withers.

"Now, please," he said. "Will you telephone Mr.

Potter? I'd be glad if you would not mention that it was my suggestion. It would come more gracefully from you."

Withers dialled the number with as bad a grace as well might be. He got Donald whose voice came over in an audible quack.

"Hullo."

"Hullo, Don, it's Wits."

"Oh, God, Wits, I'm most frightfully worried, I——"

"You'd better not talk about your worries on the telephone. I rang up to say I thought it might be as well if you stayed with your mother for a bit. She'll want you there with all this trouble. I'll send your things around."

"Yes, but listen, Wits. About the house at——"

Captain Withers said: "You stay where you are," and rang off.

"Thank you," said Alleyn. "That will do nicely. How tall are you, Captain Withers?"

"Five foot eight and a half in my socks."

"Just about Lord Robert's height," said Alleyn, watching him.

Withers stared blankly at him.

"I suppose there must be some sense in a few of the things you say," he said.

"I hope so. Can you remember what Lord Robert was saying on the telephone when you walked into the room at one o'clock this morning?"

"What room?"

"At Marsdon House."

"You're talking through your hat. I never heard him on any telephone."

"That's all right then," said Alleyn. "Were you on the top landing near the telephone-room round about one o'clock?"

"How the devil should I know? I was up there quite a bit."

"Alone?"

"No. I was there with Don sometime during the supper dances. We were in the first sitting-out room. Old Carrados was up there then."

"Did you hear anyone using a telephone?"

"Fancy I did, now you mention it."

"Ah well, that's the best we can do at the moment, I suppose," said Alleyn, collecting Taylor's *Medical Jurisprudence*. "By the way, would you object to my searching these rooms? Just to clear your good name, you know."

"You can crawl over them with a microscope, if you like."

"I see. Thank you very much. Some other time, perhaps. Good morning."

He'd got as far as the door when Withers said:

"Here! Stop!"

"Yes?"

Alleyn turned and saw a flat white finger pointed at his face.

"If you think," said Captain Withers, "that I had anything to do with the death of this buffoon you're wasting your time. I didn't. I'm not a murderer and if I was, I'd go for big game—not domestic pigs."

Alleyn said: "You are fortunate. In my job we often have to hunt the most unpleasant quarry. A matter of routine. Good morning."

12

Report from a Waiter

In the street outside Alleyn met Detective-Sergeant Thompson who did not look like a detective-sergeant. As Captain Withers's windows enjoyed an uninterrupted view of Sling Street Alleyn did not pause to speak to Thompson, but he remarked to the air as they passed:

"Don't lose him."

Fox was waiting outside the post office.

"He's a nasty customer, I should say," he remarked as they fell into step.

"Who? Withers? I believe you, my old—"

"You were pretty well down on him, Mr. Alleyn."

"I was in a fix," said Alleyn. "I'd have liked to raid this place at Leatherhead without giving him any warning but the wretched Donald is sure to let him know what he told us and Withers will close down his gambling activities. The best we can hope for in that direction is that our man will find something conclusive if he gets into the house. We'd better take a taxi to Dimitri's. What time was he to be at the Yard?"

"Midday."

"It's a quarter to twelve. He ought to have left. Come on."

They got a taxi.

"How about Withers?" asked Fox, staring solemnly at the driver's back.

"For a likely suspect? He's the right height to within an inch. Good enough in the cloak and hat to diddle the taximan. By the way, there's nowhere in the bedroom where he could have stowed them. I saw inside the wardrobe and had a quick look under the bed and in the cupboard while he was on the telephone. Anyway, he said I could crawl over the flat with a microscope if I liked and he wasn't calling my bluff either. If he's got anything to hide it's at the house at Leatherhead."

"The motive's not so hot," said Fox.

"What is the motive?"

"He knew Lord Robert had recognised him and thought he was on his trail. He wants to get hold of the money and knows young Potter is the heir."

"That's two of his motives. But well? Damn," said Alleyn, "nearly a quotation! Bunchy warned me against 'em. Associating with the peerage, that's what it is. There's a further complication. Mrs. Halcut-Hackett may think Bunchy was a blackmailer. From his notes Bunchy seems to have got that impression. He was close to her when her bag was taken and had stuck to her persistently. If Withers is having an affair with the woman, she probably confided the blackmail stunt to him. Withers is possibly the subject of the Halcut-Hackett blackmail. The letter the blackmailer has got hold of may be one from Mrs. H-H to Withers or t'other way round. If she told him she thought Lord Robert was the blackmailer——"

"That's three of his motives," said Fox.

"You may say so. On the other hand Withers may be the blackmailer. It's quite in his line."

"Best motive of all," said Fox, "if he thought Lord Robert was on to him.

"How you do drone on, you old devil. Well, if we want to, we can pull him in for having dirty novels in his beastly flat. Look at this."

Alleyn pulled the book jacket out of his pocket. It displayed in primary colours a picture of a terrible young woman with no clothes on, a florid gentleman, and a lurking harridan. It was entitled: *The Confessions of a Procuress.*

"Lor'!" said Fox. "You oughtn't to have taken it."

"What a stickler you are to be sure." Alleyn pulled a fastidious grimace. "Can't you see him goggling over it in some bolt-hole on the Côte d'Azur! I've got his nasty flat prints on my own cigarette-case. We'll see if he's handled Donald Potter's 'Taylor.' Particularly the sections that deal with suffocation and asphyxia. I fancy, Fox, that a Captain Withers who was uninstructed in the art of smothering would have made the customary mistake of using too much violence. We'll have to see if he's left any prints in this telephone-room at Marsdon House."

"The interruption," said Fox thoughtfully. "As I see it, we've got to get at the identity of the individual who came in while Lord Robert was talking to you on the telephone. If the party's innocent, well, there'll be no difficulty."

"And contrariwise. I tried to bounce Withers into an admission. Took it for granted he was the man."

"Any good?"

"Complete wash-out. He never batted an eyelid. Seemed genuinely astonished."

"It may have been Dimitri. At least," said Fox, "we know Dimitri collects the boodle. What we want to find out is whether he's on his own or working for someone else."

"Time enough. Which brings us back to Bunchy's broken sentence. 'And he's working with——' With whom? Or is it with what? Hullo, one arrives."

The taxi had pulled up at a respectable old apartment house in the Cromwell Road. On the opposite pavement sat a young man mending the seat of a wicker chair.

"That's Master James D'Arcy Carewe, detective-constable," said Alleyn.

"What, him!" cried Fox in a scandalised voice. "So it is. What's he want to go dolling himself up in that rig for?"

"He's being a detective," Alleyn explained. "His father's a parson and he learnt wicker-work with the Women's Institute or something. He's been pining to disguise himself ever since he took the oath."

"Silly young chap," said Fox.

"He's quite a bright boy really, you know."

"Why's he still there, anyway?"

"Dimitri hasn't left yet, evidently. Wait a moment."

Alleyn slid back the glass partition of the taxi and addressed the driver:

"We're police officers. In a minute or two a man will come out of this house and want a cab. Hang about for him. He will probably ask you to drive him to Scotland Yard. If he gives any other address I want you to write it quickly on this card while he is getting into the cab. Drop the card through the gear lever slit in the floor. Here's a pencil. Can you do this?"

"Right you are, governor," said the taxi-man.

"I want you to turn your car and pass that fellow mending a chair seat. Go as slow as you can, drive two hundred yards up the road and let us out. Then wait for your man. Here's your fare and all the rest of it."

"Thank you, sir. O.K., sir," said the taxi-man.

He turned, Alleyn lowered the window and, as they passed the wicker expert, leant out and said:

"Carewe! Pick us up."

The expert paid no attention.

"I told you he's not as silly as he looks," said Alleyn. "There we are."

They got out. The taxi turned once more. They heard the driver's hoarse: "Taxi, sir?" heard him pull up, heard the door slam, heard the cab drive away. "He hasn't dropped his card," said Alleyn staring after the taxi. They continued to walk up the Cromwell Road. Presently a cry broke out behind them.

"Chairs to mend! Chairs to mend!"

"There!" said Fox in exasperation. "Listen to him making an exhibition of himself! It's disgraceful. That's what it is. Disgraceful."

They turned and found the wicker-worker hard at their heels, followed by long trails of withy.

"Come here," said Alleyn. "There's no need to continue your spirited impersonation, Carewe. Your quarry has departed."

"Sir!" said the wicker-worker in consternation.

"Tell me," Alleyn went on, "why are you presenting the Cries of London to an astonished world?"

"Well, sir," said the chair-mender, "following your instructions, I proceeded——"

"Quite. But you should understand by this time that the art of disguise is very often unnecessary and is to be attained by simpler means than those which embrace a great outlay in willow wands, envious slivers, and cabriole legs. What, may I ask, would you have done with all this gear when the hunt was up?"

"There's a taxi rank round the corner, sir. If I whistled——"

"And a pretty sight you'd have looked," said Fox indignantly, "whistling cabs in that rig-out. By the time you'd wound yourself in and out of that muck and got yourself aboard, your man would have been half-way to Lord knows where. If that's the sort of stuff they teach you at——"

"Yes, all right, Fox," said Alleyn hastily. "Very true. Now, look here, Carewe, you go away and undress and report to me at the Yard. You can go back by Underground. Don't look so miserable or the old ladies will start giving you coppers."

Carewe departed.

"Now then, Fox," Alleyn continued, "give me a few minutes in that flat and then ring up as if from the Yard and keep Dimitri's servant on the telephone as long as possible. You'd better have a list of times and places. Say Dimitri has given them to you and say you will be able to confirm them. All right?"

"Right oh, Mr. Alleyn."

"You can use the call-box at the taxi rank. Then away with you to the Yard and keep Dimitri going until I come. Arrange to have him tailed when he leaves."

Alleyn returned to Dimitri's flat which was on the ground floor. The door was opened by a thin dark man who exuded quintessence of waiter.

"Is Mr. Dimitri in?" asked Alleyn.

"Monsieur has just left, sir. May I take a message?"

"He's gone, has he?" said Alleyn very pleasantly. "What a bore, I've just missed him. Do you know if he was going to Scotland Yard?"

The man hesitated.

"I'm not sure, sir. I think——"

"Look here," said Alleyn, "I'm Chief Inspector Alleyn. Here's my card. I was in this part of the world and I thought I'd save Mr. Dimitri the trouble of moving if I called. As I am here I may as well get you to clear up one or two points for me. Do you mind?"

"Please, sir! Not at all, but it is a little difficult——"

"It is rather, out here. May I come in?" asked Alleyn, and walked in without waiting for the answer.

He found himself in a sitting-room that had an air of wearing a touch of black satin at the neck and wrists but was otherwise unremarkable. The servant followed him and stood looking uneasily at his own hands.

"You will have guessed," Alleyn began, "that I am here on business connected with the death of Lord Robert Gospell."

"Yes, sir."

"The first thing I have to say is that we would be glad if you'd use great discretion in discussing this affair. Indeed it would be better if you did not discuss it at all, with anybody. Except of course, M. Dimitri himself."

The man looked relieved.

"But it is understood perfectly, sir. Monsieur has

already warned me of this himself. I shall be most discreet."

"Splendid. We feel it our duty to protect M. Dimitri and any other person of position from the unpleasant notoriety that unfortunately accompanies such accidents as these."

"Yes, certainly, sir. Monsieur himself was most emphatic."

"I'm sure he was. You will understand," Alleyn went on, "that it is also necessary to have before us a clear account of the movements of many persons. What is your name?"

"Francois, sir. Francois Dupont."

"Were you at Marsdon House last night?"

"Yes, sir. By an unusual chance I was there."

"How did that happen?"

"An important member of our staff failed M. Dimitri yesterday afternoon. It seems that he was afflicted suddenly with appendicitis. M. Dimitri was unable to replace him satisfactorily at so short notice and I took his place."

"This was unusual?"

"Yes, sir. I am M. Dimitri's personal servant."

"Where were you stationed at Marsdon House?"

A telephone rang in the entrance passage.

"Excuse me, sir," said the servant. "The telephone."

"That's all right," said Alleyn.

The man went out closing the door softly behind him.

Alleyn darted into an adjoining bedroom leaving the door ajar. He opened built-in cupboards, ran his hands between hanging suits, amongst neatly stacked shirts and under-garments, disturbing nothing, exploring everywhere. Thanking his stars that the drawers ran easily he moved with economy, swiftness and extreme precision. The adjoining bedroom was innocently naked. Dimitri's servant looked after him well. There was no hiding-place anywhere for a bulky cloth cloak. Everything was decently ordered. Alleyn returned silently to the sitting-room. He could hear the servant's voice:

"Hullo? Hullo? Yes, sir. I am still here. Yes, sir, that is quite correct. It is as Monsieur Dimitri says, sir. We returned together at three thirty in a taxi. At three-thirty. No, sir, no. At three-thirty. I am sorry, sir, I will repeat. At three-thirty we return——"

The sideboard contained only bottles and glasses, the bookcases only books. The desk was locked but it was a small one. Dimitri and his servant were tidy men with few possessions. Alleyn opened the last cupboard. It contained two suitcases. He tipped them gingerly. No sound of anything. He opened them. They were empty. Alleyn shut the cupboard door gently and returned to the middle of the sitting-room when he stood with his head slanted, listening to Dimitri's servant whose voice has risen to a painful falsetto.

"But I am telling you. Permit me to speak. Your colleague is here. He is about to ask me all these questions himself. He has given me his card. It is the Chief Inspector All-eyne. Ah, *mon Dieu! Mon Dieu!*"

Alleyn went into the passage. He found Francois with his shoulders up to his ears and his unoccupied hand sketching desperation to the air.

"What is it?" asked Alleyn. "Is it for me?"

"Here is M. l'Inspecteur!" screamed Francois into the receiver. "Will you have the goodness——"

Alleyn addressed the telephone.

"Hullo!"

"Hullo there!" said Fox's voice in accents of exasperation.

"Is that you, Fox. What's the matter?"

"Nothing, I hope, Mr. Alleyn," said Fox, falling back on an indistinct mumble.

"It's Alleyn, here. There's been a slight misunderstanding. I have missed Mr. Dimitri but will come along as soon as possible. Will you ask him to wait? Apologise for me."

"I hope there *was* time. I'll get along to the Yard now."

"Very well. That's perfectly all right," said Alleyn and rang off.

He returned to the sitting-room followed by Francois.

"A slight misunderstanding," explained Alleyn blandly. "My colleague did not quite follow you. He is unfortunately rather deaf and is about to retire."

Francois muttered.

"To resume," said Alleyn. "You were going to tell me where you were stationed last night."

"By the top landing, sir. The gallery above the ballroom. My duties were to keep the ash-trays emptied and to attend to the wishes of the guests who sat out dances on this floor."

"What are the rooms on this gallery?"

"At the stairhead, sir, one finds a green baize door leading to the servants' quarters, the back stairs and so on. Next to this door is a room which last night was employed as a sitting-room. One finds next, a bathroom, bedroom and toilet used last night for ladies. Last at the end of the gallery, a green boudoir also used as a sitting-room for the ball."

"Was there a telephone in any of these rooms?"

"In the green boudoir, sir. It was used several times during the evening."

"You are an excellent witness, Francois. I compliment you. Now tell me. You were stationed on this landing. Do you remember the names of the persons who used the telephone?"

Francois pinched his lower lip.

"It was used by Lady Jennifer Trueman to enquire for her little girl who is ill. Her ladyship requested me to get the number for her. It was used by a young gentleman who called a toll number to say that he would not be returning to the country. Early in the evening it was answered by Sir Daniel Davidson, who, I think, is a doctor. He spoke about a patient who had had an operation. It was also used, sir, by Lord Robert Gospell."

Alleyn waited a moment. With a sort of astonishment he realised his heart had quickened.

"Could you hear what Lord Robert said?"

"No, sir."

"Did you notice if anyone went into the room while Lord Robert was at the telephone?"

"No, sir. Immediately after Lord Robert entered this room I was summoned by Sir Herbert Carrados who came out of the other sitting-room and spoke to me about the lack of matches. Sir Herbert was annoyed. He sent me into this room to see for myself and ordered me to go at once and fetch more matches. There did not appear to me to be any lack of matches but I did not, of course, say so. I fetched more matches from downstairs. When I returned I went to the telephone-room and found it empty. I attended to the ash-tray and the matches in the telephone-room, also."

Alleyn sighed.

"Yes, I see. I've no doubt you made a good job of it. Any cigar-stumps in the telephone-room? You wouldn't remember, of course."

"No, sir."

"No. Francois—who was in the other sitting-room and who was on the landing before Lord Robert telephoned? Before Sir Herbert Carrados sent you away. Can you remember?"

"I will try, sir. There were two gentlemen who also sent me away."

"What?"

"I mean, sir, that one of them asked me to fetch two whiskies-and-sodas. That is not at all a usual request under the circumstances. It is not even *comme il faut* at a ball of this sort, where there is champagne at the buffet and also whisky, to order drinks as if it were an hotel. I received the impression that these two gentlemen wished to be alone on the landing. I obtained their drinks, using the back stairs. When I returned I gave them the drinks. At that time, sir, Lord Robert Gospell had just come up the stairs and when they saw him these two gentlemen moved into the first sitting-room which was unoccupied."

"Do you mean that they seemed to avoid him?"

"I received the impression, sir, that these gentlemen wished to be alone. That is why I remember them."

"Their names?"

"I do not know their names."

"Can you describe them?"

"One, sir, was a man perhaps forty-five or fifty years of age. He was a big man with a red face and thick neck. His voice was an unsympathetic voice. The other was a young gentleman, dark, rather nervous. I observed that he danced repeatedly with Miss Bridget O'Brien."

"Thank you," said Alleyn. "That is excellent. Any others?"

"I cannot recall any others, sir. Wait! There *was* someone who was there for some time."

Francois put his first finger to his chin like a sort of male dairymaid and cast his eyes to the ceiling.

"*Tiens!*" he exclaimed, "who could it have been? *Alors,* I have it. It is of no importance at all, sir. It was the little mademoiselle, the secretary, who was known to few and therefore retired often to the gallery. I have remembered too that Sir Daniel Davidson, the physician, came upstairs. That was earlier. Before Lord Robert appeared. I think Sir Daniel looked for a partner because he went quickly in and out of both rooms and looked about the landing. I have remembered now that it was for Lady Carrados he enquired but she had gone downstairs a few minutes earlier. I told Sir Daniel this and he returned downstairs."

Alleyn looked over his notes.

"See now," he said. "I am right in saying this? The persons who, as far as you know, could have gone into the telephone-room while Lord Robert was using the telephone were Sir Herbert Carrados and the two gentlemen who sent you for whisky."

"Yes, sir. And the mademoiselle. Miss Harris is her name. I believe she entered the ladies' toilet just as Lord Robert went into the telephone-room. I have remarked that when ladies are much disengaged at balls they frequently enter the dressing-room. It is," added

Francois with an unexpected flash of humanity, "a circumstance that I find rather pathetic."

"Yes," said Alleyn. "Very pathetic. I am right, then, in saying that before Lord Robert went to telephone you fetched drinks for these two men and immediately after that he began to telephone. You were sent away by Sir Herbert Carrados, having him, Miss Harris and possibly others, whom you have forgotten, on the landing, and the two gentlemen in the other sitting-out room. Sir Daniel Davidson had gone downstairs some minutes previously. Lady Carrados before Sir Daniel, who was looking for her. You're sure of that?"

"Yes, sir. It is in my memory because after her ladyship had gone I entered the telephone-room and saw she had left her bag there. Monsieur—Mr. Dimitri—came up at that time, saw it, and said he would return it to her ladyship. I told him she had gone downstairs and he returned, I think, by the back stairs."

"He fits in between Lady Carrados and Sir Daniel. Did he return?"

"No, sir. I believe, sir, that I have mentioned everyone who was on the landing. At that time nearly all the guests were at supper. Later, of course, many ladies used the cloakroom toilet."

"I see. Now for the rest of the evening. Did you see Lord Robert again?"

"No, sir. I remained on the top landing until the guests had gone. I then took a tray to Monsieur in the butler's pantry."

"Was this long after the last guest had left?"

"No, sir. To be correct, sir, I fancy there may still have been one or two left in the hall. Monsieur was in the buffet when I came down."

"Was Sir Herbert Carrados in the buffet?"

"He left as I entered. It was after he left that Monsieur ordered his little supper."

"When did you go home?"

"As I have explained to your colleague, at three-thirty, with Monsieur. The police rang up this flat before Monsieur had gone to bed."

"You carried Monsieur Dimitri's luggage for him, no doubt?"

"His luggage, sir? He had no luggage."

"Right. I think that is all. You have been very helpful and obliging."

Francois took his tip with a waiter's grace and showed Alleyn out.

Alleyn got a taxi. He looked at his watch. Twenty past twelve. He hoped Fox was keeping Dimitri for him. Dimitri! Unless Francois lied, it looked as if the odds against Dimitri being the murderer were lengthening.

"And the worst of it is," muttered Alleyn, rubbing his nose, "that I think Francois, blast his virtue, spoke nothing but the truth."

13

Dimitri Cuts His Fingers

In his room at the Yard Alleyn found Dimitri closeted with Fox. Fox introduced them solemnly.

"This is Mr. Dimitri; Chief Detective-Inspector Alleyn, who is in charge of this case."

"Ah, yes?" said Dimitri bowing. "I believe we have met before."

Alleyn said: "I have just come from your flat, Mr. Dimitri. I was up that way and hoped to save you a journey. I was, however, too late. I saw your servant and ventured to ask him one or two questions. He was most obliging."

He smiled pleasantly at Dimitri and thought: "He's looking sulky. Not a good head. Everything's a bit too narrow. He's got a mean look. No fool, though. Expensive clothes, fishy hands, uses a lot of hair oil.

Honey and flowers. Ears set very low. No lobes to them. Less than an eye's width between the two eyes. I fancy the monocle is a dummy. Dents by the nostrils. False teeth. A smooth gentleman."

Dimitri said: "Your colleague has already rung my servant, Mr. Alleyn."

"Yes," said Fox. "I just checked up the time Mr. Dimitri left. I've been explaining, sir, that we realise Mr. Dimitri doesn't want to appear more than can be avoided."

"In my position, Chief Inspector," said Dimitri, "it is most undesirable. I have been seven years building up my business and it is a specialised business. You understand that I have an extremely good clientele. I may say the very best. It is essential to my business that my clients should have complete faith in my discretion. But essential! In my position one sees and hears many things."

"I have no doubt of that," said Alleyn, looking steadily at him. "Things that with a less discreet, less scrupulous person, might be turned to advantage."

"That is a dreadful thought, Mr. Alleyn. One cannot with equanimity contemplate such a base idea. But I must tell you that in my business the finest shades of discretion must be observed."

"As in ours. I shall not ask you to repeat any scandals, Mr. Dimitri. We will confine ourselves to the simplest facts. Your own movements, for instance."

"Mine?" asked Dimitri, raising his eyebrows.

"If you please. We are anxious to get a little information about a small green boudoir on the top gallery at Marsdon House. It has a telephone in it. Do you know the room I mean?"

"Certainly." The sharp eyes were veiled, the mouth set in a thin line.

"Did you at any time visit this room?"

"Repeatedly. I make it my business to inspect all the rooms continually."

"The time in which we are interested is about one

o'clock this morning. Most of Lady Carrados's guests were at supper. Captain Maurice Withers and Mr. Donald Potter were on this top landing. So was your servant, Francois. Do you remember going upstairs at this time?"

Dimitri spread out his hands.

"It is impossible for me to remember. I am so very sorry." He removed his rimless eyeglass and began to turn it between the fingers and thumb of his left hand.

"Let me try to help you. I learnt that at about this time you returned Lady Carrados's bag to her. One of the guests noticed you. Where did you find this bag, Mr. Dimitri? Perhaps that will help."

Dimitri suddenly put his hands in his pockets and Alleyn knew that it was an unfamiliar gesture. He could see that the left hand was still secretly busy with the eyeglass.

"That is correct. I seem to think the bag was in the room you mention. I am very particular about such things. My servants may not touch any bags that are left lying about the rooms. It is incredible how careless many ladies are with their bags, Mr. Alleyn. I make it a rule that only I myself return them. Thus," said Dimitri virtuously, "am I solely responsible."

"It might be quite a grave responsibility. So the bag was in the green room. Anybody there?"

"My servant Francois. I trust there was nothing missing from this bag?" asked Dimitri with an air of alarm. "I asked her ladyship to be good enough to look at it."

"Her ladyship," said Alleyn, "has made no complaint."

"I am extremely relieved. For a moment I wondered—However."

"The point is this," said Alleyn. "At one o'clock Lord Robert telephoned from this little green room. My informant is not your servant, Mr. Dimitri. I must make that clear. At this time I think he was downstairs. My informant tells me that you were on the landing.

Perhaps it was shortly after you collected Lady Carrados's bag."

"If it was I did not hear anything of it," said Dimitri instantly. "Your informant is himself misinformed. I did not see Lord Robert on this gallery. I did not notice him at all until he was leaving."

"You saw him then?"

"Yes. He enquired if I had seen Mrs. Halcut-Hackett. I informed his lordship that she had left."

"This was in the hall?"

"Yes."

"Did you see Lord Robert leave?"

There was a marked pause and then Dimitri said:

"I have already explained all this to your colleague. After speaking to his lordship I went to the buffet on the ground floor. I remained there for a time speaking to Sir Herbert Carrados."

Alleyn took a piece of paper from his pocket-book and handed it to Dimitri.

"This is the order of departure among the last guests. We have got our information from several sources. Mr. Fox was greatly helped in compiling it by his interview with you earlier this morning. Would you mind glancing at it?"

Dimitri surveyed the list.

"It is correct, as far as I can remember, up to the time I left the hall."

"I believe you saw the encounter at the foot of the stairs between Lord Robert and his nephew, Mr. Donald Potter?"

"It was scarcely an encounter. They did not speak."

"Did you get the impression that they avoided each other?"

"Mr. Alleyn, we have already spoken of the need for discretion. Of course one understands this is a serious matter. Yes. I did receive this impression."

"Right. Then before you went to the buffet you noticed Mrs. Halcut-Hackett, Captain Withers, Mr.

Potter, and Sir Daniel Davidson leave separately, and in that order?"

"Yes."

"Do you know Captain Withers?"

"Professionally? No. He does not entertain, I imagine."

"Which left the buffet first, you or Sir Herbert?"

"I really do not remember. I did not remain very long in the buffet."

"Where did you go?"

"I was fatigued. I made certain that my staff was working smoothly and then my servant brought me a light supper to the butler's pantry which I had reserved for my office."

"How long was this after Lord Robert left?"

"I really do not know. Not long."

"Did Francois remain in the butler's pantry?"

"Certainly not."

"Did anyone come in while you were there?"

"I do not remember."

"If, on reflection, you do recall any witness to your solitary supper-party it would help us in our work and free you from further embarrassment."

"I do not understand you. Do you attempt to establish my alibi in this most regrettable and distressing fatality? Surely it is obvious that I could not have been in a taxi-cab with Lord Robert Gospell and in the buffet at Marsdon House at the same moment."

"What makes you think that this crime was committed during the short time you spent in the buffet, Mr. Dimitri?"

"Then or later, it is all the same. Still I am ready to help you, Chief Inspector. I will try and remember if I was seen in the pantry."

"Thank you. I believe you attended the Bach recital by the Sirmione Quartette in the Constance Street Hall on June 3rd?"

The silence that followed Alleyn's question was so complete that the rapid tick of his desk clock came out of obscurity to break it. Alleyn was visited by a fantastic idea. There were four clocks in the room: Fox, Dimitri, himself and that small mechanical pulse on the writing-desk.

Dimitri said: "I attended the concert, yes. I am greatly attached to the music of Bach."

"Did you happen to notice Lord Robert at this concert?"

It was as if the clock that was Dimitri was opened and the feverish little pulse of the brain revealed. Should he say yes; should he say no?

"I am trying to remember. I think I do remember that his lordship was present."

"You are quite correct, Mr. Dimitri. He was not far away from you."

"I pay little attention to externals when I listen to beautiful music."

"Did you return her bag to Mrs. Halcut-Hackett?"

Dimitri gave a sharp cry. Fox's pencil skidded across the page of his notebook. Dimitri drew his left hand out of his pocket and stared at his fingers. Three drops of blood fell from them to his striped trouser leg.

"Blood on your hand, Mr. Dimitri," said Alleyn.

Dimitri said: "I have broken my glass."

"Is the cut deep? Fox, my bag is in the cupboard there. I think there is some lint and strapping in it."

"No," said Dimitri, "it is nothing." He wrapped his fine silk handkerchief round his fingers and nursed them in his right hand. He was white to the lips.

"The sight of blood," he said, "affects me unpleasantly."

"I insist that you allow me to bandage your hand," said Alleyn. Dimitri did not answer. Fox produced iodine, lint and strapping. Alleyn unwrapped the hand. Two of the fingers were cut and bled freely. Dimitri shut his eyes while Alleyn dressed them. The hand was icy cold and clammy.

"There," said Alleyn. "And your handkerchief to hide the blood-stains which upset you so much. You are quite pale, Mr. Dimitri. Would you like some brandy?"

"No. No, thank you."

"You are recovered?"

"I do not feel well. I must ask you to excuse me."

"Certainly. When you have answered my last question. Did you ever return Mrs. Halcut-Hackett's bag?"

"I do not understand you. We spoke of Lady Carrados's bag."

"We now speak of Mrs. Halcut-Hackett's bag which you took from the sofa at the Sirmione concert. Do you deny that you took it?"

"I refuse to prolong this interview. I shall answer no more questions without the advice of my solicitor. That is final."

He rose to his feet. So did Alleyn and Fox.

"Very well," said Alleyn. "I shall have to see you again, Mr. Dimitri; and again, and I dare say again. Fox, will you show Mr. Dimitri down?"

When the door had closed Alleyn spoke into his telephone.

"My man is leaving. He'll probably take a taxi. Who's tailing him?"

"Anderson relieving Carewe, sir."

"Ask him to report when he gets a chance but not to take too big a chance. It's important."

"Right, Mr. Alleyn."

Alleyn waited for Fox's return. Fox came in grinning.

"He's shaken up a fair treat to see, Mr. Alleyn. Doesn't know if he's Mayfair, Soho, or Wandsworth."

"We've a long way to go before he's Wandsworth. How are we ever going to persuade women like Mrs. Halcut-Hackett to charge their blackmailers? Not in a lifetime unless——"

"Unless what?"

"Unless the alternative is even more terrifying. Fox, do you think it within the bounds of possibility that Dimitri ordered his trifle of caviare and champagne at Sir Herbert's expense, that Francois brought it to him in the pantry, that Francois departed and Dimitri, hurriedly acquiring a silk hat and overcoat, darted out by the back door just in time to catch Lord Robert in the mist, ask him preposterously for a lift and drive away? Can you swallow this camel of unlikelihood and, if so, can you open your ponderous and massy jaws still farther and engulf the idea of Dimitri performing his murder and subsequent masquerade, returning to Marsdon House, and settling down to his supper without anybody noticing anything out of the ordinary?"

"When you put it that way, sir, it does sound funny. But we don't know it's impossible."

"No, we don't. He's about the right height. I've a strong feeling, Fox, that Dimitri is not working this blackmail game on his own. We're not allowed strong feelings, so ignore it. If there is another scoundrel in the game they'll try to get into touch. We'll have to do something about that. What's the time? One o'clock. I'm due at Sir Daniel's at two and I'll have to see the A.C. before then. Coming?"

"I'll do a bit of work on the file first. We ought to hear from the fellow at Leatherhead any time now. You go to lunch, Mr. Alleyn. When did you last eat anything?"

"I don't know. Look here——"

"Did you have any breakfast?" asked Fox, putting on his spectacles and opening the file.

"Good Lord, Fox, I'm not a hothouse lily."

"This isn't a usual case, sir, for you. It's a personal matter, say what you like, and you'll do no good if you try and work it on your nerves."

Fox glanced at Alleyn over the top of his spectacles, wetted his thumb, and turned a page.

"Oh, God," said Alleyn, "once the wheels begin to turn, it's easier to forget the other side. If only I didn't see him so often. He looked like a child, Fox. Just like a child."

"Yes," said Fox. "It's a nasty case, personal feelings aside. If you see the Assistant Commissioner now, Mr.

Alleyn, I'll be ready to join you for a bite of lunch before we go to Sir Daniel Davidson's."

"All right, blast you. Meet me downstairs in a quarter of an hour."

"Thank you, sir," said Fox, "I'll be pleased."

And twenty minutes later he presided over Alleyn's lunch with all the tranquil superiority of a Nannie. They arrived at St. Luke's Chambers, Harley Street, at two o'clock precisely. They sat in a waiting-room lavishly strewn with new periodicals. Fox solemnly read *Punch*, while Alleyn, with every appearance of the politest attention, looked at a brochure appealing for clothes and money for the Central Chinese Medical Mission. In a minute or two a secretary told them that Sir Daniel would see them and showed them into his consulting-room.

"The gentlemen from Scotland Yard, Sir Daniel, Mr. Alleyn and Mr. Fox."

Davidson, who had apparently been staring out of the window, came forward and shook hands.

"It's very good of you to come to me," he said. "I said on the telephone that I was quite ready to report at Scotland Yard whenever it suited you. Do sit down."

They sat down. Alleyn glanced round the room and what he saw pleased him. It was a charming room with apple-green walls, an Adams fireplace and silver-starred curtains. Above the mantelpiece hung a sunny landscape by a famous painter. A silk praying-mat that would not have disgraced a collector's walls did workaday service before the fireplace. Sir Daniel's desk was an adapted spinet, his ink-well recalled the days when sanded paper was inscribed with high-sounding phrases in quill-scratched caligraphy. As he sat at his desk Sir Daniel saw before him in Chinese ceramic, a little rose-red horse. A beautiful and expensive room, crying in devious tones of the gratitude of wealthy patients. The most exalted, if not the richest, of these stared with blank magnificence from a silver frame.

Sir Daniel himself, neat, exquisite in London clothes

and a slightly flamboyant tie, with something a little exotic about his fine dark head, looked as though he could have no other setting than this. He seated himself at his desk, joined his hands and contemplated Alleyn with frank curiosity.

"Surely you are Roderick Alleyn?" he said.

"Yes."

"I have read your book."

"Are you interested in criminology?" asked Alleyn with a smile.

"Enormously! I hardly dare to tell you this because you must so often fall a victim to the enthusiasm of fools. I, too! 'Oh, Sir Daniel, it must be *too* marvellous to be able to look into the minds of people as you do.' Their minds! My God! Their stomachs are enough. But I often think quite seriously that I should have liked to follow medical jurisprudence."

"We have lost a great figure then," said Alleyn.

"That's very graceful. But it's untrue, I'm afraid. I am too impatient and altogether too much of a partisan. As in this case. Lord Robert was a friend of mine. It would be impossible for me to look at this case with an equal eye."

"If you mean," said Alleyn, "that you do not feel kindly disposed towards his murderer, no more do we. Do we, Fox?"

"No, sir, that we do not," said Fox.

Davidson's brilliant eyes rested for a moment on Fox. With a single glance he seemed to draw him into the warm circle of his confidence and regard. "All the same," thought Alleyn, "he's uneasy. He doesn't quite know where to begin." And he said:

"You very kindly rang up to say you might be able to help us."

"Yes," said Davidson, "yes, I did." He lifted a very beautiful jade paperweight and put it down. "I don't know how to begin." He darted a shrewd and somehow impish glance at Alleyn. "I find myself in the unenviable position of being one of the last people to see Lord Robert."

Fox took out his notebook. Davidson looked distastefully at it.

"When did you see him?" Alleyn asked.

"In the hall, just before I left."

"You left, I understand, after Mrs. Halcut-Hackett, Captain Withers, and Mr. Donald Potter, who went away severally about three-thirty."

Davidson's jaw dropped. He flung up his beautiful hands.

"Believe it or not," he said, "I had a definite struggle with my conscience before I made up my mind to admit it."

"Why was that?" asked Alleyn.

Again that sideways impish glance.

"I didn't want to come forward at all. No a bit. It's very bad for us parasites to appear in murder trials. In the long run, it is very bad indeed. By the way, I suppose it *is* a case of homicide. No doubt about it? Or shouldn't I ask?"

"Of course you can ask. There seems to be no doubt at all. He was smothered."

"Smothered!" Davidson leant forward, his hands clasped on the desk. Alleyn read in his face the subtle change that comes upon all men when they embark on their own subject. "Good God!" he said, "he wasn't a Desdemona! Why didn't he make a rumpus? Is he much marked?"

"There are no marks of violence."

"None? Who did the autopsy?"

"Curtis. He's our expert."

"Curtis, Curtis?—yes, of course. How does he account for the absence of violence? Heart? His heart was in a poor condition."

"How do you know that, Sir Daniel?"

"My dear fellow, I examined him most thoroughly three weeks ago."

"Did you!" exclaimed Alleyn. "That's very interesting. What did you find?"

"I found a very unpleasant condition. Evidence of fatty degeneration. I ordered him to avoid cigars like the

plague, to deny himself his port and to rest for two hours
every day. I am firmly persuaded that he paid no
attention whatsoever. Nevertheless, my dear Mr.
Alleyn, it was not a condition under which I would
expect an unprovoked heart attack. A struggle certainly
might induce it and you tell me there is no evidence of a
struggle."

"He was knocked out."

"Knocked out! Why didn't you say so before?
Because I gave you no opportunity, of course. I see.
And quietly asphyxiated? How very horrible and how
ingenious."

"Would the condition of the heart make it quicker?"

"I should say so, undoubtedly."

Davidson suddenly ran his fingers through his
picturesque hair.

"I am more distressed by this abominable, this
unspeakable crime than I would have thought possible.
Mr. Alleyn, I had the deepest regard for Lord Robert. It
would be impossible to exaggerate my regard for him.
He seemed a comic figure, an aristocratic droll with an
unusual amount of charm. He was much more than that.
He had a keen brain. In conversation he understood
everything that one left unsaid, his mind was both subtle
and firm. I am a man of the people. I adore all my smart
friends and I understand, *Christo Mio*, do I not
understand! my smart patients! But I am not, deep in
my heart, at ease with them. With Lord Robert I was at
ease. I showed off and was not ashamed afterwards that
I had done so."

"You pay him a great compliment when you confess
as much," said Alleyn.

"Do I not? Listen. If it had been anyone else, do you
know what I should have done? I should have kept quiet
and I should have said to myself *il ne faut pas réveiller
le chat qui dor*, and hoped nobody would remember that
I stood in the hall this morning at Marsdon House and
watched Lord Robert at the foot of the stairs. But as it is
I have screwed myself up to making the superb gesture of

coming to you with information you have already received. *Gros-Jean en remontre a son curé!*

"Not altogether," said Alleyn. "It is not entirely *une vielle histoire*. You may yet glow with conscious virtue. I am longing for a precise account of those last minutes in the hall. We have the order of the going but not the nature of it. If you don't mind giving us a microscopically exact version?"

"Ah!" Davidson frowned. "You must give me a moment to arrange my facts. A microscopically exact version! Wait, now." He closed his eyes and his right hand explored the surface of the carved paperweight. The deliberate movement of the fingers arrested Alleyn's attention. The piece of jade might have been warm and living so sensitively did the finger-tips caress it. Alleyn thought: "He loves his beautiful possessions." He determined to learn more of this *poseur* who called himself a man of the people and spattered his conversation with French and Italian tags, who was at once so frankly theatrical and so theatrically frank.

Davidson opened his eyes. The effect was quite startling. They were such remarkable eyes. The light grey iris, unusually large, was ringed with black, the pupil a sharp black accent. "I bet he uses that trick on his patients to some effect," thought Alleyn and then realised that Davidson was smiling. "Blast him, he's read my thoughts." And he found himself returning the smile as if he and Davidson shared an amusing secret.

"Take this down, Fox," said Alleyn.

"Very good, sir," said Fox.

"As you have noticed," Davidson began, "I have a taste for the theatrical. Let me present this little scene to you as if we watched it take place behind the footlights. I have shaken hands with my host and hostess where the double flight of stairs meet in a gallery outside the ballroom. I come down the left-hand flight of stairs, thinking of my advancing years and longing for my bed. In the hall are scattered groups of people; coated, cloaked, ready for departure. Already the great house seems exhausted and a little raffish. One feels the presence of drooping flowers, one seems to smell the dregs of champagne. It is indeed time to be gone. Among the departing guests I notice an old lady whom I wish to avoid. She's rich, one of my best patients, but her chief complaint is a condition of chronic, complicated, and acute verbal diarrhoea. I have ministered to this complaint already this evening and as I have no wish to be offered a lift in her car I dart into the men's cloakroom. I spend some minutes there, marking time. It is a little awkward as the only other men in the cloakroom are obviously engaged in an extremely private conversation."

"Who are they?" asked Alleyn.

"A certain Captain Withers who is newly come upon the town and that pleasant youth, Donald Potter. They both pause and stare at me. I make a great business of getting my coat and hat. I chat with the cloakroom attendant after I have tipped him. I speak to Donald Potter but am so poorly received that in sheer decency I am forced to leave. Lucy Lorrimer—*tiens,* there I go!"

"It's all right," said Alleyn, "I know all about Lucy Lorrimer."

"What a woman! She is still screaming out there. I pull up my scarf and lurk in the doorway, waiting for her to go. Having nothing else to do I watch the other people in the hall. The *grand seigneur* of the stomach stands at the foot of the stairs."

"Who?"

"The man who presides over all these affairs. What is his name?"

"Dimitri?"

"Yes, Dimitri. He stands there like an imitation host. A group of young people go out. Then an older woman, alone, comes down the stairs and slips through the doors into the misty street. It was very strange, all that mist."

"Was this older woman Mrs. Halcut-Hackett?"

"Yes. That is who it was," said Davidson a little too casually.

"Is Mrs. Halcut-Hackett a patient of yours, Sir Daniel?"

"It so happens that she is."

"Why did she leave alone? What about her husband and—hasn't she got a débutante attached to her?"

"The protégée who is unfortunately *une jeune fille un peu farouche,* fell a prey to toothache earlier in the evening and was removed by the General. I heard Lord Robert offer to escort Mrs. Halcut-Hackett home."

"Why did he not do so?"

"Perhaps because they missed each other."

"Come now, Sir Daniel, that's not your real opinion."

"Of course it's not, but I don't gossip about my patients."

"I needn't assure you that we shall be very discreet. Remember what you said about your attitude towards this case."

"I do remember. Very well. Only please, if you can avoid my name in subsequent interviews, I shall be more than grateful. I'll go on with my recital. Mrs. Halcut-Hackett, embedded in ermine, gives a swift look round the hall and slips out through the doors into the night. My attention is arrested by something in her manner, and while I stare after her somebody jostles me so violently that I actually stumble forward and only just save myself from falling. It is Captain Withers who has come out of the cloakroom behind me. I turn to receive his apologies and find him with his mouth set and his unpleasant eyes—I mistrust people with white lashes —goggling at the stair-head. He does not even re-alise his own incivility, his attention is fixed on Lord Robert Gospell, who has begun to descend the stairs. This Captain Withers's expression is so singular that I, too, forget our encounter. I hear him draw in his breath. There is a second's pause and then he too, thrusts his way through a party of chattering youngsters and goes out."

"Do you think Withers was following Mrs. Halcut-Hackett?"

"I have no reason to think so, but I do think so."

"Next?"

"Next? Why, Mr. Alleyn, I pull myself together and start for the door. Before I have taken three steps young Donald Potter comes out of the buffet with Bridget O'Brien. They meet Lord Robert at the foot of the stairs."

"Yes?" said Alleyn as Davidson paused.

"Donald Potter," he said at last, "says what is no doubt a word of farewell to Bridget, and then he too goes out by the front entrance."

"Without speaking to his uncle?"

"Yes."

"And Lord Robert?"

"Lord Robert is asking in that very penetrating high-pitched voice of his, if Dimitri has seen Mrs. Halcut-Hackett. I see him now and hear him—the last thing I do see or hear before the double doors close behind me."

14

Davidson Digresses

"That was a very vivid little scene," said Alleyn.

"Well, it was not so long ago, after all," said Davidson.

"When you got outside the house, did you see any of the others, or had they all gone?"

"The party of young people came out as I did. There was the usual bustle for taxis with linkmen and porters. Those linkmen! They are indeed a link with past glories. When one sees the lights from their torches flicker on the pale, almost wanton faces of guests half-dazed with dancing, one expects Millament herself to come down the steps and all the taxis to turn into sedan chairs. However, I must not indulge my passion for elaboration. The party of young people surged into the three taxis that had been summoned by the porter. He was about to call one for me when, to my horror, I saw a Rolls Royce on the other side of the road. The window was down and there, like some Sybil, mopping and mowing, was Lucy Lorrimer. 'Sir Daniel! Sir Daniel!' I

shrank further into my scarf but all in vain. An officious
flunkey cries out: 'The lady is calling you, sir.' Nothing
for it but to cross the road. 'Sir Daniel! Sir Daniel! I
have waited for you. Something most important! I shall
drive you home and on the way I can tell you——' An
impossible woman. I know what it means. She is
suffering from a curious internal pain that has just
seized her and now is the moment for me to make an
examination. I must come in. She is in agony. I think
furiously and by the time I reach her window I am
prepared. 'Lady Lorrimer—forgive me—not a moment
to spare—the Prime Minister—a sudden indisposition——!' and while she still gapes I turn and bolt
like a rabbit into the mist!"

For the first time since the tragedy of last night Alleyn
laughed. Davidson gave him a droll look and went on
with his story.

"I ran as I have not done since I was a boy in
Grenoble, pursued by that voice offering, no doubt, to
drive me like the wind to Downing Street. Mercifully the
mist thickened. On I went, looking in vain for a taxi. I
heard a car and shrank into the shadows. The Rolls
Royce passed. I crept out. At last a taxi! It was coming
behind me. I could just see the two misted headlights.
Then voices, but indistinguishable. The taxi stopped,
came on towards me. Engaged! *Mon Dieu,* what a night!
I walked on, telling myself that sooner or later I must
find a cab. Not a bit of it! By this time, I suppose, the
last guest had gone. It was God knows what time of the
morning and the few cabs I did meet were all engaged. I
walked from Belgrave Square to Cadogan Gardens and I
assure you, my dear Mr. Alleyn, I have never enjoyed a
walk more. I felt like a middle-aged harlequin in search
of adventure. That I found none made not the smallest
matter."

"Unless I'm much mistaken," said Alleyn, "you
missed it by a very narrow margin. Adventure is perhaps
not the right word. I fancy tragedy passed you by, Sir
Daniel, and you did not recognise it."

"Yes," said Davidson and his voice was suddenly

sombre. "Yes, I believe you may be right. It is not so amusing, after all."

"That taxi-cab. Which way did you turn when you fled from Lady Lorrimer?"

"To my right."

"How far had you run when you heard the taxi?"

"I don't know. It is almost impossible to judge. Perhaps four hundred yards. Not far, because I had stopped and hidden from Lucy Lorrimer."

"You tell us you heard voices. Did you recognise them?"

Davidson waited, staring thoughtfully at Alleyn.

"I realise how important this is," he said at last. "I am almost afraid to answer. Mr. Alleyn, I can only tell you that when those voices—I could hear no words, remember—reached me through the mist, I thought at first that one was a woman's voice and then I changed my mind and thought it was a man's. It was a high-pitched voice."

"And the other?"

"Definitely a man's."

"Can you remember anything else, anything at all, about this incident?"

"Nothing. Except that when the taxi passed me I thought the occupants were men."

"Yes. Will you give us a signed statement?"

"About the taxi incident? Certainly."

"Can you tell me who was left behind at Marsdon House when you went away?"

"After the noisy party that went when I did, very few remained. Let me think. There was a very drunk young man. I think his name is Percival and he came out of the buffet just before I left and went into the cloakroom. There was somebody else. Who was it? Ah, yes, it was a curious little lady who seemed to be rather a fish out of water. I had noticed her before. She was quite unremarkable and one would never have seen her if she had not almost always been alone. She wore glasses. That is all I can tell you about her except—yes—I saw her dancing with Lord Robert. I remember now that she was looking at him as he came downstairs. Perhaps she felt some sort of gratitude towards him. She would have been pathetic if she had not looked so composed. I shouldn't be surprised if she was a dependent of the house. Perhaps Bridget's ex-governess, or Lady Carrados's companion. I fancy I encountered her myself somewhere during the evening. Where was it? I forget!"

"The ball was a great success, I believe?"

"Yes. Lady Carrados was born under a star of hospitality. It is always a source of wonderment to me why one ball should be a great success and another offering the same band, caterer, and guests, an equally great failure. Lady Carrados, one would have said, was at a disadvantage last night."

"You mean she was unwell?"

"So you've heard about that. We tried to keep it quiet. Yes, like all these mothers she's overdone herself."

"Worrying about something, do you imagine?" asked Alleyn, and then in reply to Davidson's raised brows he said: "I wouldn't ask if it was not relevant."

"I can't imagine, I must confess, how Lady Carrados's indisposition can have any possible connection with Lord Robert Gospell's death. She is nervously exhausted and felt the strain of her duties." Davidson added as if to himself: "This business will do her no good, either."

"You see," said Alleyn, "in a case of this sort we have to look for any departure from the ordinary or the expected. I agree that this particular departure seems quite irrelevant. So, alas, will many of the other facts we bring to light. If they cannot be correlated they will be discarded. That is routine."

"No doubt. Well, all I can tell you is that I noticed Lady Carrados was unwell, told her to go and lie down in the ladies' cloakroom which I understand was on the top landing, and to send her maid for me if she needed me. Getting no message, I tried to find her but couldn't. She re-appeared later on and told me she felt a little better and not to worry about her."

"Sir Daniel, did you happen to see the caterer, Dimitri, return her bag to Lady Carrados?"

"I don't think so. Why?"

"I've heard that for a time last night she thought she had lost it and was very distressed."

"She said nothing to me about it. It might account for her upset. I noticed that bag. It has a very lovely emerald and ruby clasp—an old Italian setting and much too choice a piece to bedizen a bit of tinsel nonsense. But nowadays people have no sense of congruity in ornament. None." `

"I have been looking at your horse. You, at least, have an appreciation for the beautiful. Forgive me for forgetting my job for a moment but—a ray of sunshine has caught that little horse. Rose red and ochre! I've a passion for ceramics."

Davidson's face was lit from within. He embarked eagerly on the story of how he acquired his little horse. His hands touched it as delicately as if it was a rose. He and Alleyn stepped back three thousand centuries into the golden age of pottery and Inspector Fox sat as silent as stout Cortez with his official notebook open on his knees and an expression of patient tolerance on his large solemn face.

"——and speaking of Benvenuto," said Davidson who had talked himself into the Italian Renaissance, "I saw in a room at Marsdon House last night, unless I am a complete nincompoop, an authentic Cellini medallion. And where, my dear Alleyn, do you suppose it was? To what base use do you imagine it had been put?"

"I've no idea," said Alleyn, smiling.

"It had been sunk; sunk, mark you, in a machine-turned gold case with a devilish diamond clasp and it was surrounded with brilliants. Doubtless this sacrilegious abortion was intended as a receptacle for cigarettes."

"Where was this horror?" asked Alleyn.

"In an otherwise charming green sitting-room."

"On the top landing?"

"That's the one. Look for this case yourself. It's worth seeing in a horrible sort of way."

"When did you visit this room?"

"When? Let me see. It must have been about half-past eleven. I had an urgent case yesterday and the assistant surgeon rang me up to report."

"You didn't go there again?"

"No. I don't think so. No, I didn't."

"You didn't," persisted Alleyn, "happen to hear Lord Robert telephone from that room?"

"No. No, I didn't return to it at all. But it was a charming room. A Greuze above the mantelpiece and three or four really nice little pieces on a pie-crust table and with them this hell-inspired crime. I could not imagine a person with enough taste to choose the other pieces, allowing such a horror as a Benvenuto medallion—and a very lovely one—sunk, no doubt cemented, by its perfect reverse, to this filthy cigarette-case."

"Awful," agreed Alleyn. "Speaking of cigarettes, what sort of case did you carry last night?"

"Hullo!" Davidson's extraordinary eyes bored into his. "What sort of——" He stopped and then muttered to himself: "Knocked out, you said. Yes, I see. On the temple."

"That's it," said Alleyn.

Davidson pulled a flat silver case from his pocket. It was beautifully made with a sliding action and bevelled edges. Its smooth surface shone like a mirror between the delicately tooled margins. He handed it to Alleyn.

"I don't despise frank modernity, you see."

Alleyn examined the case, rubbing his fingers over the tooling. Davidson said abruptly:

"One could strike a sharp blow with it."

"One could," said Alleyn, "but it's got traces of plate powder in the tooling and it's not the right kind, I fancy."

"I wouldn't have believed it possible that I could have been so profoundly relieved," said Davidson. He waited for a moment and then with a nervous glance at Fox he added: "I suppose I've no alibi?"

"Well, no," said Alleyn, "I suppose you haven't, but I shouldn't let it worry you. The taxi-man may remember passing you."

"It was filthily misty," said Davidson peevishly. "He may not have noticed."

"Come," said Alleyn, "you mustn't get investigation nerves. There's always Lucy Lorrimer."

"There is indeed always Lucy Lorrimer. She has rung up three times this morning."

"There you are. I'll have to see her myself. Don't worry; you've given us some very useful information, hasn't he, Fox?"

"Yes, sir. It's kind of solidified what we had already."

"Anything you'd like to ask Sir Daniel, Fox?"

"No, Mr. Alleyn, thank you. I think you've covered the ground very thoroughly. Unless——"

"Yes?" asked Davidson. "Come on, Mr. Fox."

"Well, Sir Daniel, I was wondering if you could give us an opinion on how long it would take a man in Lord Robert Gospell's condition to die under these circumstances."

"Yes," said Davidson, and again that professional note sounded in his voice. "Yes. It's not easy to give you the sort of answer you want. A healthy man would go in about four minutes if the murderer completely stopped all access of air to the lungs. A man with a condition of the heart which I believe to have obtained in this instance would be most unlikely to live for four minutes. Life might become extinct within less than two. He might die almost immediately."

"Yes. Thank you, sir."

Alleyn said: "Suppose the murderer had some slight knowledge of medicine and was aware of Lord Robert's condition, would he be likely to realise how little time he needed?"

"That is rather a difficult question to answer. His slight knowledge might not embrace asphyxia. I should

say that any first year student would probably realise
that a diseased heart would give out very rapidly under
these conditions. A nurse would know. Indeed, I should
have thought most laymen would think it probable. The
actual time to within two or three minutes might not be
appreciated."

"Yes. Thank you."

Alleyn got up.

"I think that really is everything. We'll get out a
statement for you to sign, if you will. Believe me, we do
realise that it has been very difficult for you to speak of
your patients under these extremely disagreeable
circumstances. We'll word the beastly document as
discreetly as may be."

"I'm sure you will. Mr. Alleyn, I think I remember
Lord Robert telling me he had a great friend at Scotland
Yard. Are you this friend? I am sure you are. Please
don't think my question impertinent. I am sure that you
have suffered, with all his friends, a great loss. You
should not draw too much upon your nervous energy,
you know, in investigating this case. It is quite useless
for me to tell you this but I *am* a physician and I do
know something about nerves. You are subjecting
yourself to a very severe discipline at the moment. Don't
overdo it."

"Just what I'd like to tell him, sir," said Fox
unexpectedly.

Davidson turned on him a face cordial with
appreciation.

"I see we understand each other, Mr. Fox."

"It's very kind of you both," said Alleyn with a grin,
"but I'm not altogether a hothouse flower. Good-bye,
Sir Daniel. Thank you so much."

They shook hands and Fox and Alleyn went out.

"Where do we go now?" asked Fox.

"I think we'd better take a look at Marsdon House.
Bailey ought to have finished by now. I'll ring up from
there and see if I can get an appointment with the
Carrados family *en masse*. It's going to be difficult, that.
There seems to be no doubt that Lady Carrados is one

of the blackmailing victims. Carrados himself is a difficult type, a frightful old snob, he is, and as vain as a peacock. Police investigation will undoubtedly stimulate all his worst qualities. He's the sort of man who'd go to any lengths to avoid the wrong kind of publicity. We'll have to go warily if we don't want him to make fools of us and a confounded nuisance of himself."

On the way to Marsdon House they went over Davidson's evidence.

"It's a rum thing, when you come to think of it," ruminated Fox. "There was Sir Daniel looking at that taxi and wishing it wasn't booked and there inside it, were Lord Robert and the man who had made up his mind to kill him. He must have started in to do it almost at once. He hadn't got much time, after all."

"No," said Alleyn, "the time factor is important."

"How exactly d'you reckon he set about it, sir?"

"I imagine them sitting side by side. The murderer takes out his cigarette-case, if indeed it was a cigarette-case. Perhaps he says something to make Lord Robert lean forward and look through the window. He draws back his hand and hits Lord Robert sharply on the temple with the edge and point of the case—the wound seems to indicate that. Lord Robert slumps back. The murderer presses his muffled hand over the nose and mouth, not too hard but carefully. As the mouth opens he pushes the material he is using between the teeth and further and further back towards the throat. With his other hand he keeps the nostrils closed. And so he sits until they are nearly at Cheyne Walk. When he removes his hands the pulse is still, there is no attempt at respiration. The head falls sideways and he knows it is all over." Alleyn clenched his hands. "He might have been saved even then, Fox. Artificial respiration might have saved him. But there was the rest of the drive to Queens Gate and then on to the Yard. Hopeless!"

"The interview with Sir Herbert Carrados ought to clear up this business of Dimitri," Fox said. "If Sir Herbert was any length of time in the buffet with Dimitri."

"We'll have to go delicately with Carrados. I wonder if the obscure lady will be there. The lady that nobody noticed but who, since she did not dance very much, may have fulfilled the traditional office of the onlooker. Then there's the Halcut-Hackett game. We'll have to get on with that as soon as possible. It links up with Withers."

"What sort of a lady is Mrs. Halcut-Hackett? She came and saw you at the Yard, didn't she, about the blackmail business?"

"Yes, Fox, she did. She played the old, old game of pretending to be the friend of the victim. Still she had the pluck to come. That visit of hers marked the beginning of the whole miserable affair. You may be sure that I do not forget this. I asked Bunchy to help us find the blackmailer. If I hadn't done that he'd be alive now, I suppose, unless . . . unless, my God! Donald killed his uncle for what he'd get out of it. If blackmail's at the bottom of the murder, I'm directly responsible."

"Well, sir, if you'll excuse me, I don't think that's a remark to get you or anyone else much further. Lord Robert wouldn't have thanked you for it and that's a fact. We don't feel obliged to warn everybody who helps in a blackmail case that it's liable to turn to murder. And why?" continued Fox with the nearest approach to animation that Alleyn had ever seen in him. "Because up to now it never has."

"All right, Br'er Fox," said Alleyn. "I'll pipe down."

And for the rest of the way to Marsdon House they were both silent.

15

Simple Soldier - Man

Marsdon House had been put into a sort of cold-storage by the police. Dimitri's men had done a certain amount of clearing up before Alleyn's men arrived, but for the most part the great house seemed to be suffering from a severe form of carry-over. It smelt of stale cigarette-butts, greenery and alcohol. Above all, of cigarette-butts. They were everywhere bent double, stained red, stained brown, in ash-trays, fireplaces and wastepaper-boxes; ground into the ballroom floor, dropped behind chairs, lurking in dirty cups and floating in a miserable state of disintegration among the stalks of dying flowers. Upstairs in the ladies' dressing-room they lay in drifts of spilt powder, and in the green boudoir someone had allowed a cigarette to eat a charred track across the margin of a pie-crust table.

Alleyn and Fox stood in the green boudoir and looked at the telephone.

"There he sat," said Alleyn, and once more he quoted: " 'The cakes and ale feller. Might as well mix his damn brews with poison. And he's working with——' Look, Fox, he must have sat in this chair, facing the door. He wouldn't see anybody coming because of that very charming screen. Imagine our interloper sneaking through the door. He catches a word that arrests his attention, stops for a second and then, realising what Lord Robert is doing, comes round the screen. Lord Robert looks up: 'Hullo, I didn't see you,' and knowing he has just mentioned the Yard, pitches his lost property story and rings off. I've left word at the Yard that every name on that guest list is to be traced and each guest asked as soon as possible if he or she butted in on that conversation. I'm using a lot of men on this case, but the A.C.'s behaving very prettily, thank the Lord. Get that P.C., will you?"

The constable who had been left in charge reported that Detective-sergeant Bailey had been all over the room for prints and had gone to the Yard before lunch.

"Is the telephone still switched through to this room?"

"I believe so, sir. Nothing's been touched."

"Fox, ring up the Yard and see if there's anything new."

While Fox was at the telephone Alleyn prowled about the room looking with something like despair at the evidence of so many visitors. It was useless to hope that anything conclusive would be deduced from Bailey's efforts. They might find Lord Robert's prints on the telephone but what was the good of that? If they could separate and classify every print that had been left in the room it would lead them exactly nowhere.

Fox turned away from the telephone.

"They've got through the list of guests, sir. Very smart work. Five men on five telephones. None of the guests admit to having overheard Lord Robert, and none of the servants."

"That's our line, then. Find the interloper. Somehow I thought it would come to that." Alleyn wandered about the room. "Davidson was right; it's a pleasant room."

"The house belongs to an uncle of Lady Carrados, doesn't it?"

"Yes, General Marsdon. He would appear to be a fellow of taste. The Greuze is charming. And these enamels. Where's the offensive Cellini conversion, I wonder." He bent over the pie-crust table. "Nothing like it here. That's funny. Davidson said it was on this table, didn't he? It's neither here nor anywhere else in the room. Rum! Must have belonged to one of the guests. Nothing much in it. Still, we'd better check it. What a hellish bore! All through the guests again, unless we strike it lucky! Francois might have noticed it sometime when he was doing the ash-trays. Better ask him."

He rang up Francois, who said he knew nothing of any stray cigarette-case. Alleyn sighed and took out his notes. Fox cruised solemnly about the top landing.

"Hi!" called Alleyn after ten minutes. "Hi! Fox!"

"Hullo, sir?"

"I've been trying to piece these peoples' movements together. As far as I can see, it goes something like this. Now pay attention, because it's very muddly and half the time I won't know what I'm talking about. Some time during the supper interlude Lady Carrados left her bag in this room. Francois saw Dimitri collect it and go downstairs. Miss Troy, who was dancing with Bunchy, saw him return the bag to Lady Carrados in the ballroom. Miss Troy noticed it looked much emptier than before. We don't know if there were any witnesses to the actual moment when she left the bag, but it doesn't matter. Bunchy saw her receive it from Dimitri. At one o'clock he rang me up to say he had a strong line on the blackmailer and the crucial conversation took place. Now, according to Francois, there were four people who might have overheard this conversation. Withers, Donald Potter, Sir Herbert Carrados, and the colourless Miss Harris, who may or may not have been in the lavatory but was certainly on this landing.

Someone else may have come and gone while Francois
was getting matches for the enraged Carrados. On
Francois's return he went into the telephone-room and
found it empty. Sounds easier when you condense it. All
right. Our job is to find out if anyone else could have
come upstairs, listened to the telephone, and gone down
again while Francois was in the servants' quarters.
Withers says he heard the telephone when he was in the
other sitting-room. He also says Carrados was up here
at that time so, liar though no doubt he is, it looks as if
he spoke the truth about that. Come on, Fox, let's
prowl."

The gallery was typical of most large, old-fashioned
London houses. The room with the telephone was at the
far end, next it was a lavatory. This turned out to be a
Victorian affair with a small ante-room and a general
air of varnish and gloom. The inner door was half-
panelled with thick clouded glass which let through a
little murky daylight. Beyond it was a bedroom that had
been used as a ladies' cloakroom and last, at the top of
the stairs, the second sitting-out room. Beside the door
of this room was another green-baize door leading to
servants' quarters and back stairs. The other side of the
gallery was open and looked over the great well of the
house. Alleyn leant on the balustrade and stared down
the steep perspective of twisting stairs into the hall two
stories below.

"A good vantage spot this," he said. "We'll go down,
now."

On the next landing was the ballroom. Nothing could
have looked more desolate than the great empty floor,
the chairs that wore that disconcerting air of talking to
each other, the musicians' platform, littered with
cigarette-butts and programmes. A fine dust lay over
everything and the great room echoed to their footsteps.
The walls sighed a little as though the air imprisoned
behind them sought endlessly for escape. Alleyn and
Fox hunted about but found nothing to help them and
went down the great stairs to the hall.

"Here he stood," said Alleyn, "at the foot of the left-hand flight of stairs. Dimitri is not far off. Sir Daniel came out of the cloakroom over there on the left. The group of noisy young people was nearer the front entrance. And through this door, next the men's cloakroom, was the buffet. Let's have a look at it. You've seen all this before, Br'er Fox, but you must allow me to maunder on."

They went into the buffet.

"It stinks like a pot-house, doesn't it? Look at Dimitri's neat boxes of empty champagne bottles under the tables. Gaiety at ten pounds a dozen. This is where Donald and Bridget came from in the penultimate scene and where Dimitri and Carrados spoke together just before Lord Robert left. And for how long afterwards? Look, Fox, here's a Sherlock Holmes touch. A cigar stump lying by a long trace of its own ash. A damn' good cigar and has been carefully smoked. Here's the gentleman's glass beside it and here, on the floor, is the broken band. A Corona-Corona." Alleyn sniffed at the glass. "Brandy. Here's the bottle, Courvoisier '87. I'll wager that wasn't broadcast among the guests. More likely to have been kept for old Carrados. Fox, ring up Dimitri and find out if Sir Herbert drank brandy and smoked a cigar when he came in here after the party. And at the same time you might ask if we can see the Carrados family in about half an hour. Then we'll have to go on to the Halcut-Hackett group. Their house is close by here, Halkin Street. We'll have to come back. I want to see Carrados first. See if General and Mrs. Halcut-Hackett will see us in about two hours, will you, Fox?"

Fox padded off to the telephone and Alleyn went through the second door of the buffet into a back passage. Here he found the butler's pantry. Dimitri's supper tray was still there. "He did himself very well," thought Alleyn, noticing three or four little green-black pellets on a smeared plate. "Caviare. And here's the wing of a bird picked clean. Champagne, too. Sleek, Mr. Dimitri, eating away like a well-fed cat behind the scenes."

He rejoined Fox in the hall. Mr. Dimitri, said Fox, remembered giving Sir Herbert Carrados brandy from a special bottle reserved for him. He thought that Sir Herbert smoked a cigar while he took his brandy but would not swear to it.

"We'd better print the brandy-glass," said Alleyn. "I'll get Bailey to attend to it and then, I think, they can clean up here. How did you get on?"

"All right, sir. The Halcut-Hacketts will see us any time later on this afternoon."

"What about Carrados?"

"He came to the telephone," said Fox. "He'll see us if we go round now."

"How did he sound? Bloody-minded?"

"If you like to put it that way, sir. He seemed to be sort of long-suffering, more than angry, I thought, and said something about hoping he knew his duty. He mentioned that he is a great personal friend of the chief commissioner."

"Oh, Lord, Lord! Huff and grandeur! Uncertain, coy, and hard to please. Don't I know it. Fox, we must continue to combine deference with a suggestion of high office. Out with the best butter and lay it on in slabs. Miserable old article, he is. Straighten your tie, harden your heart, and away we go."

Sir Herbert and Lady Carrados lived in Green Street. A footman opened the door to Alleyn.

"Is Sir Herbert at home?" asked Alleyn.

"Sir Herbert is not at home, sir. Would you care to leave a message?"

"He has an appointment with me," said Alleyn pleasantly, "so I expect he is at home really. Here's my card."

"I beg pardon, sir," said the footman, looking at Alleyn's clothes which were admirable. "I understood it was the police who were calling."

"We are the police," said Alleyn.

Fox, who had been dealing with their taxi, advanced. The footman's eye lit on his bowler and boots.

"I beg pardon, sir," he said; "will you come this way, please?"

He showed them into a library. Three past Carradoses, full length, in oils, stared coldly into space from the walls. The firelight wavered on a multitude of books uniformly bound, behind glass doors. Sir Herbert, in staff-officer's uniform with shiny boots and wonderful breeches, appeared in a group taken at Tunbridge Wells, the centre of his war-time activities. Alleyn looked at it closely but the handsome face was as expressionless as the tightly breeched knees which were separated by gloved hands resting with embarrassing inportance on the inside of the thighs. A dumb photograph. It was flanked by two illuminated addresses of which Sir Herbert was the subject. A magnificent cigar-box stood on a side table. Alleyn opened it and noted that the cigars were the brothers of the one that had been smoked in the buffet. He gently closed the lid and turned to inspect a miniature French writing-cabinet.

Fox, completely at his ease, stood like a rock in the middle of the room. He appeared to be lost in a mild abstraction but he could have gone away and described the library with the accuracy of an expert far-gone in Pelmanism.

The door opened and Carrados came in. Alleyn found himself unaccountably reminded of bereaved royalty. Sir Herbert limped rather more perceptibly than usual and employed a black stick. He paused, screwed his glass in his eye, and said:

"Mr. Alleyn?"

Alleyn stepped forward and bowed.

"It is extremely kind of you to see us, sir," he said.

"No, no," said Carrados, "one must do one's duty however hard one is hit. One has to keep a stiff upper lip. I was talking to your chief commissioner just now, Mr. Alleyn. He happens to be a very old friend of mine—er—won't you sit down both of you, Mr.—er——?"

"This is Inspector Fox, sir."

"Oh, yes," said Carrados, extending his hand. "Do sit down, Fox. Yes"—he turned again to Alleyn when they were all seated. "Your C.O. tells me you are a son of another old friend. I knew your mother very well years ago and she sees quite a lot of my wife, I believe. She was at Marsdon House last night." He placed his hand over his eyes and repeated in an irritating whisper: "At Marsdon House. Ah, well!"

Alleyn said: "We are very sorry indeed, sir, to bother you after what has happened. This tragedy has been a great shock to you, I'm afraid."

Carrados gave him an injured smile.

"Yes," he said, "I cannot pretend that it has not. Lord Robert was one of our dearest friends. Not only have we a great sense of personal bereavement but I cannot help thinking that my hospitality has been cruelly abused."

This reduction of homicide to terms of the social amenities left Alleyn speechless. Sir Herbert appeared to regard murder as a sort of inexcusable *faux pas*.

"I suppose," he continued, "that you have come here armed with a list of questions. If that is so I am afraid you are doomed to disappointment. I am a simple soldier-man, Mr. Alleyn, and this sort of thing is quite beyond my understanding. I may say that ever since this morning we have been pestered by a crew of insolent young pups from Fleet Street. I have been forced to ask Scotland Yard, where I believe my name is not unknown, if we had no redress from this sort of damnable persecution. I talked about it to your chief who, as I think I told you, is a personal friend of mine. He agrees with me that the behaviour of journalists nowadays is intolerable."

"I am sorry you have been badgered," said Alleyn. "I will be as quick as I can with our business. There *are* one or two questions, I'm afraid, but only one or two and none of them at all formidable."

"I can assure you I am not in the least afraid of police

investigation," said Carrados with an injured laugh. His hand still covered his eyes.

"Of course not, sir. I wanted first of all to ask you if you spoke to Lord Robert last night. I mean something more than hail and farewell. I thought that if there was anything at all unusual in his manner it would not escape your notice as it would the notice of, I am afraid, the majority of people."

Carrados looked slightly less huffy.

"I don't pretend to be any more observant than the next fellow," he said, "but as a soldier-man I've had to use my eyes a bit and I think if there's anything wrong anywhere I'm not likely to miss it. Yes, I spoke to Lord Robert Gospell once or twice last night and I can assure you he was perfectly normal in every possible way. He was nice enough to tell me he thought our ball the most successful of the season. Perfectly normal."

Alleyn leant forward and fixed Carrados with a reverent glare.

"Sir Herbert," he said, "I'm going to do a very unconventional thing and I hope you won't get me my dismissal as I'm sure you very easily could. I'm going to take you wholly into our confidence."

It was pleasant to see the trappings of sorrow fall softly away from Carrados, and to watch his posture change from that of a stricken soldier-man to an exact replica of the Tunbridge Wells photograph. Up came his head. The knees were spread apart, the hands went involuntarily to the inside of the thighs. Only the gloves and breeches were lacking. A wise son of Empire sat confessed.

"It would not be the first time," said Carrados modestly, "that confidence has been reposed in me."

"I'm sure it wouldn't. This is our difficulty. We have reason to believe that the key to this mystery lies in a single sentence spoken by Lord Robert on the telephone from Marsdon House. If we could get a true report of the conversation that Lord Robert held with an unknown person at one o'clock this morning I believe we would have gone a long way towards making an arrest."

"Ah!" Carrados positively beamed. "This bears out my own theory, Mr. Alleyn. It was an outside job. You see I am conversant with your phraseology. From the moment we heard of this tragedy I said to my wife that I was perfectly satisfied that none of our guests could be in any way implicated. A telephone message from outside! There you are!"

"I had half hoped," said Alleyn modestly, "that you might have heard about this call. I suppose it was stupid of me."

"When was it?"

"At one o'clock. We've got so far."

"At one o'clock. One o'clock. Let me see!" Carrados drew his heavy brows down over his foolish eyes and scowled importantly. "At the moment I must confess I cannot quite recall——"

"Most of your guests were still at supper, I think," said Alleyn. "I've spoken to the servant on duty on the top landing and he fancies he can remember that you came upstairs round about that time."

The purple veins in Sir Herbert's red cheeks suddenly started up.

"By God, I should think the fellow did remember, confound his impudence. Certainly, I went on to the top landing and it *was* one o'clock. You are perfectly right, Mr. Alleyn. I pay these damn' caterers a fortune to organise the whole affair and I expect, not unreasonably I hope, a certain standard of efficiency. And what do I find? No matches! No matches in the sitting-out room at the end of the stairs and the damn place smothered in ash. A lighted cigarette burning the mantelpiece! It was underneath the clock. That's how I remember the time. Just on one o'clock, as you say. I trust I'm a reasonable sort of fellow, Alleyn, but I don't mind telling you I saw red. I went out on to the landing and I gave that fellow a dressing-down he won't forget in a hurry. Sent him hareing off downstairs with a flea in his ear. Damn', spoonfed dago!"

"Were you on the landing all this time, sir?"

"Of course I wasn't on the landing all the time! I was in and out of the blasted sitting-room, damn it. I went upstairs at, I suppose, about five to one, walked into this room and found it in the condition I've described. I would have looked at the other room, the one with the telephone, but I saw there was a couple sitting out in there. Behaving, I may say, more like a footman and a housemaid than the sort of people one is accustomed to receive as one's guests. However! The man came sneaking out just as I was blasting this damned waiter-fellow. He hung about the landing. This fellow Withers, I mean. Don't know if I gave you his name before. Then the lady came out and scuttled into the cloakroom. Yes, by God, sir, and Robert Gospell came upstairs and went into the telephone-room."

Carrados blew out his moustache triumphantly. "There you are!" he said. "Into the room to telephone."

"Splendid, sir. Now may I just go over this to make sure I've got it right? You came out of the first sitting-out room and spoke to the waiter. Captain Withers came out of the second room (the telephone-room) followed in a moment by Mrs. Halcut-Hackett who went into the cloakroom."

"Here!" ejaculated Carrados, "I didn't mention the lady's name, Alleyn. By God, I hope I know my manners better than to use a lady's name out of turn."

Alleyn achieved an expression of gentlemanly cunning.

"I'm afraid, sir, I rather jumped to conclusions."

"Really? D'you mean it's common talk? An American, wasn't she? Well, well, well, I'm sorry to hear that. Halcut-Hackett's a very old friend of mine. I'm very sorry to hear that."

Alleyn reflected acidly that Sir Herbert was enjoying himself thoroughly and hurried on.

"At this moment, just as you return to the sitting-room, having sent the waiter downstairs, and Mrs. Halcut-Hackett dives into the cloakroom, Lord Robert comes upstairs. What does Withers do?"

"Sheers off and comes sloping into the sitting-room after me. I had to make conversation with the fellow. Young Potter was sulking about in there too. I hope I've got as much tolerance for the youngsters as any other old fogey, Alleyn, but I must confess I——"

He stopped and looked uncomfortable.

"Yes?" murmured Alleyn.

"I—it doesn't matter. Stick to the point, eh? Withers, eh? Yes. Well now, I flatter myself, Alleyn, that I can get along with most people but I freely confess I did not enjoy Withers's company. Calls himself Captain. What was his regiment?"

"I don't know at all. Could you, by any chance, hear Lord Robert from the other room?"

"No. No, I couldn't. Now you mention it, I believe I heard the extension bell doing that damned dialling tinkle. The fact is I couldn't stand any more of that confounded outsider's conversation. I made my excuses and went downstairs."

"Did you meet anybody coming up?"

"I don't think so. Mrs. Halcut-Hackett was going down ahead of me."

"So while you were still in the sitting-room, sir, anybody might have come upstairs and gone into the room where Lord Robert sat telephoning?"

"I suppose so."

"Mrs. Halcut-Hackett might have gone in before you went downstairs. Captain Withers or Donald Potter might have done it afterwards?"

"Yes, by Gad, they might. If you want to get an account of this telephone conversation you might ask 'em. I don't like to make the suggestion about one of my guests, but upon my soul I wouldn't put it past Withers to listen to a private conversation. What's young Potter doing, cottoning on to a cad twenty years his senior, I'd like to know? However! Anything more?"

"Yes, sir. Did you by any chance notice a Miss Harris while you were upstairs? The man said something——"

"Harris? D'you mean m'wife's secretary? Yes, of

course I saw her. She bolted into the lavatory when I came up. I didn't see her come out."

"I see. Perhaps I might have a word with her before I go."

"Certainly, but you'll find her a bit difficult. She's a shy little thing—pity there aren't more like her. Nowadays they don't give a damn who sees them coming out of any door."

Sir Herbert suddenly made up his mind he had said something amusing and broke into loud baying laughter in which Alleyn was careful to join.

"Poor little Harris," Carrados said. "Well, well, well!"

"Now," continued Alleyn when the laughter had died away, "about the end of the ball. We would like to trace Lord Robert's movements, of course. I don't know, sir, if you can give us any help at all."

"Ah! Yes. Well, let me see. My wife and I stood on the ballroom gallery at the head of the stairs saying good-bye to our guests—those of them who were old-fashioned enough to think it necessary to thank their hosts. Some of the young cubs didn't take the trouble, I may tell you. Lord Robert came, of course, and was perfectly charming. Let me see, now. He went downstairs, into the cloakroom and out again wearing that extraordinary cloak of his. I remember this because I came down and passed him. I went into the buffet."

"Did you come out again before Lord Robert left?"

"No." Carrados returned for a moment to the stricken soldier-man. "No. That was the last I shall ever see of Robert Gospell. Ah, well! I don't mind admitting, Alleyn, that this thing has hit me pretty hard. Pretty hard! Still, we've got to bite on the bullet, haven't we? What were we saying? Oh, yes. I stayed in the buffet for some time. I don't mind admitting I was about all in. I smoked a cigar and had a peg of brandy. I had a word with that fellow Dimitri and then I went home."

"With Lady Carrados and Miss O'Brien?"

"What? No. No, I packed them off earlier in the other

car. My wife was absolutely fagged out. I wanted to
have a look round. Make sure everything was all right. I
wouldn't trust anybody else. These people are so
damned careless, leaving lighted cigarettes all over the
place. I satisfied myself everything was all right and then
I went home. The chauffeur came back for me. Daresay
you'd like to see him."

"No, sir, thank you. I think we may take that as
read."

"I've no wish to be treated differently from anyone
else but that's as you please, of course. Anything else?"

"If I might have a word with Lady Carrados, sir?"

"I don't think my wife can give you any information,
Alleyn. She's absolutely prostrated by this business.
Robert Gospell was a very great friend of hers and she's
taken it damn' hard. Matter of fact, she's not up."

Alleyn paused.

"I am so sorry," he said at last. "That's most
unfortunate. I wanted if possible to save her appearing
at the inquest."

"When is the inquest?"

"Tomorrow morning, sir."

Carrados glared at him.

"She will certainly be too unwell for any such thing. I
shall see that her doctor forbids it. And it is equally
impossible for her to see you this afternoon. I know that
if I were to disturb her, which I have no intention of
doing as she is asleep in bed, she would refuse. That's
definite."

The door opened and the footman came in.

"Her ladyship, sir, wishes me to say that if Mr. Alleyn
has a few minutes to spare she would be very pleased to
see him."

He waited, gently closing the door on an extremely
uncomfortable silence.

16

Lady Carrados Looks Back

Alleyn followed the footman upstairs, leaving Fox in the library to make the best of a sticky situation.

The footman handed Alleyn over to a maid who took him to Lady Carrados. She was not in bed. She was in her boudoir erect in a tall blue chair and wearing the look that had prompted Paddy O'Brien to compare her with a Madonna. She held out her hands when she saw Alleyn and as he took them a phrase came into his mind. He thought: "She is an English lady and these are an English lady's hands, thin, unsensual, on the end of delicate thin arms."

She said: "Roderick! I do call you Roderick, don't I?"

Alleyn said: "I hope so. It's a long time since we met, Evelyn."

"Too long. Your mother tells me about you some-times. We spoke to each other to-day on the telephone. She was so very kind and understanding, Roderick, and she told me that you would be too. Do sit down and smoke. I should like to feel that you are not a great detective but an old friend."

"I should like to feel that too," said Alleyn. "I must tell you, Evelyn, that I was on the point of asking to see you when I got your message."

"An official call?"

"Yes, bad luck to it. You've made everything much pleasanter by asking for me."

She pressed the thin hands together and Alleyn, noticing the bluish lights on the knuckles, remembered how Troy had wanted to paint them.

Lady Carrados said: "I suppose Herbert didn't want you to see me?"

"He wasn't very pleased with the idea. He thought you were too tired and distressed."

She smiled faintly: "Yes," she said, and it was impossible to be sure that she spoke ironically. "Yes, he is very thoughtful. What do you want to ask me, Roderick?"

"All sorts of dreary questions, I'm afraid. I'm sorry about it. I know you were one of Bunchy's friends."

"So were you."

"Yes."

"What is your first question?"

Alleyn went over the final scene in the hall and found she had nothing new to tell him. She answered him quickly and concisely. He could see that his questions held no particular significance for her and that her thoughts were lying in wait, anxiously, for what was yet to come. As soon as he began to speak of the green room on the top landing he knew that he touched her more nearly. He felt a profound distaste for his task. He went on steadily, without emphasis.

"The green sitting-room with the telephone. We know that he used the telephone and are anxious to find out if he was overheard. Someone says you left your bag there, Evelyn. Did you?"

"Yes."

"Dimitri returned it to you?"

"Yes."

"When was this?"

"Soon after I had come up from supper—about half-past twelve or a quarter to one."

"Not as late as one o'clock?"

"No."

"Why are you so certain of this, please?"

"Because," said Lady Carrados, "I was watching the time rather carefully."

"Were you? Does the peak of a successful ball come at a specific moment?"

"Well, one rather watches the time. If they don't begin to drift away after supper it looks as if it will be a success."

"Where were you when Dimitri returned your bag?"

"In the ballroom."

"Did you notice Bunchy at about this time?"

"I—don't think—I remember."

The hands were pressed closer together as if she held her secret between them; as if it might escape. Her lips were quite white.

The door opened and Bridget came in. She looked as if she had been crying.

"Oh, Donna," she said, "I'm sorry. I didn't know——"

"This is my girl, Roderick. Bridget, this is Sarah's uncle."

"How do you do," said Bridget. "The detective one?"

"The detective one."

"Sarah says you're quite human really."

"That's very kind of Sarah," said her uncle dryly.

"I hope you're not heckling my mother," said Bridget, sitting on the arm of the chair. She had an air of determined sprightliness.

"I'm trying not to. Perhaps you could help us both. We are talking about last night."

"Well, I might be able to tell you something

frightfully important without knowing it myself, sort of, mightn't I?"

"It's happened before now," said Alleyn with a smile. "We were talking about your mother's bag."

"The one she left upstairs and that I found?"

"Bridgie!" whispered Lady Carrados. "Oh, Bridgie!"

"It's all right, Donna, my sweet. That had nothing to do with Bunchy. Oh—he was there, wasn't he? In the supper-room when I brought it to you?"

Bridget, perched on the arm of the wing chair, could not see her mother's face and Alleyn thought: "Now we're in for it."

He said: *"You* returned the bag in the *supper-room,* did you?"

Lady Carrados suddenly leant back and closed her eyes.

"Yes," Bridget said, "and it was simply squashed full of money. But why the bag? Does it fit in somewhere frightfully subtle? I mean was the motive really money and did the murderer think Donna gave Bunchy the money, sort of? Or something?"

Lady Carrados said: "Bridgie darling, I'm by way of talking privately to Mr. Alleyn."

"Oh, are you, darling? I'm sorry. I'll whizz off. Shall I see you again before you go, Mr. Alleyn?"

"Please, Miss Bridget."

"Well, come along to the old nursery. I'll be there."

Bridget looked round the corner of the chair at her mother, who actually managed to give her a smile. She went out and Lady Carrados covered her face with her hands.

"Don't try to tell me, Evelyn," said Alleyn gently. "I'll see if I can tell you. Come now, it may not be so dreadful, after all. Listen. Someone has been blackmailing you. You have had letters written in script on Woolworth paper. One of them came on the morning Bunchy brought you spring flowers. You put it under your pillow. Last night you left your bag in the green room, because you had been told to leave it there. It contained the money the blackmailer demanded. It now appears that Bridget returned your bag, still full of notes, while you were in the supper-room with Bunchy. Did you replace it in the green sitting-room? You did . . . and later it was returned to you, empty—while you were in the ballroom?"

"But—you *know* all this! Roderick, do you also know what they had found out?"

"No. I have no idea what they found out. Had Bunchy?"

"That is what horrifies me. Bunchy knew, at least, that I was being persecuted. When Bridgie brought back that hideous bag last night, I nearly collapsed. I can't tell you what a shock it was to me. You are quite right, a letter, like the one you described, came a few days ago. There had been others. I didn't answer them. I destroyed them all and tried to put them out of my mind. I thought perhaps they wouldn't go on with it if I paid no attention. But this one threatened dreadful things, things that would hurt Bridgie so much—so much. It said that if I didn't do as I was ordered Herbert and Bridgie would be told about—everything. I couldn't face that. I did what they said. I put five hundred pounds in notes in that bag and left it on the little table in the green sitting-room before one o'clock.

And then Bridgie must have seen it. I shall never forget her coming into the supper-room, laughing and holding out that bag. I suppose I must have looked frightful. It's all muddled in my mind now, like the memory of a terrible dream. Somehow we got rid of Bridgie. Bunchy must have been splendid. Sir Daniel Davidson was there. I've been to see him lately about my health and he had said something to me before that evening. I got rid of him, too, and then Bunchy and I went out into the hall and Bunchy said he knew what I wanted to do with the bag and begged me not to do it. I was frantic. I broke away from him and went back again to the green sitting-room. Nobody was there. I put the bag back on the table. It was then twenty to one. I put it behind a big ormolu and enamel box on the table. Then I went down to the ballroom. I don't know how much later it was when I saw Dimitri coming through the room with the bag. At first I thought the same thing had happened again, but when I took it in my hand I knew the money had gone. Dimitri had found the bag, he said, and recognised it as mine. That's all."

"That's all," repeated Alleyn. "It's a good deal. Look here, Evelyn, I'm going to ask you point-blank, is it possible that Dimitri is the man who is blackmailing you?"

"Dimitri!" Her eyes opened wide. "Good heavens, no! No, no, it's out of the question. He couldn't possibly have any idea, any means of knowing. Not possibly."

"Are you sure of that? He is in and out of people's houses and has free access to their rooms. He has opportunities of overhearing conversations, of watching people when they are off their guard."

"How long has he been doing this work?"

"He told me seven years."

"My secret is more than twice as old as that. 'Lady Audley's Secret'! But it's not so amusing, Roderick, when you carry it about with you. And yet, do you know, there have been times when I have almost forgotten my secret. It all happened so very long ago. The years have sifted past and mounted like sand into smooth unremarkable shapes and they have gradually hidden the old times. I thought I should never be able to speak of this to anyone in the world, but, oddly enough, it is rather a relief to talk about it."

"You realise, don't you, that I am here to investigate a murder? It's my job to work out the circumstances surrounding it. I must have no consideration for anybody's feelings if they come between me and the end of the job. Bunchy knew you were the victim of a blackmailer. You are not the only victim. He was actually working with us on information we had from another source but which points directly to the same individual. It's quite possible, and to us it seems probable, that the blackmailing may be linked with the murder. So we have a double incentive to get at the blackmailer's identity."

"I know what you are going to ask me. I have no idea who it is. None. I've asked myself over and over again who it could be."

"Yes. Now see here, Evelyn, I could get up to all the old tricks, and with any luck I'd probably get a line on this secret of yours. I'd trap you into little admissions and when I got away from here I'd write them all down, add them up, and see what I could make of the answer. Probably there wouldn't be an answer so we'd begin to dig and dig. Back through those years that have sifted over your trouble and hidden it. And sooner or later we would find something. It would all be very disagreeable and I should hate it and the final result would be exactly the same as if you told me your whole story now."

"I can't. I can't tell you."

"You are thinking of the consequences. Newspaper publicity. Court proceedings. You know it wouldn't be nearly as bad as you imagine. Your name would probably never appear."

"Madame X," said Lady Carrados with a faint smile, "and everybody in court knowing perfectly well who I was. Oh, it's not for myself I mind. It's Bridgie. And Herbert. You've met Herbert and you must realise how he'd take a blow of this sort. I can think of nobody who would mind more."

"And how is he going to take it if we find out for ourselves? Evelyn, think! You're one of Bunchy's friends."

"I'm not a revengeful woman."

"Good God, it's not a question of revenge. It's a question of leaving a blackmailing murderer at large."

"You needn't go on, Roderick. I know quite well what I ought to do."

"And I know quite well that you're going to do it."

They looked squarely at each other. Her hands made a gesture of surrender.

"Very well," said Lady Carrados. "I give in. How much more dignified it would have been, wouldn't it, if I had accepted my duty at first?"

"I had no doubt about what you'd do. It's quite

possible, you know, that your side of the business need never come out. Of course, I can't promise this, but it is possible we'll work on your information without putting it in as evidence."

"That's very kind of you," she said faintly.

"You're being ironical," said Alleyn with a grin, "and that shows you're not going to mind as much as you feared, or I hope it does. Now then. It's something about Bridget, isn't it, and it happened more than fourteen years ago. Bridget's how old? Seventeen?"

Lady Carrados nodded.

"I don't believe I ever met your first husband, Evelyn. Is Bridget very like him?"

"Yes. She's got all Paddy's gaiety."

"My mother told me that. Bridget doesn't remember him, of course. Ought we to begin with him?"

"Yes. You needn't go on being delicate, Roderick. I think you've guessed, haven't you? Paddy and I were not married."

"Bless my soul," said Alleyn, "how very courageous of you, Evelyn."

"I think it was now but it didn't seem so then. Nobody knew. It's the *Jane Eyre* theme but I hadn't Miss Eyre's moral integrity. Paddy left a wife in an Australian lunatic asylum, came home, and fell in love with me. As you would say in your report, we went through a form of marriage and lived happily and bigamously together. Then Paddy died."

"Weren't you afraid it would come out?"

"No. Paddy's wife had no relations." Lady Carrados waited for a moment. She seemed to be gravely contemplating the story she had decided to relate. When she spoke again it was with composure and even, or so Alleyn fancied, an air of relaxation. He wondered if she had often marshalled the facts in her own mind and rehearsed her story to an imaginary listener. The quiet voice went on sedately: "She was a music-hall comedienne who had been left stranded in a little town in New South Wales. He married her there and took her

to Sydney. Six weeks later she became hopelessly insane.
He found out that her mother was in a lunatic asylum
somewhere in America. Paddy had not told anybody of
his marriage and he had not looked up any of his
acquaintances in Sydney. When he arranged to have her
put away it was under her maiden name. He invested a
sum of money, the interest on which was enough to pay
the fees and expenses. He left the whole thing in the
hands of the only man who knew the truth. He was
Anthony Banks, Paddy's greatest friend, and was
absolutely above suspicion, I am sure. He lived in
Sydney and helped Paddy all through that time. He held
Paddy's power of attorney. Even he did not know Paddy
had remarried. Nobody knew that."

"What about the parson who married them?"

"I remember that Paddy said he was a very old man.
The witnesses were his wife and sister. You see, we
talked it all over very carefully and Paddy was quite
certain there was no possibility of discovery."

"There is something more, isn't there?"

"Yes. Something that I find much more difficult."
The even voice faltered for a moment. Alleyn saw that
she mustered up all her fortitude before she went on.
"Five months after we were married he was killed. I had
started Bridgie and came up to London to stay with my
mother and to see my doctor. Paddy was to motor up
from our house at Ripplecote and drive me back. In the
morning I had a telegram from him. It said: 'The best
possible news from Anthony Banks.' On the way the car
skidded and crashed into the wall of a bridge. It was in a
little village. He was taken into the vicarage and then to
the cottage hospital. When I got there he was
unconscious and he didn't know that I was with him
when he died."

"And the news?"

"I felt certain that it could only be one thing. His wife
must have died. But we could find no letters or cables at
all, so he must have destroyed whatever message he had
been sent by Anthony Banks. The next thing that

happened was that Paddy's solicitors received five thousand pounds from Australia and a letter from Anthony Banks to say it was forwarded in accordance with Paddy's instructions. In the meantime I had written to Anthony Banks. I told him of Paddy's death but wrote as a cousin of Paddy's. He replied with the usual sort of letter. He didn't, of course, say anything about Paddy's wife but he did say that a letter from him must have reached Paddy just before he died and that if it had been found he would like it to be destroyed unopened. You see, Roderick, Anthony Banks must have been honest because he could have kept that five thousand pounds himself quite easily, when she died. And he didn't know Paddy had remarried."

"Yes, that's quite true. Are you certain from what you knew of Paddy that he would have destroyed Banks's letter?"

"No. I've always thought he would have kept it to show me."

"Do you think he asked the people in the vicarage or at the hospital to destroy his letters?"

"They had found his name and address on other letters in his wallet, so it wasn't that." For the first time the quiet voice faltered a little. "He only spoke once, they said. He asked for me."

Alleyn gave her a moment and then he said:

"Do you remember the name of the people at the vicarage?"

"I don't. I wrote and thanked them for what they had done. It was some very ordinary sort of name."

"And the cottage hospital?"

"It was at Falconbridge in Buckinghamshire. Quite a big hospital. I saw the superintendent doctor. He was an elderly man with a face like a sheep. I think his name was Bletherley. I'm perfectly certain that he was not a blackmailer, Roderick. And the nurses were charming."

"Do you think that he could possibly have left the letter in the case, or that it could have dropped out of his pocket?"

"I simply cannot believe that if he kept it at all it would be anywhere but in his wallet. And I was given the wallet. It was in the breast pocket of his coat. You see, Roderick, it's not as if I didn't try to trace the letter. I was desperately anxious to see the message from Anthony Banks. I asked again and again if anything could have been overlooked at the hospital and endless enquiries were made."

She stopped for a moment and looked steadily at Alleyn.

"You can see now," she said, "why I would go almost to any length to keep this from Bridget."

"Yes," said Alleyn, "I can see."

17

The Element of Youth

Alleyn saw Bridget in her old nursery which had been
converted into a very human sitting-room. She made
him take a large armchair and jiggled a box of cigarettes
under his nose.

"It's no good being official and pretending you don't.
I can see you do."

"Really!" exclaimed Alleyn with a look at his fingers
which were not stained with nicotine. "How?"

"The outline of your case shows through your coat.
You should take up detection, Mr. Alleyn, it's *too*
interesting."

Alleyn took a cigarette.

"Got me there," he said. "Have you yourself any
ideas about being a police-woman?" He fingered the
outline that showed through his breast pocket.

"I suppose one has to begin at the bottom," said Bridget. "What's the first duty of a police-woman?"

"I don't know. We are not allowed to hang round the girls in the force."

"What a shame," said Bridget, "I won't join. I should like you to hang round me, Mr. Alleyn."

Alleyn thought: "She's being just a bit too deliberately the audacious young charmer. What's up with her? Young Donald, damn his eyes!"

He said: "Well, so I must for the moment. I want to talk to you about last night, if I may."

"I'm afraid I won't be much good," said Bridget. "I hope you find whoever it was. It's worrying Donna to death, and Bart's being absolutely lethal over it. Bart's my stepfather. You've met him, haven't you? All pukka sahib and horsewhips. Is a horsewhip any worse than an ordinary one, do you know?"

"You knew Lord Robert pretty well, didn't you?" asked Alleyn.

"Yes. He was a great friend of Donna's. I suppose you think I'm being hard and modern about him. I'd have been sorrier if it had happened longer ago."

"That's rather cryptic," said Alleyn. "What does it mean?"

"It doesn't mean I'm not sorry now. I am. We all loved him and I mind most dreadfully. But I found out I didn't really know him well. He was harder than you'd ever believe. In a way that makes it worse; having been out of friends with him. I feel I'd give anything to be able to tell him I—I—I'm sorry."

"Sorry for what?"

"For not being very nice to him last night. I snubbed him."

"Why did you snub poor Bunchy?"

"Because he was beastly to his nephew who happens to be rather a particular friend of mine."

"Donald Potter? Yes, I know about that. Don't you think it's possible that Donald was rather hard on his uncle?"

"No, I don't. Donald's a man now. He's got to stand on his own feet and decide things for himself. Bunchy simply wouldn't understand that. He wanted to choose Donald's friends, settle his career, and treat him exactly as if he was a schoolboy. Bunchy was just hopelessly Victorian and conventional."

"Do you like Captain Withers?" asked Alleyn suddenly.

"What?" Bridget became rather pink. "I can't say he's exactly my cup of tea. I suppose he is rather ghastly in a way, but he's a marvellous dancer and he can be quite fun. I can forgive anybody almost anything if they're amusing, can't you?"

"What sort of amusement does Captain Withers provide?"

"Well, I mean he's gay. Not exactly gay but he goes everywhere and everybody knows him, so he's always quite good value. Donald says Wits is a terribly good business man. He's been frightfully nice about advising Donald and he knows all sorts of people who could be useful."

"Useful in what way? Donald is going in for medicine, isn't he?"

"Well——" Bridget hesitated. "Yes. That was the original idea, but Wits rather advises him not to. Donald says there's not much in medicine nowadays and, anyway, a doctor is rather a dreary sort of thing to be."

"Is he?" asked Alleyn. "You mean not very smart?"

"No, of course I don't mean that," said Bridget. She glared at Alleyn. "You *are* a pig," she said. "I suppose I do. I hate drab, worthy sort of things and, anyway, it's got nothing to do with the case."

"I should like to know what career Captain Withers has suggested for Donald."

"There's nothing definite yet. They've thought of starting a new night club. Wits has got wonderfully original ideas."

"Yes," agreed Alleyn, "I can quite imagine it. He's doing quite well with the place at Leatherhead, isn't he? Why doesn't he take Donald in there?"

Bridget looked surprised.

"How did you know about that?" she asked.

"You must never say that to policemen," said Alleyn. "It steals their thunder. As a matter of fact, I have been talking to Withers and the Leatherhead venture cropped up."

"Well, I dare say you know more about it than I do," said Bridget. "Donald says it's just a small men's club. More for fun than to make money. They play bridge and things. I don't think there's any opening there."

"Have you spoken to Donald since his uncle died?"

Bridget clenched her hands and thumped them angrily on her knees.

"Of course, he rang me up. I'd just got to the telephone when Bart came in looking like a beastly old cochin-chinarooster and took the receiver from me. I could have killed him, he was so infuriating! He was all sort of patient and old-world. He sympathised with Donald and then he said: 'If you don't mind an old fellow speaking frankly, I think it would be better if you didn't communicate with my stepdaughter for the time being!' I said: 'No! Give it to me,' but he simply turned his back on me and went on: 'You understand. I'm afraid I must forbid it,' and put the receiver down. I stormed at him but we were in Donna's room and she was so upset I had to give in and promise I wouldn't write or anything. It's so beastly, *beastly* unfair. And it's all because Bart's such a filthy old snob and is afraid of all the reporters and scandal and everything. Horrid bogus old man. And he's absolutely *filthy* to darling Donna. How she ever married him! After daddy, who must have been so gay, and charming, and who loved her so much. How she could! And if Bart thinks I'm going to give Donald up he's jolly well got another think coming."

"Are you engaged?"

"No. We're waiting till Donald begins to earn."

"And how much must Donald earn before he is marriageable?"

"You don't put it very nicely, do you? I suppose you

think I'm hard and modern and beastly. I dare say I am but I can't bear the idea of everything getting squalid and drab because we have to worry about money. A horrid little flat, second-rate restaurants, whitewood furniture painted to look fresh and nice. Ugh! I've seen these sorts of marriages," said Bridget looking worldly-wise, "and I *know*."

"Donald is his uncle's heir, you know."

Bridget was on her feet, her eyes flashing.

"Don't you dare," she said, "don't you dare say that because Donald gets the money he had anything to do with this. Don't you dare."

"And don't you go putting ideas into people's heads by getting on the defensive before you've been given cause," said Alleyn very firmly indeed. He put his hand inside his breast pocket. The slight bulge disappeared and out came Alleyn's notebook. In the midst of her fury Bridget's glance fell on it. She looked from the notebook to Alleyn. He raised one eyebrow and screwed his face into an apologetic grimace.

"The idea was perfectly magnificent," he said. "It did look like a cigarette-case. The edges of the bulge weren't quite sharp enough."

"Pig!" said Bridget.

"Sorry," said Alleyn. "Now then. Three or four official questions, if you please. And look here, Miss Bridget, will you let me offer you a very dreary piece of advice? It's our set-piece for innocent witnesses. Don't prevaricate. Don't lose your temper. And don't try any downright thumping lies, because if you do, as sure as eggs is eggs, you'll be caught out and it'll look very nasty indeed for anyone whom you thought you were going to protect. You think Donald is innocent, don't you?"

"I *know* he is innocent."

"Right. Then you have nothing in the wide world to fear. Away we go. Did you sit out in the green sitting-room on the top gallery?"

"Yes. Lots of times."

"During the supper hour? Between twelve and one?"

Bridget pondered. As he watched her Alleyn looked back at youth and marvelled at its buoyancy. Bridget's mind bounced from thoughts of death to thoughts of love. She was sorry Bunchy was murdered, but as long as Donald was not suspected she was also rather thrilled at the idea of police investigation. She was sincerely concerned at her mother's distress and ready to make sacrifices on Lady Carrados's behalf. But ready to meet all sorrow, anger, or fright was her youth, like a sort of pneumatic armour that received momentary impressions of these things but instantly filled out again. Now, when she came to her mother's indisposition she spoke soberly, but it was impossible to escape the impression that on the whole she was rather stimulated than unnerved by tragedy.

"I was up there with Donald until after most people had gone in to the supper-room. We both came down together. That was when I returned her bag to Donna. Donna wasn't well. She's awfully tired. She nearly fainted when I found her in the supper-room. She said afterwards it was the stuffiness."

"Yes?"

"It was a queer sort of night. Hot indoors, but when any of the windows were opened the mist came in and it brought a kind of dank chilliness. Donna asked me to fetch her smelling-salts. I ran upstairs to the ladies' cloakroom. Donna's maid Sophie was there. I got the smelling-salts from Sophie and ran downstairs. I couldn't find Donna but I ran into Bunchy who said she was all right again. I had booked that dance with Percy Percival. He was a bit drunk and was making a scene about my having cut him out. So I danced with him to keep him quiet."

"Did you go up to the green sitting-room again?"

"Not for some time. Donald and I went up there towards the end of the party."

"Did you at any stage of the proceedings leave your cigarette-case on the pie-crust table in that room?"

Bridget stared at him.

"I haven't got a cigarette-case; I don't smoke. Is there something about a cigarette-case in the green sitting-room?"

"There may be. Do you know if anybody overheard Bunchy telephone from that room at about one o'clock?"

"I haven't heard of it," said Bridget. He saw that her curiosity was aroused. "Have you asked Miss Harris?" she said. "She was on the top landing a good deal last night. She's somewhere in the house now."

"I'll have a word with her. There's just one other point. Lord Robert was with your mother when you returned her bag, wasn't he? He was there when she felt faint?"

"Yes. Why?"

"Did he seem upset in any way?"

"He seemed very concerned about Donna but that was all. Sir Daniel—Donna's doctor—came up. Bunchy opened a window. They all seemed to want me out of the way. Donna asked for her smelling-salts, so I went and got them. That's all. What about a cigarette-case? Do tell me."

"It's gold with a medallion sunk in the lid and surrounded by brilliants. Do you know it?"

"It sounds horribly grand. No, I don't think I do."

Alleyn got up.

"That's all, then," he said. "Thank you so much, Miss Bridget. Good-bye." He had got as far as the door before she stopped him.

"Mr. Alleyn!"

"Yes?"

She was standing very erect in the middle of the room, her chin up and a lock of hair falling across her forehead.

"You seem to be very interested in the fact that my mother was not well last night. Why?"

"Lord Robert was with her at the time——" Alleyn began.

"You seem equally interested in the fact that I

returned my mother's bag to her. Why? Neither of these incidents had anything to do with Bunchy Gospell. My mother's not well and I won't have her worried."

"Quite right," said Alleyn. "I won't either if I can help it."

She seemed to accept that but he could see that she had something else to say. Her young, beautifully made-up face in its frame of careful curls had a frightened look.

"I want you to tell me," said Bridget, "if you suspect Donald of anything."

"It is much too soon for us to form any definite suspicion of anybody," Alleyn said. "You shouldn't attach too much significance to any one question in police interrogations. Many of our questions are nothing but routine. As Lord Robert's heir—no, don't storm at me again, you asked me and I tell you—as Lord Robert's heir Donald is bound to come in for his share of questions. If you are worrying about him, and I see you are, may I give you a tip? Encourage him to return to medicine. If he starts running night clubs the chances are that sooner or later he will fall into our clutches. And then what?"

"Of course," said Bridget thoughtfully, "it'll be different now. We could get married quite soon, even if he was at a hospital or something all day. He will have *some* money."

"Yes," agreed Alleyn, "yes."

"I mean I don't want to be heartless," continued Bridget looking at him quite frankly, "but naturally one can't help thinking of that. We're terribly, terribly sorry about Bunchy. We couldn't be sorrier. But he wasn't young like us."

Into Alleyn's mind came suddenly the memory of a thinning head, leant sideways, of fat hands, of small feet turned inwards.

"No," he said, "he wasn't young like you."

"I think he was stupid and tiresome over Donald," Bridget went on in a high voice, "and I'm not going to pretend I don't, although I am sorry I wasn't friends with him last night. But all the same I don't believe he'd have minded us thinking about the difference the money would make. I believe he would have understood that."

"I'm sure he would have understood."

"Well then, don't look as if you're thinking I'm hard and beastly."

"I don't think you're beastly and I don't believe you are really very hard."

"Thank you for nothing," said Bridget and added immediately: "Oh, damn, I'm sorry."

"That's all right," said Alleyn. "Good-bye."

"Yes, but——"

"Well?"

"Nothing. Only, you make me feel shabby and it's not fair. If there was anything I could do for Bunchy I'd do it. So would Donald, of course. But he's dead. You can't do anything for dead people."

"If they have been murdered you can try to catch the man that killed them."

"'An eye for an eye.' It doesn't do them any good. It's only savagery."

"Let the murderer asphyxiate someone else if it's going to suit his book," said Alleyn. "Is that the idea?"

"If there was any real thing we could do——"

"How about Donald doing what his uncle wanted so much? Taking his medical? That is," said Alleyn quickly, "unless he really has got a genuine ambition in another direction. Not by way of Captain Withers's night clubs."

"I've just said he might be a doctor, now, haven't I?"

"Yes," said Alleyn, "you have. So we're talking in circles." His hand was on the door-knob.

"I should have thought," said Bridget, "that as a detective you would have wanted to make me talk."

Alleyn laughed outright.

"You little egoist," he said, "I've listened to you for the last ten minutes and all you want to talk about is yourself and your young man. Quite right too, but not the policeman's cup of tea. You take care of your mother who needs you rather badly just now, encourage your young man to renew his studies, and if you can, wean him from Withers. Good-bye, now, I'm off."

18

Predicament of a Secretary

When he had closed the nursery door behind him, Alleyn made for the stairs. If Fox was still closeted in the library with Carrados conversation must be getting a bit strained. He passed Lady Carrados's room and heard a distant noise.

"It's insufferable, my dear Evelyn, that——"

Alleyn grimaced and went on downstairs.

He found Fox alone in the library.

"Hullo, Br'er Fox," said Alleyn. "Lost the simple soldier-man?"

"Gone upstairs," said Fox. "I can't say I'm sorry. I had a job to keep him here at all after you went."

"How did you manage it?"

"Asked him if he had any experience of police investigation. That did it. We went from there to how he helped the police catch a footman that stole somebody's pearls in Tunbridge and how if he just hadn't happened to notice the man watching the vase on the piano nobody would ever have thought of looking in the

Duchess's pot-pourri. Funny how vain some of these old gentlemen get, isn't it?"

"Screamingly. As we seem to have this important room all to ourselves we'd better see if we can get hold of Miss Harris. You might go and ask——"

But before Fox got as far as the door it opened and Miss Harris herself walked in.

"Good afternoon," she said crisply, "I believe you wished to see me. Lady Carrados's secretary."

"We were on the point of asking for you, Miss Harris," said Alleyn. "Won't you sit down? My name is Alleyn and this is Inspector Fox."

"Good afternoon," repeated Miss Harris and sat down. She was neither plain nor beautiful, short nor tall, dark nor fair. It crossed his mind that she might have won a newspaper competition for the average woman, that she represented the dead norm of femininity. Her clothes were perfectly adequate and completely without character. She was steeped in nonentity. No wonder that few people had noticed her at Marsdon House. She might have gone everywhere, heard everything like a sort of upper middle-class Oberon at Theseus's party. Unless, indeed, nonentity itself was conspicuous at Marsdon House last night.

He noticed that she was not in the least nervous. Her hands rested quietly in her lap. She had laid a pad and pencil on the arm of her chair exactly as if she was about to take notes at his dictation. Fox took his own notebook out and waited.

"May we have your name and address?" asked Alleyn.

"Certainly, Mr. Alleyn," said Miss Harris crisply. "Dorothea Violet Harris. Address—town or country?"

"Both, please."

"Town: fifty-seven, Ebury Mews, S.W. Country: The Rectory, Barbicon-Bramley, Bucks." She glanced at Fox. "B—a—r—b—i——"

"Thank you, miss, I think I've got it," said Fox.

"Now, Miss Harris," Alleyn began, "I wonder if you can give me any help at all in this business."

To his tense astonishment Miss Harris at once opened her pad on which he could see a column of shorthand hieroglyphics. She drew out from her bosom on a spring extension a pair of rimless pince-nez. She placed them on her nose and waited with composure for Alleyn's next remark.

He said: "Have you some notes there, Miss Harris?"

"Yes, Mr. Alleyn. I saw Miss O'Brien just now and she told me you would be requiring any information I could give about Lord Robert Gospell's movements last night and this morning. I thought it better to prepare what I have to say. So I just jotted down one or two little memos."

"Admirable! Let's have 'em."

Miss Harris cleared her throat.

"At about twelve-thirty," she began in an incisive monotone, "I met Lord Robert Gospell on the ballroom landing. I was speaking to Miss O'Brien. He asked me to dance with him later in the evening. He went downstairs. I remained on the landing until a quarter to one. I happened to glance at my watch. I then went upstairs to top landing. Remained there. Period of time unknown but I returned to ballroom landing before one-thirty. Lord Gospell—I mean Lord Robert Gospell—then asked me to dance."

Miss Harris's voice stopped for a moment. She moved her writing-pad on the arm of her chair.

"We danced," she continued. "Three successive dances with repeats. Lord Robert introduced me to several of his friends and then he took me into the buffet on the street-level. We drank champagne. He then remembered that he had promised to dance with the Duchess of Dorminster——" Here Miss Harris appeared to lose her place for a moment. She repeated "Had promised to dance with the Duchess of Dorminster," and cleared her throat again. "He took me to the ballroom and asked me for the next Viennese waltz. I remained in the ballroom. Lord Robert danced with the Duchess and then with Miss Agatha Troy, the portrait painter, and then with two ladies whose names I do not know. Not at once, of course," said Miss Harris in parenthesis. "That would be ridiculous. I still remained in the ballroom. The band played the 'Blue Danube.' Lord Robert was standing in a group of his friends close to where I sat. He saw me. We danced the 'Blue Danube' together and revisited the buffet. I noticed the time. I had intended leaving much earlier and was surprised to find that it was nearly three o'clock. So I stayed till the end."

She glanced up at Alleyn with the impersonal attentive air proper to her position. He felt so precisely that she was indeed his secretary that there was no need for him to repress a smile. But he did glance at Fox who, for the first time in Alleyn's memory, looked really at a loss. His large hand hovered uncertainly over his own notebook. Alleyn realised that Fox did not know whether to take down Miss Harris's shorthand in his own shorthand.

Alleyn said: "Thank you, Miss Harris. Anything else?"

Miss Harris turned a page.

"Details of conversation," she began. "I have not made memos of *all* the remarks I have remembered. Many of them were merely light comments on suitable subjects. For instance, Lord Robert spoke of Lady Carrados and expressed regret that she seemed to be tired. That sort of thing."

"Let us have his remarks under this heading," said Alleyn with perfect gravity.

"Certainly, Mr. Alleyn. Lord Robert asked me if I had noticed that Lady Carrados had been tired for some time. I said yes, I had, and that I was sorry because she was so nice to everybody. He asked if I thought it was entirely due to the season. I said I expected it was because many ladies I have had posts with have found the season very exhausting, although in a way Lady Carrados took the entertaining side very lightly. Lord Robert asked me if I liked being with Lady Carrados. I replied that I did, very much. Lord Robert asked me several questions about myself. He was very easy to talk to. I told him about the old days at the rectory and how we ought to have been much better off, and he was very nice, and I told about my father's people in Bucks and he seemed quite interested in so many of them being parsons and what an old Buckinghamshire family we really are."

"Oh, God," thought Alleyn on a sudden wave of painful compassion. "And so they probably are and because for the last two or three generations they've had to haul down the social flag inch by inch their children are all going to talk like this and nobody's going to feel anything but uncomfortably incredulous."

He said: "You come from Barbicon-Bramley? That's not far from Bassicote, is it? I know that part of Bucks fairly well. Is your father's rectory anywhere near Falconbridge?"

"Oh, no. Falconbridge is thirty miles away. My Uncle Walter was rector at Falconbridge."

Alleyn said: "Really? Long ago?"

"When I was a small girl. He's retired now and lives in Barbicon-Bramley. All the Harrises live to ripe old ages. Lord Robert remarked that many of the clergy do. He said longevity was one of the more dubious rewards of virtue," said Miss Harris with a glance at her notes.

Alleyn could hear the squeaky voice uttering this gentle epigram.

"He *was* amusing," added Miss Harris.

"Yes. Now, look here, Miss Harris, we're coming to something rather important. You tell me you went up to the top landing between, say, a quarter to one and one-fifteen. Do you think you were up there all that time?"

"Yes, Mr. Alleyn, I think I was."

"Whereabouts were you?"

Miss Harris turned purple with the rapidity of a pantomime fairy under a coloured spotlight.

"Well, I mean to say, I sat on the gallery, I went into the ladies' cloakroom on the landing to tidy and see if everything was quite nice, and then I sat on the gallery again and—I mean I was just about."

"You were on the gallery at one o'clock, you think?"

"I—really I'm not sure if I——"

"Let's see if we can get at it this way. Did you go into the cloakroom immediately after you got to the landing?"

"Yes. Yes, I did."

"How long were you in the cloakroom?"

"Only a few minutes."

"So you were back on the gallery again well before one."

"Yes," said Miss Harris without enthusiasm, "but——"

"At about the time I am trying to get at, Captain Withers and Mr. Donald Potter were on the gallery from where they moved into the sitting-room on that landing. Sir Herbert Carrados was in and out of the sitting-room and you may have heard him order the servant on duty up there to attend to the ash-trays and matches. Do you remember this?"

"No. Not exactly. I think I remember seeing Captain Withers and Mr. Potter through the sitting-room door as I passed to go downstairs. The larger sitting-room—not the one with the telephone. Lord Robert was in the telephone-room."

"How do you know that?"

"I—I heard him."

"From the cloakroom?"

"The—I mean——"

"The room between the cloakroom and the telephone-room, perhaps," said Alleyn, mentally cursing the extreme modesty of Miss Harris.

"Yes," said Miss Harris looking straight in front of her. Her discomfiture was so evident that Alleyn himself almost began to feel shy.

"Please don't mind if I ask for very exact information," he said. "Policemen are rather like doctors in these instances. Things don't count. When did you go into this ladies' room?"

"As soon as I got upstairs," said Miss Harris. "Hem!"

"Right. Now let's see if we can get things straight, shall we? You came upstairs at, say, about ten or fifteen minutes to one. You went straight to this door next the green sitting-room with the telephone. Did you see anyone?"

"Captain Withers was just coming out of the green sitting-room. I think there was a lady in there. I saw her through the open door as I—as I opened the other."

"Yes. Anyone else?"

"I think I noticed Sir Herbert in the other sitting-room, the first one, as I passed the door. That's all."

"And then you went into the ladies' room?"

"Yes," admitted Miss Harris, shutting her eyes for a moment and opening them again to stare with something like horror at Fox's pencil and notebook. Alleyn felt that already she saw herself being forced to answer these and worse questions shouted at her by celebrated counsel at the Old Bailey.

"How long did you remain in this room?" he asked.

White to the lips Miss Harris gave a rather mad little laugh. "Oh," she said, "oh, quayte a tayme. You know."

"And while you were there you heard Lord Robert telephoning in the next room?"

"Yes, I did," said Miss Harris loudly with an air of defiance.

"She's looking at me," thought Alleyn, "exactly like a trapped rabbit."

"So Lord Robert probably came upstairs after you. Do you suppose the lady you had noticed was still in the green room when he began telephoning?"

"No. I heard her come out and—and she—I mean she tried to—tried to——"

"Yes, yes," said Alleyn, "quite. And went away?"

"Definitely."

"And then Lord Robert began to telephone? I see. Could you hear what he said?"

"Oh, no. He spoke in a low tone of course. I made no attempt to listen."

"Of course not."

"I could not have heard if I had tried," continued Miss Harris. "I could only hear the tone of the voice and that was quite unmistakable."

"Yes?" said Alleyn encouragingly. "Now," he thought, "now at last are we getting to it?" Miss Harris did not go on, however, but sat with her mouth done up in a maddening button of conscious rectitude.

"Did you hear the end of the conversation?" he said at last.

"Oh, yes! The end. Yes. At least, someone came into the room. I heard Lord Robert say: 'Oh, hello!' Those were the only words I did distinguish, and almost immediately I heard the telephone tinkle, so I knew he had rung off."

"And the other person? Was it a man?"

"Yes. Yes, a man."

"Could you," said Alleyn in a level voice, "could you recognise this man?"

"Oh, *no*," cried Miss Harris with an air of relief. "No *indeed*, Mr. Alleyn, I haven't the faintest idea. You see, after that I didn't really hear anything at all in the next room. Nothing at all. Really."

"You returned to the landing?"

"Not immediately. No."

"Oh?" said Alleyn. He could think of nothing else to say. Even Fox seemed to have caught the infection of extreme embarrassment. He cleared his throat loudly. Miss Harris, astonishingly, broke into a high-pitched prattle, keeping her eyes fixed on the opposite wall and clenching and unclenching her hands.

"No. Not for some minutes and then, of course, when I did return they had both gone. I mean when I finally returned. Of course Lord Robert went before then and—and—so that was perfectly all right. Perfectly."

"And the other man?"

"He—it was most unfortunate. A little mistake. I assure you I did not see who it was. I mean as soon as he realised it was the wrong door he went out again. Naturally. The inner door being half-glass made it even more unfortunate though of course there being two rooms was—was better for all concerned than if it was the usual arrangement. And I mean that he didn't see me so that in a way it didn't matter. It didn't really matter a scrap. Not a scrap."

Alleyn, listening to this rigmarole, sent his memory back to the top gallery of Marsdon House. He remembered the Victorian ante-room that opened off the landing, the inner gloomy sanctum beyond. The chaotic fragments of Miss Harris's remarks joggled together in his brain and then clicked into a definite pattern.

"Not a scrap, really," Miss Harris still repeated.

"Of course not," agreed Alleyn cheerfully. "I think I understand what happened. Tell me if I go wrong. While you were still in the inner room the man who had interrupted Lord Robert's telephone conversation came out of the green sitting-room and blundered through the wrong door into the ante-room of the ladies' lavatory. That it?"

Miss Harris blanched at the unfortunate word but nodded her head.

"Why are you so sure it was this same man, Miss Harris?"

"Well, because, because I heard their voices as they came to the door of the next room and then Lord Robert's voice on the landing and then—then it happened. I just knew that was who it was."

Alleyn leant forward.

"The inner door," he said, "is half-glass. Could you see this intruder?"

"Dimly, dimly," cried Miss Harris. "Greatly obscured, I assure you. I'm sorry to say I forgot for some seconds to switch off my light. The other was on."

"So you actually could see the shape of this person, however shadowy, through the clouded glass?"

"Yes. For a second or two. Before he went away. I think perhaps he was feeling unwell."

"Drunk?"

"No, no. Certainly not. It was not a bit like that. He looked more as if he'd had a shock."

"Why?"

"He—the shape of him put its hands to its face and it

swayed towards the glass partition and for a moment leant against it. Thank God," said Miss Harris with real fervour, "I had locked the door."

"The silhouette would be clearer, more sharply defined, as it came closer to the door?"

"I suppose so. Yes, it was."

"Still you did not recognise it?"

"No. Never for an instant."

"Suppose—for the sake of argument, I was to say this man was either Sir Herbert Carrados, Captain Withers, the waiter on the landing, Mr. Donald Potter, or Dimitri the caterer. Which would you think most likely?"

"I don't know. Perhaps Dimitri. I don't know."

"What height?"

"Medium."

"Well," said Alleyn, "what happened next?"

"He took his hands from his face. He had turned away with his back against the door. I—I got the impression he suddenly realised where he was. Then the shape moved away and turned misty and then disappeared. I heard the outer door shut."

"And at last you were able to escape?"

"I waited for a moment." Miss Harris looked carefully at Alleyn. Perhaps she saw something in his eye that made her feel, after all, her recital had not been such a terrible affair.

"It *was* awkward," she said, "wasn't it? Honestly?"

"Honestly," said Alleyn, "it was."

19

The General

"Then your idea is," said Fox as they headed again for
Belgrave Square, "that this chap in the W.C. was the
murderer."

"Yes, Fox, this *is* my idea. There's no earthly reason
why an innocent person should not admit to interrupting
the telephone call and nobody has admitted to it. I'm
afraid we'll have to go again through the whole damn'
boiling, guests, servants and all to make sure of our
ground. *And* we'll have to ask every man jack of 'em if
they burst across the threshold of Miss Harris's outer
sanctuary. Every *man* jack. Thank the Lord there's no
need for the women, though from what I know of my
niece Sarah we wouldn't meet with many mantling
cheeks and conscious looks among the débutantes. If
nobody admits to the telephone incident, or to the
sequel in the usual offices, then we can plot another
joint in our pattern. We can say there is at least a strong
probability that our man overheard Bunchy telephone
to me, interrupted the sentence: 'and he's working

218

with——' waited in the green sitting-room until Bunchy had gone and then blundered into the ante-room."

"But why would he do that?" said Fox. "Did he think it was a man's, or was he trying to avoid somebody? Or what?"

"It's a curious picture, isn't it? That dim figure seen through the thick glass. Even in her mortal shame Miss Harris noticed that he seemed to be agitated. The hands over the face, the body leaning for a moment against the door. And then suddenly he pulls himself together and goes out. He looked, said Miss Harris, as though he'd had a shock. If he's our man he had indeed had a shock. He'd just intercepted a telephone call to the Yard from a man who apparently knew all there was to know about his blackmailing activities. He might well feel he must blunder through the first door he came to and have a moment alone to pull himself together."

"Yes," agreed Fox, "so he might. I'd like something a bit more definite to hinge it on, though."

"And so, I promise you, would I. The detestable realms of conjecture! How I hate them."

"Miss Harris didn't get us any further with the business down in the hall."

"The final departures? No, she didn't. She simply bore out everything we'd already been told."

"She's an observant little lady, isn't she?" said Fox.

"Yes, Fox, she's no fool, for all her tender qualms. And now we have a delightful job ahead of us. We've got to try and bamboozle, cajole, or bully Mrs. Halcut-Hackett into giving away her best young man. A charming occupation."

"Will we be seeing the General, too? I suppose we'll have to. I don't think the other chaps will have tackled him. I told them not to touch any of our lot."

"Quite right," said Alleyn, with a sigh. "We shall be seeing the General. And here we are at Halkyn Street. The Halcut-Hacketts of Halkyn Street! An important collection of aspirates and rending consonants. The General first, I suppose."

The General was expecting them. They walked

through a hall which, though it had no tongue, yet it did speak of the most expensive and most fashionable house decorator in London. They were shown into a study smelling of leather and cigars and decorated with that pleasant sequence of prints of the Nightcap Steeplechase. Alleyn wondered if the General had stood with his cavalry sabre on the threshold of this room, daring the fashionable decorator to come on and see what he would get. Or possibly Mrs. Halcut-Hackett, being an American, caused her husband's study to be aggressively British. Alleyn and Fox waited for five minutes before they heard a very firm step and loud cough. General Halcut-Hackett walked into the room.

"Hullo! Afternoon! What!" he shouted.

His face was terra cotta, his moustache formidable, his eyes china blue. He was the original ramrod brass-hat, the subject of all army jokes kindly or malicious. It was impossible to believe his mind was as blank as his face would seem to confess. So true to type was he that he would have seemed unreal, a two-dimensional figure that had stepped from a coloured cartoon of a regimental dinner, had it not been for a certain air of solidity and a kind of childlike constancy that was rather appealing. Alleyn thought: "Now, *he* really *is* a simple soldier-man."

"Sit down," said General Halcut-Hackett. "Bad business! Damn' blackguardly killer. Place is getting no better than Chicago. What are you fellows doing about it? What? Going to get the feller. What?"

"I hope so, sir," said Alleyn.

"Hope so! By Gad, I should hope you hope so. Well, what can I do for you?"

"Answer one or two questions, if you will, sir."

" 'Course I will. Bloody outrage. The country's going to pieces in my opinion and this is only another proof of it. Men like Robert Gospell can't take a cab without gettin' the life choked out of them. What it amounts to. Well?"

"Well, sir, the first point is this. Did you walk into the green sitting-room on the top landing at one o'clock this morning while Lord Robert Gospell was using the telephone?"

"No. Never went near the place. Next!"

"What time did you leave Marsdon House?"

"Between twelve and one."

"Early," remarked Alleyn.

"My wife's charge had toothache. Brought her home. Whole damn' business has been too much for her. Poodle-faking and racketing! All people think of nowadays. Goin' through her paces from morning till night. Enough to kill a horse."

"Yes," said Alleyn. "One wonders how they get through it."

"Is your name Alleyn?"

"Yes, sir."

"George Alleyn's son, are you? You're like him. He was in my regiment. I'm sixty-seven," added General Halcut-Hackett with considerable force. "Sixty-seven. Why didn't you go into your father's regiment? Because you preferred this. What?"

"That's it, sir. The next point is——"

"What? Get on with the job, eh? Quite right."

"Did you return to Marsdon House?"

"Why the devil should I do that?"

"I thought perhaps your wife was——"

The General glared at the second print in the Nightcap series and said:

"M'wife preferred to stay on. Matter of fact, Robert Gospell offered to see her home."

"He didn't do so, however?"

"Damn it, sir, my wife is not a murderess."

"Lord Robert might have crossed the square as escort to your wife, sir, and returned."

"Well, he didn't. She tells me they missed each other."

"And you, sir. You saw your daughter in and then——"

"She's not my daughter!" said the General with a good deal of emphasis. "She's the daughter of some friend of my wife's." He glowered and then muttered half to himself: "Unheard of in my day, that sort of thing. Makes a woman look like a damn' trainer. Girl's no more than a miserable scared filly. Pah!"

Alleyn said: "Yes, sir. Well, then, you saw Miss——?"

"Birnbaum. Rose Birnbaum, poor little devil. Call her Poppet."

"——Miss Birnbaum in and then——"

"Well?"

"Did you stay up?"

To Alleyn's astonishment the General's face turned from terra-cotta to purple, not, it seemed, with anger, but with embarrassment. He blew out his moustache several times, pouted like a baby, and blinked. At last he said:

"Upon my soul, I can't see what the devil it matters whether I went to bed at twelve or one."

"The question may sound impertinent," said Alleyn. "If it does I'm sorry. But, as a matter of police routine, we want to establish alibis——"

"*Alibis!*" roared the General. "*Alibis!* Good God, sir, are you going to sit there and tell me I'm in need of an alibi? Hell blast it, sir——"

"But, General Halcut-Hackett," said Alleyn quickly, while the empurpled General sucked in his breath, "every guest at Marsdon House is in need of an alibi."

"Every guest! Every guest! But, damn it, sir, the man was murdered in a bloody cab, not a bloody ballroom. Some filthy bolshevistic fascist," shouted the General, having a good deal of difficulty with this strange collection of sibilants. He slightly dislodged his upper plate but impatiently champed it back into position. "They're all alike!" he added confusedly. "The whole damn' boiling."

Alleyn hunted for a suitable phrase in a language that General Halcut-Hackett would understand. He glanced at Fox who was staring solemnly at the General over the top of his spectacles.

"I'm sure you'll realise, sir," said Alleyn. "that we are simply obeying orders."

"What?"

"That's done it," thought Alleyn.

"Orders! I can toe the line as well as the next fellow," said the General, and Alleyn, remembering Carrados had used much the same phrase, reflected that in this instance it was probably true. The General, he saw, *was* preparing to toe the line.

"I apologise," said the General. "Lost my temper. Always doing it nowadays. Indigestion."

"It's enough to make anybody lose their temper, sir."

"Well," said the General, "you've kept yours. Come on, then."

"It's just a statement, sir, that you didn't go out again after you got back here and, if possible, someone to support the statement."

Once again the General looked strangely embarrased.

"I can't give you a witness," he said. "Nobody saw me go to bed."

"I see. Well then, sir, if you'll just give me your word that you didn't go out again."

"But, damme, I did take a—take a—take a turn round the square before I went to bed. Always do."

"What time was this?"

"I don't know."

"You can't give me an idea? Was it long after you got home?"

"Some time. I saw the child to her room and stirred up my wife's maid to look after her. Then I came down here and got myself a drink. I read for a bit. I dare say I dozed for a bit. Couldn't make up my mind to turn in."

"You didn't glance at the clock on the mantelpiece there?"

Again the General became acutely self-conscious.

"I may have done so. I fancy I did. Matter of fact, I remember now I did doze off and woke with a bit of a start. The fire had gone out. It was devilish chilly." He glared at Alleyn and then said abruptly: "I felt wretchedly down in the mouth. I'm getting an old fellow nowadays and I don't enjoy the small hours. As you say, I looked at the clock. It was half-past two. I sat here in this chair trying to make up my mind to go to bed. Couldn't. So I took a walk round the square."

"Now that's excellent, sir. You may be able to give us the very piece of information we're after. Did you by chance notice anybody hanging about in the square?"

"No."

"Did you meet anybody at all?"

"Constable."

Alleyn glanced at Fox.

"P.C. Titheridge," said Fox. "We've got his report, sir."

"All right," said Alleyn. "Were people beginning to leave Marsdon House when you passed, sir?"

The General muttered something about "might have been," paused for a moment and then said: "It was devilish murkey. Couldn't see anything."

"A misty night; yes," said Alleyn. "Did you happen to notice Captain Maurice Withers in the mist?"

"No!" yelled the General with extraordinary vehemence. "No, I did not. I don't know the feller. No!"

There was an uncomfortable pause and then the General said: "Afraid that's all I can tell you. When I got in again I went straight to bed."

"Your wife had not returned?"

"No," said the General very loudly. "She had not."

Alleyn waited for a moment and then he said:

"Thank you very much, sir. Now, we'll prepare a statement from the notes Inspector Fox has taken, and if you've no objection, we'll get you to sign it."

"I—um—um—um—I'll have a look at it."

"Yes. And now, if I may, I'd like to have a word with Mrs. Halcut-Hackett."

Up went the General's chin again. For a moment Alleyn wondered if they were in for another outburst. But the General said: "Very good. I'll tell her," and marched out of the room.

"Crikey!" said Fox.

"That's Halcut-Hackett that was," said Alleyn. "Why the devil," he added rubbing his nose, "why the devil is the funny old article in such a stew over his walk round the square?"

"Seems a natural thing for a gentleman of his kind to do," Fox ruminated. "I'm sure I don't know. I should have thought he's the sort that breaks the ice on the Serpentine every morning as well as walking round the square every night."

"He's a damn bad liar, poor old boy. Or is he a poor old boy? Is he not perhaps a naughty old boy? Blast! Why the devil couldn't he give us a nice straight cast-iron alibi? Poking his nose into Belgrave Square; can't tell us exactly when or exactly why or for exactly how long. What did the P.C. say?"

"Said he'd noticed nothing at all suspicious. Never mentioned the General. I'll have a word with Mr. P.C. Titheridge about this."

"The General is probably a stock piece if he walks round Belgrave Square every night," said Alleyn.

"Yes, but not at half-past two in the morning," objected Fox.

"Quite right, Fox, quite right. Titheridge must be blasted. What the devil was old Halcut-Hackett up to last night! We can't let it go, you know, because, after all, if he suspects——"

Alleyn broke off. He and Fox stood up as Mrs. Halcut-Hackett made her entrance.

Alleyn, of course, had met her before, on the day she came to his office with the story of Mrs. X and the blackmailing letters. He reflected now that in a sense she had started the whole miserable business. "If it hadn't been for this hard, wary, stupid woman's visit," he thought, "I shouldn't have asked Bunchy to poke his head into a death-trap. Oh, God!"

Mrs. Halcut-Hackett said: "Why, Inspector, they didn't tell me it was you. Now, do you know I never realised, that day I called about my poor friend's troubles, that I was speaking to Lady Alleyn's famous son."

Inwardly writhing under his blatant recognition of his

snob-value Alleyn shook hands and instantly introduced
Fox to whom Mrs. Halcut-Hackett was insufferably
cordial. They all sat down. Alleyn deliberately waited for
a moment or two before he spoke. He looked at Mrs.
Halcut-Hackett. He saw that under its thick patina of
cream and rouge her face was sagging from the bones of
her skull. He saw that her eyes and her hands were
frightened.

He said: "I think we may as well begin with that same
visit to the Yard. The business we talked about on that
occasion seems to be linked with the death of Lord
Robert Gospell."

She sat there, bolt upright in her expensive stays and
he knew she was terrified.

"But," she said, "that's absurd. No, honestly, Mr.
Alleyn, I just can't believe there could be any possible
connection. Why, my friend——"

"Mrs. Halcut-Hackett," said Alleyn, "I am afraid we
must abandon your friend."

She shot a horrified glance at Fox, and Alleyn
answered it.

"Mr. Fox is fully acquainted with the whole story,"
he said. "He agrees with me that your friend had better
dissolve. We realise that beyond all doubt you yourself
were the victim of these blackmailing letters. There is no
need for you to feel particularly distressed over this. It is
much better to tackle this sort of thing without the aid of
an imaginary Mrs. X. She makes for unnecessary
confusion. We now have the facts——"

"But—how do you——?"

Alleyn decided to take a risk. It was a grave risk.

"I have already spoken to Captain Withers," he said.

"My God, has Maurice confessed!"

Fox's notebook dropped to the floor.

Alleyn, still watching the gaping mouth with its wet
red margin, said: "Captain Withers has confessed
nothing." And he thought: "Does she realise the damage
she's done?"

"But I don't mean that," Mrs. Halcut-Hackett
gabbled. "I don't mean that. It's not that. You must be

crazy. He couldn't have done it." She clenched her hands and drummed with her fists on the arms of the chair. "What did he tell you?"

"Very little I'm afraid. Still we learned at least that it was not impossible——"

"You must be crazy to think he did it. I tell you he couldn't do it."

"He couldn't do what, Mrs. Halcut-Hackett?" asked Alleyn.

"The thing—Lord Robert . . ." She gaped horridly and then with a quick and vulgar gesture, covered her mouth with her ringed hand. Horrified intelligence looked out of her eyes.

"What did you think Captain Withers had confessed?"

"Nothing to do with this. Nothing that matters to anyone but me. I didn't mean a thing by it. You've trapped me. It's not fair."

"For your own sake," said Alleyn, "you would be wise to try and answer me. You say you did not mean to ask if Captain Withers had confessed to murder. Very well, I accept that for the moment. What might he have confessed? That he was the author of the letter your blackmailer had threatened to use. Is that it?"

"I won't answer. I won't say anything more. You're trying to trap me."

"What conclusion am I likely to draw from your refusal to answer? Believe me, you take a very grave risk if you refuse."

"Have you told my husband about the letters?"

"No. Nor shall I do so if it can be avoided. Come now." Alleyn deliberately drew all his power of concentration to a fine point. He saw his dominance drill like a sort of mental gimlet through her flabby resistance. "Come now. Captain Withers is the author of this letter. Isn't he?"

"Yes, but——"

"Did you think he had confessed as much?"

"Why, yes, but——"

"And you suppose Lord Robert Gospell to have been

the blackmailer? Ever since that afternoon when he sat behind you at the concert?"

"Then it was Robert Gospell!" Her head jerked back. She looked venomously triumphant.

"No," said Alleyn. "That was a mistake. Lord Robert was not a blackmailer."

"He was. I know he was. Do you think I didn't see him last night, watching us. Why did he ask me about Maurice? Why did Maurice warn me against him?"

"Did Captain Withers suggest that Lord Robert was a blackmailer?" In spite of himself a kind of cold disgust deadened Alleyn's voice. She must have heard it because she cried out:

"Why do you speak of him like that? Of Captain Withers, I mean. You've no right to insult him."

"My God, this is a stupid woman," thought Alleyn. Aloud he said: "Have I insulted him? If so I have gone very far beyond my duty. Mrs. Halcut-Hackett, when did you first miss this letter?"

"About six months ago. After my charade party in the little season."

"Where did you keep it?"

"In a trinket-box on my dressing-table."

"A locked box?"

"Yes. But the key was sometimes left with others in the drawer of the dressing-table."

"Did you suspect your maid?"

"No. I can't suspect her. She has been with me for fifteen years. She's my old dresser. I know she wouldn't do it."

"Have you any idea who could have taken it?"

"I can't think, except that for my charade party I turned my room into a buffet, and the men moved everything round."

"What men?"

"The caterer's men. Dimitri. But Dimitri superintended them the whole time. I don't believe they had an opportunity."

"I see," said Alleyn.

He saw she now watched him with a different kind of

awareness. Alleyn had interviewed a great number of Mrs. Halcut-Hacketts in his day. He knew very well that with such women he carried a weapon that he was loath to use, but which nevertheless fought for him. This was the weapon of his sex. He saw with violent distaste that some taint of pleasure threaded her fear of him. And the inexorable logic of thought presented him to himself, side by side with her lover.

He said: "Suppose we get the position clear. In your own interest I may tell you that we have already gathered a great deal of information. Lord Robert was helping us on the blackmail case, and he has left us his notes. From them and from our subsequent enquiries we have pieced this much together. In your own case Captain Withers was the subject of the blackmailing letters. Following our advice you carried out the blackmailer's instructions and left your bag in the corner of the sofa at the Constance Street Hall. It was taken. Because Lord Robert deliberately sat next to you and because Captain Withers had, as you put it, warned you against him, you came to the conclusion that Lord Robert took the bag and was therefore your blackmailer. Why did you not report to the police the circumstances of the affair at the concert? You had agreed to do so. Were you advised to let the case drop as far as the Yard was concerned?"

"Yes."

"By Captain Withers? I see. That brings us to last night. You say you noticed that Lord Robert watched you both during the ball. I must ask you again if Captain Withers agrees with your theory that Lord Robert was a blackmailer."

"He—he simply warned me against Lord Robert."

"In view of these letters and the sums of money the blackmailer demanded, did you think it advisable to keep up your friendship with Captain Withers?"

"We—there was nothing anybody could—I mean ——"

"What do you mean?" asked Alleyn sternly.

She wetted her lips. Again he saw that look of

subservience and thought that of all traits in an ageing
woman this was the unloveliest and most pitiable.

She said: "Our friendship is partly a business
relationship."

"A business relationship?" Alleyn repeated the words
blankly.

"Yes. You see Maurice—Captain Withers—has very
kindly offered to advise me and—I mean right now
Captain Withers has in mind a little business venture in
which I am interested, and I naturally require to talk
things over so—you see——?"

"Yes," said Alleyn gently, "I do see. This venture of
Captain Withers is of course the club at Leatherhead,
isn't it?"

"Why, yes, but——"

"Now then," said Alleyn quickly, "about last night.
Lord Robert offered to see you home, didn't he? You
refused or avoided giving an answer. Did you go home
alone?"

She might as well have asked him how much he knew,
so clearly did he read the question in her eyes. He
thanked his stars that he had made such a fuss over
Withers's telephone. Evidently Withers had not rung her
up to warn her what to say. Frightened his call would be
tapped, thought Alleyn with satisfaction, and decided to
risk a further assumption. He said:

"You saw Captain Withers again after the ball, didn't
you?"

"What makes you think that?"

"I have every reason to believe it. Captain Withers's
car was parked in a side street off Belgrave Square. How
long did you sit there waiting for him?"

"I don't admit I sat there."

"Then if Captain Withers tells me he took a partner
to the Matador last night after the ball I am to conclude
that it was not you?"

"Captain Withers would want to protect me. He's
very, very thoughtful."

"Can you not understand," said Alleyn, "that it is
greatly to your advantage and his, if you can prove that

you both got into his car and drove to the Matador last night?"

"Why? I don't want it said that——"

"Mrs. Halcut-Hackett," said Alleyn: "Do you want an alibi for yourself and Captain Withers or don't you?"

She opened her mouth once or twice like a gaping fish, looked wildly at Fox and burst into tears.

Fox got up, walked to the far end of the room, and stared with heavy tact at the second print of the Nightcap series. Alleyn waited while scarlet claws scuffled in an elaborate handbag. Out came a long piece of monogrammed tulle. She jerked at it violently.

Something clattered to the floor. Alleyn darted forward and picked it up.

It was a gold cigarette-case with a medallion set in the lid and surrounded by brilliants.

20

Rose Birnbaum

Mrs. Halcut-Hackett dabbed at the pouches under her eyes as if her handkerchief was made of blotting-paper.

"You frighten me," she said. "You frighten me so. I'm just terrified."

Alleyn turned the cigarette-case over in his long hands.

"But there is no need to be terrified, none at all. Don't you see that if you can give me proof that you and Captain Withers motored straight from Marsdon House to the Matador, it clears you at once from any hint of complicity in Lord Robert's death?"

He waited. She began to rock backwards and forwards, beating her hands together and moving her head from side to side like a well-preserved automaton.

"I can't. I just can't. I won't say anything more. I just won't say another thing. It's no good. I won't say another thing."

"Very well," said Alleyn, not too unkindly. "Don't try. I'll get at it another way. This is a very magnificent case. The medallion is an old one. Italian Renaissance, I should think. It's most exquisitely worked. It might almost be Benvenuto himself who formed those minute scrolls. Do you know its history?"

"No. Maurice picked it up somewhere and had it put on the case. I'm crazy about old things," said Mrs. Halcut-Hackett with a dry sob. "Crazy about them."

Alleyn opened the lid. An inscription inside read "E. from M.W." He shut the case but did not return it to her.

"Don't lose it, Mrs. Halcut-Hackett. The medal is a collector's piece. Aren't you afraid to carry it about with you?"

She seemed to take heart of grace at his interest. She dabbed again at her eyes and said: "I'm just terribly careless with my things. Perhaps I ought not to use it. Only last night I left it lying about."

"Did you? Where?"

She looked terrified again the moment he asked her a question.

"Some place at the ball," she said.

"Was it in the green sitting-room on the top landing?"

"I—yes—I think maybe it was."

"At what time?"

"I don't know."

"During the supper hour didn't you sit in that room with Captain Withers?"

"Yes. Why not? Why shouldn't I?" She twisted the handkerchief round her hands and said: "How do you know that? My husband—I'm not—*he's not having me watched?*"

"I don't for a moment suppose so. I simply happened to know that you sat in this room some time just before one o'clock. You tell me you left your cigarette-case there. Now when you came out of that room what did you do?"

"I went into the cloakroom to tidy. I missed the case when I opened my bag in the cloakroom."

"Right. Now as you went from the green sitting-room to the cloakroom two doors away, did you happen to notice Lord Robert on the landing? Please don't think I am trying to entrap you. I simply want to know if you saw him."

"He was coming upstairs," she said. Her voice and manner were more controlled now.

"Good. Did you hear the dialling sound on the telephone extension while you were in the cloakroom?"

"Yes. Now you remind me I did hear it."

"When you came out of the cloakroom did you go back for your case?"

"No. No, I didn't."

"Why not?"

"Why? Because I forgot."

"You forget it again!"

"I didn't just forget but I went to the head of the stairs and Maurice was in the other sitting-out room at the stair-head, waiting for me. I went in there, and then I remembered my case and he got it for me."

"Had the telephone rung off?" asked Alleyn.

"I don't know."

"Was anyone else on the landing?"

"I guess not."

"Not by any chance, a short rather inconspicuous lady sitting alone?"

"No. There wasn't anybody on the landing. Donald Potter was in the sitting-room."

"Was Captain Withers long fetching your case?"

"I don't think so," she said nervously. "I don't remember. I talked to Donald. Then we all went downstairs."

"Captain Withers did not say whether there was anyone else in the telephone-room when he got the cigarette-case?"

"No, he didn't say anything about it."

"Will you be very kind and let me keep this case for twenty-four hours?"

"Why? Why do you want it?"

Alleyn hesitated and at last he said: "I want to see if anybody else recognises it. Will you trust me with it?"

"Very well," she said. "I can't refuse, can I?"

"I'll take great care of it," said Alleyn. He dropped it in his pocket and turned to Fox who had remained at the far end of the room. Fox's notebook was open in his hand.

"I think that's all, isn't it?" asked Alleyn. "Have I missed anything, Fox?"

"I don't fancy so, sir."

"Then we'll bother you no longer, Mrs. Halcut-Hackett," said Alleyn, standing before her. She rose from her chair. He saw that there was a sort of question in her eyes. "Is there anything you would like to add to what you have said?" he asked.

"No. No. But you said a little while ago that you would find out about what you asked me before. You said you'd trace it another way."

"Oh," said Alleyn cheerfully, "you mean whether you went from Marsdon House to the Matador in Captain Withers's car, and if so, how long it took. Yes, we'll ask the commissionaire and the man in the office at the Matador. They may be able to help."

"My God, you mustn't do that!"

"Why not?"

"You can't do that. For God's sake say you won't. For God's sake . . ."

Her voice rose to a stifled, hysterical scream, ending in a sort of gasp. Fox sighed heavily and gave Alleyn a look of patient endurance. Mrs. Halcut-Hackett drew breath. The door opened.

A plain girl, dressed to go out, walked into the room.

"Oh, I'm sorry," she said, "I didn't know——"

Mrs. Halcut-Hackett stared round her with the air of a trapped mastodon and finally blundered from the room as fast as her French heels would carry her.

The door slammed behind her.

The plain girl, who was most beautifully curled, painted and dressed, looked from Alleyn to Fox.

"I'm so sorry," she repeated nervously. "I'm afraid I shouldn't have come in. Ought I to go and see if there's anything I can do?"

"If I were you," said Alleyn, "I don't think I should.

Mrs. Halcut-Hackett is very much distressed over last night's tragedy and I expect she would rather be alone. Are you Miss Birnbaum?"

"Yes, I am. You're detectives, aren't you?"

"That's us. My name is Alleyn and this is Mr. Fox."

"Oh, how d'you do?" said Miss Birnbaum hurriedly. She hesitated and then gave them her hand. She looked doubtfully into Alleyn's face. He felt the chilly little fingers tighten their grip like those of a frightened child.

"I expect you've found it rather upsetting too, haven't you?"

"Yes," she said dutifully. "It's dreadful, isn't it?" She twisted her fingers together. "Lord Robert was very kind, wasn't he? He was very kind to me."

"I hope your toothache's better," said Alleyn.

She looked at her hands and then up into his face.

"I didn't have toothache," she said.

"No?"

"No. I just wanted to go home. I *hate* coming out," added Miss Birnbaum with extraordinary vigour. "I knew I would and I do."

"That's bad luck. Why do you do it?"

"Because," said Miss Birnbaum with devastating frankness, "my mother paid Mrs. Hackett, I mean Mrs. Halcut-Hackett, five hundred pounds to bring me out."

"Hi!" said Alleyn, "aren't you talking out of school?"

"You won't tell anybody I said that, will you? I've never breathed a word about it before. Not to a single soul. But you look my kind of person. And I'm absolutely fed up. I'm simply not the social kind. Golly, what a relief to get that off my chest!"

"What would you like to do?"

"I want to be an art student. My grandfather was a painter, Joseph Birnbaum. Have you ever heard of him?"

"I think I have. Didn't he paint a thing called 'Jewish Sabbath'?"

"That's right. He was a Jew, of course. I'm a Jewess. My mother isn't, but I am. That's another thing I'm not supposed to say. I'm only sixteen. Would you have thought I was older?"

"I think I should."

"That," said Miss Birnbaum, "is because I'm a Jewess. They mature very quickly, you know. Well, I suppose I mustn't keep you."

"I should like to keep *you* for a minute, if I may."

"That's all right then," said Miss Birnbaum and sat down. "I suppose Mrs. Halcut-Hackett won't come back, will she?"

"I don't think so."

"I don't mind so much about the General. He's stupid, of course, but he's quite kind. But I'm *terrified* of Mrs. Halcut-Hackett. I'm such a failure and she hates it."

"Are you sure you're such a failure?"

"Oh, yes. Last night, only four people asked me to dance. Lord Robert, when I first got there, and a fat man, and the General, and Sir Herbert Carrados."

She looked away for a moment and her lips trembled.

"I tried to pretend I had a soul above social success," she said, "but I haven't at all. I minded awfully. If I could paint and get out of it all it wouldn't matter, but when you're in a thing it's beastly to be a failure. So I got toothache. I must say it *is* queer me saying all this to you."

"The General took you home, didn't he?"

"Yes. He *was* kind. He got Mrs. Halcut-Hackett's maid whom I hate worse than poison, to give me oil of cloves and Ovaltine. *She* knew all right."

"Did you go to sleep?"

"No. I tried to think of a way to write to mother so that she would let me give it up. And then everything began to go through and through my head. I tried to think of other things but all the failure-parties kept coming up."

"Did you hear the others return?"

"I heard Mrs. Halcut-Hackett come in. It was frightfully late. She goes past my door to her room and she's got diamante shoe buckles that make a clicking noise with every step. I had heard the clock strike four. Did the General go back to the dance?"

"He went out again, I think."

"Well then it must have been the General I heard come along the passage at a quarter past three. Just after. I heard every clock chime from one till six. Then I fell asleep. It was quite light then."

"Yes."

Alleyn took a turn up and down the room.

"Have you met Agatha Troy?" he asked.

"The painter? She was there last night. I wanted awfully for someone to introduce us but I didn't like to ask. I think she's the best living English painter, don't you?"

"Yes, I believe I do. She teaches, you know."

"Does she? Only geniuses, I suppose."

"I think only students who have gone a certain distance."

"If I were allowed to go a certain distance first, I wonder if she would ever have me."

"Do you think you would be good?" asked Alleyn.

"I'm sure I would be able to draw. I'm not so sure of paint. I see everything in line. I say."

"Hallo?"

"D'you think this will make any difference to the coming-out game? Is she going to be ill? I've thought so lots of times lately. She's so bloody-minded."

"Don't say 'she' and don't say 'bloody-minded.' The one's common and you're too young for the other."

Miss Birnbaum grinned delightedly.

"Well," she said, "it's what I think anyway. And she's not even virtuous. Do you know the Withers person?"

"Yes."

"He's her boy-friend. Don't pretend to be shocked. I wrote and told mother about it. I hoped it'd shake her a bit. My father wrote and asked me if he was called Maurice and was like a red pig—that's a frightful insult, you know—because if he was I wasn't to stay. I like my father. But mother said if he was a friend of Mrs.

Halcut-Hackett he must be all right. I thought that frightfully funny. It's about the only thing that is at all funny in the whole business. I don't think it can be very amusing to be frightened of your boy-friend and your husband, do you?"

Alleyn rubbed his head and stared at Miss Birnbaum.

"Look here," he said, "you're giving us a good deal of information, you know. There's Mr. Fox with his notebook. What about that?"

The dark face was lit with an inward smouldering fire. Two sharp lines appeared at the corners of the thick lips.

"Do you mean she may get into trouble? I hope she does. I hate her. She's a wicked woman. She'd murder anyone if she wanted them out of the way. She's felt like murdering me pretty often. She says things to me that twist me up inside, they hurt so. 'My dear child, how can you expect me to do anything with you if you stare like a fish and never utter.' 'My God. what have I done to be saddled with a burden like this?' 'My dear child, I suppose you can't help looking what you are, but at least you might make some effort to sound a little less like Soho.' And then she imitates my voice. Yesterday she told me there was a good deal to be said for the German point of view, and asked me if I had any relations among the refugees because she heard quite a number of English people were taking them as maids. I hope she is a murderess. I hope you catch her. I hope they hang her by her beastly old neck until she's dead."

The thick soft voice stopped. Miss Birnbaum was trembling very slightly. A thin line of damp appeared above her upper lip.

Alleyn grimaced, rubbed his nose and said:

"Do you feel any better for that?"

"Yes."

"Vindictive little devil! Can't you get on top of it all and see it as something intensely disagreeable that won't last for ever? Have you tried drawing as a counter-irritant?"

"I've done a caricature of Her. When I get away from

here I'll send it to her if she's not in gaol by that time."

"Do you know Sarah Alleyn?"

"She's one of the successes. Yes, I know her."

"Do you like her?"

"She's not bad. She actually remembers who I am when she sees me."

Alleyn decided to abandon his niece for the moment.

"Well," he said, "I dare say you're nearer to escape than you imagine. I'll be off now. I hope we meet again."

"So do I. I suppose you think I'm pretty ghastly."

"That's right. Make up your mind everybody hates you and you'll always be happy."

Miss Birnbaum grinned.

"Think you're clever," she said, "don't you? Good-bye."

They shook hands in a friendly manner, and she saw them out into the hall. Alleyn had a last glimpse of her standing stocky, dark, and truculent against a background of restrained and decorous half-tones and beautiful pseudo-Empire curtains.

21

Statement by Lucy Lorrimer

It was nearly six o'clock in the evening when Alleyn and Fox returned to Scotland Yard. They went to Alleyn's room. Fox got to work on his notes, Alleyn tackled the reports that had come in while they were away. They both lit pipes and between them was established that pleasant feeling of unexpressed intimacy that comes to two people working in silence at the same job.

Presently Alleyn put down the reports and looked across at his friend. He thought: "How often we have sat like this, Fox and I, working like a couple of obscure clerks in the offices of the Last Judgment concern, filing and correlating the misdeeds of men. Fox is getting quite grizzled and there are elderly purple veins in his cheeks. I shall go home later on, a solitary fellow, to my own hole." And into his thoughts came the image of a woman who sat in a tall blue chair by his fire, but that was too domestic a picture. Rather, she would sit on the hearth-rug. Her hands would be stained with charcoal and they would sweep beautiful lines across a white surface. When he came in she would look up from her drawing and Troy's eyes would smile or scowl. He jerked the image away and found that Fox was looking at him wth his usual air of bland expectancy.

"Finished?" asked Alleyn.

"Yes, sir. I've been trying to sort things out. There's the report on the silver cleaning. Young Carewe took that on and he seems to have made a fair job of it. Got himself up as a Rat and Mice Destruction Officer and went round all the houses and palled up with the servants. All the Carrados silver was cleaned this morning including Sir Herbert's cigar-case which isn't the right shape anyway, because he saw it in the butler's pantry. Sir Daniel's man does his silver cleaning on Mondays and Fridays so it was all cleaned up yesterday. Francois does Dimitri's stuff every day or says he does. Young Potter and Withers are looked after by the flat service and only their table silver is kept polished. The Halcut-Hacketts' cases are cleaned once a week—Fridays—and rubbed up every morning. That's that. How's the report from Bailey?"

"Bailey hasn't much. There's nothing in the taxi. He got Withers's prints from my cigarette-case but, as we expected, the green sitting-room was simply a mess. He *has* found Withers's and young Potter's prints on the pages of Taylor's *Medical Jurisprudence*. The pages that refer to asphyxiation."

"By gum, that's something."

"Not such a great deal, Fox. They will tell us that when the newspaper report came out they were interested and turned up Taylor on suffocation; and who is to call them liars? The man who went to Leatherhead had a success. Apparently Withers keeps a married couple there. Our man pitched a yarn that he had been sent by the borough to inspect the electrical wiring in the house, and got in. What's more he seems to have had a good look round. He found a roulette wheel and had the intelligence to examine it pretty closely. The middle dozen slots had been very slightly opened. I expect the idea is that Master Donald or some other satellite of

Withers should back the middle dozen. The wheel seems brand new. There was an older one that showed no signs of irregularity. There were also several packs of cards which had been lightly treated with the favourite pumice-stone. Luckily for us the married couple had had a violent row with the gallant Captain and were prepared to talk. I think we've got enough to pull him in on a gambling-hell charge. Thompson reports that Withers has stayed in all day. The telephone was disconnected as soon as we left. Donald Potter's clothes were returned to him by taxi. Nobody has visited Withers. Dimitri comes next. Dimitri went home after he left here, visiting a chemist on the way to get his hand bandaged. He, too, has remained indoors, and has made no telephone calls. Most exemplary behaviour. How the blazes are we going to get any of these victims to charge Dimitri?"

"You're asking me!" said Fox.

"Yes. Not a hope in a hundred. Well now, Fox, I've been over this damnable, dreary, involved, addling business of the green sitting-room. It boils down to this. The people who could have overheard Lord Robert's telephone conversation were Withers, Sir Herbert Carrados, Miss Harris, Mrs. Halcut-Hackett, and Donald. They were all on or about the top landing and wouldn't have to lie particularly freely in avoiding any reference to a brief dart in and out of the telephone-room. But, but, but, and a blasted but it is, it is quite possible that while Lord Robert telephoned, someone came upstairs and walked into the telephone-room. Mrs. Halcut-Hackett was in the cloak-room; Withers, Donald, and Carrados, in the other sitting-room, Miss Harris in the lavatory. Dimitri says he was downstairs but who the devil's to prove it? If the others are speaking the truth, anybody might have come up and gone down again unseen."

"The gentleman who burst into the lavatory?"

"Precisely. He may even have hidden in there till the coast was clear though I can't see why. There's nothing particularly fishy in coming out of a sitting-room."

"Ugh," said Fox.

"As I see the case now, Fox, it presents one or two highlights. Most of them seem to be concentrated on cigarette-cases. Two cigarette-cases. The murderer's and Mrs. Halcut-Hackett's."

"Yes," said Fox.

"After the cigarette-cases comes the lost letter. The letter written by Paddy O'Brien's friend in Australia. The letter that somebody seems to have stolen eighteen years ago in Buckinghamshire. It's odd, isn't it, that Miss Harris's uncle was sometime rector of Falconbridge, the village where Paddy O'Brien met with his accident? I wonder if either Miss Harris or Lady Carrados realises there is this vague connection. I think our next move after the inquest is to go down to Barbicon-Bramley where we may disturb the retirement of Miss Harris's uncle. Then we'll have to dive into the past history of the hospital in Falconbridge. But what a cold trail. A chance in a thousand."

"It's a bit of a coincidence Miss Harris linking up in this way, isn't it?" ruminated Fox.

"Are you building up a picture with Miss Harris as the agent of an infamous old parson who has treasured a compromising letter for eighteen years, and now uses it? Well, I suppose it's not so impossible. But I don't regard it as a *very* great coincidence that Miss Harris had drifted into Lady Carrados's household. Coincidences become increasingly surprising as they gain in importance. One can imagine someone telling Miss Harris about Paddy O'Brien's accident and Miss Harris saying the parson at Falconbridge was her uncle. Everybody exclaims tiresomely at the smallness of the world and nobody thinks much more of it. Mix a missing letter up in the story and we instantly incline to regard Miss Harris's remote connection with Falconbridge as a perfectly astonishing coincidence."

"She'd hardly have mentioned it so freely," admitted Fox, "if she'd had anything to do with the letter."

"Exactly. Still, we'll have to follow it up. And, talking of following things up, Fox, there's Lady Lorrimer.

We'll have to check Sir Daniel Davidson's account of himself."

"That's right, sir."

Fox unhooked his spectacles and put them in their case.

"On what we've got," he asked, "have you any particular leaning to anyone?"

"Yes. I've left it until we had a moment's respite to discuss it with you. I wanted to see if you'd arrived independently at the same conclusion yourself."

"The cigarette-case and the telephone call."

"Yes. Very well, Fox: 'in a contemplative fashion and a tranquil frame of mind,' let us discuss the cigarette-cases. Point one."

They discussed the cigarette-cases.

At seven o'clock Fox said:

"We're not within sight of making an arrest. Not on that evidence."

Alleyn said: "And don't forget we haven't found the cloak and hat."

Fox said: "It seems to me, Mr. Alleyn, we'll have to ask every blasted soul that hasn't got an alibi if we can search their house. Clumsy."

"Carrados," began Alleyn, "Halcut-Hackett, Davidson, Miss Harris. Withers and Potter go together. I swear the hat and cloak aren't in the flat. Same goes for Dimitri."

"The garbage-tins," said Fox gloomily. "I've told the chaps about the garbage-tins. They're so unlikely they're enough to make you cry. What would anybody do with a cloak and hat, Mr. Alleyn, if they wanted to get rid of 'em? We know all the old dodges. You couldn't burn 'em in any of these London flats. It was low tide, as you've pointed out, and they'd have had to be dropped off the bridge which would have been a pretty risky thing to do. D'you reckon they'll try leaving 'em at a railway office?"

"We'll have to watch for it. We'll have to keep a good man to tail our fancy. I don't somehow feel it'll be a left-luggage affair, Br'er Fox. They've been given a little too

much publicity of late years. Limbs and torsos have
bobbed up in corded boxes with dreary insistence, not
only up and down the L.N.E.R. and kindred offices, but
throughout the pages of detective fiction. I rather fancy
the parcels post myself. I've sent out the usual request.
If they were posted it was probably during the rush hour
at one of the big central offices, and how the suffering
cats we're to catch up with that is more than I can tell.
Still, we'll hope for a lucky break, whatever that may
be."

The desk telephone rang. Alleyn, suddenly and
painfully reminded of Lord Robert's call, answered it.

His mother's voice asked if he would dine with her.

"I don't suppose you can get away, my dear, but as
this flat is only five minutes in a taxi it might suit you to
come in."

"I'd like to," said Alleyn. "When?"

"Eight, but we can have it earlier if you like. I'm all
alone."

"I'll come now, mama, and we'll have it at eight. All
right?"

"Quite all right," said the clear little voice. "So glad,
darling."

Alleyn left his mother's telephone number in case
anybody should want him, and went by taxi to the flat
she had taken in Catherine Street for the London
season. He found Lady Alleyn surrounded by news-
papers and wearing horn-rimmed glasses.

"Hullo, darling," she said. "I shan't pretend I'm not
reading about poor Bunchy, but we won't discuss it if
you don't want to."

"To tell you the truth," said Alleyn, "I rather feel I
want to sit in an armchair, stare at nothing, and scarcely
speak. Charming company for you, mama."

"Why not have a bath?" suggested Lady Alleyn
without looking up from her paper.

"Do I smell?" asked her son.

"No. But I always think a bath is rather a good idea
when you've got to the staring stage. What time did you
get up this morning?"

"*Yesterday* morning. But I have bathed and shaved since then."

"No bed at all last night? I should have a bath. I'll run it for you. Use my room. I've sent for a change of clothes."

"Good Lord!" said Alleyn, and then: "You're something rather special in the maternal line, aren't you?"

He bathed. The solace of steaming water wrapped him in a sort of luxurious trance. His thoughts, that for sixteen hours had been so sharply concentrated, became blurred and nebulous. Was it only "this morning" that he had crossed the courtyard to a taxi, half hidden by wreaths of mist? This morning! Their footsteps had sounded hollow on the stone pavement. "I got to look after meself, see?" A door opened with a huge slow movement that was full of horror. "Dead, ain't 'e? *Dead, ain't 'e?* DEAD, AIN'T 'E?" "Suffocated!" gasped Alleyn and woke with his nose full of bath-water.

His man had sent clean linen and a dinner-suit. He dressed slowly, feeling rarefied, and rejoined his mother in the sitting-room.

"Help yourself to a drink," she said from behind her newspaper.

He got his drink and sat down. He wondered vaguely why he should feel so dog-tired. He was used to missing a night's sleep and working straight through the twenty-four hours. It must be because it was Bunchy. And the thought came into his mind that there must be a great many people at this hour who with him remembered that comic figure and regretted it.

"He had a great deal of charm," said Alleyn aloud and his mother's voice answered him tranquilly.

"Yes, a great deal of charm. The most unfair of all the attributes."

"You don't add: 'I sometimes think,' " said Alleyn.

"Why should I?"

"People so often use that phrase to water down their ideas. You are too positive to use it."

"In Bunchy's case the charm was one of character

and then it is not unfair," said Lady Alleyn. "Shall we dine? It's been announced."

"Good Lord," said Alleyn, "I never noticed."

Over their coffee he asked: "Where's Sarah?"

"She's dining and going to a play with a suitably chaperoned party."

"Does she see anything of Rose Birnbaum?"

"My dear Roderick, who on earth is Rose Birnbaum?"

"She's Mrs. Halcut-Hackett's burden for the season. Her professional burden."

"Oh, that gel! Poor little thing, yes. I've noticed her. I don't know if Sarah pays much attention. Why?"

"I wish you'd ask her here some time. Not a seasonable party. She's got an inferiority complex about them. She's one of the more unfortunate by-products of the season."

"I see. I wonder why that singularly hard woman has involved herself with a paying protégée. Are the Halcut-Hacketts short of money?"

"I don't know. I should think she might be at the moment."

"Withers," said Lady Alleyn.

"Hullo. You know all about Withers, do you?"

"My dear Rory, you forget I sit in chaperones' corner."

"Gossip," said Alleyn.

"The gossip is not as malicious as you may think. I always maintain that men are just as avid scandalmongers as women."

"I know you do."

"Mrs. Halcut-Hackett is not very popular, so they don't mind talking about her in chaperones' corner. She's an opportunist. She never gives an invitation that will not bring its reward and she never accepts one that is likely to lower her prestige. She is not a kind woman. She's extremely common, but that doesn't matter. Lots of common people are charming. Like bounders. I believe no woman ever falls passionately in love with a man unless he has just the least touch of the bounder somewhere in his composition."

"Really, mama!"

"I mean in a very rarefied sense. A touch of arrogance. There's nothing like it, my dear. If you're too delicately considerate of a woman's feelings she may begin by being grateful, but the chances are she'll end by despising you."

Alleyn made a wry face. "Treat 'em rough?"

"Not actually, but let them think you *might*. It's humiliating but true that ninety-nine women out of a hundred like to feel their lover is capable of bullying them. Eighty of them would deny it. How often does one not hear a married woman say with a sort of satisfaction that her husband won't let her do this or that? Why do abominably written books with strong silent heroes still find a large female public? What do you suppose attracts thousands of women to a cinema actor with the brains of a mosquito?"

"His ability as a cinema actor."

"That, yes. Don't be tiresome, Roderick. Above all, his arrogant masculinity. That's what attracts ninety-nine out of a hundred, you may depend upon it."

"There is, perhaps unfortunately, always the hundredth woman."

"And don't be too sure of her. I am *not,* I hope, one of those abominable women who cries down her own sex. I'm by way of being a feminist, but I refuse to allow the ninety-nine (dear me this begins to sound like a hymn) to pull the wool over my elderly eyes."

"You're an opinionated little party, mama, and you know it. But don't suppose you can pull the wool over my eyes either. Do you suggest that I go to Miss Agatha Troy, hale her about her studio by her hair, tuck her under my arrogant masculine arm, and lug her off to the nearest registry office?"

"Church, if you please. The Church knows what I'm talking about. Look at the marriage service. A direct and embarrassing expression of the savagery inherent in our ideas of mating."

"Would you say the Season came under the same heading?"

"In a way I would say so. And why not? As long as one recognises the more savage aspects of the Season, one keeps one's sense of proportion and enjoys it. As I do. Thoroughly. And as Bunchy Gospell did. When I think of him," said Lady Alleyn, her eyes shining with tears, "when I think of him this morning, gossiping away to all of us, so pleased with Evelyn's ball, so gay and—and *real,* I simply cannot realise——"

"I know."

"I suppose Mrs. Halcut-Hackett comes into the picture, doesn't she? And Withers?"

"What makes you think so?"

"He had his eye on them. Both there and at the Halcut-Hackett's cocktail-party. Bunchy knew something about Captain Withers, Roderick. I saw that and I remarked on it to him. He told me not to be inquisitive, bless him, but he admitted I was right. Is there anything more in it than that?"

"A good deal. Withers has a bad record and Bunchy knew it."

"Is that a motive for murder?" asked Lady Alleyn.

"It might be. There are several discrepancies. I've got to try and settle one of them to-night."

"To-night? My dear, you'll fall asleep with the customary warning on your lips."

"Not I. And I'm afraid there's no occasion as yet for the customary warning."

"Does Evelyn Carrados come into the picture at all?" Alleyn sat up.

"Why do you ask that?"

"Because I could see that Bunchy had his eye on her too."

"We'd better change jobs, darling. You can go into the Yard and watch people having their eyes on each other and I'll sit in chaperones' corner, pounce at young men for Sarah, and make conversation with Lady Lorrimer. I've got to see her some time soon, by the way."

"Lucy Lorrimer! You don't mean to tell me she's in this business. I can well understand somebody murdering *her* but I don't see her on the other side of the picture. Of course she is mad."

"She's got to supply half an alibi for Sir Daniel Davidson."

"Good heavens, who next! Why Davidson?"

"Because he was the last man to leave before Bunchy."

"Well, I hope it's not Sir Daniel. I was thinking of showing him my leg. Roderick, I suppose I can't help you with Lucy Lorrimer. I can easily ring her up and ask her to tea. She must be seething with excitement and longing to talk to everybody. Bunchy was to dine with her to-night."

"Why?"

"For no particular reason. But she kept saying she knew he wouldn't come, that he'd forget. I can easily ring her up and she shouts so loudly you need only sit beside me to hear every word."

"All right," said Alleyn, "let's try. Ask her if she saw anything of Bunchy as she was leaving."

"You sit in the chair here, darling, and I'll perch on the arm. We can have the receiver between us."

Lady Lorrimer's telephone was persistently engaged but at last they got through. Her ladyship, said a voice, was at home.

"Will you say it's Lady Alleyn. Thank you."

During the pause that followed Lady Alleyn eyed her son with a conspiratorial air and asked him to give her a cigarette. He did so and provided himself with pencil and paper.

"We'll be *ages*," she whispered, waving the receiver to and fro rather as if it were a fan. Suddenly it emitted a loud cracking sound and Lady Alleyn raised it gingerly to within four inches of her right ear.

"Is that you, Lucy?"

"My *dear!*" shouted the receiver, "I'm *so* glad. I've been *longing* to speak to you for of course you can tell us *everything*. I've always thought it was *such* a pity that

goodlooking son of yours turning himself into a
policeman because, say what you will, it must be
frightfully bad for them so long in the one position only
moving their arms and the internal organs taking *all* the
strain which Sir Daniel tells me is the cause of half the
diseases of woman, though I must own I think his
practice is getting rather beyond him. Of course in the
case of the Prime Minister everything must be excused."

Lady Alleyn looked an enquiry at her son who
nodded his comprehension of this amazing paradiddle.

"Yes, Lucy?" murmured Lady Alleyn.

"Which brings me to this *frightful* calamity,"
continued the telephone in a series of cracks and
splutters. *"Too* awful! And you know he was to dine
with me to-night. I put my other guest off because I felt
I could never accustom myself to the idea that there but
for the Grace of God sat Bunchy Gospell. Not perhaps
the Grace of God but His ways are inscrutable indeed
and when I saw him come down the staircase humming
to himself I little thought that he was going to his grave.
I shall *never* forgive myself, of course, that I did not
offer to drive him and as it turned out with the Prime
Minister being so ill I might have done so."

"Why do you keep introducing the Prime Minister
into this story, Lucy?" asked Lady Alleyn. She clapped
her hand over the mouthpiece and said crossly: "But I
want to know, Roderick."

"It's all right," said Alleyn. "Davidson pretended
—do listen, darling, she's telling you."

"—I can't describe the agony. Helena," quacked the
telephone, "I really thought I should *swoon* with it. I felt
Sir Daniel must examine me without losing a moment,
so I told my chauffeur to look out for him because I
promise you *I* was too ill to distinguish one man from
another. Then I saw him coming out of the door. 'Sir
Daniel, Sir Daniel!' He did not hear me and all would
have been lost if one of the linkmen had not seen my
distress and drawn Sir Daniel's attention to me. He
crossed the street and as a very old patient I don't mind
admitting to you, Helena, I *was* rather *disappointed* but

of course with the country in the state it is one must make sacrifices. He was extremely agitated. The Prime Minister had developed some terrible complaint. Please tell nobody of this, Helena. I know you are as silent as the grave but Sir Daniel would no doubt be gravely compromised if it were ever to leak out. Under those conditions I could do nothing but bear my cross in silence and it was not until he had positively *run* away that I thought of driving him to Downing Street. By the time my fool of a chauffeur had started the car, of course, it was too late. No doubt Sir Daniel had raced to the nearest taxicab and although I have rung up to enquire tactfully, he is continually engaged, so that one fears the worst."

"Mad!" said Lady Alleyn to her son.

"—I can't tell you how much it has upset me but I hope I know my duty, Helena, and having just recollected that your boy was a constable I said to myself that he should learn of this extraordinary man whom I am firmly persuaded is an assassin. What other explanation can there be?"

"Sir Daniel Davidson!" exclaimed Lady Alleyn.

"Good heavens, Helena, are you mad! For pity's sake tell your son to come and see me himself in order that there may be no mistake. How could it be my poor Sir Daniel, who was already on his way to Downing Street? I attribute my appalling condition at this moment to the shock I received. Do you remember a play called *The Face at the Window*? I was reminded of it. I assure you I screamed aloud—my chauffeur will bear witness. The nose was flat and white and the moustache quite frightful, like some hairy monster gummed to the window-pane. The eyes rolled. I could do nothing but clutch my pearls. 'Go away!' I screamed. My chauffeur, fool that he is, had seen nothing and by the time he roused himself it had disappeared."

Alleyn held a sheet of paper before his mother's nose. On it he had written: "Ask her who it was."

"Have you any idea who it was, Lucy?" asked Lady Alleyn.

"There is no doubt whatsoever in my mind, Helena, and I should have thought little in yours. These appalling cases that have occurred! The papers are full of them. The Peeping Tom of Peckham, though how he has managed to go there every night from Halkyn Street——"

Alleyn gave a stifled exclamation.

"From Halkyn Street?" repeated Lady Alleyn.

"There is no doubt that his wife's appalling behaviour has turned his head. He suspected poor Robert Gospell. You must have heard, as I did, how he asked her to let him take her home. No doubt he was searching for them. The jury will bring in a strong recommendation for mercy or perhaps they will find him guilty but insane, as no doubt he is."

"But Lucy! Lucy, listen. *Who are you talking about?*"

"Don't be a fool, Helena, who should it be but George Halcut-Hackett?"

22

Night Club

"Well, Roderick," said Lady Alleyn when she had at last got rid of Lucy Lorrimer, "you may be able to make something of this but it seems to me that Lucy has at last gone completely insane. Do you for an instant suppose that poor old General Halcut-Hackett is the Peeping Tom of Peckham? And who *is* the Peeping Tom of Peckham?"

"Some case the Press has made into a front-page story—no, of course, it's completely irrelevant. But all the same it does look as though old Halcut-Hackett flattened his face against the window of Lucy Lorrimer's car."

"But Lucy stayed till the end, she says, and I know he took that unfortunate child away soon after midnight. What was the poor old creature doing in Belgrave Square at half-past three?"

"He told me he went for a constitutional," murmured Alleyn.

"Rubbish. One doesn't peer into old ladies' cars when one takes constitutionals at half-past three in the morning. The whole thing's preposterous."

"It's so preposterous that I'm afraid it must be included in my dreary programme. Would you care to come to a night-club with me, mama?"

"No, thank you, Rory."

"I thought not. I must go alone to the Matador. I imagine they open at about eleven."

"Nobody goes until after midnight or later," said Lady Alleyn.

"How do you know?"

"Sarah is forever pestering me to allow her to 'go on to the Matador.' She now hopes to produce a chaperone, but I imagine it is scarcely the haunt of chaperones. I have no intention of letting her go."

"It's one of those places that offer the attractions of a tiny dancing-floor, a superlative band, and a crowd so dense that you spend the night dancing cheek-to-cheek with somebody else's partner. It is so dimly lit that the most innocent visitor takes an air of intrigue and the guiltiest has at least a sporting chance of going unrecognised."

"You seem to be remarkably familiar with its amenities," said his mother dryly.

"We've had our eye on the Matador for some time. It will meet with one of three fates. The smartest people will get tired of it and it will try to hold them by relaxing its vigilance in the matter of drink; or the smartest people will get tired of it and it will gradually lose its prestige and continue to make money out of the less exclusive but equally rich; or the smartest people will get tired of it and it will go bust. We are interested in the first contingency and they know it. They are extremely polite to me at the Matador."

"Shall you be long there?"

"No. I only want to see the commissionaire and the

secretary. Then I'll go home and to bed. May I use your telephone?"

Alleyn rang up Fox and asked him if he had seen the constable on night duty in Belgrave Square.

"Yes," said Fox. "I've talked to him. He says he didn't report having seen the General, you know who—double aitch—because he didn't think anything of it, knowing him so well. He says he thought the General had been at the ball and was on his way home."

"When was this?"

"About three-twenty when most of the guests were leaving Marsdon House. Our chap says he didn't notice the General earlier in the evening when he took the young lady home. He says he still had his eye on the crowd outside the front door at that time, and might easily have missed him. He says it's right enough that the old gentleman generally takes a turn round the Square of an evening but he's never noticed him as late as this before. I've told him a few things about what's expected of him and why sergeants lose their stripes," added Fox. "The fact of the matter is he spent most of his time round about the front door of Marsdon House. Now, there's one other thing, sir. One of these linkmen has reported he noticed a man in a black overcoat with a white scarf pulled up to his mouth and a black trilby hat, standing for a long time in the shadow on the outskirts of the crowd. The linkman says he was tall and looked like a gentleman. Thinks he wore evening clothes under his overcoat. Thinks he had a white moustache. He says this man seemed anxious to avoid notice and hung about in the shadows, but he looked at him several times and wondered what he was up to. The linkman reckons this man was hanging about on the other side of the street in the shadow of the trees, when the last guests went away. Now, sir, I reckon that's important."

"Yes, Fox. Are you suggesting that this lurker was the General?"

"The description tallies, sir. I thought I'd arrange for

this chap, who's still here at the Yard, to get a look at
the General and see if he can swear to him."

"You do. Better take your linkman off to the Square.
See if you can catch the General doing his evening
march. He'll be able to see him in the same light under
the same conditions as last night's."

"That's right."

"I'm going to the Matador and then home. Ring me
up if there's anything."

"Very good, Mr. Alleyn. Good night."

"Good night, Br'er Fox."

Alleyn turned from the telephone and stared at his
mother.

"It looks as if Lucy Lorrimer isn't altogether dotty,"
he said. "Old Halcut-Hackett seems to have behaved in
a very curious manner last night. If, indeed, it was the
General, and I fancy it must have been. He was so
remarkably evasive about his own movements. Do you
know him at all well?"

"Not very, darling. He was a brother-officer of your
father's. I rather think he was one of those large men
whom regimental humour decrees shall be called 'Tiny.'
I can't remember ever hearing that he had a violent
temper or took drugs or seduced his colonel's wife or
indeed did anything at all remarkable. He didn't marry
this rather dreadful lady of his until he was about fifty."

"Was he rich?"

"I rather think he was fairly rich. Still is, I should
have thought from that house. He's got a country place
too, I believe, somewhere in Kent."

"Then why on earth does she bother with paying
débutantes?"

"Well, you know, Rory, if she's anxious to be asked
everywhere and do everything she's more likely to
succeed with something young behind her. Far more
invitations would come rolling in."

"Yes. I rather think there's more to it than that. Good
night, darling, you are the best sort of mama. Too

astringent to be sweet, thank God, but nevertheless comfortable."

"Thank you, my dear. Come in again if you want to. Good night."

She saw him out with an air of jauntiness, but when she returned to her drawing-room she sat still for a long time thinking of the past, of her son, of Troy, and of her own fixed determination never to meddle.

Alleyn took a taxi to the Matador in Soho. The Matador commissionaire was a disillusioned giant in a plum-coloured uniform. He wore beautiful gloves, a row of medals, and an expression of worldly wisdom. He stood under a representation in red neon lights of a capering bull-fighter, and he paid the management twenty pounds for his job. Alleyn gave him good evening and walked into the entrance-hall of the Matador. The pulsation of saxophones and percussion instruments hung on the air, deadened in this ante-room by draperies of plum-coloured silk caught up into classic folds by rows of silvered tin sunflowers. A lounge porter came forward and directed Alleyn to the cloakroom.

"I wonder if you know Captain Maurice Withers by sight," asked Alleyn. "I'm supposed to join his party and I'm not sure if I've come to the right place. He's a member here."

"I'm sorry, sir. I've only just taken this job myself and I don't know the members by sight. If you ask at the office, sir, they'll tell you."

With a silent anathema on this ill chance Alleyn thanked the man and looked for the box-office. He found it beneath a large sunflower and surrounded by richer folds of silk. Alleyn peered into it and saw a young man in a beautiful dinner-jacket, morosely picking his teeth.

"Good evening," said Alleyn.

The young man abandoned the toothpick with lightning sleight-of-hand.

"Good evening, sir," he said brightly in a cultured voice.

"May I speak to you for a moment—Mr.——?"

The young man instantly looked very wary.

"Well—ah—I am the manager. My name is Cuthbert."

Alleyn slid his card through the peep-hole. The young man looked at it, turned even more wary, and said:

"Perhaps if you wouldn't mind walking round to the side door, Mr.—oh! Inspector—ah!—Alleyn. Simmons!"

A cloakroom attendant appeared. On the way to the side door Alleyn tried his story again but neither the cloakroom attendant nor the commissionaire, who was recalled, knew Withers by sight. The attendant conducted Alleyn by devious ways into a little dim room behind the box-office. Here he found the manager.

"It's nothing very momentous," said Alleyn. "I want you to tell me, if you can, about what time Captain Maurice Withers arrived at this club last night—or rather this morning?"

He saw Mr. Cuthbert glance quickly at an evening paper on which appeared a quarter-page photograph of Robert Gospell. During the second or two that elapsed before he replied, Alleyn heard again that heavy insistent thudding of the band.

"I'm afraid I have no idea at all," said Mr. Cuthbert at last.

"That's a pity," said Alleyn. "If you can't tell me I suppose I'll have to make rather a business of it. I'll have to ask all your guests if they saw him and when and so on. I'm afraid I shall have to insist on seeing the book. I'm sorry. What a bore for you."

Mr. Cuthbert looked at him with the liveliest distaste.

"You can understand," he began, "that in our position we have to be extremely tactful. Our guests expect it of us."

"Oh, rather," agreed Alleyn. "But there's not going to be nearly such a fluster if you give me the information I want quietly, as there will be if I have to start asking all sorts of people all sorts of questions."

Mr. Cuthbert stared at his first finger-nail and then bit it savagely.

"But if I don't know," he said peevishly.

"Then we're just out of luck. I'll try your commissionaire and—Simmons, is it? If that fails we'll have to start on the guests."

"Oh, damn!" ejaculated Mr. Cuthbert. "Well, he came in late. I do remember that."

"How do you remember that, please?"

"Because we had a crowd of people who came on from—from the Marsdon House Ball at about half-past three or a quarter to four. And then there was a bit of a lull."

"Yes."

"Yes, well, and then a good deal later Captain Withers signed in. He ordered a fresh bottle of gin."

"Mrs. Halcut-Hackett arrived with him, didn't she?"

"I don't know the name of his partner."

"A tall, big, blonde woman of about forty to forty-five, with an American accent. Perhaps you wouldn't mind calling——"

"All right, then, all right. She did."

"Was it as late as half-past four when they arrived?"

"I don't—look here, I mean——"

"It's quite possible you may hear no more of this. The more exact your information, you know, the less troublesome our subsequent enquiries."

"Yes, I know, but we owe a DUTY to our guests."

"Do you know actually to within say ten minutes when this couple arrived? I think you do. If so, I most strongly advise you to tell me."

"Oh, all right. As a matter of fact it was a quarter-past four. There'd been such a long gap with nobody coming in—we were practically full anyway of course—that I *did* happen to notice the time."

"That's perfectly splendid. Now if you'll sign a statement to this effect I don't think I need bother you any more."

Mr. Cuthbert fell into a profound meditation. Alleyn

lit a cigarette and waited with an air of amiability. At
last Mr. Cuthbert said:

"Am I likely to be called as a witness to anything?"

"Not very. We'll spare you if we can."

"I could refuse."

"And I," said Alleyn, "could become a member of
your club. You couldn't refuse that."

"Delighted, I'm sure," said Mr. Cuthbert unhappily.
"All right. I'll sign."

Alleyn wrote out a short statement and Mr. Cuthbert
signed it. Mr. Cuthbert became more friendly and
offered Alleyn a drink which he refused with the greatest
amiability. Mr. Cuthbert embarked on a long eulogistic
account of the Matador and the way it was run and the
foolishness of night-club proprietors who attempted to
elude the lawful restriction imposed on the sale of
alcoholic beverages.

"It never pays," cried Mr. Cuthbert. "Sooner or later
they get caught. It's just damn' silly."

A waiter burst into the room, observed something in
Mr. Cuthbert's eye, and flew out again. Mr. Cuthbert
cordially invited Alleyn to accompany him into the
dance-room. He was so insistent that Alleyn allowed
himself to be ushered through the entrance-hall and
down a plum-coloured tunnel. The sound of the band
swelled into a rhythmic all-pervading rumpus. Alleyn
was aware of more silver sunflowers; of closely ranked
tables and faces dimly lit from below, of a more distant
huddle of people ululating and sliding in time to the
band. He stood just inside the entrance, trying to
accustom his eyes to this scene, while Mr. Cuthbert
prattled innocently of the blameless charm of his club.
Alleyn was reminded of "Ruddigore"—"We only cut
respectable capers." He was about to turn away when he
knew abruptly that someone was watching him. His eyes
followed this intangible summons. He turned slowly to
the left and there at a corner table sat Bridget O'Brien
and Donald Potter.

They were both staring at him and with such intensity
that he could not escape the feeling that they had wished

to attract his attention. He deliberately met their gaze and returned it. For a second or two they looked at each other and then Bridget made a quick gesture, inviting him to join them.

He said: "I see some friends. Do you mind if I speak to them for a moment?"

Mr. Cuthbert was delighted and melted away on a wave of tactfulness. Alleyn walked over to the table and bowed.

"Good evening."

"Will you sit down for a minute?" said Bridget. "We want to speak to you."

One of Mr. Cuthbert's waiters instantly produced a chair.

"What is it?" asked Alleyn.

"It's Bridgie's idea," said Donald. "I can't stand it any longer. I've said I'll do whatever Bridgie says. I suppose I'm a fool but I give in. In a way I want to."

"He's got nothing to fear," said Bridget. "I've told him——"

"Look here," said Alleyn, "this doesn't seem a particularly well-chosen spot for the kind of conversation that's indicated."

"I know," said Bridget. "If Donna or Bart ever finds out I've been here there'll be a row of absolutely horrific proportions. The Matador! Unchaperoned! With Donald! But we were desperate—we *had* to see each other. Bart has driven me stark ravers, he's been so awful. I managed to ring Donald up from an outside telephone and we arranged to meet here. Donald's a member. We've talked it all over and we were coming to see you."

"Suppose you do so now. The manager here knows I'm a policeman so we'd better not leave together. Here's my address. Come along in about fifteen minutes. That do?"

"Yes, thank you," said Bridget, "won't it, Donald?"

"All right, all right," said Donald. "It's your idea, darling. If it lands me in——"

"It won't land you anywhere but in my flat," said

Alleyn. "You've both come to a very sensible decision."

He rose and looked down at them. "Good Lord," he thought, "they *are* young." He said: "Don't weaken. *Au revoir,*" and walked out of the Matador.

On the way to his flat he wondered if the loss of the best part of another night's sleep was going to get him any nearer a solution.

23

Donald on Wits

Alleyn walked restlessly about his sitting-room. He had
sent Vassily, his old servant, off to bed. The flat, at the
end of a cul-de-sac behind Coventry Street, was very
silent. He was fond of this room. It had a contradictory
air of monastic comfort that was, if he had realised it, a
direct expression of himself. Dürer's praying hands were
raised above his mantelpiece. At the other end of the
room Troy's painting of the wharf at Suva uttered, in
sharp cool colours, a simple phrase of beauty. He had
bought this picture secretly from one of her exhibitions
and Troy did not know that it hung there in his room.
Three comfortable elderly chairs from his mother's
house at Bossicote, his father's desk, and waist-high all
round the walls, a company of friendly books. But this
June night his room seemed chilly. He put a match to
the wood fire and drew the three armchairs into the

circle of its radiance. Time those two arrived. A taxi came up the cul-de-sac and stopped. The door banged. He heard Bridget's voice and went to let them in.

He was reminded vividly of two small children entering a dentist's waiting-room. Donald was the victim, Bridget the not very confident escort. Alleyn tried to dispel this atmosphere, settled them in front of the fire, produced cigarettes, and remembering they were grown-up offered them drinks. Bridget refused. Donald with an air of grandeur accepted a whiskey and soda.

"Now then," said Alleyn, "what's it all about?" He felt he ought to add: "Open wide!" and as he handed Donald his drink: "Rinse, please."

"It's about Donald," said Bridget in a high determined voice. "He's promised to let me tell you. He doesn't like it but I say I won't marry him unless he does, so he's going to. And besides, he really thinks he ought to do it."

"It's a damn' fool thing to do," said Donald. "There's no reason actually why I should come into it at all. I've made up my mind but all the same I don't see——"

"All the same, you are in it, darling, so it doesn't much matter if you see why or not, as the case may be."

"All right. That's settled anyway, isn't it? We needn't go on arguing. Let's tell Mr. Alleyn and get it over."

"Yes, let's. Shall I?"

"If you like."

Bridget turned to Alleyn.

"When we met to-night," she began, "I asked Donald about Captain Withers, because the way you talked about him this afternoon made me think perhaps he's not a good idea. I made Donald tell me *exactly* what he knows about Wits."

"Yes?"

"Yes. Well, Wits is a crook. Isn't he, Donald?"

"I suppose so."

"He's a crook because he runs a gambling hell at Leatherhead. Don says you know that or anyway you suspect it. Well, he does. And Donald said he'd go in with him only he didn't know then how crooked Wits was. And then Donald lost money to Wits and couldn't pay him back and Wits said he'd better stand in with him because he'd make it pretty hot for Donald if he didn't. What with Bunchy and everything."

"But Bunchy paid your debts to Withers," said Alleyn.

"Not all," said Donald with a scarlet face but a look of desperate determination. ("First extraction," thought Alleyn.) "I didn't tell him about all of it."

"I see."

"So Donald said he'd go in with Wits. And then when he quarreled with Bunchy and went to live with Wits he found out that Wits was worse of a crook than ever. Don found out that Wits was getting money from a woman. Do I have to tell you who she was?"

"Was it Mrs. Halcut-Hackett?"

"Yes."

"Was it much?" Alleyn asked Donald.

"Yes, sir," said Donald. "I don't know how much. But she—he told me she had an interest in the Leatherhead club. I thought at first it was all right. Really I did. It's hard to explain. I just got sort of used to the way Wits talked. Everything is a ramp nowadays—a racket—that's what Wits said and I began rather to think the same way. I suppose I lost my eye. Bridget says I did."

"I expect she's right, isn't she?"

"I suppose so. But—I don't know. It was all rather fun in a way until—well, until to-day."

"You mean since Bunchy was murdered?"

"Yes. I do. But—you see——"

"Let me," said Bridget. "You see, Mr. Alleyn, Donald got rather desperate. Wits rang up and told him to keep away. That was this morning."

"I know. It was at my instigation," said Alleyn. "I was there."

"Oh," said Donald.

"Well, anyway," said Bridget, "Donald got a bit of a shock. What with your questions and Wits always rubbing it in that Donald was going to be quite well off when his uncle died."

"Did Captain Withers make a lot of that?"

Bridget took Donald's hand.

"Yes," she said, "he did. Didn't he, Donald?"

"Anyone would think, Bridget, that you wanted to hang one of us, Wits or me," said Donald and he raised her hand to his cheek.

Bridget said: "I'm going to tell *everything*. You're innocent, and if you're innocent you're safe. My mother would say that. You say it, don't you, Mr. Alleyn?"

"Yes," said Alleyn.

"Well, this afternoon," Bridget went on, "Donald's things came back from Wits's flat. His clothes and his books. When he unpacked them he saw one book was missing."

"The first volume of Taylor's *Medical Jurisprudence?*"

Donald wetted his lips and nodded.

"That upset Donald, awfully," Bridget continued, growing rather white in the face, "because of one chapter in the book. After they read the papers this morning Donald and Wits had an argument about how long it took to—to——"

"Oh God!" said Donald suddenly.

"To asphyxiate anybody?" asked Alleyn.

"Yes. And Donald looked it up in this book."

"Did Captain Withers handle the book?"

Donald looked quickly at Bridget and said: "Yes he did. He read a bit of it and then lost interest. He thought it would have taken longer, he said."

"Donald was puzzled about the book not arriving, and about Wits telling him not to come to the flat," said Bridget. "He thought about it all the afternoon, and the more he thought the less he liked it. So he rang up. Wits answered but when he heard Donald's voice he simply cut him off without another word. Didn't he, darling?"

"Yes," said Donald. "I rang again and he didn't answer. I—I couldn't think clearly at all. I felt stone cold in the pit of my stomach. It was simply ghastly to find myself cut dead like that. *Why* shouldn't he answer me, *why!* Why hadn't he sent the book? Only that morning we'd been together in his flat, perfectly friendly. Until the news came—after that I didn't listen to anything Wits said. As soon as I knew Uncle Bunch had been murdered I couldn't think of anything else. I wasn't dressed when the papers came. Mother had known for hours, but the telephone being disconnected then, she couldn't get hold of me. I hadn't told her my address. Wits kept talking. I didn't listen. And then, when I did get home, you were there, getting at me, getting at me. And then my mother crying, and the flowers, and everything. And on top of it all this business of Wits not wanting to speak to me. I couldn't think. I just *had* to see Bridget."

"Yes," said Bridget, "he had to see me. But you're muddling things, Donald. We ought to keep them in their right order. Mr. Alleyn, we've got as far as this afternoon. Well, Donald got so rattled about the telephone and the missing book that in spite of what Wits had said, he felt he *had* to see him. So after dinner he took a taxi to Wits's flat and he could see a light under the blind, so he knew Wits was in. Donald still had his own latch-key so he went straight in and up to the flat. Now you go on, Donald."

Donald finished his whiskey and soda and with unsteady fingers lit a fresh cigarette. "All right," he said. "I'll tell you. When I walked into the sitting-room he was lying on the divan bed. I stood in the middle of the room looking at him. He didn't move, and he didn't speak at all loudly. He called me a foul name and told me to get out. I said I wanted to know why he'd behaved as he did. He just lay there and looked at me. I said something about you, sir—I don't know what—and in a split second he was on his feet. I thought he was going to start a fight. He asked me what the bloody hell I'd said to you about him. I said I'd avoided speaking about him as much as possible. But he began to ask all sorts of questions. God, he did look ugly. You often read about the veins swelling with rage in people's faces. They did in his. He sat on the edge of the table swinging one foot and his face got sort of dark."

"Yes," said Alleyn. "I can see Captain Withers. Go on."

"He said——" Donald caught his breath. Alleyn saw his fingers tighten round Bridget's. "He said that unless I kept my head and held my tongue he'd begin to talk himself. He said that after all I had quarrelled with Uncle Bunch and I had been in debt and I was Uncle Bunch's heir. He said if he was in this thing up to his knees I was in it up to my neck. He pulled his hand out of his pocket and pointed his flat finger at my neck. Then he told me to remember, if I didn't want to commit suicide, that when he left Marsdon House he went to his car and drove to the Matador. I was to say that I'd seen him drive off with his partner."

"Did you see this?"

"No. I left after him. I did think I saw him walking ahead of me towards his car. It was parked in Belgrave Road."

"Why do you suppose, did Withers take this extraordinary attitude when you saw him to-night?"

"He thought I'd given him away to you. He told me so."

"About Leatherhead?"

"Yes. You said something about—about——"

"Fleecing lambs," said Bridget.

"Yes. So I did," admitted Alleyn cheerfully.

"He thought I'd lost my nerve and talked too much."

"And now you are prepared to talk?"

"Yes."

"Why?"

"We've told you——" Bridget began.

"Yes, I know. You've told me that you persuaded Donald to come to me because you thought it better for him to explain his association with Withers. But I rather think there's something more behind it than that. Would I be wrong, Donald, if I said that you were at least encouraged to take this decision by the fear that Withers himself might get in first and suggest that you had killed your uncle?"

Bridget cried out: "No! *No!* How can you be so cruel? How can you think that of Donald! Donald!"

But Donald looked steadily at Alleyn and when he spoke again it was gravely and with a certain dignity that became him very well.

He said: "Don't, Bridget. It's perfectly natural Mr. Alleyn should think that I'm afraid of Wits accusing me. I *am* afraid of it. I didn't kill Uncle Bunch. I think I was fonder of him than anyone else in the world except you, Bridgie. But I had quarrelled with him. I wish to God I hadn't. I didn't kill him. The reason I agreed to come and talk to you like this—the reason I'm quite ready now to answer any questions about Wits, even if it means implicating myself——" He stopped and took a deep breath.

"Yes?" asked Alleyn.

"—is that after seeing Wits this evening I believe he murdered my uncle."

There was a long silence.

"Motive?" asked Alleyn at last.

"He thought he had a big enough hold over me to get control of the money."

"Proof?"

"I've none. Only the way he spoke to-night. He's afraid I believe he'd murder anyone if he'd enough incentive."

"That's not proof, nor anything like it."

"No. It seemed good enough," said Donald, "to bring me here when I might have kept quiet."

The telephone rang. Alleyn went over to the desk and answered it.

"Hullo?"

"Roderick, is that you?"

"Yes. Who is it, please?"

"Evelyn Carrados."

Alleyn looked across to the fireplace. He saw Bridget bend forward swiftly and kiss Donald.

"Hullo!" he said. "Anything the matter?"

"Roderick, I'm so worried. I don't know what to do. Bridgie has gone out without saying a word to anyone. I've rung up as many people as I dared and I haven't an inkling where she is. I'm so terrified she's done something wild and foolish. I thought she might be with Donald Potter and I wondered if you could tell me his telephone number. Thank Heaven Herbert is out at a regimental dinner, at Turnbridge. I'm distraught with anxiety."

"It's all right, Evelyn," said Alleyn. "Bridget's here with me."

"With you?"

"Yes. She wanted to talk to me. She's quite all right. I'll bring her back——"

"Is Donald Potter there?"

"Yes."

"But why? What have they *done* it for? Roderick, I want to see you. I'll come and get Bridget, may I?"

"Yes, do," said Alleyn and gave her his address.

He hung up the receiver and turned to find Bridget and Donald looking very startled.

"Donna!" whispered Bridget. "Oh, Golly!"

"Had I better go?" asked Donald.

"I think perhaps you'd better," said Alleyn.

"If Bridgie's going to be hauled over the coals I'd rather stay."

"No, darling," said Bridget, "it will be better not, honestly. As long as Bart doesn't find out I'll be all right."

"Your mother won't be here for ten minutes," said Alleyn. "Look here, Donald, I want a full account of this gambling business at Leatherhead. If I put you in another room will you write one for me? It will save us a great deal of time and trouble. It must be as clear as possible with no trimmings and as many dates as you can conjure up. It will, I hope, lead to Captain Withers's conviction."

Donald looked uncomfortable.

"It seems rather a ghastly sort of thing to do. I mean——"

"Good heavens, you have just told me you think the man's a murderer and you apparently know he's a blackguard. He's used you as a cat's-paw and I understand his idea has been to swindle you out of your money!"

"All right," said Donald. "I'll do it."

Alleyn took him into the dining-room and settled him there with pen and paper.

"I'll come in later on and see what sort of fist you've made of it. There will have to be witnesses to your signature."

"Shall I be had up as an accomplice?"

"I hardly think so. How old are you?"

"Twenty-one in August. It's not that I mind for myself. At least it would be pretty bloody, wouldn't it? But I've said I'll go through with it."

"So you have. Don't make too big a sainted martyr of yourself," said Alleyn good-naturedly. Donald looked up at him and suddenly the ghost of Lord Robert's twinkle came into his eyes.

"All right," he said. "I won't."

Alleyn returned to Bridget and found her sitting on the hearth-rug. She looked very frightened.

"Does Bart know?"

"No, but your mother's been very worried."

"Well, that's not all me. Bart's nearly driving her dotty. I can't tell you what he's like. Honestly it would never astonish me if Bart had an apoplectic fit and went crazy."

"Dear me," said Alleyn.

"No, honestly. I don't know what he told you when you interviewed him but I suppose you saw through the famous Carrados pose, didn't you? Of course you did.

But you may not have realised what a temper he's got. I didn't for a long time. I mean not until I was about fifteen."

"Two years ago?" asked Alleyn with a smile. "Tell me about it."

"It was simply frightful. Donna had been ill and she was sleeping very badly. Bart was asked if he'd mind going into his dressing-room. I didn't realise then, but I do now, that that was what annoyed him. He always gets the huff when Donna's ill. He takes it as a sort of personal insult and being a beastly old Victorian Turk the dressing-room idea absolutely put the tin cupola on it. Are you shocked?"

"I suppose not," said Alleyn cautiously. "Anyway, go on."

"Well, you're not. And so he went into his dressing-room. And then Donna got really ill and I said we must have Sir Daniel because she *was* so ill and he's an angel. And Bart rang him up. Well, I wanted to get hold of Sir Daniel first to tell him about Donna before Bart did. So I went downstairs into Bart's study because I told the butler to show Sir Daniel in there. Bart was up with Donna telling her how 'seedy' he felt, and it didn't matter, she wasn't to notice. And then Sir Dan came in and was angelic and I told him about Donna. Did you notice in the study there's a French escritoire thing on a table?"

"Yes."

"Well, Sir Dan adores old things and he saw it and raved about it and said it was a beautiful piece and told me when it was made and how they used sometimes to put little secret drawers in them and you just touch a screw and they fly out. He said it was a museum piece and asked me if I didn't think some of the vanished ladies might come back and open the secret drawer with ghostly fingers. So I thought I'd like to see, and when Sir Dan had gone up to Donna I tried progging the screws with a pencil and at last a little drawer did fly out triangularly, sort of. There was a letter in it. I didn't touch it, naturally, but while I was looking at the drawer, Bart must have come in. What did you say?"

"Nothing," said Alleyn. "Go on."

"I can't *tell* you what he was like. He went absolutely stark *ravers,* honestly. He took hold of my arm and twisted it so much I screamed before I could stop myself. And then he turned as white as the washing and called me a little bastard. I believe he'd have actually hit me if Sir Dan hadn't come down. I think Sir Dan had heard me yell and he must have guessed what had happened because he had one glance at my arm—I had short sleeves—and then he said in a lovely *dangerous* sort of voice: 'Are you producing *another* patient for me, Carrados?' Bart banged the little drawer shut, began to splutter and try to get up some sort of explanation. Sir Daniel just looked at him through his glasses—the ones with the black ribbon. Bart tried to pretend I'd slipped on the polished floor and he'd caught me by the arm. Sir Daniel said: 'Very curious indeed,' and went on looking at my arm. He gave me a prescription for some stuff to put on it and was frightfully nice to me, and didn't ask questions, but just ignored Bart. It made me absolutely *crawl* with shame to hear Bart trying to do his simple soldier stuff and sort of ingratiate himself with Sir Dan. And when he'd gone Bart apologised to me and said he was really terribly nervy and ill and had never recovered from the war, which was pretty good as he spent it in Tunbridge Wells. That was the worst of all, having to hear him apologise. He said there was a letter from his mother in the drawer and it was very sacred. Of course I felt simply *septic*. He's never forgiven me and I've never forgotten. My private belief is there was something about his miserable past in that drawer."

Bridget's voice at last stopped. Alleyn, who had sat in his chair, was silent for so long, that at last she turned from the fire and looked into his face.

"It's a queer story, isn't it?" she said.

"Very queer, indeed," said Alleyn. "Have you ever told anyone else about it?"

"No. Well, only Donald." She wriggled across the hearth-rug. "It's funny," she said. "I suppose I ought to be frightened of you, but I'm not. Why's Donna coming?"

"She wants to collect you, and see me," said Alleyn absently.

"Everybody wants to see you." She clasped her hands over his knees. "Don't they?" insisted Bridget.

"For no very flattering reason, I'm afraid."

"Well, I think you're really rather a lamb," said Bridget.

"Tell me," said Alleyn, "do you think anyone else knows the secret of that French writing-case?"

"I shouldn't think so. You'd never know unless somebody showed you."

"None of the servants?"

"I'm sure not. Bart slammed the drawer shut as soon as Sir Daniel came in."

"Has Sir Daniel ever been alone in that room?"

"Sir Dan? Good heavens, you don't think my angelic Sir Dan had anything to do with Bart's beastly letter?"

"I simply want to clear things up."

"Well, as a matter of fact I don't think he's been in the study before or since and he was never alone there that day. When Sir Dan comes, the servants always show him straight upstairs. Bart hates his room to be used for visitors."

"Has Dimitri, the catering man ever been alone in that room?"

"Why—I don't know. Yes, now you come to mention it he *did* interview Donna there, about a month before our ball-dance. I went down first and he was alone in the room."

"When was this? Can you remember the date?"

"Let me see. I'll try. Yes. Yes, I can. It was on the tenth of May. We were going to Newmarket and Dimitri came early in the morning because of that."

"Would you swear he was alone in the room?"

"Yes, yes, I would. But, please, what does it mean?"

"See here," said Alleyn. "I want you to forget all about this. Don't speak of it to anyone, not even to Donald. Understood?"

"Yes, but——"

"I want your promise."

"All right, I promise."

"Solemnly?"

"Solemnly."

The front-door bell rang.

"Here's your mother," said Alleyn.

24

The Dance is Wound Up

When Alleyn opened the door to Evelyn Carrados, he
saw her as a dark still figure against the lighted street.
Her face was completely shadowed and it was
impossible for him to glean anything from it. So that
when she walked into the sitting-room he was not
prepared for her extraordinary pallor, her haunted eyes,
and the drawn nervousness of her mouth. He
remembered that she had gone to her room before she
missed Bridget, and he realised with compassion that
she had removed her complexion and neglected to
replace it. Perhaps Bridget felt something of the same
compassion for she uttered a little cry and ran to her
mother. Lady Carrados using that painful gesture of all
distracted mothers, held Bridget in her arms. Her thin
hands were extraordinarily expressive.

"Darling," she murmured. With a sort of hurried

intensity she kissed Bridget's hair. "How could you frighten me like this Bridgie, how *could* you?"

"I thought you wouldn't know. Donna, *don't*. It's all right, really it is. It was only about Donald. I didn't want to worry you. I'm so sorry, *dear* Donna." Lady Carrados gently disengaged herself and turned to Alleyn.

"Come and sit down, Evelyn," he said. "There's nothing to worry about. I would have brought your daughter home, but she had some interesting news and I thought you would trust her with me for half an hour."

"Yes, Roderick, of course. If only I had known. Where's Donald? I thought he was here."

"He's in the next room. Shall we send Bridget to join him for a minute or two?"

"Please."

"Don't interrupt him," said Alleyn as Bridget went out.

"All right."

The door closed behind her.

Alleyn said: "Do you ever drink brandy, Evelyn?"

"Never, why?"

"You're going to do so now. You're quite done up. Warm your hands at my fire while I get it for you."

He actually persuaded her to drink a little brandy, and laughed at her convulsive shudder.

"Now then," he said, "there's no need for you to fuss about Bridget. She's been, on the whole, a very sensible young person and her only fault is in giving a common place visit the air of a secret elopement."

"My nerves have gone, I think. I began to imagine all sorts of horrible things. I even wondered if she suspected Donald of this crime."

"She is, on the contrary, absolutely assured of Donald's innocence."

"Then why did she do this?"

"I'd better tell you the whole story. The truth is, Evelyn, they were longing for each other's bright eyes. Bridget wanted to convince me of Donald's innocence.

She also wanted him to tell me this and that about a third person who doesn't matter at the moment. They met, most reprehensibly, at the Matador."

"The Matador! Roderick, how naughty of them! It just simply isn't done by débutantes. No, really that was *very* naughty."

Alleyn was both relieved and surprised to find that this departure from débutantes' etiquette took momentary precedence over Lady Carrados's other troubles.

"They had only just arrived, I imagine, when I ran into them there. The place was only half-full, Evelyn. It was too early for the smart people. I shouldn't think anyone else saw them. I brought them on here."

"I'm very glad you did," she said doubtfully.

"Was that all that worried you?"

"No. It's Herbert. He's been so extraordinary, Roderick, since this tragedy. He's stayed indoors all day and he never takes his eyes off me. I was afraid he would give up this dinner to-night, but, thank Heaven, he didn't. It is followed by the annual regimental dance and he has to present trophies or something so it will keep him quite late. I should have gone too, but I couldn't face it. I couldn't face another hour with him. He keeps making curious hints as if he—Roderick, almost as if he suspected me of something."

"Tell me what he says."

She leant back in her chair and relaxed. He saw that, not for the first time, he was to play the part of confidant. "An odd role for a C.I.D. man," he thought, "and a damn' useful one." He settled himself to listen.

"It began soon after you left. While we were at tea. We had tea in my boudoir. I asked my secretary, Miss Harris, to join us, because I thought if she was there it might be a little easier. Naturally enough, but most unfortunately, poor Miss Harris began to speak to Bridget about Bunchy. She said she'd been reading a book on famous trials and somehow or other the word 'blackmail' cropped up. I—I'm afraid I was startled and showed it. The very word was enough as you may imagine. I looked up to find Herbert's eyes fixed on me with an expression of—how can I describe it?—of knowing terror. He didn't go with the others after tea but hung about the room watching me. Suddenly he said: 'You were very friendly with Robert Gospell, weren't you?' I said: 'Of course I was.' Then he asked me to show him my bank-book. It sounded perfectly insane, right on top of his other question. Almost funny—as if he suspected I'd been keeping poor Bunchy. But it wasn't very funny. It terrified me. He never worries about my money as a rule. He generally makes rather a point of not doing so, because, apart from the allowance he gives me, I've got my own, and what Paddy left me. I knew if he saw my bank-book it would show that I had been drawing large sums—five hundred pounds, to meet the demands of—to——"

"The five hundred that went into that big bag of yours last night. How did you draw it out, Evelyn?"

"I drew some myself. I cashed a cheque for five hundred. I can't think that Herbert knew, or that he could have suspected the truth, if he did know. It's all so terribly disturbing. I put him off by saying I couldn't find the book, that I thought I had sent it back to the bank. He hardly seemed to listen. Suddenly he asked me if Bunchy had ever called when I was out? It seemed a perfectly inane question. I said I didn't know. He sat glaring at me till I could have screamed, and then he said: 'Did he know anything about old furniture?' "

Alleyn glanced up quickly: "Old furniture?"

"I know! It sounds demented, doesn't it? I repeated it like you, and Herbert said: 'Well, antiques. Pieces like the escritoire in my study.' And then he leaned forward and said: 'Do you think he knew anything about that?' I said: 'Herbert, what *are* you talking about?' and he said: 'I suppose I'm going to pieces. I feel I have been surrounded by treachery all my life!' It sounds just silly, but it frightened me. I rather lost my head, and asked him how he could talk like that. I began to say that

Bridget was always loyal, when he burst out laughing. 'Your daughter,' he said, 'loyal! How far do you suppose her loyalty would take her? Would you care to put it to the test?' "

Lady Carrados pressed her hands together.

"He's always disliked Bridgie. He's always been jealous of her. I remember once, it must be two years ago now, they had some sort of quarrel, and Herbert actually hurt her. He hurt her arm. I should never have found out if I hadn't gone to her room and seen the marks. I think he sees some reflection of Paddy in her. Roderick, do you think Herbert can know about Paddy and me? Is there the smallest possibility that the blackmailer has written to him?"

"It is possible, of course," said Alleyn slowly, "but I don't think it quite fits in. You say this extraordinary change in Carrados began after Miss Harris and Bridget talked of blackmail, and you showed you were startled?"

"Yes."

"Do you think your obvious dismay could have suggested to him that you yourself were the victim of blackmail?"

"I don't know. It certainly suggested something pretty ominous," said Lady Carrados, with the ghost of a smile. "He's in the most extraordinary state of mind, it terrifies me."

"When did you marry him, Evelyn?"

"When? Two years after Paddy died. He had wanted me to marry him before. Herbert was a very old friend of my family's. He had always been rather attached to me."

"He's never given any sign of this sort of behaviour before?"

"Not *this* sort. Of course, he's rather difficult sometimes. He's very touchy. He's eighteen years older than I am, and he hates to be reminded of it. One has to be rather tactful. I suppose he's vain. Bridgie thinks so, I know."

The gentle voice, with its tranquil, level note, faltered for a moment, and then went on steadily. "I suppose you wonder why I married him, don't you?"

"A little, yes. Perhaps you felt that you needed security. You had had your great adventure."

"It was exactly that. But it wasn't right, I see that now. It wasn't fair. Although Herbert knew quite well that he was not my great love, and was very chivalrous and humble about it, he couldn't really resign himself to the knowledge, and he grew more and more inclined to be rather a martyr. It's pathetically childish sometimes. He tries to draw my attention to his little ailments. He gets a sort of patient look. It irritates Bridgie dreadfully, which is such a pity. And yet, although Herbert seems simple, he's not. He's a mass of repressions, and queer twisted thoughts. Do you know, I think he is still intensely jealous of Paddy's memory."

"Did you see much of him before Paddy died?"

"Yes. I'm afraid, poor Herbert, that he rather saw himself as the faithful, chivalrous friend who continued to adore me quite honourably after I was—married. You see, I still think of myself as Paddy's wife. We used to ask Herbert to dine quite often. He bored Paddy dreadfully but—well, I'm afraid Paddy rather gloried in some of Herbert's peculiarities. He almost dined out on them. It was very naughty of him, but he was so gay always and so charming that he was forgiven everything. Everything."

"I know."

"Herbert rather emphasised the sacrificial note in his friendship, and of course Paddy saw that, and used to tease me about him. But I was very attached to him. No, he wasn't quite so touchy in those days, poor fellow. He was always very kind indeed. I'm afraid both Paddy and I rather got into the way of making use of him."

"You are sure he suspected nothing?"

"Absolutely. In a way he was our greatest friend. I told you that I was staying with my mother when Paddy was hurt. She rang Herbert up when the news came through. Almost instinctively we turned to him. He was with us in a few minutes. Why, I suppose in a way I owe it to Herbert that I was in time to see Paddy before he died."

Alleyn opened his mouth, and shut it again. Lady Carrados was staring into the fire, and gave no sign that she realised the significance of this last statement. At last Alleyn said: "How did that come about?"

"Didn't I tell you this afternoon? It was Herbert who drove me down to the Vicarage at Falconbridge on the day Paddy died."

It was one o'clock in the morning when Alleyn saw Lady Carrados, Bridget and Donald into a taxi, thankfully shut his door, and went to bed. Less than twenty-four hours had passed since Robert Gospell met with his death, yet in that short time all the threads but one of the most complicated homicide cases he had ever dealt with had been put into his hands. As he waited for sleep, so long delayed, he saw the protagonists as a company of dancers moving in a figure so elaborate that the pattern of their measure was almost lost in the confusion of individual gestures. Now it was Donald and Bridget who met and advanced through the centre of the maze; now Withers, marching on the outskirts of the dance, who turned to encounter Mrs. Halcut-Hackett. Evelyn Carrados and her husband danced back to back into the very heart of the measure. Sir Daniel Davidson, like a sort of village master of ceremonies, with a gigantic rosette streaming from his buttonhole, gyrated slowly across and across. Dimitri slipped like a thief into the dance, offering a glass of champagne to each protagonist. Miss Harris skipped in a decorous fashion round the inner figure, but old General Halcut-Hackett, peering anxiously into every face, seemed to search for his partner. To and fro the figures swam more and more dizzily, faster and faster, until the confusion was intolerable. And then, with terrifying abruptness, they were stricken into immobility, and before he sank into oblivion, Alleyn, in a single flash, saw the pattern of the dance.

25

Benefit of Clergy

The inquest on Lord Robert Gospell was held at eleven
o'clock the next morning. It was chiefly remarkable for
the circumstance that more people were turned away
from it than had ever been turned away from any
previous inquest in the same building. The coroner was
a cross-grained man with the poorest possible opinion of
society with a small s and a perfectly venomous hatred
of Society with a large one. He suffered from chronic
dyspepsia and an indeterminate but savage conviction
that somebody was trying to get the better of him. The
proceedings were coloured by his efforts to belittle the
whole affair when he thought of the fashionable
spectators, and to make the very most of it when he
reflected that this sort of things was the direct outcome
of the behaviour of those sorts of people. However,

apart from this personal idiosyncrasy, he was a good coroner. He called Donald, who, very white-faced, gave formal evidence of identification. He then heard the evidence of the taxi-driver, was particular about time, place and route, and called Alleyn.

Alleyn described his first view and examination of the body. In formal phrases he gave a precise account of the injuries he had found on the body of his friend. Dr. Curtis followed with his report on the post-mortem. One of Dimitri's men gave evidence on the time Lord Robert left Marsdon House. The coroner with a vindictive glance at the audience said he saw no reason to call further evidence, addressed the jury in words that left them in no possible doubt as to the verdict they should return and when they had duly returned it, ordered an adjournment. He then fixed a baleful blue eye on the farthest wall and pronounced an expression of sympathy with the relatives. The whole proceedings had lasted twenty minutes.

"Swish!" said Fox when he met Alleyn in the street outside. "That's old 'Slap-Bang, Here-we-are-again.' You can't beat him for speed can you, sir?"

"Mercifully, you can't. Fox, we're off to Barbicon-Bramley. I've borrowed my mother's car and I've a hell of a lot to tell you, and I rather think the spell is wound up."

"Sir?"

"You are quite right, Fox. Never quote, and if you do certainly not from Macbeth."

Lady Alleyn's car was parked in a side street. Fox and Alleyn got into it and headed for the Uxbridge Road. On the way Alleyn related Bridget's and Donald's and Lady Carrados's stories. When he had finished Fox grunted and they were both silent for ten minutes.

"Well," said Fox at last, "it all points to the same thing doesn't it, Mr. Alleyn?"

"Yes, Fox. In a dubious sort of way it does."

"Still, I don't quite see how we can exclude the others."

"Nor do I unless we get something definite from these people. If necessary we'll have to go on to Falconbridge and visit the hospital but I'm in hopes that Miss Harris's uncle will come out of his retirement and go back to his gay young rectorish days seventeen years ago."

"What a hope!" said Fox.

"As you indicate, the chances are thin."

"If they couldn't find this chap O'Brien's letter on the premises then how can we expect to trace it now, seventeen years later?"

"Well urged, Br'er Fox, well urged. But I fancy we know something now that they didn't know then."

"Oh, well," conceded Fox. "Maybe. But all the same I wouldn't give you a tuppeny damn for our chances and that's flat."

"I'm a little more sanguine than that. Well, if we fail here we'll have to peg away somewhere else."

"There's the missing cloak and hat."

"Yes. Any report come in this morning from the postal people?"

"No. I've followed your suggestion and asked them to try and check yesterday's overseas parcels post. Our chaps have gone into the rubbish-bin game and there's nothing there. Chelsea and Belgrave bins were emptied this morning and there's been no cloaks or hats in any of them. Of course something may come in from further afield."

"I don't fancy the rubbish-bins, Fox. Too risky. For some reason he wanted those things to be lost completely. Hair oil, perhaps. Yes, it might be hair oil. I'm afraid, you know, that we *shall* have to ask all these people if we may search their houses."

"Carrados is sure to object, sir, and you don't want to have to get search warrants yet, do you?"

"I think we can scare him by saying that Dimitri, Withers, Davidson, Halcut-Hackett and Lady Mildred Potter are all going to be asked to allow a search of their houses. He'll look a bit silly if he refuses on top of that."

"Do you think the cloak and hat may still be hidden away in—well, in the guilty party's house?"

"No, blast it. I think they got rid of them yesterday before we had covered the first phase of investigation."

"By post?"

"Well, can you think of a better method? In London? We've decided the river's barred because of the tide. We've advertised the damn' thing well enough—they haven't been shoved down anyone's area. We've searched all the way along the Embankment. The men are still at it but I don't think they'll find them. The murderer wouldn't have time to do anything very elaborate in the way of hiding them and anyway, if we're right, it's off his beat."

"Where would he send them?" ruminated Fox.

"Put yourself in his place. What address would you put on an incriminating parcel?"

"Care of Private Hoo Slung Dung, forty-second battalion, Chop Suey, Mah Johng, Manchuria, to wait till called for," suggested Fox irritably.

"Something like that," said Alleyn. "Something very like that, Br'er Fox."

They drove in silence for the rest of the way to Barbicon-Bramley.

Miss Harris's natal village proved to be small and rather self-consciously picturesque. There was a preponderance of ye olde-ness about the few shops and a good deal of pseudo Tudor half-timbering on the outlying houses. They stopped at the post office and Alleyn asked to be directed to the Reverend Mr. Walter Harris's house.

"I understand he is not the rector but his brother."

"Oo, yes," agreed the post office lady rattling her basket cuffs and flashing a smile. "That will be the old gentleman. Quayte an aydentity in the district. First to the left into Oakapple Lane and straight on to the end. 'The Thatch.' It's ever so unmistakable. The last residence on the left, standing back in its own grounds."

"Thank you so much," said Alleyn.

As they drove away he noticed that the post office was semi-detached from the local land-and-estate office and he wondered if the basket cuffs had an interest in both.

They found "The Thatch" as she had predicted, without any difficulty. The grounds of its own in which it stood back were an eighth of an acre of charming cottage garden. Alleyn and Fox had only got half-way up the cobbled path when they came upon two rumps up-ended behind a tall border of rosemary and lavender. The first was clad in patched trousers of clerical grey, the second in the navy blue decency of a serge skirt. Fragrant herbs hid the rest of these two gardeners from view.

"Good afternoon, sir," said Alleyn, removing his hat.

With a slow upheaving movement, the Reverend and Mrs. Walter Harris became wholly vertical and turned about.

"Oh!" they said gently. "Good afternoon."

They were very old indeed and had the strange marital likeness that so often comes upon a man and woman who have worked together all their lives. Their faces, though they differed in conformation, echoed each other in expression. They both had mild grey eyes surrounded by a network of kindly lines; they were both weather-beaten, and each of their mouths in repose, curved into a doubtful smile. Upon Mrs. Harris's hair rather than her head was a wide garden hat with quite a large rent in the crown through which straggled a straight grey lock or two. Her husband also wore well over his nose a garden hat, an ancient panama with a faded green ribbon. His long crepey neck was encircled by a low clerical collar, but instead of the usual grey jacket an incredibly faded All Souls blazer hung from his sharp shoulder-blades. He now tilted his head backwards in order to look at Alleyn under his hat-brim and through his glasses which were clipped halfway down his nose.

Alleyn said: "I'm so sorry to bother you, sir."

"No matter," said Mr. Harris, "no matter." His voice had the authentic parsonic ring.

"There's nothing more maddening than to be interrupted when you've settled down to a good afternoon's gardening," Alleyn added.

"Twitch!" said Mr. Harris violently.

"I beg your pardon?"

"Twitch! It's the bane of my existence. It springs up like veritable dragon's teeth and I assure you it's a great deal more difficult to extract. Three wheelbarrow loads since last Thursday forenoon."

"Walter," said his wife, "these gentleman want to speak to you."

"We won't keep you more than a few minutes, sir," said Alleyn.

"Yes, dear. Where shall I take them?"

"Into your den," said Mrs. Harris, as if her husband was a carnivorous ravager.

"Certainly, certainly. Come along. Come along," said Mr. Harris in the patient voice of vicarage hospitality. "Come along."

He took them through a french window into a little faded red room where old dim photographs of young men in cassocks hung beside old dim photographs of famous cathedrals. The shelves were full of dusty volumes of sermons and the works of Mrs. Humphrey Ward, Charles Kingsley, Charlotte M. Younge, Dickens and Sir Walter Scott. Between a commentary and an *Imitation of Christ* was a copy of *The Martyrdom of Man,* truculently solid. For Mr. Harris had once been an earnest undergraduate and had faced things. It was a shabby, friendly, old room.

"Sit down, sit down," said Mr. Harris.

He hurriedly gathered up from the chairs, parish magazines, *Church Times,* and seed catalogues. With his arms full of these papers, he wandered vaguely about his den.

Alleyn and Fox sat down on the horsehair chairs.

"That's right, said Mr. Harris. He incontinently dropped all his papers on the floor and sat down.

"Now, what can I have the pleasure——? Um?"

"First, sir, I must tell you we are police officers."

"Dear me," said Mr. Harris, "not young Hockley again, I hope. Are you sure it's not my brother you want? The rector of Barbicon-Bramley? He's been very interested in the case and he told me that if the poor lad was not charged he could find a post for him with some kind souls who are prepared to overlook——"

"No, sir," interrupted Alleyn gently, "it's you we want to see."

"But I'm retired," said Mr. Harris opening his eyes very wide. "I'm quite retired, you know."

"I am going to ask you to go back to the days when you were rector of Falconbridge."

"Of Falconbridge!" Mr. Harris beamed at them. "Now, this is really the greatest pleasure. You come from dear old Falconbridge! Let me see, I don't recollect either of your faces though, of course, I have been retired now for fifteen years and I'm afraid my memory is not what it used to be. Now tell me your names."

"Mr. Harris, we don't come from Falconbridge, we are from Scotland Yard. My name is Alleyn and this is Inspector Fox."

"How do you do? I hope nothing has gone wrong in the dear old village," ejaculated Mr. Harris anxiously. He suddenly remembered his panama hat and snatched it from his head revealing a shining pink pate with an aura of astonished white fluff.

"No, no," said Alleyn hastily. "At least, not recently." He darted a venomous glance at Fox who was grinning broadly. "We are investigating a case, sir, and are anxious to trace a letter which we believe to have been lost in Falconbridge between seventeen and eighteen years ago."

"A letter! Dear me, I'm afraid if it was addressed to me there is very little hope of recovery. Only this morning I found I had mislaid a most important letter from a very dear old friend, Canon Worsley of All Saints, Chipton. It's a most *extraordinary* thing where that letter has gone. I distinctly remember that I put it in the pocket of this jacket and——"

He thrust his hands in the side pockets of his blazer and pulled out a collection of string, seed-packets, pencils and pieces of paper.

"Why, there it is!" he exclaimed, staring at an envelope that had fallen to the floor. "There, after all, it is! I am ASTOUNDED."

"Mr. Harris," said Alleyn loudly. Mr. Harris instantly threw his head back and looked at Alleyn through his glasses. "Eighteen years ago," continued Alleyn very rapidly, "there was a motor accident on the bridge outside the rectory at Falconbridge. The driver, Captain O'Brien, was severely injured and was taken into the rectory. Do you remember?"

Mr. Harris had opened his mouth in astonishment but he said nothing. He merely continued to gape at Alleyn.

"You were very kind to him," Alleyn went on; "you kept him at the rectory and sent for help. He was taken to the hospital and died there a few hours later."

He paused but Mr. Harris's expression had not changed. There was something intensely embarrassing in his posture and his unexpected silence.

"Do you remember?" asked Alleyn.

Without closing his mouth Mr. Harris slowly shook his head from side to side.

"But it was such a serious accident. His young wife motored down from London. She went to the hospital but he died without regaining consciousness."

"Poor fellow!" said Mr. Harris in his deepest voice. "Poor fell-oh!"

"Can't you remember, now?"

Mr. Harris made no reply but got to his feet, went to the french window, and called into the garden.

"Edith! Edith!"

"Hoo-ee?" replied a wavering voice close at hand.

"Can you spare-ah a moment?"

"Coming."

He turned away from the window and beamed at them.

"Now we shan't be long," he announced.

But when Alleyn saw Mrs. Harris amiably blunder up the garden path he scarcely shared in this optimistic view. They all stood up. She accepted Alleyn's chair and drew her gardening gloves from her old hands. Mr. Harris contemplated her as if she was some rare achievement of his own.

"Edith, my dear," he said loudly, "would you tell these gentlemen about an accident?"

"Which accident?"

"That, I'm afraid, I don't know, dear. Indeed we are depending upon you to inform us."

"I don't understand you, Walter."

"I don't understand myself very well, I must admit, Edith. I find it all very puzzling."

"What?" said his wife. Alleyn now realised that she was slightly deaf.

"Puzzling," shouted Mr. Harris.

"My husband's memory is not very good," explained Mrs. Harris smiling gently at Alleyn and Fox. "He was greatly shaken by his cycling accident some months ago. I suppose you have called about the insurance."

Raising his voice Alleyn embarked once more on his recital. This time he was not interrupted but as neither of the Harrises gave any sign of understanding, it was impossible to tell whether or not he spoke in vain. By the time he had finished, Mr. Harris had adopted his former disconcerting glare. Mrs. Harris, however, turned to her husband and said:

"You remember the blood on the carpet, Walter? At dear old Falconbridge?"

"Dear me, yes. Now *that's* what I was trying to recollect. Of course it was. Poor fellow. Poor fell-oh!"

"Then you *do* remember?" Alleyn cried.

"Indeed, I do," said Mrs. Harris reproachfully. "The

poor young wife wrote us such a charming letter, thanking us for the little we had been able to do for him. I would have liked to answer it but unfortunately my husband lost it."

"Edith, I have discovered dear old Worsley's letter. It was in my pocket. Fancy!"

"Fancy, dear, yes."

"Talking of letters," said Alleyn to Mrs. Harris. "Can you by any chance remember anything about a letter that was lost on the occasion of Captain O'Brien's accident? I think you were asked if it had been found in the vicarage."

"I'm afraid I didn't catch——"

Alleyn repeated it.

"To be sure I do," said Mrs. Harris. "Perfectly."

"You were unable to give any information about this letter?"

"On the contrary."

"What!"

"On the contrary," repeated Mrs. Harris firmly. "I sent it after him."

"After who?" roared Fox so loudly that even Mrs. Harris gave a little jump. "I'm sure I beg pardon, sir," said Fox hastily, "I don't know what came over me." He opened his notebook in some confusion.

"Mrs. Harris," said Alleyn, "will you please tell us everything you can remember about this letter?"

"Yes, please do, Edith," said her husband unexpectedly. "She'll find it for you," he added in an aside. "Don't distress yourselves."

"Well," began Mrs. Harris. "It's a long time ago now and I'm afraid I'm rather hazy. It was after they had taken him away, I fancy, that we found it under the couch in the study. That was when we noticed the stain on the carpet you remember, Walter. At first, of course, I thought it was one of my husband's letters—it was not in an envelope. But when I glanced at it I realised at once that it was not, as it began 'Dear Daddy' and we have no children."

" 'Dear Daddy,' " repeated Alleyn.

"I decided afterwards that it was perhaps 'Dear Paddy' but as my husband's name is Walter Bernard it didn't signify. 'Why,' I said, or something of that sort. 'Why, it must have dropped out of that poor fellow's coat when the ambulance man examined him.' And—of course, I remember it now as clearly as if it was yesterday—and I said to little Violet: 'Pop on your bicycle and take it to the hospital as quickly as you can, dear, because they may be looking for it.' So little Violet——"

"Who was she, please?" asked Alleyn rather breathlessly.

"I beg your pardon?"

"Who was little Violet?" shouted Alleyn.

"My small niece. My husband's brother's third daughter. She was spending her holidays with us. She is grown up now and has a delightful post in London with a Lady Carrados."

"Thank you," said Alleyn. "Please go on."

26

Alleyn Plots a Denouement

But there was not much more to tell. Apparently Violet
Harris had bicycled off with Paddy O'Brien's letter and
had returned to say she had given it to the gentleman
who had brought the lady in the motor-car. The
gentleman had been sitting in the motor-car outside the
hospital. As far as Mrs. Harris could state, and she and
her husband went into a mazed avuncular family history
to prove their point, little Violet had been fifteen years
old at the time. Alleyn wrote out her statement, shorn of
its interminable parentheses, and she signed it.
Throughout the interview neither she nor her husband
gave the faintest sign of any form of curiosity.
Apparently it did not strike either of them as singular
that the interest in a letter lost eighteen years ago should
suddenly be cited to such a pitch that C.I.D. officers

thought it necessary to seek for a signed statement in the heart of Buckinghamshire.

They insisted on taking Alleyn and Fox round their garden. Alleyn hadn't the heart to refuse and besides he had a liking for gardens. Mrs. Harris gave them each a bunch of lavender and rosemary, which flowers, she said, were less conspicuous for gentlemen to carry than the gayer blossoms of summer. The sight of Fox solemnly grasping a posy in his enormous fist and examining a border of transplanted pansies, was almost too much for his superior officer. It was two o'clock when the tour of the garden was completed.

"You must come in whenever you are passing," said Mrs. Harris, blinking cordially at Alleyn, "and I shall remember what you say about your mother's herb garden."

"Yes, yes," agreed Mr. Harris. "Whenever you are passing. Of course. Anybody from dear old Falconbridge is doubly welcome."

They stood side by side at the gate and waved, rather in the manner of children, as Alleyn turned the car and drove away down Oakapple Lane.

"Well!" ejaculated Fox. "Well!"

"Not another word," said Alleyn, "until we get to that pub outside Barbicon-Bramley. Do you realise we've had no lunch? I refuse to utter another word until I've drunk a pint of bitter."

"And some bread and cheese and pickles," said Fox. "Pickles with plenty of onions in them."

"Lord! Lord! Fox, what a choice! Now I come to think of it, though, it sounds damn' good. 'Bread and cheese and pickles,' Fox, it's what we need. New white bread, mousetrap cheese, home-made pickles and bitter."

"That's the idea, Mr. Alleyn. You're a great gourmet," said Fox who had taught himself French, "and don't think I haven't enjoyed some of those dinners you're given me when everything seemed to sort of slide into something else. I have. But when you're famished and in the English countryside you can't beat bread and cheese and pickles."

The pub provided them with these delicacies. They took about a quarter of an hour over their meal and then set out again.

"Now then," said Alleyn.

"The thing that beats me," said Fox, wiping his short moustache with his handkerchief, "is little Violet. We knew she was a niece of this old gentleman's but, by gum, we didn't know she was staying there at the time, now, did we?"

"No, Br'er Fox, we didn't."

"I suppose she may not know it herself," continued Fox. "I mean to say, Miss Violet Harris may not realise that Lady Carrados was this Mrs. O'Brien whose husband was brought into her uncle's vicarage when she was a kid of fifteen."

"Quite possible. I hope she remembers the bicycle ride. We'll have to jog her memory, I dare say."

"Yes. Now I reckon, on what we've heard, that it was Carrados who took that letter from little Violet. Carrados, sitting in the car outside the hospital, while the poor chap who'd got the letter from Australia was dying inside. And then, later on, when there's all the fuss about a missing letter, what does he do?"

Alleyn knew this question was purely rhetorical and didn't interrupt.

"He tells the widow," said Fox; "he tells the widow that he's made every enquiry and there isn't a letter to be found."

"Yes," agreed Alleyn. "No doubt he tells her that."

"Right. Now, why does he do that? I reckon it's because Sir Herbert Carrados is what you might call a bit of a moral coward with a kind of mental twist. What these psycho-johnnies call a repression or some such thing. As I see it he didn't want to admit to having seen the letter because he'd actually read it. This Australian bloke knew Captain O'Brien had married a loony and

wrote to tell him he was now a widower. If what Lady
Carrados told you was correct and he'd fancied her for a
long time, that letter must have shaken him up a bit.
Now perhaps he says to himself, being a proud snobbish
sort of chap and yet having set his heart on her, that he'll
let sleeping dogs lie."

"Cut the whole thing dead? Yes. That's sound
enough. It's in character."

"That's what I mean," said Fox in a gratified voice.
"But all the same he doesn't destroy the letter. Or does
he?"

"That," said Alleyn, "is exactly what we've got to
find out."

"Well, sir, we've got our suspicions, haven't we?"

"Yes. Before this evening, Fox, I want to make
certainties of our suspicions."

"By gum, Mr. Alleyn, if we can do that we'll have
made a tidy job of this case. Don't count your chickens,
as I well know, but if we can get an arrest within two
days after the crime, in a complicated case like this,
we're not doing too badly, now are we?"

"I suppose not, you old warrior, I suppose not."
Alleyn gave a short sigh. "I wish——" he said. "Oh
God, Fox, I do wish he hadn't died. No good
maundering. I also wish very much that we'd been able
to find some trace of something, just *something* in the
taxi. But not a thing."

"The funeral's at three o'clock to-morrow, isn't it?"
asked Fox.

"Yes. Lady Mildred has asked me to be one of the
bearers. It's pretty strange under the circumstances, but
I'd like to do it. And I'd like to think that we had our
killer locked up before then. When we get back, Fox,
we'll have to arrange for these people to come round to
the Yard. We'll want Miss Harris, Bridget Carrados, her
mother, Carrados himself, Davidson, Withers, Dimitri
and Mrs. Halcut-Hackett. I'll see Lady Carrados alone
first. I want to soften the shock a little if it's possible."

"When shall we get them to come, sir?"

"It'll be four o'clock by the time we're back to the Yard. I think we'll make it this evening. Say nine o'clock. It's going to be devilish tricky. I'm counting on Dimitri losing his head. It's a cool head, blast it, and he may keep his wits about him. Talking of wits, there's the gallant Captain to be reckoned with. Unless I'm a Dutchman, Donald Potter's given me enough in his statement to lock the gallant Captain up for a nice long stretch. That's some comfort."

They were silent until they got as far as the Cromwell Road and then Fox said: "I suppose we are right, Mr. Alleyn. I know that seems a pretty funny thing to say at this stage, but it's a worrying business and that's a fact. It's the trickiest line of evidence I've *ever* come across. We seem to be hanging our case on the sort of things you usually treat with a good deal of suspicion."

"Don't I know it. No, Fox, I think it'll hold firm. It depends on what these people say in their second interviews to-night, of course. If we can establish the facts about the two cigarette-cases, the secret drawer, the telephone conversation and the stolen letter, we're right. Good Lord, that sounds like a list of titles from the old Sherlock Holmes stories. I think part of the charm of those excellent tales lies in Watson's casual but enthralling references to cases we never hear of again."

"The two cigarette-cases," repeated Fox slowly, "the secret drawer, the telephone conversation, and the stolen letter. Yes. Yes, that's right. You may say we hang our case on those four hooks."

"The word 'hang,' " said Alleyn grimly, "is exceedingly apposite. You may."

He drove Fox to the Yard.

"I'll come up with you and see if anything fresh has come in," he said.

They found reports from the officers who were out on the job. Dimitri's men reported that Francois had gone to the local stationers and bought a copy of this morning's *Times*. The stationer had told the Yard man that Dimitri as a rule took the *Daily Express*.

Alleyn laid the report down.

"Beat up a *Times* Br'er Fox."

Fox went out. He was away for some time. Alleyn brought his file up to date and lit his pipe. Then he rang up Lady Carrados.

"Evelyn? I've rung you up to ask if you and your husband and Bridget will come to my office at the Yard to-night. It's some more tidying up of this affair. If possible I'd like to have a word with you first. Would you rather it was here or in your house?"

"In your office, *please,* Roderick. It would be easier. Shall I come now?"

"If you will. Don't be fussed. I'm so sorry to bother you."

"I'll come at once," said the faint voice.

Fox returned with a *Times* which he laid on Alleyn's desk. He pointed a stubby finger at the personal column.

"What about the third from the top?" he said.

Alleyn read it aloud.

" 'Childie Darling. Living in exile. Longing. Only want Daughter. Daddy.' "

"Um," said Alleyn. "Has daddy had anything else to say to Childie during the last week or so?"

"Not during the last fortnight, anyway. I've looked up the files."

"There's nothing else in the agony column. The others are old friends, aren't they?"

"That's right."

"We'd better ask Father *Times* about daddy."

"I'll do that," said Fox, "and I'll get going on these people for to-night."

"Thank you, Fox. I've tackled Lady Carrados who is coming to see me now. If you've time I'd be glad if you'd fix the others. I ought to go and see Lady Mildred about the arrangements for to-morrow."

"You'll have time for that later on."

"Yes. I must report to the A.C. before this evening. I'll go along now, I think, and see if he's free. Ask them to show Lady Carrados up here, Fox, and ring through when she arrives."

"Very good, Mr. Alleyn."

Alleyn saw the Assistant Commissioner's secretary, who sent him in to the great man. Alleyn laid the file on the desk. The A.C. disregarded it.

"Well, Rory, how goes it? I hear you've got half the Yard mudlarking on Chelsea Embankment and the other half tailing the aristocracy. What's it all about?" asked the A.C., who had been kept perfectly *au fait* with the case but whose favourite pose was one of ignorance. "I suppose you want me to read this damn' nonsense?" he added, laying his hand on the file.

"If you will, sir. I've summed-up at the end. With your approval I'm collecting the relevant people here to-night and if the interviews go the right way I hope to be able to make an arrest. If you agree, I'd like a blank warrant."

"You're a pretty cool customer, aren't you?" grunted the A.C. "And if the interviews go all wrong you return the warrant and think of something else? That it?"

"Yes, sir. That's it."

"See here, Rory, our position in this affair is that we've got to have a conviction. If your customer gets off on this sort of evidence, opposing counsel is going to make us look like so many Aunt Sallies. It's so damn' shaky. Can't you hear what old Harrington-Barr will do with you if he's briefed? Make you look like a boiled egg, my good man, unless you've got a damning admission or two to shove at the jury. *And* all this blackmail stuff. How are you going to get any of these people to charge their blackmailer? You know what people are over blackmail."

"Yes, sir. I do rather hope for a damning admission."

"Do you, by Gad! All right, all right. See them in here. In my room. I'd better know the worst at once, I suppose." He scowled at Alleyn. "This goes a bit close to you, doesn't it? Lord Robert was a friend of yours, wasn't he?"

"He was, sir, yes."

"Ugh! He was a nice little chap. I understand the F.O. is making tender enquiries. In case a foreign power remembers him pottering about twenty years ago and has decided to assassinate him. Silly asses. Well, I'm sorry you've had this knock, Rory. It doesn't seem to have cramped your style. Quick work, if it's accurate."

"If!" said Alleyn. "I hope to Heaven we haven't gone wrong."

"What time's the denouement to-night?"

"Nine o'clock, sir."

"All right. Trot 'em along here. Thank you, Rory."

"Thank you, sir."

On his return to his own room he found Fox was waiting for him.

"Lady Carrados is downstairs, sir."

"Go and bring her up, Fox, will you?"

Fox turned in the doorway.

"I've got on to *The Times*," he said. "They were a bit dignified about it but I know one of the chaps who deals with the agony-column notices and got hold of him. He told me the Childie Darling thing came by mail with a postal order for double rates and a request that it should appear, very particular, in this morning's edition. The note said the advertiser would call to collect the change, if any, and was signed W. A. K. Smith, address G.P.O., Erith."

"Postmark?"

"They'd lost the envelope but he'll look for it. The writing," said Fox, "was in script on common notepaper."

"Was it indeed?" murmured Alleyn.

"There's one other thing," said Fox. "The reports have come through from the post offices. A clerk at the Main Western District says that during the rush hour yesterday someone left a parcel on the counter. He found it later on in the day. It was soft, about the right weight and had five bob in tuppenny stamps on it, one and fivepence more than was necessary. He remembers

the address was to somewhere in China and it was
written in script. So my Private Hoo Flung Dung may
have been a fair guess. We've got on to Mount Pleasant
and it's too late. A parcels post went out to China this
afternoon."

"Blast!" said Alleyn.

"I'll be off," said Fox, "and get her ladyship."

While he waited for Lady Carrados, Alleyn cut the
little notice out of *The Times*. After a moment's
consideration he unlocked a drawer in his desk and took
out Mrs. Halcut-Hackett's gold cigarette-case. He
opened it and neatly gummed the notice inside the lid.

Fox showed Lady Carrados in and went away.

"I'm so sorry, Evelyn," said Alleyn. "I've been
closeted with my superior. Have you been here long?"

"No. What is it now, please, Roderick?"

"It's this. I want you to allow what may seem a rather
drastic step. I want you to give me permission to talk to
your husband, in front of you, about Paddy O'Brien."

"You mean—tell him that we were not married?"

"If it seems necessary."

"I can't!"

"I shouldn't do it if it wasn't vitally necessary. I
do not believe, Evelyn, that he would"—Alleyn
hesitated—"that he would be as shocked as you
imagine."

"But I *know* he would be terribly shocked. Of course
he would."

"I think I can promise you that you have nothing to
fear from this decision. I mean that Carrados's attitude
to yourself and Bridget will not be materially affected by
it."

"I cannot believe that. I cannot believe that he will
not be dreadfully wounded. Even violent."

"I promise you that I honestly believe that it may help
you both to a better understanding."

"If only I could think that!"

"It will certainly help us to see justice done on your
blackmailer. Evelyn, I don't want to be intolerably

priggish, but I do believe it is your duty to do this."

"I had almost made up my mind to tell him."

"All the better. Come now. Look at me! Will you let me deal with it?"

She looked at him. Quite deliberately he used the whole force of that thing people call personality and of which he knew—how could he not know?—he had his share. He imposed his will on hers as surely as if it was a tangible instrument. And he saw her give way.

She raised her hands and let them fall limply back on her lap.

"Very well, I'm so bemused and puzzled, I don't know, I give up. My house is falling about my ears. I'll do whatever you think best, Roderick."

"You need say very little." He went into details. She listened attentively and repeated his instructions. When that was over he rose and looked down at her. "I'm so sorry," he said. "It's no good my trying to make light of this. It *is* a very upsetting business for you. But take heart of grace. Bridget need not know, although I think if I were you I should tell her. She's got plenty of courage and the moderns don't make nearly such heavy weather of that sort of thing as we did. My niece Sarah prattles away about people born in and out of wedlock as if it was a fifty-fifty chance. Upon my word, Evelyn, I wouldn't be surprised if your daughter found a certain amount of romantic satisfaction in the story you have been at such pains to hide from her."

"That would be almost funny, wouldn't it?" Lady Carrados looked into Alleyn's compassionate eyes. She reached out her hand and he took it firmly between both of his.

"Roderick," she said, "how old are you?"

"Forty-three, my dear."

"I'm forty," and absent-mindedly she added, as women do: "Isn't it awful?"

"Dreadful," agreed Alleyn, smiling at her.

"Why haven't you married?"

"My mother says she tried to make a match of it

between you and me. But Paddy O'Brien came along and I hadn't a chance."

"That seems odd, now, doesn't it? If it's true. I don't remember that you ever paid me any particular attention."

He saw that she had reached that lull in the sensibilities that sometimes follows extreme emotional tension. She spoke idly with an echo of her customary gentle gaiety. She sounded as if her mind had gone as limp as the thin hand he still held.

"You ought to marry," she said vaguely and added: "I must go."

"I'm coming down. I'll see you to your car."

As she drove away he stood looking after her for a second or two, and then shook his head doubtfully and set out for Cheyne Walk.

27

Interlude for Love

Alleyn wondered if it was only because he knew the body of his friend had come home that he felt its presence. Perhaps the house was not more quiet than it had been that morning. Perhaps the dead did not in truth cast about them so deep a spell. And then he smelt lilies and all the hushed chill of ceremonial death closed about his heart. He turned to Bunchy's old butler who was in the condition so often found in the faithful retainers of Victorian melodrama. He had been weeping. His eyes were red and his face blotted with tears, and his lips trembled. He showed Alleyn into Mildred's sitting-room. When she came forward in her lustreless black clothes, he found in her face the same unlovely reflection of sorrow. Mildred wore the customary expression of bereavement, and though he knew it to be the stamp of sincere grief, he felt a kind of impatience. He felt a profound loathing of the formalities of death. A dead body was nothing, nothing but an intolerable caricature of something someone had loved. It was a reminder of unspeakable indignities, and yet people surrounded their dead with owlish circumstances, asked you, as Mildred was asking him now, in a special muted voice, to look at them.

"I know you'd like to see him, Roderick."

He followed her into a room on the ground floor. The merciless scent of flowers was so heavy here that it hung like mist on the cold air. The room was crowded with flowers. In the centre, on three shrouded trestles, Robert Gospell's body lay in its coffin.

It was the face of an elderly baby, dignified by the possession of some terrific secret. Alleyn was not troubled by the face. All dead faces looked like that. But the small fat hands which in life had moved with staccato emphasis, were obediently folded, and when he saw these his eyes were blinded by tears. He groped in his overcoat pocket for a handkerchief and his fingers found the bunch of rosemary from Mr. Harris's garden. The grey-green spikes were crisp and unsentimental and they smelt of the sun. When Mildred turned aside, he gave them to the dead.

He followed her back to her drawing-room and she began to tell him about the arrangements for the funeral.

"Broomfield, who as you know is the head of the family, is only sixteen. He's abroad with his tutor and can't get back in time. We are not going to alter his plans. So that Donald and I are the nearest. Donald is perfectly splendid. He has been such a comfort all day. Quite different. And then dear Troy has come to stay with me and has answered all the letters and done everything."

Her voice, still with that special muted note, droned on, but Alleyn's thoughts had been arrested by this news of Troy and he had to force himself to listen to Mildred. When she had finished he asked her if she wished to know anything about his side of the picture and discovered that she was putting all the circumstances of her brother's death away from her. Mildred had adopted an ostrich attitude towards the murder and he got the impression that she rather hoped the murderer would never be caught. She wished to cut the whole thing dead and he thought it was rather clever and rather nice of her to be able to welcome him so cordially as a friend and pay no attention to him as a policeman.

After a minute or two there seemed to be nothing more to say to Mildred. Alleyn said good-bye to her, promised to attend the memorial service at eleven and to do his part at the funeral. He went out into the hall.

In the doorway he met Troy.

He heard his own voice saying: "Hullo, you're just in time. You're going to save my life."

"Whatever do you mean?"

"It's nearly five. I've had six hours' sleep in the last fifty-eight hours. That's nothing for us hardy coppers but for some reason I'm feeling sorry for myself. Will you take tea or a drink or possibly both with me? For God's sake say you will."

To himself his voice sounded hideously false and jaunty. It seemed to have adopted the manner of the assured philanderer without his assurance. He was astonished when Troy said:

"Very well, where shall we go?"

"I thought," said Alleyn, who up to that moment had thought nothing of the sort, "that we might have tea at my flat. Unless you object to my flat."

"I'm not a débutante," said Troy. "I don't think I need coddle my reputation. Your flat let it be."

"Good," said Alleyn. "I've got my mother's car. I'll just warn my servant and tell the Yard where to find me. Do you think I may use the telephone?"

"I'm sure you may."

He darted to telephone and was back in a minute.

"Vassily is tremendously excited," he said. "A lady to tea! Come on."

On the way Alleyn was so filled with astonishment at finding himself agreeably alone with Troy that he fell into a trance from which he only woke when he pulled the car up outside his own flat. He did not apologise for his silence: he felt a tranquillity in Troy that had accepted it, and when they were indoors he was delighted to hear her say: "This is peaceful," and to see her pull off her cap and sit on a low stool before the fireplace.

"Shall we have a fire?" asked Alleyn. "Do say yes. It's not a warm day, really."

"Yes, let's," agreed Troy.

"Will you light it while I see about tea?"

He went out of the room to give Vassily a series of rather confused orders, and when he returned there was Troy before the fire, bareheaded, strangely familiar.

"So you're still here," said Alleyn.

"It's a nice room, this."

He put a box of cigarettes on the floor beside her and took out his pipe. Troy turned and saw her own picture of Suva at the far end of the room.

"Oh, yes," said Alleyn, "there's that."

"How did you get hold of it?"

"I got someone to buy it for me."

"But why——?"

"I don't know why I was so disingenuous about it except that I wanted it so very badly for reasons that were not purely aesthetic and I thought you would see through them if I made a personal business of it."

"I should have been rather embarrassed, I suppose."

"Yes." Alleyn waited for a moment and then he said: "Do you remember how I found you that day, painting and cursing? It was just as the ship moved out of Suva. Those sulky hills and that ominous sky were behind you."

"We had a row, didn't we?"

"We did."

Troy's face became rather pink.

"In fact," said Alleyn, "there is scarcely an occasion on which we have met when we have not had a row. Why is that, do you suppose?"

"I've always been on the defensive."

"Have you? For a long time I thought you merely disliked me."

"No. You got under my guard."

"If it hadn't been for that damned case, things might have gone better," said Alleyn. "What a pity it is that we cannot sometimes react to situations like characters in the less honest form of novel. The setting should have been ideal, you know. A murder in your house. You with just enough motive to make a 'strong situation' and not enough seriously to implicate you. Me, as the grim detective finding time for a bit of Rochester stuff. You should have found yourself drawn unwillingly into love, Troy. Instead of which I merely acquired a sort of post-mortem disagreeableness. If you painted a surrealist picture of me I would be made of Metropolitan Police notebooks, one eye would be set in a keyhole, my hands would be occupied with somebody's else's private correspondence. The background would be a morgue and the whole pretty conceit wreathed with festoons of blue tape and hangman's rope. What?"

"Nonsense," said Troy.

"I suppose so. Yes. The vanity of the male trying to find extraordinary reasons for a perfectly natural phenomenon. You don't happen to love me. And why the devil should you?"

"You don't happen to understand," said Troy shortly, "and why the devil should you?"

She took a cigarette and tilted her face up for him to give her a light. A lock of her short dark hair had fallen across her forehead. Alleyn lit the cigarette, threw the match into the fire and tweaked the lock of hair.

"Abominable woman," he said abruptly. "I'm so glad you've come to see me."

"I tell you what," said Troy more amiably. "I've

always been frightened of the whole business. Love and so on."

"The physical side?"

"Yes, that, but much more than that. The whole business. The breaking down of all one's reserves. The mental as well as the physical intimacy."

"My mind to me a kingdom is."

"I feel it wouldn't be," said Troy.

"I feel it rather terrifyingly still would be. Don't you think that in the closest possible union there must always be moments when one feels oneself completely separate, completely alone. Surely it must be so, otherwise we would not be so astonished on the rare occasions when we read each other's thoughts."

Troy looked at him with a sort of shy determination that made his heart turn over.

"Do you read my thoughts?" she asked.

"Not very clearly, Troy. I dare not wish I could."

"I do yours, sometimes. That is one of the things that sends my defences up."

"If you could read them now," said Alleyn, "you might well be frightened."

Vassily came in with tea. He had, Alleyn saw at a glance, excitedly rushed out to his favourite delicatessen shop round the corner and purchased caviare. He had made a stack of buttered toast, he had cut up many lemons, and he had made tea in an enormous Stuart pot of Lady Alleyn's, which her son had merely borrowed to show to a collector. Vassily had also found time to put on his best coat. His face was wreathed in smiles of embarrassing significance. He whispered to himself as he set this extraordinary feast out on a low table in front of Troy.

"Please, please," said Vassily. "If there is anysink more, sir. Should I not perhaps——"

"No, no," said Alleyn hastily, "that will do admirably."

"Caviare!" said Troy. "Oh, how glad I am—a heavenly tea."

Vassily broke into a loud laugh, excused and bowed himself out, and shut the doors behind him with the stealth of a soubrette in a French comedy.

"You've transported the old fool," said Alleyn.

"What is he?"

"A Russian carry-over from a former case of mine. He very nearly got himself arrested. Can you really eat caviare and drink Russian tea? He's put some milk there."

"I don't want milk and I shall eat any quantity of caviare," said Troy.

When they had finished and Vassily had taken away the tea things, Troy said: "I must go."

"Not yet."

"Oughtn't you to be at Scotland Yard?"

"They'll ring me up if I'm wanted. I'm due there later on."

"We've never once mentioned Bunchy," said Troy.

"No."

"Shall you get an early night to-night?"

"I don't know, Troy."

Alleyn sat on the footstool by her chair. Troy looked down on his head propped between his long thin hands.

"Don't talk about the case if you'd rather not. I only wanted to let you know that if you'd like to, I'm here."

"You're here. I'm trying to get used to it. Shall you ever come again, do you think? Do you know I swore to myself I would not utter one word of love this blessed afternoon? Well, perhaps we'd better talk about the case. I shall commit a heinous impropriety and tell you I may make an arrest this evening."

"You *know* who killed Bunchy?"

"We believe we do. If to-night's show goes the right way we shall be in a position to make the arrest."

He turned and looked into her face.

"Ah," he said, "my job again! Why does it revolt you so much?"

Troy said: "It's nothing reasonable—nothing I can attempt to justify. It's simply that I've got an absolute horror of capital punishment. I don't even know that I agree with the stock arguments against it. It's just one of those nightmare things. Like claustrophobia. I used to adore the Ingoldsby Legends when I was a child. One day I came across the one about my Lord Tomnoddy and the hanging. It made the most extraordinary impression on me. I dreamt about it. I couldn't get it out of my head. I used to turn the pages of the book, knowing that I would come to it, dreading it, and yet—I had to read it. I even made a drawing of it."

"That should have helped."

"I don't think it did. I suppose most people, even the least imaginative, have got a bogy man in the back of their minds. That has always been mine. I've spoken of it before. And so you see when you and I met in that other business and it ended in your arrest of someone I knew——" Her voice wavered. "And then there was the trial and—the end——"

With a nervous movement she touched his head.

"It's not you. And yet I mind so much that it is you."

Alleyn pulled her hand down against his lips.

There was complete silence. Everything he had ever felt; every *frisson,* the most profound sorrow, the least annoyance, the greatest joy and the smallest pleasure had been but preparation for this moment when her hand melted against his lips. Presently he found himself leaning over her. He still held her hand like a talisman and he spoke against the palm.

"This must be right. I swear it must be right. I can't be feeling this alone. Troy?"

"Not now," Troy whispered. "No more, now. Please."

"Yes."

"Please."

He stooped, took her face between his hands, and kissed her hard on the mouth. He felt her come to life beneath his lips. Then he let her go.

"And don't think I shall ask you to forgive me," he

said. "You've no right to let this go by. You're too damn' particular by half, my girl. I'm your man and you know it."

They stared at each other.

"That's the stuff to give the troops," Alleyn added. "The arrogant male."

"The arrogant turkey-cock," said Troy shakily.

"I know, I know. But at least you didn't find it unendurable. Troy, for God's sake can't we be honest with each other? When I kissed you just then you seemed to meet me like a flame. Could I have imagined that?"

"No."

"It was as if you shouted with your whole body that you loved me. How can I not be arrogant?"

"How can I not be shaken?"

When he saw that she was indeed greatly shaken an intolerable wave of compassion drowned his thoughts. He stammered. "I'm sorry. I'm sorry."

Troy began to speak slowly.

"Let me go away now. I want to think. I will try to be honest. I promise you I did not believe I loved you. It seemed to me that I couldn't love you when I resented so much the feeling that you made some sort of demand whenever we met. I don't understand physical love. I don't know how much it means. I'm just plain frightened and that's a fact."

"You shall go. I'll get a taxi. Wait a moment."

He ran out and got a taxi. When he returned she was standing in front of the fire holding her cap in her hand and looking rather small and lost. He brought her coat and dropped it lightly across her shoulders.

"I've been very weak," said Troy. "When I said I'd come I thought I would keep it all very peaceful and impersonal. You looked so worn and troubled and it was so easy just to do this. And now see what's happened?"

"The skies have opened and the stars have fallen. I

feel as if I'd run round the world in the last hour. And now you must leave me."

He took her to the taxi. Before he shut the door he said: "Your most devoted turkey-cock."

28

Alleyn Marshals the Protagonists

The assistant commissioner's clock struck a quarter to nine as Alleyn walked into the room.

"Hullo, Rory."

"Good evening, sir."

"As you have no doubt observed with your trained eye my secretary is not present. So you may come off the official rocks. Sit down and light your pipe."

"Thank you," said Alleyn.

"Feeling a bit shaky?"

"A bit. I shall look such an egregious ass if they don't come up to scratch."

"No doubt. It's a big case, Chief Inspector."

"Don't I know it, sir!"

"Who comes first?"

"Sir Herbert and Lady Carrados."

"Any of 'em arrived yet?"

"All except Dimitri. Fox has dotted them about the place. His room, mine, the waiting-room, and the

318

charge-room. As soon as Dimitri arrives, Fox'll come
and report."

"Right. In the meantime, we'll go over the plan of
action again."

They went over the plan of action.

"Well," said the Assistant Commissioner, "it's
ticklish, but it may work. As I see it, everything depends
on the way you handle them."

"Thank you, sir," said Alleyn grimly, "for those few
reassuring words.".

The Assistant Commissioner's clock struck nine.
Alleyn knocked out his pipe. There was a tap on the
door and Fox came in.

"We are all ready, sir," he said.

"All right, Mr. Fox. Show them in."

Fox went out. Alleyn glanced at the two chairs
under the central lamp, and then at the Assistant
Commissioner sitting motionless in the green-shaded
light from his desk. Alleyn himself stood before the
mantelpiece.

"Stage set," said the quiet voice beyond the green
lamp. "And now the curtain rises."

There was a brief silence, and then once more the
door opened.

"Sir Herbert and Lady Carrados, sir."

They came in. Alleyn moved forward, greeted them
formally, and then introduced them to the Assistant
Commissioner. Carrados's manner as he shook hands
was a remarkable mixture of the condescension of a
viceroy and the fortitude of an early Christian martyr.

The Assistant Commissioner was crisp with them.

"Good evening, Lady Carrados. Good evening, Sir
Herbert. In view of certain information he has received,
Chief Detective-Inspector Alleyn and I decided to invite
you to come and see us. As the case is in Mr. Alleyn's
hands, I shall leave it to him to conduct the
conversation. Will you both sit down?"

They sat. The light from the overhead lamp beat
down on their faces, throwing strong shadows under the

eyes and cheek-bones. The two heads turned in unison to Alleyn.

Alleyn said: "Most of what I have to say is addressed to you, Sir Herbert."

"Indeed?" said Carrados. "Well, Alleyn, as I fancy I told you yesterday afternoon, I am only too anxious to help you to clear up the wretched business. As Lord Robert's host on that fatal night——"

"Yes, we quite realise that, sir. Your attitude encourages one to hope that you will understand, or at any rate excuse, my going over old ground, and also breaking into new. I am in a position to tell you that we have followed a very strange trail since yesterday—a trail that has led us to some remarkable conclusions."

Carrados turned his eyes, but not his head, towards his wife. He did not speak.

"We have reason to believe," Alleyn went on, "that the murder of Lord Robert Gospell is the outcome of blackmail. Did you speak, sir?"

"No. No! I cannot see, I fail to understand——"

"I'll make myself clearer in a moment, I hope. Now, for reasons into which I need not go at the moment, the connection between this crime and blackmail leads us to one of two conclusions. Either Lord Robert was a blackmailer, and was killed by one of his victims, or possibly someone wishing to protect his victim——"

"What makes you say that?" asked Carrados hoarsely. "It's impossible!"

"Impossible? Why, please?"

"Because, Lord Robert, Lord Robert was not—it's impossible to imagine—have you any proof that he was a blackmailer?"

"The alternative is that Lord Robert had discovered the identity of the blackmailer, and was murdered before he could reveal it."

"You say this," said Carrados, breathlessly, "but you give no proof."

"I ask you, sir, simply to accept my statement that rightly or wrongly we believe our case to rest on one or the other of those alternatives."

"I don't pretend to be a detective, Alleyn, but——"

"Just a minute, sir, if you don't mind. I want you now to go back with me to a day nearly eighteen years ago, when you motored Lady Carrados down to a village called Falconbridge in Buckinghamshire. You were not married then."

"I frequently motored her into the country in those days."

"You will have no difficulty in remembering this occasion. It was the day on which Captain Paddy O'Brien met with his accident."

Alleyn waited. He saw the sweat round Carrados's eyes shine in the strong lamplight.

"Well?" said Carrados.

"You do remember that day?" Alleyn asked.

"But Herbert," said Lady Carrados, "of course you do."

"I remember, yes. But I fail to see——"

"Please, sir! I shall fire point-blank in a moment. You remember?"

"Naturally."

"You remember that Captain O'Brien was taken first to the vicarage and from there, in an ambulance, to the hospital, where he died a few hours later?"

"Yes."

"You remember that, after he died, your wife, as she is now, was very much distressed because she believed that a certain letter which Captain O'Brien carried had been lost?"

"I have no recollection of this."

"Let me help you. She said that he had probably carried it in his pocket, that it must have fallen out, that she was most anxious to recover it. Am I right, Lady Carrados?"

"Yes—quite right."

Her voice was low, but perfectly steady. She was looking at Alleyn with an air of shocked bewilderment.

"Did you ask Sir Herbert if he had enquired everywhere for this missing letter?"

"Yes."

"Do you remember now, Sir Herbert?"

"I think—I—remember—something. It was all very distressing. I tried to be of some use; I think I may have been of some use."

"Did you succeed in finding the letter?"

"I—don't think so."

"Are you sure?"

A little runnel of sweat trickled down each side of his nose into that fine moustache.

"I am tolerably certain."

"Do you remember sitting in your car outside the hospital while Lady Carrados was with Captain O'Brien?"

Carrados did not speak for a long time. Then he swung round in his chair, and addressed that silent figure in the green lamplight.

"I can see no possible reason for this extraordinary procedure. It is most distressing for my wife, and I may say, sir, it strikes me as being damnably offensive and outside the duties of your office."

"I don't think it is, Sir Herbert," said the Assistant Commissioner. "I advise you to answer Mr. Alleyn, you know."

"I may tell you," Carrados began, "that I am an intimate friend of your chief's. He shall hear about this."

"I expect so," said the Assistant Commissioner. "Go on, Mr. Alleyn."

"Lady Carrados," said Alleyn, "did you, in point of fact, leave Sir Herbert in the car when you went into the hospital?"

"Yes."

"Yes. Now, Sir Herbert, while you waited there, do you remember a schoolgirl of fifteen or so coming up on her bicycle?"

"How the devil can I remember a schoolgirl on a bicycle eighteen years ago?"

"Only because she gave you the letter that we have been discussing."

Evelyn Carrados uttered a stifled cry. She turned and looked at her husband, as though she saw him for the first time. He met her with what Alleyn thought one of the most extraordinary glances he had ever seen—accusation, abasement, even a sort of triumphant misery, were all expressed in it; it was the face of a mean martyr. "The mask of jealousy," thought Alleyn. "There's nothing more pitiable or more degrading. My God, if ever I——" He thrust the thought from him, and began again.

"Sir Herbert, did you take that letter from the schoolgirl on the bicycle?"

Still with a sort of smile on his mouth, Carrados turned to Alleyn.

"I have no recollection of it," he said.

Alleyn nodded to Fox, who went out. He was away for perhaps two minutes. Nobody spoke. Lady Carrados had bent her head, and seemed to look with profound attention at her gloved hands, clasped tightly together in her lap. Carrados suddenly wiped his face with his palm, and then drew out his handkerchief. Fox came back. He ushered in Miss Harris.

"Good evening, Miss Harris," said Alleyn.

"Good evening, Mr. Alleyn. Good evening, Lady Carrados. Good evening, Sir Herbert. Good evening," concluded Miss Harris with a collected glance at the Assistant Commissioner.

"Miss Harris," said Alleyn, "do you remember staying with your uncle, Mr. Walter Harris, when he was vicar at Falconbridge? You were fifteen at the time I mean."

"Yes, Mr. Alleyn, certainly," said Miss Harris.

Carrados uttered some sort of oath. Lady Carrados said: "But—what do you mean, Miss Harris?"

"Certainly, Lady Carrados," said Miss Harris, brightly.

"At that time," said Alleyn, "there was a fatal motor accident."

"To Captain O'Brien. Pardon me, Lady Carrados. Yes, Mr. Alleyn."

"Good Lord!" ejaculated Alleyn, involuntarily. "Do you mean to say that you have realised that——"

"I knew Captain 'Paddy' O'Brien was Lady Carrados's first husband, naturally."

"But," said Alleyn, "did you never think of telling Lady Carrados that there was this, well, this link, between you?"

"Oh, no," said Miss Harris, "naturally not, Mr. Alleyn. It would not have been at all my place to bring it up. When I was given the list of vacant posts at the Friendly Cousins Registry Office I thought this seemed the most suitable, and I—please excuse me, Lady Carrados—I made enquiries, as one does, you know. And I said to my friend Miss Smith: 'What an extraordinary coincidence,' because when I learned of Lady Carrados's former name I realised it must be the same, and I said to Smithy: 'I think that must be an omen,' so I applied for the post."

"I see," said Alleyn, "and do you remember Sir Herbert too?"

"Oh, yes. At least, I wasn't quite sure at first, but afterwards I was. Sir Herbert was the gentleman in the car. Perhaps I should explain?"

"Please do."

"I had actually spoken to him." She looked apologetically at Carrados. "I'm quite sure Sir Herbert has quite forgotten, because I was just a gawky schoolgirl at the time."

"That will do, Miss Harris," said Carrados violently. "You will please not answer any further questions."

Miss Harris looked extremely startled, turned bright pink, and opened her eyes very wide indeed. She closed her lips in a prudent button.

"Go on, Miss Harris," said Alleyn.

"Which do you wish me to do, Lady Carrados?" asked her secretary.

"I think you had better go on," said the faint voice.

"Very well, Lady Carrados. You see, I had the pleasure of returning a letter that had been left behind at the vicarage."

"That is an absolute lie," said Carrados, loudly.

"Pardon me," said Miss Harris, "but I cannot let that pass. I am speaking the truth."

"Thank you, Miss Harris," said Alleyn, quickly. "Would you mind waiting outside for a moment? Fox."

Fox shepherded her out.

"By God!" began Carrados. "If you take the word of a——"

"Wait a moment," said Alleyn. "I think I shall go on with my story. Our case, Sir Herbert, is that you did, in fact, take this letter, and for some reason never gave it to the lady who afterwards married you. Our case is that, having read the letter, you kept it for eighteen years, in the drawer of a miniature writing-desk in your study."

"I protest. I absolutely deny——"

"You deny this, too?"

"It is outrageous! I tell you this, sir, if I have any influence——"

"Just a moment," said Alleyn. "Lady Carrados is speaking."

The focus of attention shifted to the woman. She sat there as if she attended a meeting of some society in which she was interested. Her furs, her expensive, unnoticeable clothes, her gloves, her discreet make-up, might have been taken as symbols of controlled good-breeding. It was the fierce rigidity of her figure that gave expression to her emotion. Her voice scarcely wavered. Alleyn realised that she was oblivious to her surroundings, and to the presence of other people in the room, and that seemed to him to be the most significant indication of her distress. She spoke directly to her husband.

"You knew! All these years you have watched me, and known how much I suffered. Why did you hide the letter? Why did you marry me, knowing my past history? It seems to me you must be mad. I understand now why you have watched me, why, since this awful business, you have never taken your eyes off me. You knew. You knew I was being blackmailed." She caught her breath, and moved round stiffly until she faced her husband. "You've done it," she whispered. "It's you. You're mad, and you've done it to torture me. You've always been jealous of Paddy. Ever since I told you it could never be the same with anyone else. You were jealous of dead Paddy."

"Evelyn," said Alleyn gently. She made a slight impatient gesture, but she spoke only to Carrados.

"You wrote those letters. It's you."

Carrados stared at her like an idiot. His mouth was open. His eyebrows were raised in a sort of imbecile astonishment. He shook his head from side to side.

"No," he said. "No, Evelyn, no."

"Make him tell you, Roderick," she said, without turning her head.

"Sir Herbert," said Alleyn. "Do you deny you kept this letter in the secret drawer of that desk?"

"Yes."

Fox glanced at Alleyn, went out, and returned, after another deadly silence, with Bridget.

Lady Carrados gave a little moaning cry, and caught at her daughter's hand.

"Miss O'Brien," said Alleyn, "I've asked you to come here in order that the Assistant Commissioner may hear of an incident you related to me yesterday. You told me that on one occasion, when you were alone in the study of your stepfather's house, you examined the miniature writing-cabinet in that room. You told me that when you pressed a tiny screw a triangular drawer opened out of the cabinet and that there was a letter in it. Is this true?"

"Donna?" Bridget looked anxiously at her mother.

"Yes, yes, darling. Tell them. Whatever it is, tell them."

"It's quite true," said Bridget.

"Your stepfather came into the study at this juncture?"

"Yes."

"What was his attitude when he saw what you had done?"

"He was very angry indeed."

"What did he do?"

"He twisted my arm, and bruised it."

"A lie. The child has always hated me. Everything I have tried to do for her—— A lie, a wicked spiteful lie!"

"Fox," said Alleyn, "will you ask Sir Daniel to come in?"

Sir Daniel had evidently been sitting in the secretary's office, as he came in almost immediately. When he saw the two Carradoses and Bridget, he greeted them exactly as if they were fellow guests at a party. He then shook hands with the Assistant Commissioner, and turned to Alleyn.

"Sir Daniel," said Alleyn. "I've asked you to come in as I understand you were witness to a scene which Miss O'Brien has just described to us. It took place about two years ago. Do you remember that Miss O'Brien rang you up and asked you to come and see her mother who was unwell?"

"That has happened more than once," said Davidson.

"On this particular visit you went into the study and talked to Miss O'Brien about a small French writing-cabinet."

Davidson moved his eyebrows.

"Oh, yes?"

"Do you remember it?"

"I do. Very well."

"You told her that there was probably a secret drawer in the box. Then you went upstairs to see Lady Carrados."

"Yes. That's how it was, I think."

"When you returned, were Miss O'Brien and Sir Herbert together in the study?"

"Yes," said Davidson, and set his lips in an extremely firm line.

"Will you describe the scene that followed?"

"I am afraid not, Mr. Alleyn."

"Why not?"

"Let us say, for reasons of professional etiquette."

Lady Carrados said: "Sir Daniel, if you are thinking of me, I implore you to tell them what they want to know. I want the truth as much as anyone here. If I don't know the truth now, I shall go to pieces."

Davidson looked at her in astonishment.

"*You* want me to tell them about that afternoon?"

"Yes, yes, I do."

"And you, Carrados?" Davidson stared at Carrados, as if he were a sort of curiosity.

"Davidson, I implore you to keep your head. I am sure you saw nothing that could be construed—that could be regarded as evidence—that——Davidson, you know me. You know that I'm not a vindictive man. You know."

"Come," said Alleyn, "we can cut this short. Sir Daniel, did you examine Miss O'Brien's arm when you returned to the study?"

"I did," said Davidson, turning his back on Carrados.

"What did you find?"

"A certain amount of contusion, for which I prescribed a lotion."

"To what cause did you attribute these bruises?"

"They suggested that the arm had been tightly held, and twisted."

"What were the relative position of Sir Herbert and his step-daughter when you came into the study?"

"He held her by the arm."

"Would it be correct to say he was storming at her?"

Davidson looked thoughtfully at Bridget. They exchanged half-smiles. "He was shouting a good deal, certainly," said Davidson dryly.

"Did you notice the writing-desk?"

"I don't think I noticed it the second time I went into

the room. I realised that Sir Herbert Carrados was talking about it when I came in."

"Yes. Thank you, Sir Daniel. Will you and Miss O'Brien wait outside? We'll see Mr. Dimitri, if you please, Fox."

Davidson and Bridget both went out. Dimitri was ushered in by Fox. He was very sleek, with a clean bandage round his cut finger, oil on his hair, scent on his person. He looked out of the corners of his eyes, and bowed extensively.

"Good evening, my lady. Good evening, gentlemen."

"Mr. Dimitri," Alleyn began, "I have———"

"Stop!"

Carrados had got to his feet. He stood with his hand raised before his face in a curious gesture, half defensive, half declamatory. Then he slowly extended his arm, and pointed to Dimitri. The action was both ridiculous and alarming.

"What's the matter, Sir Herbert?" asked Alleyn.

"What's he doing here? My God, now I know—I know———"

"Well, Sir Herbert? What do you know?"

"Stop! I'll tell you. I did it! I did it! I confess. I confess everything. I did it!"

29

Climax

"You did what, Sir Herbert?"

It was the A.C.'s voice, very quiet and matter-of-fact.

"I kept the letter." Carrados looked directly at his wife. "You know why. If ever you had spoken of him, if ever you had compared me to that fellow, if I had found you—— You know why."

"Yes," said Lady Carrados. "I know why."

"For God's sake," Carrados said, "for God's sake, gentlemen, let this go no further. It's a private matter between my wife and myself."

"It has gone much further than that," said Alleyn. "Did you not in fact write blackmailing letters to your wife purely in order to torture her mind? Did you not do this?"

"You fool," shouted Carrados. "You fool! It's I who have suffered. It's I who have dreaded what might happen. The letter was stolen. It was stolen. It was stolen."

"Now," said Alleyn, "it seems we are going to get the truth. When did you miss the letter?"

Carrados looked from one face to the other. For a frightful moment Alleyn thought he was going to burst into tears. His lips were shaking. He seemed an old man. He began to speak.

"It was when we came back from Newmarket. That evening I was alone in my study. Bridget had been very inconsiderate all day, leaving us and going off with a young man of whom I could not approve. My wife had taken her part against me. I was alone in my study. I found myself looking at the French writing-cabinet. There was something different in the arrangement of the pieces in front of it. I went to rearrange them, and being there I tried the hidden drawer. It was empty! I tell you the letter was there the day before. I saw it there. The day before I had been very angry with my wife. She had been cruel to me. I am very sensitive and my nerves are shattered. I am alone. Terribly lonely. Nobody cares what becomes of me. She was so thoughtless and cruel. So I looked at the letter because the letter gave me comfort. It was there the night before. And do you know who was alone in my room on May the ninth?"

"Yes," said Alleyn. "I am glad you, too, remember. It was Mr. Colombo Dimitri."

"Ah," said Carrados shakily. "Ah, now we're getting at it. Now, we're getting at it."

"I am afraid I do not understand," said Dimitri. "Is Sir Herbert perhaps ill?"

Carrados slewed round and again he pointed at Dimitri.

"You stole it, you filthy dago. I know you stole it. I have suspected it from the first. I could do nothing—nothing."

"Excuse me, Mr. Alleyn," said Dimitri, "but I believe that I may charge Sir Herbert Carrados with libel on this statement. Is it not so?"

"I don't think I advise you to do so, Mr. Dimitri. On the other hand I shall very strongly advise Lady Carrados to charge you with blackmail. Lady Carrados, is it a fact on the morning of May the twenty-fifth, when Lord Robert Gospell paid you a visit, you received a blackmailing letter?"

"Yes."

"Do you believe that the only source from which the blackmailer could have got his information was the letter lost on the day of Captain O'Brien's accident?"

"Yes."

Alleyn took an envelope from his pocket, handed it to her.

"Was the blackmailing letter written in a similar style to this?"

She glanced at it and turned her head away.

"It was exactly like that."

"If I tell you that the lady to whom this letter is addressed had been blackmailed as you have been blackmailed and that we have positive evidence that the man who wrote this address was Colombo Dimitri, are you prepared to charge him with blackmail?"

"Yes."

"It is completely false," said Dimitri. "I shall certainly sue for libel."

His face was ashen. He put his bandaged hand to his lips and pressed it against them.

"Before we go any further," said Alleyn, "I think I should explain that Lord Robert Gospell was in the confidence of Scotland Yard as regards these blackmailing letters. He was working for us on the case We've got his signed statement that leaves no doubt at all that Mr. Dimitri collected a sum of money at a concert held at the Constance Street Hall on Thursday, June the third. Lord Robert actually watched Mr. Dimitri collect this money."

"He——" Dimitri caught his breath, his lips were drawn back from his teeth in a sort of grin. "I deny everything," he said. "Everything. I wish to send for my lawyer."

"You shall do so, Mr. Dimitri, when I have finished. On June the eighth, two nights ago, Lady Carrados gave a ball at Marsdon House. Lord Robert was there. As he knew so much about Mr. Dimitri already, he thought he would find out a little more. He watched Mr. Dimitri. He now knew the method employed. He also knew that Lady Carrados was the victim of blackmail. Is that right, Lady Carrados?"

"Yes. I had a conversation with him about it. He knew what I was going to do."

"What were you going to do?"

"Put my bag containing five hundred pounds in a certain place in the green sitting-room upstairs."

"Yes," said Alleyn. "Now, Lord Robert saw Mr. Dimitri return her empty bag to Lady Carrados shortly before one o'clock. At one o'clock he rang me up and told me he now had enough evidence. The conversation was interrupted by someone who must have overheard at least one very significant phrase. Two and a half hours later Lord Robert was murdered."

The quiet of the room was blown into piercing clamour. Dimitri had screamed like a woman, his mouth wide open. This shocking rumpus lasted for a second and stopped. Alleyn had a picture of an engine-driver pulling a string and then letting it go. Dimitri stood, still with a gaping mouth, wagging his finger at Alleyn.

"Now then, now then," said Fox and stepped up to him.

"False!" said Dimitri, frantically snapping his fingers in Fox's face and then shaking them as if they were scorched. "False! You accuse me of murder. I am not an assassin. I am innocent. *Christo mio,* I am innocent, innocent, innocent!"

For a moment it looked as if he'd try to bolt from the room. He might have been a tenor giving an excruciatingly bad performance in a second-rate Italian opera. He mouthed at Alleyn, tore his hair, crumpled on to a chair, and burst into tears. Upon the five English people in the office there descended a heavy aura of embarrassment.

"I am innocent," sobbed Dimitri. "As innocent as a child. The blessed saints bear witness to my innocence. The blessed saints bear witness——"

"Unfortunately," said Alleyn, "their evidence is not acceptable in a court of law. If you will keep quiet for a moment, Mr. Dimitri, we can get on with our business. Will you ask Mrs. Halcut-Hackett to come in, please, Fox?"

The interval was enlivened by the sound of Dimitri biting his nails and sobbing.

Mrs. Halcut-Hackett, dressed as if she was going to a Continental restaurant and looking like a beauty-specialist's mistake, came into the office. Fox followed with an extra chair which he placed for her. She sat down and drew up her bust until it seemed to perch like some super-structure on a rigid foundation. Then she saw Lady Carrados. An extraordinary look passed between the two women. It was as if they had said to each other: "You, too?"

"Mrs. Halcut-Hackett," said Alleyn. "You have told me that after a charade party you gave in December you found that a document which you valued was missing from a box on your dressing-table. Had this man, Colombo Dimitri, an opportunity of being alone in this room?"

She turned her head and looked at Dimitri who flapped his hands at her.

"Why, yes," she said. "He certainly had."

"Did Lord Robert sit near you at the Sirmione Quartette's concert on June the third?"

"You know he did."

"Do you remember that this man, Colombo Dimitri, sat not very far away from you?"

"Why—yes."

"Your bag was stolen that afternoon?"

"Yes." She looked again at Lady Carrados who suddenly leant forward and touched her hand.

"I'm so sorry," she said. "I, too. Indeed you have nothing to fear from us. We have suffered, too. I have made up my mind to hide nothing now. Will you help by also hiding—nothing?"

"Oh, my dear!" said Mrs. Halcut-Hackett in a whisper.

"We need not ask for very much more," said Alleyn. "Would it have been possible for Dimitri to have taken your bag while you were out of the concert-room?"

"Lord Robert might have seen," said Mrs. Halcut-Hackett.

"Lord Robert did see," said Alleyn.

"The dead!" cried Dimitri. "I cannot be accused by the dead."

"If that was true," said Alleyn, "as it often is, what a motive for murder! I tell you we have a statement, written and signed by the dead."

Dimitri uttered a sort of moan and shrank back in his chair.

Alleyn took from his pocket the cigarette-case with the medallion.

"This is yours, isn't it?" he asked Mrs. Halcut-Hackett.

"Yes. I've told you so."

"You left it in the green sitting-room at Marsdon House?"

"Yes—only for a few minutes."

"A minute or two, not more, after you came out of that room you heard the dialling tinkle of the telephone?"

"Yes."

"You had seen Lord Robert coming upstairs?"

"Yes."

Alleyn nodded to Fox who again left the room.

"After you had joined your partner in the other sitting-out room, you discovered the loss of your case?"

"Yes, I did."

"Your partner fetched it."

She wetted her lips. Dimitri was listening avidly. Carrados had slumped down in his chair with his chin on his chest. Alleyn felt he was giving, for anybody that had time to notice it, a quiet performance of a broken man. Lady Carrados sat upright, her hands folded in her lap, her face looked exhausted. The A.C. was motionless behind the green lamp.

"Well, Mrs. Halcut-Hackett? Your partner fetched your case from the green sitting-room, didn't he?"

"Yes."

The door opened and Withers walked in after Fox. He stood with his hands in his pockets and blinked his white eyelashes.

"Hallo," he said. "What's the idea?"

"I have invited you to come here, Captain Withers, in order that the Assistant Commissioner may hear your statement about your movements on the night of the ball at Marsdon House. I have discovered that although you left Marsdon House at three-thirty you did not arrive at the Matador Night Club until four-fifteen. You therefore have no alibi for the murder of Lord Robert Gospell."

Withers looked at Mrs. Halcut-Hackett with a sort of sneer.

"She can give me one," he said.

She looked at him and spoke to Alleyn. Her voice was quite expressionless.

"I'd made up my mind it would have to come out. Between the time we left the ball and the time we got to the Matador, Captain Withers drove me about in his car. I was afraid of my husband. I had seen him watching me. I wanted to talk to Captain Withers. I was afraid to say this before."

"I see," said Alleyn. "You accept that, Captain Withers?"

"It's true enough."

"Very well. Now, to return to Marsdon House. You told me that at about one o'clock you were in the sitting-room at the head of the stairs."

"So I was."

"You did not tell me you were also in the telephone-room."

Withers stared at Mrs. Halcut-Hackett. She had been watching him like a frightened animal but as soon as his eyes turned towards her she looked away from him.

"Why should I?" said Withers.

"You were in the telephone-room with Mrs. Halcut-Hackett before you went to the other room. You returned to it from the other room to fetch this."

Alleyn's long arm shot up. Seven heads followed the movement. Seven pairs of eyes were concentrated on the gold cigarette-case with the jewelled medallion.

"And what if I did?"

"Where did you find this case?"

"On a table in the room with the telephone."

"When I asked you yesterday if you overheard Lord Robert telephoning in this room, as we know he did at one o'clock, you denied it."

"There wasn't anybody in the room when I fetched the case. I told you I heard the dialling tinkle on the extension a bit before then. If it was Gospell I suppose he'd gone when I got there."

"Is there any reason why anybody, say Mr. Dimitri in the corner there, should not have gone into the telephone-room after you left it with Mrs. Halcut-Hackett, and before you returned for the case?"

"No reason at all as far as I'm concerned."

"Dimitri," said Alleyn, "have you seen this case before? Look at it. Have you seen it before?"

"Never. I have never seen it. I do not know why you ask. I have never seen it."

"Take it in your hands. Look at it."

Dimitri took the case.

"Open it."

Dimitri opened it. From where Alleyn stood he could see the little cutting taken from *The Times*. Dimitri saw it too. His eyes dilated. The case dropped through his hands to the floor. He pointed a shaking finger at Alleyn.

"I think you must be the devil himself," he whispered.

"Fox," said Alleyn, "will you pass the case round?"

It passed from hand to hand. Withers, Evelyn Carrados and Carrados, all looked at it. Withers handled it as if he had done so before, but seemed quite unmoved by the cutting. The Carradoses both looked blankly at it and passed it on. Mrs. Halcut-Hackett opened the case and stared at the scrap of paper.

"This wasn't here before," she said. "What is it? Who put it here?"

"I'm sorry," said Alleyn. "It's done no damage. It will come off quite easily."

He took the case from her.

Dimitri suddenly leapt to his feet. Fox who had never taken his eyes off him moved in front of the door.

"Sit down, Mr. Dimitri," said Alleyn.

"I am going. You can keep me here no longer against my will. You accuse, you threaten, you lie! I say I can endure it no longer. I am an innocent man, a man of standing with a clientele of great excellence. I will see a lawyer. My God, let me pass!"

He plunged forward. Alleyn caught him by one arm, Fox by the other. He struggled violently. The A.C. pressed a bell on his desk, the door was opened from the outside and two plain-clothes men walked into the room. Beyond, in the brightly lit secretary's room three startled faces, Bridget's, Davidson's, and Miss Harris's, peered over the shoulders of more Yard men, and through the doorway.

"Look after him," said Alleyn.

Dimitri, mouthing and panting, was taken over by the two officers.

"Now then," they said. "Now then."

"Lady Carrados," said Alleyn, "will you formally charge this man?"

"I do charge him."

"In a moment," said Alleyn to Dimitri, "you will be taken to the charge-room but before we talk about the exact nature of the charge——" He looked through the door: "Sir Daniel? I see you're still there. May I trouble you again for a moment?"

Davidson, looking very startled, came through.

"Good God, Alleyn!" he said, staring at Dimitri. "What's this?"

Alleyn said: "You can, I believe, give me the final piece of evidence in an extremely involved affair. You see this cigarette-case?"

Davidson took it.

"My dear fellow," he said, "that's the abortion. I told you about it. It's part of the collection at Marsdon House. You remember?"

He moved to the light and after another startled glance at Dimitri who had gone perfectly still and stared at him like a lost soul, Davidson put up his glasses and examined the case.

"You know, I believe it *is* Benvenuto," he said, looking over his glasses at Alleyn.

"Yes, yes, I dare say. Will you tell us where you saw it?"

"Among a collection of *objets d'art* on a pie-crust table in an upstairs room at Marsdon House."

"At what time, Sir Daniel?"

"My dear Alleyn, I told you. About eleven-thirty or so. Perhaps earlier."

"Would you swear you noticed it no later than eleven-thirty?" insisted Alleyn.

"But of course I would," said Davidson. "I did not return to that room. I am quite ready to swear it."

He held the cigarette-case up in his beautifully shaped hand.

"I swear I saw this case on the table in the green sitting-room not later than eleven-thirty. That do?"

The silence was broken only by Dimitri's laboured breathing.

And then, surprisingly clear and firm, Mrs. Halcut-Hackett's voice:

"But that can't be true."

Alleyn said: "Will you open the case?"

Davidson, who was gazing in amazement at Mrs.

Halcut-Hackett, opened the cigarette-case and saw the notice.

"Will you read that press cutting?" said Alleyn. "Aloud, please."

The deep expressive voice read the absurd message.

" 'Childie Darling. Living in exile. Longing. Only want Daughter. Daddy.'

"What in the name of all wonders is this?"

"We believe it to be a murderer's message," said Alleyn. "We think this man, Dimitri, can translate it."

Davidson shut the case with a snap.

Something had gone wrong with his hands. They shook so violently that the diamonds on the gold case seemed to have a separate flashing life of their own.

"So Dimitri is a murderer," he said.

"Look out!" said Alleyn loudly.

Dimitri flung himself forward with such extreme and sudden violence that the men who held him were taken off their guard and his hands were at Davidson's throat before they had regained their hold on him. In a moment the room was full of struggling men. Chairs crashed to the floor, a woman screamed. Fox's voice shouted urgently: "Get to it. What are you *doing!*" There was a concerted upheaval against the edge of the desk. The green-shaded lamp smashed into oblivion.

"That's better," said Alleyn's voice. "Now then. Hands together."

A sharp click, a cry from Dimitri, and then the figures resolved themselves into a sort of tableaux: Dimitri, hand-cuffed and held by three men, against the desk; Davidson in the centre of the room with Alleyn, Fox and a plainclothes man grasping his arms behind his back; the Assistant Commissioner, between the two groups, like a distinguished sort of referee.

"Murderer!" screamed Dimitri. "Treacherous, filthy assassin! I confess! Gentlemen, I confess! I have worked for him for seven years and now, now, *now* he will stand aside and let me go to the gallows for the crime he has himself committed. I will tell you everything. *Everything.*"

"Speak up, Rory," said the A.C.

"Daniel Davidson," said Alleyn, "I arrest you for the murder of Lord Robert Gospell, and I warn you . . ."

30

Confession from Troy

"I thought," said Alleyn, "that you would like to know at once, Mildred."

Lady Mildred Potter shook her head, not so much in disagreement as from a sort of general hopelessness.

"It was nice of you to come, Roderick. But I'm afraid I simply cannot take it in. Sir Daniel has always been perfectly charming to both of us. Bunchy liked him very much. He told me so. And there's no doubt Sir Daniel did wonders with my indigestion. Quite cured it. Are you sure you are not mistaken?"

"Quite sure, I am afraid, Mildred. You see, Dimitri has confessed that Davidson has been in a sort of infamous partnership with him for seven years. Davidson knew something about Dimitri in the first instance, I think. That's probably how he managed to get his hold over Dimitri. Davidson has been extremely careful. He has found the data but he has left Dimitri to carry out the practical work. Davidson saw the open drawer and the letter in Carrados's writing-cabinet.

Davidson came in on the scene between Carrados and Bridget. He was careful never to be left alone in the room himself but he told Dimitri about the secret drawer and instructed Dimitri how to steal the letter. He told Dimitri that there might be something interesting there. Dimitri did all the dirty work. He collected the handbags of the blackmailed ladies. He wrote the letters. Sometimes he got the ideas. Mrs. Halcut-Hackett's trinket-box was one of Dimitri's brightest ideas, I imagine."

"I'm lost in it, Roderick. Troy, darling, do *you* understand?"

Alleyn looked at Troy, sitting on the floor at Mildred's feet.

"I think I'm beginning to understand," said Troy.

"Well, go on, Roderick," said Mildred drearily.

"There were three things that I could not fit into the pattern," said Alleyn, and he spoke more to Troy than to Mildred. "It seemed at first that if Dimitri overheard the telephone call he had an overwhelming motive. We knew he was a blackmailer, and we knew Bunchy was on his track. But we found that Dimitri literally could not have done the murder. His alibi stood up to the time factor and came out on top.

"Withers is a bad lot, and Bunchy knew that too, but somehow I could not see Withers as the killer. He's hard, wary, and completely unscrupulous. If he did ever murder it would be deliberately, and with forethought. The whole thing would be worked out to the last second. This job was, we believed, unpremeditated until within two and a half hours of its execution. Still Withers had to be considered. There was a gap in his alibi. I now know that he spent that gap driving his woman-dupe about in his car in order to discuss a situation which had become acute. Into this department, and again I implore your silence because I certainly shouldn't tell you about it, came old General Halcut-Hackett like an elderly harlequin dodging about in the fog of Belgrave Square at the crucial time when the guests left Marsdon House. He, of course, was looking for his wife. Next came

Carrados. Old Carrados was an infernal bore. His alibi, which overlapped Dimitri's, held good, but his behaviour was rum in the extreme. It was not until I heard of an incident eighteen years old that I managed to fit him into the pattern. And all the time there were three things about Davidson for which I could find only one explanation. He told me that he saw a certain cigarette-case in the green sitting-room at about eleven-thirty. Certainly not later. We found that the cigarette-case in question was only in this room for about four minutes round about one o'clock during which the telephone conversation took place. Why should Davidson lie? He had thought the case was a set-piece—one of the Marsdon House possessions; he had *not* realised that it was the personal property of one of the guests. He stated most emphatically that he did not overhear the conversation and indeed did not return to the room after eleven-thirty. But there is a curious point about the telephone conversation. Bunchy said to me: 'He might as well mix his damn brews with poison.' Davidson must have overheard that sentence because it came just before Bunchy broke off. Bunchy was talking about Dimitri, of course, but I believe Davidson thought he was talking about him. The broken sentence: 'And he's working with——' would probably have ended: 'with such filthy ingenuity,' or something of that sort. Davidson probably thought the next word Bunchy spoke would be his (Davidson's) name. That's odd, isn't it? As for the figure Miss Harris saw beyond the glass panel undoubtedly it was Davidson. At his wits' end he must have dived through the nearest door and there, I suppose, pulled himself together and decided to murder Bunchy. Then there is the other cigarette-case."

Alleyn looked at Lady Mildred. Her head nodded like a mandarin's. He turned back to Troy and spoke softly.

"I mean the weapon. On the morning after the murder I asked to see Davidson's case. He showed me a cigarette-case that was certainly too small for the job and said it was the one he had carried last night. I noticed how immaculate it was, looked closely at it, and found traces of plate-powder in the tooling. We learnt that Davidson's cases were cleaned the morning before the ball and had not been touched after the ball. It seemed to me that this case had certainly not been out all night. It shone like a mirror and I would have sworn had not been used since it was put in his pocket. It was a thin bit of evidence but it did look as if he had lied when he said it was the case he took to Marsdon House. And then there was the condition—is Mildred asleep?"

"Yes," said Lady Mildred. "Do you mind very much, dear Roderick, if I go to bed? I'm afraid I shall never understand, you see, and I am really so very tired. I think sorrow is one of the most tiring things, don't you? Troy, my dear, you will look after poor Roderick, won't you? Donald will be in late and I don't know where he is just now."

"I think he took Bridget Carrados home," said Alleyn, opening the door for Mildred. "Evelyn and her husband wanted to be alone and Donald was in the waiting-room looking hopeful."

"He seems to be very attached to her," said Mildred, pausing at the door and looking at Alleyn with tear-stained eyes. "Is she a nice girl, Roderick?"

"Very nice. I think she'll look after him. Good night, Mildred."

"Good night."

Alleyn shut the door after her and returned to Troy.

"May I stay for a little longer?"

"Yes, please. I want to hear the end of it all." Troy looked sideways at him. "How extraordinarily well-trained your eye must be! To notice the grains of plate-powder in the tooling of a cigarette-case; could anything be more admirable? What else did you notice?"

"I notice that although your eyes are grey there are little flecks of green in them and that the iris is ringed with black. I notice that when you smile your face goes crooked. I notice that the third finger of your left hand has a little spot of vermilion on the inside where a ring should hide it; and from that, Miss Troy, I deduce that you are a painter in oils and are not so proud as you should be of your lovely fingers."

"Please tell me the end of the case."

"I would rather tell you that since this afternoon in the few spare moments I have had to spend upon it I have considered your case and that I have decided to take out a warrant for your arrest. The charge is impeding an officer of the law in the execution of his duty."

"Don't be so damned facetious," said Troy.

"All right. Where was I?"

"You had got to the third point against Davidson."

"Yes. The third point was in the method used in committing the crime. I don't think Bunchy would mind if he knew that even while I described his poor little body I was thinking of the woman to whom I spoke. Do you? He was such an understanding person, wasn't he, with just the right salty flavour of irony? I'm sure he knew how short-lived the first pang of sorrow really is if only people would confess as much. Well, Troy, the man who killed him knew how easy it was to asphyxiate people and I didn't think many killers would know that. The only real mark of violence was the scar made by the cigarette-case. A doctor would realise how little force was needed and Bunchy's doctor would know how great an ally that weak heart would be. Davidson told me about the condition of the heart because he knew I would discover he had examined Bunchy. He kept his head marvellously when I interviewed him, did Sir Daniel. He's as clever as paint. We're searching his house tonight. Fox is there now. I don't think we'll find anything except perhaps the lethal cigarette-case, but I've more hopes of Dimitri's desk. I couldn't get in to that yesterday."

"What about the cloak and hat?"

"That brings us to a very curious episode. We have searched for the cloak and hat ever since four o'clock yesterday morning and we have not found them. We did our usual routine stuff, going round all the dust-bin experts and so on and we also notified the parcels-post offices. This afternoon we heard of a parcel that had been dumped at the Main Western office during the rush hour yesterday. It was overstamped with tuppenny stamps and addressed to somewhere in China. The writing was script which was our blackmailer's favourite medium of expression. It's gone, alas, but I think there's just a chance we may trace it. It's a very long chance. Now who is likely to have an unlimited supply of tuppenny stamps, my girl?"

"Somebody who gives receipts?"

"Bless me, if you're not a clever old thing. Right as usual, said the Duchess. And who should give receipts but Sir Daniel, the fashionable physician? Who but he?"

"Dimitri for one."

"I'm sorry to say that is perfectly true, darling. But when I was in Davidson's waiting-room, I saw several of those things that I think are called illustrated brochures. They appealed for old clothes for the Central Chinese Medical Mission at God knows where. It is our purpose, my dear Troy, to get one of those brochures and write to the Central Chinese Mission asking for further information."

"I wonder," murmured Troy.

"And so, you may depend upon it, do I. There's one other point which has been kindly elucidated by the gibbering Dimitri. This morning he sent his servant out for a *Times*. When we heard of this we had a look at *The Times*, too. We found the agony column notice that I talked about when poor Mildred was trying not to go to sleep, and before I could tell you how much I approve of the solemn way you knit your brows when you listen to me. Now, this notice read like this: 'Childie Darling. Living in exile. Longing. Only want Daughter. Daddy.' A rum affair, we thought, and we noticed in our brilliant way that the initial letters read 'C.D. Lie low. D.D.' which might not be too fancifully elaborated into 'Colombo Dimitri, lie low, Daniel Davidson.' And, in fact, Mr. Dimitri has confessed to this artless device. It was arranged, he says, that if anything unprecedented, untoward, unanticipated, ever occurred, Davidson would communicate with Dimitri in precisely this manner. It was a poor effort, but Sir Daniel hadn't much time. He must have composed it as soon as he got home after his night's work. Anything more?"

"What about Dimitri and Withers?"

"They were taken to the charge-room, and duly charged. The one with blackmail, the other with running a gaming-house. I'll explain the gaming-house some other time. They are extremely nasty fellows, but if Dimitri hadn't been quite such a nasty fellow, we wouldn't have stood as good a chance of scaring him into fits and getting the whole story about Davidson. I gambled on that, and by jingo, Troy, it *was* a gamble."

"What would have happened if Dimitri had kept quiet even though he did think you were going to arrest him for murder?"

"We would still have arrested him for blackmail, and would have had to plug away at Davidson on what we'd got. But Dimitri saw we had a clear case on the blackmail charge. He'd nothing to gain in protecting Davidson."

"Do you think he really *knows* Davidson did the murder?"

"I think we shall find that Davidson tried to warn him against collecting Evelyn Carrados's bag at the ball. Davidson saw Bunchy was with Evelyn, when Bridget returned her bag the first time."

"You didn't tell me about that."

Alleyn told her about it.

"And isn't that really all?" he asked.

"Yes. That's all."

"Troy, I love you more than anything in life. I've tried humility: God knows, I am humble. And I've tried effrontery. If you can't love me, tell me so, and please let us not meet again because I can't manage meeting you unless it is to love you."

Troy raised a white face and looked solemnly at him.

"I know my mind at last," she said. "I couldn't be parked."

"Darling, darling Troy."

"I do love you. Very much indeed."

"Wonder of the world!" cried Alleyn, and took her in his arms.

Epilogue

Down a sun-baked mud track that ran through the middle of the most remote of all the Chinese Medical Mission's settlements in Northern Manchuria, walked a short, plump celestial. He was followed by six yellow urchins upon each of whose faces was an expression of rapt devotion, and liveliest envy. If his face and legs had been visible, it would have been seen that sweat poured down them in runnels. But his face was hidden by a black hat, and his legs by the voluminous folds of a swashbuckling cloak. There was glory in his gait.

In the receiving-office of the mission, a jaded young Englishman gazed in perplexity at a telegram a month old. It had been forwarded from the head depot and had done the rounds of most of the settlements. It was from New Scotland Yard, London.

The young Englishman gazed blankly through the open door at the little procession in the sun-baked track outside.